RAYBEARER

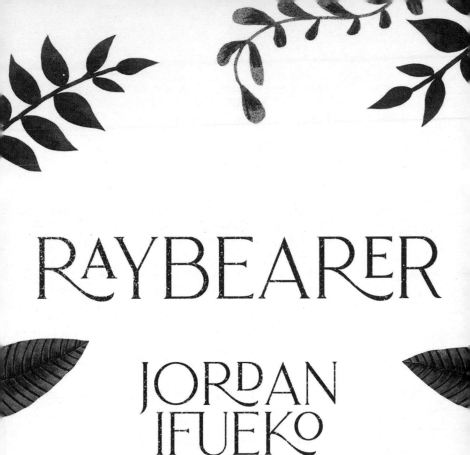

RAYBEARER

JORDAN
IFUEKO

HOT
KEY
BOOKS

First published in Great Britain in 2020 by
HOT KEY BOOKS
80–81 Wimpole St, London W1G 9RE
www.hotkeybooks.com

Text copyright © Jordan Ifueko, 2020

A CIP catalogue record for this book is available from the British Library.

ISBN: 978-1-4714-0927-1
Also available as an ebook and audiobook

1

Printed and bound by Clays Ltd, Elcograf S.p.A.

Hot Key Books is an imprint of Bonnier Books UK
www.bonnierbooks.co.uk

*For the kid scanning fairy tales
for a hero with a face like theirs.*

*And for the girls whose stories
we compressed into pities and wonders,
triumphs and cautions, without asking,
even once, for their names.*

PART 1

CHAPTER 1

I SHOULDN'T HAVE BEEN SURPRISED THAT fairies exist.

When elephants passed by in a lumbering sea beneath my window, flecks of light whispered in the dust, dancing above the rows of tusks and leather. I leaned precariously over the sill, hoping to catch a fleck before a servant wrestled me inside.

"Shame-shame, Tarisai," my tutors fretted. "What would The Lady do if you fell?"

"But I want to see the lights," I said.

"They're only *tutsu* sprites." A tutor herded me away from the window. "Kind spirits. They guide lost elephants to watering holes."

"Or to lion packs," another tutor muttered. "If they're feeling less kind."

Magic, I soon learned, was capricious. When I squinted at the swollen trunk of our courtyard boab tree, a cheeky face appeared. *Kye, kye, killer-girl*, it snickered before vanishing into the bark.

1

I was seven when the man with cobalt-fire wings found me. That night, I had decided to search Swana, the second-largest realm in the Arit empire, for my mother. I had crept past my snoring maids and tutors, stuffed a sack with mangoes, and scaled our mudbrick wall.

The moon hung high above the savannah when the *alagbato*, the fairy, appeared in my path. The light glinted in his gold-flecked eyes, which slanted all the way to his dark temples. He seized the back of my garment, hoisting me up for examination. I wore a wrapper the color of banana leaves wound several times beneath my arms, leaving my shoulders bare. The alagbato watched me, amused, as I punched and kicked the air.

I'm in bed at Bhekina House, I told myself. My heart pounded like a fist on a goatskin drum. I bit my cheek to prove I was dreaming. *I'm wrapped in gauzy mosquito nets and the servants are fanning me with palm fronds. I can smell breakfast in the kitchens. Maize porridge. Stewed matemba fish . . .*

But my cheek began to throb. I was not in bed. I was lost in the balmy Swanian grasslands, and this man was made of flames.

"Hello, Tarisai." His Sahara breath warmed my beaded braids. "Just where do you think you're going?"

"How do you know my name?" I demanded. Were alagbatos all-knowing, like Am the Storyteller?

"I am the one who gave it to you."

I was too angry to absorb this reply. Did he have to

be so *bright*? Even his hair shimmered, a luminous thicket around his narrow face. If our compound guards spotted him . . .

I sighed. I had barely made it a mile into the savannah. Capture now would be humiliating. My tutors would lock me up again—and this time, *every* window in Bhekina House would be nailed shut.

"I'm not allowed to be touched," I snapped, clawing at the alagbato's grip. His skin felt smooth and hot, like clay left to harden in the sun.

"Not allowed? You are small enough to be carried. I am told human children need affection."

"Well, I'm not human," I shot back in triumph. "So put me down."

"Who told you that, little girl?"

"No one," I admitted after a pause. "But they all say it behind my back. I'm not like other children."

This was possibly a lie. The truth was, I'd never *seen* other children, except in the market caravans that passed Bhekina House from a distance. I would wave from my window until my arms grew sore, but they never waved back. The children would stare straight past me, as if our compound—manor, orchard, and houses enough to make a small village—were invisible to anyone outside.

"Yes," the alagbato agreed grimly. "You are different. Would you like to see your mother, Tarisai?"

I stopped resisting at once, and my limbs hung limp as vines. "Do you know where she is?"

My mother was like morning mist: here, then gone, vanished in clouds of jasmine. My tutors bowed superstitiously whenever they passed her wood carving in my study. They called her *The Lady*. I delighted in our resemblance: the same high cheekbones, full lips, and fathomless black eyes. Her carving watched as my study brimmed with scholars from sun-up to moonrise.

They chattered in dialects from all twelve realms of the Arit empire. Some faces were warm and dark, like mine and The Lady's. Others were pale as goat's milk with eyes like water, or russet and smelling of cardamom, or golden with hair that flowed like ink. The tutors plied me with riddles, shoving diagrams into my hands.

Can she solve it? Try a different one. She'll have to do better than that.

I didn't know what they were looking for. I only knew that once they found it, I would get to see The Lady again.

This will be the day, the tutors gushed when I excelled at my lessons. *The Lady will be so pleased.* Then the palisade gates of Bhekina House opened, and my mother glided inside, detached as a star. Her shoulders glowed like embers. Wax-dyed cloth clung to her torso like a second skin, patterns zigzagging in red, gold, and black. She held me to her breast, a feeling so lovely I wept as she sang: *Me, mine, she's me and she is mine.*

The Lady never spoke when I demonstrated my skills. Sometimes she nodded as if to say, *Yes, perhaps.* But in the end, she always shook her head.

No. Not enough.

I recited poems in eight different languages, hurled darts into miniscule targets, solved giant logic puzzles on the floor. But each time it was no, no, and no again. Then she vanished in that haze of heady perfume.

At age five I had begun to sleepwalk, padding barefoot through the smooth plaster halls of our manor. I would peer in each room, walking and whimpering for my mother until a servant carried me back to bed.

They were always careful never to touch my skin.

"I cannot find your mother," the alagbato told me the night of my attempted escape. "But I can show you a memory. Not in my head." He dodged my attempt to seize his face. "I never store secrets on my person."

The Lady had forbidden people from touching me for a reason. I could steal the story of almost anything: a comb, a spear, a person. I touched something and knew where it had been a moment before. I saw with their eyes, if they had eyes; sighed with their lungs; felt what their hearts had suffered. If I held on long enough, I could see a person's memories for months, even years.

Only The Lady was immune to my gift. I knew every story in Bhekina House, except hers.

"You will have to take my memory from the place where it happened," said the alagbato, setting me lightly in the tall grass. "Come. It is not far."

He offered a bony hand, but I hesitated. "You're a stranger," I said.

"Are you sure?" he asked, and I felt the odd sensation of peering into a mirror. He smiled, lips pursed like a meerkat's. "If it makes you feel any better, my name is Melu. And thanks to *that woman*, I am not an alagbato." His smile soured into a grimace. "Not anymore."

Fear rose in my belly like smoke from a coal pit, but I silenced my worries. *Do you want to find The Lady or not?*

I picked up my sack, from which most of the mangoes had fallen, and took Melu's hand. Though gentle, his grip felt hard around mine, as though his muscles were made of bronze. An emerald-studded cuff glinted on his forearm, and when I grazed the cuff by accident, it seared me.

"Careful," he murmured.

We walked to a clearing hedged in acacia trees. Herons flapped above a vast, still pool. The air hung with lilies and violets, and the brush rustled and *shhh*ed in a wordless lullaby.

"Is this where you live?" I asked in awe.

"In a manner of speaking," he said. "It was beautiful for the first few thousand days. After that, it grew tedious." I blinked up at him in confusion, but he did not explain. He only pointed to the soft red earth. "The story is here."

Cautiously, I pressed my ear to the ground. I'd never tried to take the memory of any place larger than my bedroom. A familiar heat flushed my face and hands as my mind stole into the dirt, latching onto whatever memory was strongest. The winged man and the flock of herons disappeared.

The clearing is younger now, with fewer brush and acacia trees. It is daytime in this memory, and the amber pool is clear, free of fish and mayflies. My heart skips a beat: The Lady, my Lady, reclines on a rock by the water.

The sun makes a mosaic of her reflection on the pool's surface, distorting her face, rippling her cloud of midnight hair. Her wrapper is frayed, and her sandals are worn to the soles. I worry, wondering: *What were you running from, Mother?*

The Lady dips an emerald cuff into the water. She murmurs over the jewel, kissing it tenderly, and the emerald glows and fades. Then she sets the cuff down and calls out, "Melu." My mother tastes the word on her full lips, drawing out the syllables like a song. "Melu, my dear. Won't you come out and play?"

The clearing is silent. The Lady laughs, a deep, throaty sound. "The seers say that alagbatos dislike humans. Some doubt you even exist, Great Melu, guardian of Swana. But I think you do hear." She produces a green vial from her pocket and tips it precariously toward the pool. "I think you hear just fine."

A hot wind rushes into the clearing, swirling up dirt and clay into a tall, lean man. His wings smolder cobalt blue, like a young fire, but his voice is frost cold. "*Stop.*"

"I would tell you my name," The Lady tells him.

"But as you know, my father never gave me one." She pauses, still dangling that vial over the pool. "How quickly does *abiku* blood spread through earth and water, Melu? How much would poison every living thing within a fifty-mile radius? Two drops? Three?"

"Don't," Melu barks. "Wait."

The Lady points to the emerald cuff.

Melu's features contort with defeat. Stone-jawed, he picks up the cuff and snaps it on his forearm.

"If I've done that right," says The Lady, "you are no longer Swana's alagbato. You are my ehru . . . my djinn."

"Three wishes," Melu spits. "And I am bound to this grassland until your wishes are complete."

"How convenient." The Lady sits, thoughtfully dangling her muscular brown legs in the water. "Melu, I wish for a stronghold that no one may see or hear unless I desire it. A place my friends and I will always be safe. A place . . . befitting royalty. That is my first command."

Melu blinks. "It is done."

"Where?"

"A mile from here." Melu points, and the newly blossomed plaster walls of Bhekina House shimmer in the distance.

The Lady glows with pleasure. "Now," she breathes, "I wish for Olugbade's death—"

"Not allowed," Melu snaps. "Life and death are beyond my power. *Especially* that life. Even fairies may not kill a Raybearer."

The Lady's mouth hardens, then relaxes. "I thought that might be the case," she says. "Fine. I wish for a child who will do, think, and feel as I tell it. An extension of myself. A gifted child, sure to stand out in a contest of talent. This is my second command."

"Not allowed," Melu intones again. "I cannot force a human to love or hate. You may not *own* a child as you own an ehru."

"Can't I?" The Lady steeples her fingers in thought. A smile spreads across her face, and her teeth are coldly white.

"What if," she says, "my child *was* an ehru? What if my child was yours?"

Melu grows as rigid as a tree in dry season. "Such a union would go against nature. You are human, not of my kind. You ask for an abomination."

"Oh no, Melu." The Lady's brilliant black eyes dance over the ehru's horrified ones. "I command that abomination."

They performed a ritual then, one I didn't understand at seven years old. It looked painful, the way his body folded over hers in the grass. Two species never meant to unite, dissimilar as flesh against metal. But the memory told me that nine months later, my infant cries rang through Bhekina House. And The Lady's third ungranted wish—her abomination—ran through my veins.

"Do you understand now?" Melu muttered over my drowsy form, once the memory had run its course. "Until you grant her third wish, neither you nor I will be free." He touched my forehead with a long, slender finger. "I bargained with The Lady for the privilege of naming you Tarisai. It is a Swana name: *behold what is coming.* Your soul is hers for now. But your name, I insisted, must be your own."

He sounded far away. Stealing The Lady's story had exhausted me. I barely sensed Melu cradle me in his narrow arms, soar through the night, and deposit me back at the palisade gates of Bhekina House. He whispered, "I've been bound to this savannah for seven years. For my sake, I hope that woman claims her wish. But for your sake, daughter, I hope that day never comes." Then servants clambered toward the gates, and Melu was gone.

A dozen anxious hands put me to bed, and syrupy voices soothed me when I babbled about Melu the next day. *It was all a dream,* the tutors said. But their dilated pupils and terse smiles told a different story. My adventure had confirmed their most sinister suspicions.

My mother was the devil, and I, her puppet demon.

CHAPTER 2

THE SWANA GRASSLANDS WERE WARM EVEN in the rainy season. But the air around me always chilled. As birthdays passed—eight, nine, ten—I shivered through Bhekina House, coddled by servants who never broke the surface of my bubble. Sometimes I longed for human touch so much, I would bend my cheek to open flames. The tendrils would sear my skin, but I would smile, pretending to feel The Lady's fingers.

Eventually, I fell in the kitchen firepit by accident. The servants dragged me out, sobbing, shrieking prayers to Am the Storyteller. I shook all over and rasped, *"I can't die, I can't die, Mother's going to come back, so I can't die."*

But I had not burned. My clothes hung in ruined smolders, but my coily black hair had not even singed.

As my maids looked on in shock, I remembered the wording from The Lady's wish for Bhekina House: *a place my friends and I will always be safe.*

"It's Mother," I said breathlessly. "She protected me."

From that day on, I multiplied the gray hairs of my

servants by jumping off walls, submerging my head in buckets of water, and catching venomous spiders, encouraging them to bite.

"I didn't die," I would laugh as the servants set my broken bones and poured antidotal teas down my throat.

"Yes," a nursemaid would say through gritted teeth. "That's because we reached you in time."

"No," I would insist dreamily. "It's because my mother loves me."

My tutors grew more relentless. The sooner they could make me into what The Lady wanted, after all, the sooner they would be rid of me. So the lessons continued, lectures droning in my ears like gadflies. Ink fumes stung my nose each day, and the scent of jasmine haunted me each night. But Melu's memory had awoken a hunger inside me, one the mango orchards of Bhekina House could not satiate. I dreamed and lusted for the world beyond the gate.

An enormous globe rested on a wooden stand in my study. Jagged continents curved around a deep blue ocean I had never seen. The largest continent, which included Swana, was a patchwork of savannahs, forests, deserts, and snowy tundras. This was Aritsar, my tutors said. *The Deathless Arit empire, may Kunleo live forever.*

Most of the history scrolls in my study were edited. My tutors would blot out lines and sometimes whole pages with black ink, refusing to tell me why. Once, I managed to hold papers to the light, reading several paragraphs before a tutor snatched them away.

Long ago, the papers said, Aritsar had not existed. In its place, a jumble of isolated islands had floated on a vast sea. The twelve weak, rivaling lands were ravaged by abiku: demons from the Underworld. Then a warlord named Enoba "the Perfect" Kunleo had unleashed a power from the earth, uniting the lands into one massive continent. He had crowned himself emperor, enlisting twelve of the continent's rulers as his vassals. Then he battled the abiku with his newly christened Army of Twelve Realms. The mortal and immortal armies had been so evenly matched that Enoba's war dragged on for decades before, at last, the exhausted forces struck a truce.

Enoba was celebrated as Aritsar's savior. The continent rulers credited him for bringing peace, and so, for centuries, his line had ruled Aritsar from their home realm of Oluwan, uniting twelve cultures in a network of art, science, and trade. Whenever caravans passed by Bhekina House, I heard merchant families singing of the empire, rocking infants on their hips as children skipped across the savannah:

Oluwan and Swana bring his drum; nse, nse
Dhyrma and Nyamba bring his plow; gpopo, gpopo
Mewe and Sparti see our older brother dance—
Black and gold, isn't he perfect!

Quetzala sharpens his spear; nse, nse
Blessid Valley weaves his wrapper; gpopo, gpopo
Nontes and Biraslov see our older brother dance!
Black and gold, isn't he perfect?

Djbanti braids his hair; nse, nse
Moreyao brings his gourd; gpopo, gpopo
Eleven moons watch our older brother dance:
Black and gold, isn't he perfect?

Aritsar's current *older brother*, or emperor, was Olugbade
Kunleo: a direct descendant of Enoba the Perfect. I used
to croon the patriotic anthem in our mango orchards.
As I wove between branches, I would talk to an invisible
emperor, sharing my thoughts on Arit history and
governance. Sometimes I imagined him gazing down like
the sun through the clouds, warming my bare shoulders
with approval. How perfect he must be, to unite so
many lands!

Dhyrma. Nontes. Djbanti. The names of the Arit realms
tasted spicy on my tongue. My bones ached for those far
places, described by my tutors in rainbow colors: *The silk
farms of Moreyao. The night festivals of Nyamba. The snowy
peaks of Biraslov, the booby-trapped rainforests of Quetzala.* I
lay on my back, gazing up at the mango trees, trying to
imagine the high-rises of Oluwan City: the seat of our
divine emperor. Even Swana held its mystery. I had never
left our grassland, but heard tales of lush cacao fields,

and markets where women hawked candied papaya from baskets on their heads.

But more than cities and rainforests, I craved voices that would not call me *demon*.

I envied the children who passed by Bhekina House, with their grandparents who jostled them on their knees, their siblings who chased and teased them. The Lady was the only person in the world who touched me willingly.

One morning, as I watched the caravans from my study window, I learned another song.

> *Eleven danced around the throne,*
> *Eleven moons in glory shone,*
> *They shone around the sun.*

> *But traitors rise and empires fall,*
> *And Sun-Ray-Sun will rule them all,*
> *When all is said-o, all is said*
> *And done-heh, done-heh, done.*

I liked the ominous rhyme. I whispered it around the manor like an incantation until a tutor overheard me. She asked, voice quavering, where I had heard such nonsense. I told her . . . and the next day, every window in my study was nailed shut.

I pried at the wooden slats until my small fingers were scratched and torn. That glimpse of the outside had been my lifeline. My portal to Aritsar—to feeling less alone.

How dare they make my windows vanish? As The Lady had vanished, and Melu, and everything else I longed for?

I threatened to set the study aflame. "I'll do it," I howled at the servants. "Why not? I won't burn. But your scrolls will. *You* will."

My tutors had blanched. "There are things we simply can't teach you," they said, looking hunted as they bound my bloodied hands. "It is forbidden." Like The Lady, my tutors had a habit of disappearing for months. This usually occurred after one of The Lady's visits, when she found my learning to be unsatisfactory. Then new, nervous faces would replace the old ones.

On my eleventh birthday, two such faces arrived at Bhekina House, and accompanying them was the only birthday present I wanted.

"Mother!" I cried, launching myself at her. The Lady wore a richly patterned wax-dyed wrapper, which scratched my cheek as I clung to her. She cupped my face, a feeling so wonderful I shivered.

"Hello, Made-of-Me," she said, and hummed that chilling lullaby: *Me, mine, she's me and she is mine.*

We stood in Bhekina House's open-air great hall. Sunlight streamed from our chicken-scattered courtyard, glowing across the hall's clay tiles and illuminating The Lady's black cloud of hair. The two strangers flanked her, standing so close to The Lady, I was jealous.

"Friends," The Lady said, "please tell my daughter

that you are her new, permanent guardians." She seldom addressed me directly. When she did, her words were sparse and halting. I would later realize she was afraid of commanding me by accident—afraid of wasting her third precious wish, which still lay dormant inside me.

The word *permanent* piqued my interest. I had never kept a servant for more than a few months. The older stranger, a feline woman about The Lady's age, was dressed entirely in green. Tawny brown skin contrasted with hard green eyes. Curly hair burst from beneath her cloak's hood, which she wore even in the heat. An *isoken*, I realized. Isoken people had mixed blood, parents from different Arit realms. To hasten empire unity, the Kunleo imperial treasury rewarded families for every isoken child born.

"I'm Kathleen," the woman sighed at me, then turned back to The Lady. "I hope this creature won't be trouble. Does it have a name besides Made-of-You?"

"The ehru calls her something else," The Lady said.

I had been trained to recognize accents. Kathleen's lisp echoed her home realm, Mewe: a land of green, craggy hills in the distant northern fingers of Aritsar.

"My name is Tarisai," I piped up, and greeted Kathleen in Mewish, hoping to impress. "May your autumn leaves grow back green!" I didn't know what autumn was, and had never lived in a place where trees changed color, but it sounded like a nice thing to say.

"Am's Story, Lady," the isoken woman snorted. "Did

you teach the kid *all twelve* realm tongues?"

"No harm in outshining the competition," The Lady said smugly.

"They don't test children on different languages," Kathleen retorted. "Not anymore. Every realm speaks Arit now. That's the point of being an empire."

"Only Arit citizens," droned the second stranger, "take pride in their cultures being erased. Why be unique, when you could all be the same?" He looked much younger than Kathleen—perhaps twenty, and more boy than man. His voice reminded me of a spider's web, soft and gossamer. I could not place his accent anywhere in Aritsar.

He scanned me with eyes like half-moons, lifting a tan, angular jaw. A blue cape draped over his arm. Besides that, he wore nothing but trousers, and every inch of his body— face, arms, chest, and feet—was covered in what appeared to be geometric purple tattoos. I probably imagined it, but for a moment, they seemed to glow.

He gave a sardonic bow, straight jet hair shining over his shoulder. "A pleasure, Lady's Daughter. My name is Woo In. My homeland, thank the Storyteller, lies outside this unnaturally unified empire."

I gaped. "You're from Songland!"

"You make it sound like a fairy world." He rolled his eyes. "Of course I'm from Songland. I'm covered in these pretty pictures, aren't I?"

His tone was sarcastic. But I *did* think they were pretty, if a little unsettling. Patterns twisted up his face and neck, like a logic puzzle with no solution. I gulped: Woo In was a Redemptor.

Songland was a poor peninsula nation on the edge of our continent. Their ancestors had refused to recognize Enoba as emperor—and as a result, the tiny realm was excluded from Aritsar's bustling trade. A jagged range of mountains cut Songland off from the mainland. Aritsar might have ignored Songland altogether, if not for the Redemptors.

Enoba the Perfect had bought peace for our world at a steep price. Every year, three hundred children were sent into the Oruku Breach: the last known entrance to the Underworld. In exchange for this sacrifice, the abiku refrained from ravaging human cities and villages. The children, known as Redemptors, were born with maps on their skin, meant to guide them through the Underworld and back to the realm of the living. Few survived the journey. As a result, some families hid their Redemptor children at birth. But for every missed sacrifice, the abiku would send a horde of beasts and plagues to raze the continent.

Redemptors were supposedly born at random, to any race and class. But for some reason, every Redemptor in the last five hundred years had been born in Songland.

No one knew why. But guilt-ridden Arits, relieved from the burden of sacrificing their own children, had plenty of theories to help them sleep at night. The Songlanders had offended the Storyteller, they guessed. The Redemptor children were punishment for some historical sin of Songland's. Or perhaps, Songland was *blessed* by the Storyteller, and their children were saints, chosen to sacrifice themselves for the greater good. The greater good, of course, was Aritsar.

I peered at Woo In. He did not strike me as particularly saintly. But he must have been special to survive the Oruku Breach. In the rare event that Redemptor children came back alive, they were scarred in mind, if not body.

I smiled at him and Kathleen. Maybe if these strangers—my *permanent guardians*—liked me, then I could stop talking to invisible emperors. Maybe, for the first time, I could have friends. Real ones.

Don't think I'm a demon, I prayed. *Think I'm a girl. A normal, market-caravan, not-scary girl.*

"Do we *have* to nanny her?" Kathleen whined to The Lady. "Can't you hire some mute nursemaid, or bribe one into secrecy?"

"No," The Lady snapped. "Once my daughter leaves Bhekina House for Oluwan City, I cannot control what she sees and hears. She must be with people I trust."

Leave?

Leave Bhekina House?

Kathleen crossed her arms. "You're sure this . . . wish-creature is ready?"

"We are running out of time. Children are already being chosen. If we are not quick, there will be no more room on the Prince's Council—" The Lady broke off abruptly, tossing me a nervous glance.

"Don't fret, Lady," said Kathleen with a smirk. "We can always *make* room."

The Lady frowned. "I'm hoping that won't be necessary. The emperor and his Elev—" She stopped again, glancing at me. "The emperor's . . . friends . . . are too smart for that. My daughter's selection must happen as naturally as possible."

Kathleen laughed. "Do we have to keep censoring what we say? She's going to find out eventually."

"Ignorance will make her seem pure," The Lady said grimly. "The emperor loves girls like that."

"Then you're making the wish today?" Woo In asked. The Lady nodded, and to my shock, she cupped Woo In's face just as she had cupped mine. He leaned into the touch, kissing her palm. I was jealous immediately.

She said, "I know you'll keep her safe."

He scanned her features with hunger, a moth before a candle. "I believe in this cause," he said.

She fondled his hair. "And I believe in you."

"Why are we going to Oluwan?" I demanded. "Mother, are you coming too?"

"No, Made-of-Me." The Lady reclined on one of our hall's broad window seats. The sun backlit her frame in a halo. "I will come for you when the time is right." She patted her lap, nodding at me.

For the rest of my life, I wished the universe had given me a sign then. A warning of what was about to happen. But no—the air was warm and serene, and honeybirds sang

21

in the distance as I scrambled, eagerly, into my mother's arms.

She stroked my back for a moment, gazing at the hazy Swanian sky. "How frightened you must be," she told someone I could not see. "You caged me like a bird, but you could not make me sing." Then she told Kathleen, "Give her the portrait."

A gilded oval frame was placed in my hands. A boy stared back at me, with tightly curled hair and the brightest smile I'd ever seen. Naive brown eyes shone from a dark, broad-featured face.

"Why is he happy?" I asked.

The Lady raised an eyebrow. "Aren't you curious who he is?" I shrugged, and so she answered my question. "He is happy because he has everything you want. Power. Wealth. Legacy. His father stole those things from you, and gave them to him."

"Be careful, Lady," Kathleen muttered. "Remember: She must fall in love with him."

My brow creased with confusion. I couldn't remember ever wanting power or wealth. And why did I have to love him? But The Lady's pressing arms and the scent of jasmine jumbled my thoughts. I snuggled against her, forgetting the boy with his stolen happiness. I would trade all the wealth in Aritsar to be held. To be touched without fear. To never be called *dangerous*.

"Are you listening, Made-of-Me?" The Lady whispered. I closed my eyes and nodded, resting my cheek on her breast. Her heart raced like a hummingbird. Her next words were halting, cautious. "When you meet this boy in the portrait . . ."

Something that had slept for years rose in my belly, searing my skin, like the cuff on Melu's arm had done. I opened my eyes. For a moment, in my reflection on the portrait's surface, my pupils glowed like emeralds.

"When you love him the most, and when he anoints you as his own . . ." The Lady touched the boy's face, blotting out his dazzling smile. "I command you to kill him."

CHAPTER 3

I RETCHED INTO THE BOWL BETWEEN MY LEGS, stomach lurching with the jostle of the mule-and-box.

"I *told* you traveling by lodestone was a bad idea," Kathleen snapped at Woo In as she emptied my sick bowl out the window. "We should have taken camels. Lodestones are nasty powerful. She's never been exposed to magic before."

"She was raised in an invisible manor house," Woo In pointed out dryly. "She'll be fine. Besides, from the looks of it, the kid would have been sick however we traveled."

It was my first time in a mule-and-box—in anything with wheels. After leaving Bhekina House, we had crossed two realms in two weeks. By mule, camel, or river barge, the trip would have taken months. But we had traveled by lodestone: a powerful, hazardous magic that dissolved bodies and reformed them leagues away. Ports were scattered throughout Aritsar, guarded by imperial soldiers. Whenever we passed through them, Kathleen had forced my face beneath a hood.

"Stay down," she had grunted. "You're The Lady's spitting image."

I didn't understand why resembling my mother was dangerous. In fact—in the thrill of adventure—I often forgot all about The Lady's wish. Her lethal words grew hazy as I witnessed marvels from my books and scrolls. *Town. Market. Mountain. Lake. Forest.* In a world so big, what were the chances of meeting that boy in the portrait?

After the first lodestone crossing, I had vomited my breakfast onto Kathleen's boots. The Imperial Guard warriors had warned against traveling by lodestone more than once a month, but Woo In had insisted on two crossings a week.

After the fourth crossing, my left arm vanished.

I had nearly fainted in terror, and the limb flickered a few times before deciding, at last, to return. Woo In had relented then, switching us to a mule-and-box. We endured hours of stiff, dusty travel, stopping only to sleep at mudbrick village inns. I inhaled ginger soup to settle my stomach before collapsing onto a straw bedroll, too exhausted to dream.

Today, the lodestone nausea had finally begun to subside. After retching into the bowl, I felt much better, and I leaned curiously from the mule-and-box window. Our destination of Oluwan was coastal, a land of ferny palms and orange groves, with long, warm days and cool, rain-kissed nights. My heart thrummed as the unfamiliar landscape rushed by: bumpy plains of green and gold, dotted with lakes and palm trees. I gulped the morning air. It tasted like citrus and salt water.

"Little demon," hissed Kathleen when she noticed me. She tried to pull me back, grappling with my blue cotton wrapper. "For Am's sake—someone could *see*, you brat. Stay down!"

"I won't," I said, gasping in laughter as the wind whipped my beaded braids. "I'll never stay away from a window again."

"You won't live to see another," Kathleen threatened, managing to wrestle me down at last. "Not if you keep making a spectacle. You're a secret, brat. You're not supposed to exist."

I frowned. "Because my father's an ehru?"

"It would not matter if your father was the devil," Kathleen said. "To the emperor, your mother will always be the greater threat."

I pressed her, but Kathleen refused to say anything more. So I sulked, scooting away from her and joining Woo In on his side of the cramped sitting space.

I still hadn't forgiven Woo In for kissing The Lady's hand, but at least he left me alone. Half the time he hardly spoke at all, except to mutter sarcastic remarks, or to curse when his birthmarks glowed.

"Those pictures hurt you, don't they?" I frowned up at him. "Why didn't the map go away when you came back from the Breach?"

26

Woo In stiffened. "The map will disappear when the nightmares do," he said sourly.

I knew better than to ask more questions, but curiosity gnawed at me. How old had Woo In been when his parents gave him up to the abiku? What had the Underworld been *like*?

Once, at an inn, I had pretended to sleep as Woo In gazed through our second-story window. His shoulders had trembled, and after a moment, I realized he was sobbing. As if fleeing from monsters only he could see, he threw on his silk cape and leapt from the window. Then he soared above the dark rooftops, his lean body silhouetted against the moon.

"Can all Songlanders fly?" I asked him, jostling his shoulder in the mule-and-box.

His smooth brow furrowed, displeased that I knew his secret. "No. It's my Hallow."

"Hallow?"

"My birth gift. Only those with Hallows may serve The Lady. All of us have one."

All of us. The phrase made me curious: How many friends did The Lady have? "Do you have a Hallow?" I asked Kathleen.

She nodded. "I can change the appearance of whoever I please. Including you, though I think the lodestones have jumbled your insides quite enough already." She scowled out the window, growing thoughtful. "My gift comes in handy, since Mewish people gawk at *isokens*. At least in

Oluwan City, no one cares if I'm striped or spotted."

"Show me," I begged, and suddenly, instead of Kathleen, a second Woo In sat across from me. I jumped, grabbing the first Woo In's arm in fright. But now *he* was Kathleen.

"Greetings, Lady's Daughter," droned the illusion Woo In, flipping its straight jet hair. "It is I, your sullen nanny prince. Watch as I brood over my tragic childhood."

Illusion Kathleen rolled its eyes. "Very funny."

Kathleen shimmered back into her own skin and restored Woo In's face.

"Prince?" I echoed, frowning. My tutors had made me memorize the living members of every dynasty on the continent, and I'd never heard of a Prince Woo In. Queen Hye Sun of Songland had only one heir: Crown Princess Min Ja.

"I didn't make it onto many records," Woo In said flatly. "It's something they avoid when you're born cursed."

Our box neared the city gates. The roads grew broad, and the air rang with hoofbeats and voices. A highway ran alongside the broad Olorun River, and cargo-laden barges floated up and down on the current. Drums and laughter sounded as men rowed and sang. Now Kathleen hid me more than ever, but I managed a peek at the horizon, and my heart raced with wonder.

The skyline swelled with golden domes and ghostly white high-rises. Mist shrouded the towering city walls, and the Olorun River curved around the city like a steaming blue serpent. When the roads grew too crowded for our mule-and-box, we switched to a tasseled palanquin. I peered, breathless, through the gauzy curtains as runners carried us through the gates and into the city.

Streets and lofty skyways bustled with merchants and pack mules, jeering children and haughty scholars, storytelling priests and streetside hair braiders. Hawkers sold everything from kola nuts to kaftans, caged sprites to mewling hyena cubs. Obsidian tributes to Enoba the Perfect glittered in every square.

The oldest and most wealthy Oluwan families, Kathleen told me, were known as bluebloods: blue, because their skin was so black, it shone like precious cobalt. But as the Arit empire had grown, so too had Oluwan City. Now it sported every complexion under the sun, every tongue, every spice and fabric. Curry, lavender, and cayenne pepper mixed curiously in the air. Tartan wool from the north, silk from the south, and traditional wax-dyed cloth from the center realms hung side by side on clotheslines. Music and dialects from ten thousand miles apart melted together in one deafening din.

"Don't let her see the Watching Wall," Kathleen barked as we passed deeper into the city. Woo In obeyed her, seizing my protesting limbs and planting a hand over my eyes. I still managed to peek through his fingers . . . but I didn't understand what I saw.

A wall several stories high cut through the city. Murals of crowned figures stared imposingly from the plaster, one of whom I recognized: Enoba Kunleo, the handsome, broad-nosed hero of whom statues were sculpted all over Oluwan. Painted close around him were other men and women, dressed almost as grandly as the emperor. On impulse I counted them: *eleven*.

Why did that number strike a chord in my memory? The number hung over my head, like a cloud threatening thunder.

Woo In didn't let go until the streets grew quieter and the houses grander. Among the sound of trickling fountains and satiny murmurs, plump Oluwan bluebloods glided out of villas into palanquins. I noticed with curiosity that Bhekina House had been modeled after Oluwan mansions. White walls and red roofs sparkled proudly in the morning sun.

"This is Ileyoba," Kathleen murmured, both reverent and wary. "District of the emperor and all who can afford to live near him." On a green terraced hill, the domes of a sprawling palace rose to the sky. "And that," Kathleen said, "is An-Ileyoba, where the emperor lives. That's your last stop, little demon."

"Why?" I asked, but by then I did not expect an answer. At the palace gates, our palanquin was checked for weapons. Black flags ten stories tall spilled over the sandstone walls of An-Ileyoba. The flags were emblazoned with the imperial Kunleo seal: a swirling gold sun encircled by eleven moons.

"Business?" grunted a guard.

Kathleen pointed at me. "She's one of the candidates."

We descended from the palanquin, and the guard waved us into a vast, noisy chamber with yellow suns chiseled into the marble floor. Children from every Arit realm filled the room in various states of undress. Some scrubbed in tubs and were inspected for lice. Others ran drills with wooden spears, or recited poems from scrolls, or plucked frantic scales on instruments. Some even preened before hand mirrors, smiling and simpering, "An honor to meet you, Your Imperial Highness." Most of them wore black tunics, pinned at the shoulders with polished sun-and-moon clasps. Palace servants in brocaded wrappers supervised the children's preparations, and once each boy or girl was deemed suitable—for *what* I didn't know—guards ushered them into a line, which wound dizzyingly around a stone spiral staircase.

"Age," a clerk with a large book and quill droned, looking up at me from a low kneeling desk.

"Eleven," Kathleen replied. "Same age as His Imperial Highness. Her name is Tarisai, and she hails from Swana."

The clerk peered up at me suspiciously. "Are you sure? She might have a Swanian name, but she *looks* Oluwani."

Kathleen prodded me in the back, and I yelped and berated her. My Swanian accent convinced the clerk. He nodded to a gaggle of palace servants, who seized me. I fought back, clinging to Woo In's hand, but he whispered, "You are on your own now, Lady's Daughter. We can't stay."

"What's going on? What will these people do to me?"

He looked uncomfortable but squeezed my hand. "You'll be fine," he muttered. "We will always be near, even when you can't see us. And you have been prepared."

"Prepared? For what?" But then Kathleen and Woo In were herded away by guards, and my last tie to home, to Bhekina House, to everything I knew—disappeared.

Five pairs of hands removed my clothes and scrubbed my skin with plantain ash soap. My hair was washed with sweet-smelling water, combed, and twisted with shea butter until every coil shined. They pinned the flowing black tunic over my shoulders and draped me with a sash representing my home realm. The cloth was rich indigo, like the Swanian sky, and patterned with elephants and herons. Within hours I had joined the file of children on the winding stairs, our sandals slapping on the stone.

Curiosity tempered my fear. I'd never stood close to people my age before. A girl with enormous hazel eyes paced ahead of me. Her hair and neck were covered by a sheer red veil, and camels patterned her sash. I guessed that she was from Blessid Valley: a desert realm of nomadic herders and craftsmen. She twisted a gold ring on her smallest finger, singing absently to herself, "*Sleep, daughter; today you will leave me. Tonight I cannot sleep. Sleep and never forget your mother . . .*"

Her voice was like a grown woman's, deep and jangling, wrapping around me like a thick wool robe. Immediately I relaxed, but when I yawned, she stopped singing.

"Sorry," she said, and flashed a smile. "Mama says I

should be more careful. That chant puts my sister Miryam to sleep in a camel's wink. I sing it when I'm afraid: It helps my heart remember home."

"You must be cold," I said politely, nodding my head at her veil.

She laughed. "This is my prayer scarf. Blessids are People of the Wing, and we all wear a covering of some sort. It shows our devotion to the Storyteller."

My tutors had not brought me up in one of the Arit religious sects, though I knew there were four. "Can all . . . Wing-People do what you do? Magic with their voices?"

She snorted. "No. And it's not magic. I just remind bodies of what they need most; it's my Hallow."

"A birth gift," I murmured, echoing Woo In.

"Of course. Hallows are a requirement for all candidates. I hope mine is enough. I wonder—" She shot an anxious glance up the stairwell. "I wonder if Mama was right. Maybe I never should have left our caravan."

Screeches pierced the air, and suddenly guards clambered down the staircase, grappling with a blond boy with the palest skin I'd ever seen.

"It is not fair! It is not *fair*—unhand me!" the boy railed in a thick Nontish accent, gargled and breathy. Unless he had traveled by lodestone, it would have taken him almost a year to reach Oluwan. The cold, gray realm of Nontes lay within the farthest reaches of the Arit empire. "I did not even get to meet His Highness. I will send for my father. I was *born* for this! It is not fair—"

The Blessid girl snickered behind her hand. "Looks like someone didn't pass the first trial. And that's just an interview. The hard part comes after."

I stared after the Nontish boy as his screams grew distant and clutched at my indigo sash. The sensation of several pairs of child-size hands leeched from the cloth: recent memories. Within the last month, dozens of other Swanian children had worn the sash, donning and removing it with shaking fingers. Had they been excited or frightened? The cloth did not tell. "What are they going to do to us?"

"When we're tested? Oh . . ." The Blessid girl waved a hand. "Nothing *too* dangerous. The real trouble is if they like us. We never get to see our parents again. Not till we're grown up."

"*What?*" I hollered.

Several other children turned and whispered. The Blessid girl shushed me, looking embarrassed. "Of course we can't see our parents. Council members sever blood ties and swear loyalty only to the prince. Didn't anyone tell you?" At my terrified expression, she softened. "What's your name, Swana-girl? Mine's Kirah." She extended a hand, which I gaped at. She dimpled. "No point in being shy. If we both pass the trials, we're stuck together for life."

"I'm Tarisai," I said after a confused pause, and my hand slid into hers. The touch, warm and calloused, felt so natural I didn't want to let go. I stole a portion of Kirah's story, just for a moment. Two smiling older faces flashed into my mind, their prayer scarves worn and smelling of cinnamon. *Mama. Baba.*

Kirah had parents who loved her. They hadn't wanted her to come here: She had chosen this strange, chaotic place for herself.

Why? I wanted to ask, but we had reached the staircase landing. Two intricately carved doors rose up before us, guarded by warriors on either side. I had seen very few wooden doors in my life. In warm Arit realms, cloth door flaps allowed airflow, and therefore were more convenient than wood—unless one was very wealthy, private, or both. One of the warriors nodded brusquely at Kirah, and she gulped as the door swung inward. Before disappearing through the opening, she pressed my hand.

"Don't be scared, Tarisai," she murmured. Her gaze was starry. "It might be hard at first, but if they pick us . . . think of what we could *learn.* All the books in the world. No lodestone port closed. Just think: We'll practically rule the world."

Then she was gone.

Hours could have passed before the door creaked open again, and it still would have felt too soon. The guard nodded at me. When my legs didn't budge, I was unceremoniously pushed inside. The door boomed shut behind me.

I stood in an antechamber hung with purple tapestry. A cluster of men and women sprawled on divans and high-backed chairs, murmuring softly. Matching gold circlets gleamed on their brows. Their accents were as different as their complexions, but they gave the impression of a family, or something closer.

Much closer.

When I entered, they turned their heads in eerie unison. I shrank into the entryway shadows, expecting them to rise as one, like a multiheaded beast. But only one of them moved. A man with broad nostrils and deep laugh lines sat in the room's center, enthroned on a cushioned chair. The wax-dyed cloth of Oluwan, geometric patterns of red, black, and gold, draped across his solid frame. A mask hung from a cord over his chest. It was too small for anyone to wear, and I wondered at its purpose. It was black obsidian, carved in the shape of a lion with a mane of twelve stripes, each shimmering a different color.

The man reclined, examining me. "Well? Who is this?" His baritone was cheery, intended to put me at ease. His crown, an upright disc of solid gold, encircled his face like a rising sun. Over his head, three words were carved into the back of his chair: KUNLEO—OBA—ETERNAL.

In a violent flood, years of lectures filled my head. This was Olugbade Kunleo. *The* Olugbade Kunleo, from my tiresome months of genealogy lessons. The direct descendent of Enoba the Perfect.

The King of Oluwan, and High Emperor of Aritsar.

My tongue turned to lead.

"Don't be afraid, little one," sighed the emperor. "Wash your hands in the bowl. It is custom."

A gilded basin stood at my elbow, smelling strongly of herbs. The basin was engraved with pelicans, the sacred avatar of Am the Storyteller, and the birds' eyes gleamed with sapphires. I dipped my hands in the water, which was amber, like the enchanted pool near Bhekina House. My fingers tingled and I wiped them on my tunic, shrinking back into the shadows.

"Good," said Olugbade Kunleo. But as he squinted from across the room, his face drained of cheer. "Come into the light, child."

There was something familiar about his voice: a melodious timbre that drew me to obey without question. My feet advanced. The light from a tall, unglazed window fell full across my face . . . and the room gave a collective gasp.

"Am's Story," one of the courtiers swore. "She's *her* spitting image."

Another courtier scoffed, "It can't be. Not even The Lady would be reckless enough to send us her child."

"You know my mother?" I asked.

The strangers jumped, as if surprised I could speak. Why was everyone always so afraid of me?

"I'm Tarisai," I said awkwardly when their silence continued. "My home is Bhekina House, Swana. Excuse me, but—why am I here?"

Another echoing pause. "You tell us," the emperor replied dryly.

"I don't know, Your Imperial Majesty," I stammered.

"My guardians brought me to Oluwan, and my mother said she'd come for me when . . ."

Emperor Olugbade leaned forward, his tone ominously calm. "When . . . what?"

"When the time is right," I whispered. "That's all she said."

Olugbade tented his hands, considering me with a stillness that made my palms sweat. Then he laughed, a startling bark. His eyes crinkled at the corners. "Come here, Tarisai of Swana."

I crept forward, staring warily at the emperor's companions, some of whom placed hands on their weapon hilts. The emperor smelled of palm oil and oranges. The folds of his wax-dyed robe rustled, and the obsidian mask dangled from his neck as he leaned down to my ear.

"Here's what I think," he said evenly, like a father telling a bedtime story. "I think that The Lady sent you to kill me. But first, she would have you kill my son, Crown Prince Ekundayo, heir to the imperial throne."

"What?" I stared at him in horror. "Your Imperial Majesty, I don't want to—"

"I think you should try," he said, drawing a knife from his robe and thrusting it into my hand. "Go on. Try to kill me." I trembled, but he clenched my fingers around the knife hilt and brought the blade to his neck. "Try," he repeated, with a smile that warned me not to disobey. The blood drained from my face. Squeezing my eyes shut, I put pressure on the blade.

It didn't budge.

At Olugbade's urging, my hand pressed the knife hilt harder, then with all my strength. But the knife did not touch the emperor's neck. A hair's width of space lay between the blade and his skin: a thin, invisible barrier that no amount of force would make yield.

Olugbade chuckled, releasing my hand. The knife clattered to the floor.

"Do you know what this is, Tarisai?" he asked, gesturing to the lion on his chest. After my reluctant attack, one of the stripes in the lion's mane had begun to pulse with lurid light.

"It's a mask," I stammered. "Is that—is that why I couldn't hurt you?"

"No." Olugbade laughed. "This mask is merely proof of my right to rule Aritsar. Proof of the power inside me. Every stripe in the lion's mane is a death I cannot die. The only people in Aritsar who may kill me," he said, "the only people in the *entire universe*—are here in this room." He gestured to the group of eleven men and women, who clustered protectively around him. "I will not die until this body crumbles with old age. That is the power of the Ray, child. That power filled my father before me, and fills my son now. Only a Raybearer's Council of Eleven may kill him. Such is the divine protection of heaven. And none shall thwart it." He smiled tightly. "Not even your clever, clever Lady."

CHAPTER 4

THE RHYME FROM THE SWANIAN CARAVANS echoed in my head:

> *Eleven danced around the throne,*
> *Eleven moons in glory shone,*
> *They shone around the sun.*

"Eleven what?" I blurted. "What are the Eleven? Why does everyone keep talking about them?"

I could have heard a feather drop. The courtiers of the purple chamber stared, mouths agape.

Then Olugbade's laugh boomed. "You are a good mummer, Tarisai of Swana."

"I don't think she's acting," said a Mewish man. A tartan mantle draped across his pale chest, and he stroked a short red beard. He examined me with deep-set green eyes, alert with humor. "Am's Story. The Lady is a *genius*."

Olugbade continued to chuckle, though it sounded forced. "Don't be absurd, Thaddace."

"It's not absurd. It's brilliant." The man called Thaddace shook his head. "Consider: The Lady knew each child must be found pure of heart. So she raised a child in complete ignorance of the Imperial Councils. Unless we can prove she's faking her innocence, the law requires us to let her meet Prince Ekundayo. A diabolical plan, to be sure—but brilliant all the same."

"She will meet the prince over my dead body," hissed a lady seated at Olugbade's side. Her face reminded me of a spearhead: long with a pointed chin, beady eyes darting from me to the emperor. Her accent was from Nyamba, Oluwan's neighboring realm, where people read futures in the stars. "Olugbade. You will not let this girl, this *thing* anywhere near our son."

"It's the law," Thaddace interjected. "Divine law, Nawusi. She washed in the basin. We at least have to check if she has a Hallow; we can't get rid of her without breaking the rules—"

"Hang the rules," snapped Nawusi. "If Ekundayo anoints this brat onto his council, his Ray won't be able to protect him. We might as well sign his death warrant."

"And you know this to be fate?"

The woman paused, pressing her lips together. "I did not see it in the stars," she admitted. "But the girl is *that woman's* spawn."

Thaddace sighed. "If we deny her a chance, we profane holy rites. Dayo's council could be cursed forever. Is that your suggestion?"

Nawusi gripped the arms of her chair, fixing me with her spearhead stare. "Murder is in that child's *blood*," she whispered, and I shivered.

"It seems," said a fluting voice, "we must determine if this girl is truthful. Shall I examine her?"

The speaker was lounging on a couch in front of Thaddace. She was Swanian, and the loveliest person I had ever seen. Her coily curls were shorn close to her scalp, and gold powder shimmered on high, dark cheekbones. Dots of white paint adorned the bridge of her nose and arched above each eyelid, and the pelican pendant worn by priests of Am twinkled on her willowy neck.

"I am Mbali," she said. "Come here, Tarisai."

A tattooed line on her chin marked Mbali as a griot. I had only ever heard of them in story scrolls—griots were singers of histories and stories, the most sacred of Arit priests. As I approached, Thaddace's hands closed protectively on Mbali's shoulders.

She tilted my chin so her mirror-black eyes poured into mine. I warmed, as I always did when touched. Then my head swam, and my vision blurred. Scrambling for control, I placed my hand over Mbali's and tried to steal her story. But the priestess's mental shields were made of adamant. Her mind *pushed back* . . . and won.

Calm flooded my thoughts like smoke over a beehive. My arms hung limp at my sides.

"Now," intoned Mbali, "we shall have the truth. Tarisai, did your mother send you here to kill the emperor?"

I could not lie, even if I wished to do so. "No," I said.

A relieved murmur rippled through the room. "Very well," she continued. "Did your mother send you here to kill Ekundayo, Crown Prince of Aritsar?"

"I've never heard of him," I said truthfully. "Not until today."

Mbali beamed and stroked my cheek. "Am be praised," she sighed. "I ached to imagine that The Lady might have corrupted a child. If your soul is pure, we shall strive to keep it so."

I glanced around the room. Apparently Mbali's power could convince a room full of skeptics. Previously hostile faces had now softened with interest . . . except for Olugbade's and Nawusi's, which looked as wary as ever.

"It doesn't matter how innocent she is," Nawusi said, perking up. "She can't join the Prince's Council without a Hallow."

Olugbade nodded, looking relieved. "The Lady could not have force-bred a Hallowed child. That would be an act of the gods." He leaned forward with a pitying smile. "There is a difference between a talent and a Hallow, you see. Hallows are unteachable: an ability so vast, it could only be bestowed at birth. Few children qualify, but to please the law, we will let you try. Did The Lady train you to recite epic poems? That's a popular one." He chuckled. "Or let me guess: You're a juggler, or a master hyena-tamer."

"Mother didn't teach me anything," I retorted. "I can see your memories."

Again the room fell silent. Fear returned to the courtiers' faces.

"You mean," Olugbade said slowly, "that you can imagine what you *think* happened years ago. Memories that your mother has fed you."

I shook my head. "I told you—The Lady doesn't tell me anything. And I don't like going back years; it makes my head hurt."

"Why don't you demonstrate?" said Mbali.

I touched her cheek, as she had touched mine. Her skin was smooth and cool, though the tattoo on her chin thrummed with heat. I closed my eyes. The first memory was from early this morning. Thaddace's face leaned toward Mbali. He smiled warmly, his beard prickling her cheek—then his lips were on Mbali, and then—

I jerked back from her, my eyes wide as moons.

"Well?" She cocked her head.

"I . . . didn't see anything that time," I stuttered. "I'll try again." I touched her tentatively, hoping the next memory would not include the strange games adults played. I was lucky. "You were at a banquet last night," I told Mbali. "A party with just your council and the emperor. There was lots of food. You told a story." I snuck a glance at Olugbade. "The story made His Imperial Highness angry."

The griot priestess froze, and the pulse at her temple quickened.

"She could have learned that from servants talking," Nawusi said quickly. "This proves nothing."

"But no one else heard the story," Mbali whispered. "No one but our council."

"Let's see her repeat it," demanded Nawusi.

I touched Mbali's face again, reliving the private banquet. The griot priestess had accompanied herself on a talking drum, holding the goatskin-covered gourd in the crook of her arm. The drum's pitch had risen and fallen with Mbali's voice. My hips swayed with the pulsing beat as I repeated the story.

"There is a farmer's son with a mango tree, *aheh*. He keeps it in a pot by his sleeping mat. So frail, his tree! He whispers to it day and night. He enjoys the perfume of its branches, *ashe, ashe*. Most children keep dogs, goats, chickens. But not our farmer's son. For he fears any beast that can bark, *aroo*, or bite, *gnatche*.

"His tree has no mouth. His tree has no claws. His tree depends on him, only him, for water, *wishe*, for light, *ra*.

"'Poor tree,' he murmurs. See him caress the branches. 'You are too small for fruit. You are useless for the farm. You are useless for the market. You are useless to everyone but me.'

"But the branches thicken and grow, *aheh*! Up, up, up, in one night! 'Poor tree,' scoffs our farmer's son. He plucks the single mango. 'I am surprised you can blossom at all.'

"The next morning, three mangoes greet him: *za, za, za!* 'You will never make fruit for the market,' says our farmer's son.

"Up, up—our tree, she grows in the night. See her

branches make shadows, long and thick. The boy watches and his knees shake, *didun, didun*. 'It's just my little tree,' he says. 'It would be dead without me.'

"The next morning, there are twenty mangoes.

"*Ka! Ka!* The farmer's son hacks off every branch. 'It is for the tree's own good,' he says. 'The weight would strain its little boughs.' But the tree keeps growing: *gung-gung, gung-gung*. 'I will move it to a smaller pot,' he says. The roots creep over the tiny clay pot. See them burrow deep, deep into the dirt floor. 'I will stop watering it,' says our farmer's son.

"But the tree, she has learned to blossom on her own.

"The boy hacks—*ka! ka!*—but the tree grows, *gung-gung, gung-gung*. See her branches fill the boy's room! See him cower in her shadow!

"*Ehmm-ehmm*, the neighbors smell the mango perfume. They come to gape at the boy's tree. '*Aheh!* What wonder! The fruit will feed the whole village!'

"*Krah! Krah!* The boy cuts the tree down.

"*Rra!* He burns her branches.

" 'The neighbors were wrong,' he says as the blaze grows high. 'The tree could never be useful without me.'

"How peacefully he sleeps now, *ashh, ashh*. There are no branches. There are no shadows. But smell . . .

"Was that a hint of mango?

"Perhaps we imagine it, *kye, kye!*

"Or perhaps a seed survived the flames. *Whish*—see it drift on the wind, and fly where the boy cannot find it.

See it take root in the earth. See children lounge in its shadow.

"See as the boy's name is forgotten.

"Aheh: my story is done."

My voice had grown hoarse by the ending line. When my hand fell at last from Mbali's cheek, the griot priestess was trembling. Confused, I followed her gaze to Olugbade.

The emperor of Aritsar was staring at me with cold, simmering hatred.

Mbali's arm slipped around me protectively. Energy vibrated through the room, and the men and women exchanged looks, speaking without words. Their mouths remained closed, but the faint voices floated in the air, like chattering leaves on overhead branches.

"It doesn't matter whether or not she wants to kill Dayo," Nawusi finally said out loud. "If this brat has that woman's power, then she is just as dangerous as any assassin."

"The girl does not have power," Olugbade insisted. "And neither does her mother. That woman is an imposter. I will not hear any speculation of her legitimacy."

"Olu." Mbali sighed. "No matter how we examine this, the safest place for Tarisai is on Dayo's council."

"Have you lost your mind?" shrilled Nawusi.

"We already know she has a Hallow," Mbali insisted. "If Tarisai has another power—"

"She doesn't," Olugbade said.

"If she does," Mbali persisted, "this is the only way we can guarantee she never uses it against Dayo.

The Children's Palace is secure, isolated from the outside world. On Dayo's council, we could shield her from The Lady's influence more effectively than anywhere else."

After a long deliberation, several begrudging voices spoke around the room: "Dayo's council . . . Mbali's right . . . Her memory gift could be useful . . . Strict surveillance . . . Give it a try . . ."

"Fine," Nawusi said finally, rigid in her chair. "She can meet the prince. But only after we have tried our *last* option." She stood and approached me, back straight as a palace spire. Her face twitched as she tried, unconvincingly, to look friendly. "Are you hungry, child?"

"I don't know." I fidgeted. "A little."

She reached into her robe pocket and produced a shiny red fruit. The room tensed immediately.

"Nawusi . . ." Thaddace growled. "Don't be rash—"

"Do you know what this is, Tarisai?" Nawusi cooed. "No, you don't have these in Swana. But in Oluwan City, we eat delicacies from all over the empire. This is called an *apple*. They grow far to the north. Won't you take a bite?"

"No!" Mbali exclaimed, rising to her feet. "Nawusi, how could you?"

"You're the one who's so sure of her power, Mbali," Nawusi retorted. "If you're right, then perhaps she has nothing to fear from me."

"We must obey the law, Nawusi," Thaddace objected. "And for Am's sake, she's a child."

"Olugbade?" Nawusi turned to the emperor, raising an expectant eyebrow.

Olugbade leaned back in his chair, tenting his hands over the obsidian mask. At last, he said weakly, "Give it to her."

Mbali's face slackened with horror. "Olu."

But the emperor ignored the priestess, wincing at me. "I fear we are frightening you, little one. Sometimes, adults argue over silly things. But you need not fear. Take the apple."

A small voice in my head told me to run.

But where would I go? There were guards outside the door, and these people were powerful in ways I dared not guess. What if they chased me? Besides . . . Arit emperors were good. They were *perfect*.

I took the apple. Everyone in the room held their breath. I raised the smooth-skinned fruit, opened my mouth, and . . .

Mbali reached me in two strides, knocked the apple out of my hand, then kneeled and pressed me to her chest.

"Am will punish us for this," she whispered. "Poisoning a child is an unclean game to play. No matter how powerful that child may be."

I recoiled, staring at the apple on the floor with horror. What was this place, where adults tried to kill children? Why had The Lady sent me here?

I began to cry. Mbali made a soothing noise, pushing a wayward coil from my face. "Let us start again," she said.

"I am the High Priestess of Aritsar. Everyone in this room is a member of Olugbade's Eleven. And really—it's lovely to meet you, Tarisai."

"I don't understand," I hiccupped.

"Aritsar is ruled by twelve people. When the emperor is a young boy, he anoints eleven children, one from each realm, to rule beside him until death. These children are gifted, special, and loyal only to the emperor."

"And," Thaddace murmured, "to each other."

Mbali shot him what appeared to be a warning look . . . but she nodded. "A child on the council gains not only power, but a family."

Curiosity crept into my fear. I remembered Kirah's joke on the stairs: *If we both pass the trials, we're stuck together for life.* My whole life, I had longed for friends who stayed. For the people I loved to never disappear. I glanced at the men and women clustered around Olugbade, faces animated in silent conversation. That was how I had always imagined being part of a family: draped across one another like a pride of lions, trading giggles and secrets.

"If I want to join the prince's Eleven," I said slowly, "what do I have to do?"

"Well . . . above all, you must love Crown Prince Ekundayo, and devote your life to his service."

I raised an eyebrow. "Love the prince? That's it?"

"In summary." Mbali waved a hand. "There are other tests, to be sure. But what matters most is your connection with the Ray: the power of Kunleo emperors. It allows them to join eleven minds to their own. If you succeed, the prince will offer you both the Ray and his hand in councilhood. Your choice is permanent. Nothing is more important than your love—than your *loyalty*. Do you understand, Tarisai?" She stood and reached for me. "Good. I think you'll like the prince. He's—"

"Wait," I said. "How do you all know Mother? Has she been here before?"

Another pause from Mbali. "The Lady lived at the Children's Palace a long time ago, when Emperor Olugbade was a boy. It would be best, Tarisai, if you do not speak of your mother while at An-Ileyoba. Few people are old enough to remember when she lived here, but those who do may not look . . . kindly on your connection. If anyone asks, your parents are middling gentry, prosperous farmers from the Owatu region in Swana. Can you remember that?"

I nodded reluctantly. Then I scanned the room with new interest, trying to imagine The Lady as a child. "Was my mother a candidate? Did she fail?"

"She failed in every way," Olugbade intoned. "She was not aspiring to be a council member."

"Oh. Then why did she—"

"It's no use bringing up the past," Mbali said briskly. "You write your story, not the people who came before you. Come."

We crossed the room to a gilded set of doors behind Olugbade's Eleven. My hand in hers, we entered a place that made me dizzy from gazing.

"Welcome to the Children's Palace," said Mbali. "The happiest place in An-Ileyoba."

Sunlight streamed into a high-domed chamber of blue and gold. Rays glinted off a mountain of toys and a menagerie of rideable wooden animals from every Arit realm. Children on zebras and tigers scooted past me, jeering and screaming in chase. Servants in brocade wrappers bustled about, holding fruit trays and water pitchers.

Mbali caught a child by the arm: the girl I had met on the stairs. I smiled at Kirah, relieved that she had passed the mysterious trial. She beamed back and curtsied to Mbali. "Anointed Honor! Is it time for another test?"

"Not yet, my dear," Mbali replied. "But can you help me find Ekundayo? I can't pick him out in this crowd."

Kirah's round face flushed. "None of us can, Your Anointed Honor. He's been hiding since I got here." She gestured at a large group of children, who were throwing open cabinets and peeking under tables. As the groups of searchers disemboweled the room, shrieking the prince's name . . . I felt a pang of familiarity.

My tutors had often searched for me in Bhekina House. I had hidden for hours, plugging my ears to the sound of my name as it echoed through every hall. My tutors feared The Lady, and so their lives had revolved around me: my every success and failure.

Empathy surged inside me for this prince I had never met.

"He's not in here," I said.

Mbali looked down at me in surprise. "How do you know?"

I shrugged, scanning the room. "Too many people. And the cabinets would be too easy."

Mbali's mouth twitched. "Then we had better look somewhere else."

We left Kirah and passed through the brightly painted halls of the Children's Palace. It was a miniature version of An-Ileyoba's central wing, Mbali told me, and in one room, the floor was a giant marble checkerboard, where giggling children stood in place of the pieces. In another, dining tables brimmed with oranges, fried plantains, sticky fig cakes, and mountains of treats I couldn't name. The wing even had a mock throne room—a chamber with mirrored ceilings and twelve child-size thrones. At last, I lingered in a large, airy room with a dais in the center. Murals of long-dead councils glittered overhead, depicted as flower-crowned children, smiling beatifically as they danced in a circle.

"This is the Hall of Dreams," said Mbali. "You will conduct much of your training here during the day, and sleep here at night." Rolled sleeping mats lay stacked in neat piles against the walls. Tied-up mosquito nets hung in gauzy festoons from the ceiling, and embroidered constellations shimmered in silver and blue across the netting. When the nets were let down, they would look like the heavens, tumbling to the bodies of children below.

"At night, a screen separates the boys from the girls.

The prince sleeps there, in the middle." She pointed to the raised platform. "Someday, his council will sleep close beside him."

Lofty unglazed windows sank into arches along one wall, shielded by white damask curtains, which glowed with sunlight and shuddered in the breeze.

"Here," I murmured. "He's in here."

Mbali raised an eyebrow. "How do you know?"

"It's where I would hide. It's so open that no one would look very hard." One of the curtains wrinkled more than the others. I approached it, spying dark brown toes and the tips of golden sandals at the curtain's edge.

"Don't worry," I said softly. "I won't tell the others." Then I drew back the curtain. A young Oluwani boy stood before me, parting his full lips into a curious, familiar smile.

I saw red. Heat tore through me, and my pulse thrummed with the same word, over and over and over.

Kill.

CHAPTER 5

I WANTED TO WRING HIS NECK. I WANTED TO smother his mouth and soft broad nose. I wanted the light to vanish from those naive, curious eyes.

Another part of me, struggling for breath, reeled in horror. I didn't want this. I didn't hate this boy; I'd never met him in my life. What was happening to me? My ehru half, the part born of wishes and fire, calmed down as The Lady's voice echoed in my ear.

When he anoints you as his own.

My shoulders sagged in relief. It wasn't time yet. Something else had to happen before I could hurt this boy. Perhaps I could escape before it did.

"Dayo," said Mbali, "this is Tarisai of Swana, your newest candidate. Tarisai, this is His Imperial Highness Ekundayo Kunleo of Oluwan, Crown Prince of Aritsar." She added gently, without accusation, "You will be watched."

Then she made to leave. I clutched at her, afraid to be left alone with this stranger. Afraid of what I might do to him.

Mbali chuckled, misunderstanding my fear. "He won't

bite, dear. Sometimes, I wonder if our Dayo has any teeth at all." Fondly, she ruffled the boy's tightly curled hair. "Have fun." Then she slipped a key from her neck, unlocked a subtle door painted into the chamber wall, and slipped through without a sound. Strangely, Mbali's gaze still pressed on me even after she had disappeared.

Ekundayo and I stared at each other. I was taller than him, though he drowned in robes of blue-gold wax-dyed cloth. He shifted from foot to foot, looking as awkward as I felt.

"Well," he said. "Aren't you going to try and touch me?"

I blinked. "Why would I?"

"The rest of them do. They all try to hug me or kiss my fingers and sandals. They say—" He shrugged. "They say they love me."

"Well, I don't love you."

He cocked his head, aghast. "Not even a little?"

"Of course not." He looked so heartbroken, I wanted to comfort him. "It's just, I've never met you before," I stammered.

"But *everyone* loves me. Though I guess they could be lying. Father thinks I trust people too much." Ekundayo frowned, then brightened with comical speed. "Maybe *you're* lying, Tarisai of Swana. Maybe you do love me after all."

My mouth curved up. I couldn't help it: Just like in the portrait, his broad, gap-toothed smile was infectious.

"I don't have any secrets," I said, and then a fist twisted

56

my insides. I stepped away from him. "I should go. Your Imperial Highness—"

"My friends call me Dayo," he said eagerly. "Or they will. When I have friends."

In my backward shuffle I stumbled on the tasseled edge of a rug. Dayo caught my arm to steady me. I jerked away.

"Did I do something wrong again?" he asked.

"No. But people don't usually touch me. They avoid it."

"Why?"

Maybe if I scared him, he would stay away from me. "Because I'm a half-demon," I whispered, wiggling my eyebrows for effect. "A spy. I can see everything—*everything*—you've ever done."

Dayo's gaze widened. "That's amazing."

That wasn't right. He should have been frightened. No one liked having light cast on the shadows of their thoughts. Unless . . . Perhaps, they had no shadows to hide.

Why in Am's name did The Lady want me to hurt him?

"Do it," he said, taking both my hands and placing them on his face. "Do it, Tarisai. Try your spy trick on me."

I paused, feeling shy. No one had ever been *excited* about my Hallow before. I ran a thumb over his cheek, then remembered what my hands had itched to do just minutes earlier.

My mouth went dry.

No, I protested silently. That girl wasn't me. I didn't have to hurt anyone. I didn't. I *wouldn't*.

My body relaxed, and I let Dayo's memories flood my

vision. Hundreds of small faces barreled toward mine, drowning me in presents and kisses, sickly sweet voices feverish with desire: *I love you, Ekundayo . . . I'd die for you, Ekundayo . . . Pick me, Ekundayo . . . pickmepickmepickme—*

Most of the children had frightened him. Every now and then, a child made him feel safe, but they almost always failed some strange test I didn't understand. Then Mbali would take the child away, and Dayo would return to his hiding place behind the curtain, heaving quiet sobs that no one ever heard.

My feelings began to mix with Dayo's and I grew dizzy, pulling out of his mind. Just like Dayo, I had also watched the people I liked walk away. I had wondered why no one ever stayed—why I was surrounded, yet always alone. I tried to drop my hands from Dayo's face, but he held them there, eyes pouring wistfully into mine.

"You're going to be another one, aren't you?" the prince murmured. "A person I like. A person they take away."

"Maybe I won't," I said. Though our minds had separated, a strange energy hung in the air between us, tethering me to him. "Maybe I won't go anywhere."

He let me go. "There's only one way to make sure. There are lots of tests, but only one really matters." He dimpled. "If you pass, you *have* to stay with me."

I frowned. "Do not."

"Do too."

"Do not—"

"All right," he admitted. "You don't. But you'll want to; I

just know it. When there's twelve of us, they send us to Yorua Keep, a castle far away by the ocean. We'll live there all by ourselves, and train to rule Aritsar, and go on adventures. I'll see you every day. Forever, until we're dead."

"But won't our parents miss us?" I frowned at the carpet. "Why do they always send us away?"

"They don't," Dayo laughed. "Not *normal* parents. But Father's the emperor. He's preparing me to rule."

For what future, I wondered, was The Lady preparing me?

"Won't your mother miss you?" I asked.

"Oh . . ." He looked uncomfortable. "I don't have one. I mean—I know who she *is*." I noticed then that his chin strongly resembled Nawusi's. "But I'm not supposed to show favoritism to any of Father's council members. I call them all 'uncle' or 'auntie'—even my mother. It's best for diplomacy. There are lots of rules here," he admitted, "but don't worry. If you pass the test, we'll make our own rules. Far away, at Yorua."

My stomach fluttered in spite of my crossed arms. A castle full of friends who never left? A chance to see the world? To see the *sea*?

"Well?" I said. "What's the test?"

The answer was a jarring bolt ripping through my body, hurling me to the ground. Spots of light swirled painfully in my vision, and I could barely sense Dayo's anxious voice as he knelt beside me, shaking my shoulders.

"Tarisai? I'm so sorry; I shouldn't have tried it. I shouldn't—"

"What happened?" I moaned, shoving him away.

"I tried to unite your mind with mine," he said. "It's what emperors do with their councils. But it only works if you love me."

"I sure don't love you *now*," I said, rubbing my throbbing temples.

The hidden door burst open and Mbali swept in, making *tut* sounds. Dayo flew at her, blubbering, "It wasn't her fault, Auntie Mbali, I swear it wasn't; don't take her away . . ."

"Dayo," Mbali said, extracting herself from his grip and helping me up. "You administered the test. She failed. I've warned you about trying the Ray too early."

Dayo sob-hiccupped. "I—I just wanted her to stay."

"You know the rules. Candidates have only one chance to succeed."

"But—"

"Say goodbye, children." She took my hand firmly in hers and walked me toward the door.

I had wanted to get away from Dayo. To keep us both safe. But now my heart was torn. I'd never had a friend in my life, and—I *liked* him. How could I let him vanish like The Lady, and Melu, and Woo In, and Kathleen?

Why did everyone always leave me?

The memory of the screaming Nontish boy, wrestled away by guards, still lay fresh in my mind. I knew I couldn't fight Mbali. Heart racing, my mind shifted solutions like puzzle pieces. Invisible tutors breathed down my neck, and Woo In's words echoed.

You have been prepared for this.

I crossed my arms and told Mbali, "I take orders from the prince, not you."

She fixed her large dark eyes on mine. "Say that again, child."

I swallowed hard. "I don't take orders from you. 'Nothing is more important than loyalty.' You said that earlier. So I'm not going anywhere . . ." I pointed a finger at Dayo. ". . . unless *he* wants me to."

Mbali gave a slow, cunning smile. "Congratulations, Dayo. Your friend has passed a test that no candidate has before her."

Dayo gaped. "That was a test?" Mbali nodded, and Dayo's features grew puzzled. "So all the candidates you took away before . . . None of them had to go?"

"None of them understood directions as well as Tarisai."

Directions. I shuddered, wondering how many hidden commands and tests I had already missed. I swallowed hard. "So?" I asked Dayo. "Do you want me to leave?"

He wagged his head. "Never! Can she really stay, Auntie Mbali?" When the priestess nodded, Dayo cried out and tackled me in a hug. "Do you love me now, Tarisai of Swana?"

"Of course not. Stop it." I snorted, pushing him off. But both of us giggled, breathless with our newfound power. If a member of the Emperor's Council couldn't command us, who could?

"Her mind must still connect with your Ray," Mbali

reminded Dayo. "You may not offer Tarisai your hand in councilhood until it does. But give her time. If she succeeds in this and other trials, you may anoint her."

Anoint her: The words set off warning bells in my head. My happiness cooled.

Dayo bounced up and down after Mbali left. "It'll be easy, Tarisai. All you have to do is solve puzzles, and learn weapons, and science, and god-studies, and statecraft, and when you finally love me . . ." From beneath his tunic, he pulled a gold-encrusted vial dangling from a chain around his neck. "Oil from a pelican's wing," he said reverently. "If you accept my hand, I'll anoint you with it. Then you'll be one of my Eleven. Forever."

My blood ran hot. The room wheeled as The Lady's voice broke over me like searing oil:

When he anoints you as his own.

"No," I rasped. "No!"

Dayo's face wrinkled in confusion. "Tarisai? What's wrong? I didn't mean to . . ."

His words drowned in the shadows looming around me, voices that invaded my thoughts no matter how tightly I plugged my ears. *When you meet this boy in the portrait—when he anoints you as his own—I command you to kill—kill—kill—*

"I won't," I rasped, swiping at phantom fairies only I could see. "I won't. You can't make me."

"If that's what you want," said Dayo, sounding crestfallen. "I can't force you to join."

"I didn't mean you," I told him. "I meant—" My body

broke out in cold sweat as the air hung with the scent of jasmine, filling my nostrils until I gagged. With one last strangled *You can't make me, Mother* . . . , my vision rainbowed, and the room disappeared.

In a dreamworld the color of Swanian grasslands, Melu hovered above me. His spirit rode where his imprisoned body could not go, coursing through riverbanks, seeping into the bedrock of An-Ileyoba Palace. His pleading voice reverberated through the walls: *It is a shame you must hurt the boy. But an ehru may not resist a master's wish. Give in. Give in, daughter, and we will both be free.*

"I have no master," I snarled.

The apparition gave a ghostly sigh, long and grim. *Yes, you do.*

CHAPTER 6

I AWOKE WITH A LURCH, EXPECTING TO BE blinded by Melu's cobalt blue wings. But the ehru wasn't there.

Instead, a pair of lamp-like hazel eyes blinked down at me. Kirah's red veil wrapped around her hair and neck, nestling her tan, moon-shaped face. Her soothing chant had coaxed me from my nightmare.

"Oh, good." She laughed. "You're awake. The way you were twisting and turning, Mama would have said you had a demon. I almost tried a spirit-binding song, and I'm not very good at those."

At the word *demon* I shuddered and curled my knees up to my chest. I was still in the enormous hall. We were the only ones present, and it was nighttime. Sconces flickered patterns on the muraled walls. I was lying on Dayo's sleeping platform, cushioned with panther-fur blankets. Kirah sat on the edge, feet dangling over the side.

"You've been out for hours. The prince insisted on giving you his pallet. You're famous with the other children, you know. The 'Prince's Favorite.'" She paused. "Around here, that's not the safest thing to be."

"I'm thirsty." My throat was dry. She handed me a chalice from the floor. I sniffed at the liquid—it was mango juice, pulpy and cool. I sipped, vaguely glad it wasn't apple. Then slippery white rocks attacked my face.

"Ice," Kirah informed me. "Weird, right? I hear it keeps meat from going bad. Oluwan imports blocks from places like Nontes and Biraslov—cold realms up north."

I sucked down the liquid, enjoying the curious chill in my throat. "Where's everyone else?"

"They're off solving a puzzle. In the middle of the night! I guess that's how things are here. We were all sleeping, then we heard drums, and the testmakers made an announcement. They've staged a kidnapping of Prince Ekundayo. Whoever finds him gets a chance with Dayo's Ray. But you didn't wake up, so I stayed to see if you were all right."

"Thanks," I said. "But you're missing the test."

She shrugged. "There'll be others. And it's not proper to leave the sick unattended. Mama says, 'A caravan mustn't travel faster than its slowest camel.' Besides," she added with a sheepish smile, "I'm nervous about trying the Ray."

"You should be," I snorted. "I never want to try *that* again."

Her gaze grew sharp. "Then the rumors are true? The prince really tried the Ray right after meeting you?"

I wrinkled my nose. "It gave me a headache."

"It'll feel good after you love him," Kirah said fervently. "After you're anointed, you can't live without the Ray. Even my singing can't cure council sickness." She took in my blank expression, then dimpled again. "I forgot you were raised under a rock. When you're anointed, the Ray binds your body to the council. So if you ever get separated—or abandon the council—you get sick. Sweating, fever. Eventually you go mad." Her voice dropped to a murmur. "That's why no council has ever committed treason. And that's why the Emperor's Eleven are always together, touching and kissing like that. If they stay apart for long, they get the sickness."

I shuddered, remembering my feverish sleepwalking through Bhekina House. Did I miss The Lady because I was her daughter, or because I was her ehru?

Maybe all love was a bit like council sickness.

"It's a great honor to try the Ray," said Kirah. "If you succeed at uniting minds with the prince, you're sure to be one of his Eleven. Well. Unless you're *him*." She pointed at a shadow across the room.

I realized with a jolt that we weren't alone after all.

A tall, broad-backed figure leaned against a pillar, so still that I had mistaken him for a piece of furniture. He faced away from us, hunched, as if in a vain attempt to look smaller.

"What's a man doing in here?" I whispered.

"He's not a man." Kirah snorted through her nose. "He's just *big*. I heard he's only thirteen, a year older than me. Some boys get their grown-up legs early. It happened to my brothers; their voices got all cracked and funny . . ." She shot a glance at the hunched boy, then shivered. "I'd feel sorry for him, if he didn't scare me so much."

"Why? Is he mean?"

"Mama says it's unholy to gossip," Kirah said primly. "But . . . they say he's killed people. A pit fighter. The others call him the Prince's Bear, because he's very protective of Ekundayo. Also, he's been here longer than any of us. When Ekundayo tried the Ray on him, it worked immediately."

To my surprise, jealousy pricked. "So the Bear's already anointed? He's the first of Dayo's Eleven?"

"No. He refused the prince's offer. *Refused* to be anointed, can you believe it? But the Emperor's Council still won't let him leave. They think he'll change his mind."

I frowned. What sane child would turn down a permanent family? I could not imagine a rosier life. "I wonder why he said no."

Kirah tossed her head. "Thinks he's too good for us, probably. That's what kids from rich realms are like, you know. I mean . . . not *all* of them," she added awkwardly. "You're different, I guess."

"I'm not rich."

She snorted. "You're from Swana. Mama says Swana has more maize than blades of grass. Or at least, it used to. A powerful alagbato used to guard your savannahs, so the harvests never failed. But he disappeared some ten, eleven years ago. No one knows why." My skin ran cold; Melu was trapped in his grassland, unable to serve as Swana's guardian until I fulfilled The Lady's wish. I bit my lip with guilt, but Kirah didn't seem to notice. "You're lucky to come from fertile land instead of desert. I bet you've never gone hungry a day in your life."

"I haven't," I admitted. "Where's the Prince's Bear from?"

"Dhyrma," Kirah whispered. "Where they ride elephants in the streets, and the roads are paved with coins." She slipped off the bed and fussed maternally over my bedding. "If you're feeling better, I guess I should go join the others."

"Maybe I should come too."

"No; the healer said you should rest. Besides, you're already the 'Prince's Favorite.' Give the rest of us a chance, huh?" She winked, then jerked her head over at the Dhyrmish boy. "And don't worry about the Bear. We've chained him to the bedpost."

Alarmed, I squinted at the boy's gloomy corner of the room. Something silver glinted in the sconce light—a chain of metal links, wrapped around the pillar and ending in a cuff on the boy's burly arm. "It was a joke," said Kirah, looking sheepish. "The other kids started it. He's the 'Prince's Bear,' and bears are baited, so . . ."

My brow knit. "Doesn't seem to very funny to him."

"He could have stopped us if he wanted to. Besides, Mama says Dhyrmish people are like rabid dogs. I'm not going near him." She refilled my goblet from a pitcher—

Mama says sick children ought to drink lots—patted my arm, then hurried from the room.

I watched the figure in the far corner, unnerved by how still he was. He hadn't budged even when the bedroom doors slammed behind Kirah. But I lay quietly, afraid of spooking him.

Then pressure weighed on my bladder. I winced; I hadn't relieved myself for hours. Come to think of it, I was hungry too. I wriggled from the pile of panther skins and stood. The pressure intensified. After a fruitless glance around the room, I cleared my throat.

"E-excuse me," I said. "Do you ever . . . I mean . . . Do you know where they keep the chamber pots?" My face heated. The figure tensed, as though surprised I had addressed him. "Never mind," I mumbled. "I'll just—"

"The pots are kept in the corner."

I froze in surprise. The boy had not moved, but his voice filled the room, soft and implausibly deep.

"Put it back when you're done. Servants take them away in the morning."

"Oh. Thank you." I crept to a corner and retrieved a brightly painted clay pot. I paused again. "Are the privy screens outside?"

The boy made a growling sound, almost a laugh. "Privacy is illegal here, new girl. Council members aren't allowed to have secrets. Most candidates relieve themselves in the morning or late at night, when the gender screen is still drawn." His Dhyrmish accent slid in a musical scale.

Plosive consonants skipped across the boy's tongue, like stones on a pond. He added, "Don't worry. I won't look."

I did the deed as quickly as possible, stashing the pot in one of the window alcoves. My stomach gurgled. I remembered the feast I had seen in the dining hall earlier, and asked, "Where can I find food?"

"I wouldn't know," the boy replied. "I missed dinner hours ago."

"My servants tied me up like you once," I blurted awkwardly. "They were afraid I would steal their memories while they slept. I always give memories back after I take them. But they didn't trust me."

For the first time, the Dhyrmish boy turned.

Due to his size, I had expected him to look older, but a startlingly young face flickered in the candlelight, with a heavy jawline, reddish-brown skin, and steeply slanted eyebrows. His ears stuck out, as though he'd yet to grow into them, though the idea of him growing *more* was hard to imagine. "Stealing memories," he said. "That's your Hallow?"

I nodded. "Like this." Feeling a strange urge to impress him, I placed a hand on Dayo's dais. The marble groaned as my mind invaded its pores. The stone remembered a boy who had slept there decades ago. Over and over, he had rasped into the blankets: *The Lady . . . The Lady . . . The Lady.*

I snatched my hand from the dais as if it had burned me.

The Dhyrmish boy raised an eyebrow. "Something wrong?"

"Emperor Olugbade slept here before Dayo," I explained.

"When the emperor was young, he had bad dreams. I think Dayo gets bad dreams here too."

"You see all that?" asked the Dhyrmish boy. "Just by touching things?"

"People leave stories everywhere. It's easier to take them from living things. Trees, soil. Objects and dead things don't have very clear memories."

The boy ran a hand through large, soft curls. "When you take memories, could you take them for good?" The chain on his arm rattled. "Could you make someone's memories disappear forever?"

"No!" I said. "I mean, I don't know. I've never tried that before." To my surprise, the boy looked disappointed. "My name's Tarisai of Swana," I said. "What's yours?"

"Sanjeet of Dhyrma." He tensed when I came near, hiding his shackled arm. "Aren't you afraid of me?"

"Should I be?"

"You heard the Blessid girl," he said dryly. "I'm *the 'Prince's Bear.'*"

I looked down, sheepish that he had overheard us. "Kirah said you were able to connect with Dayo's Ray. That means you love him. So you can't be all bad."

"Bears are dangerous, even if they don't want to be." He stared hard at his calloused hands. "It's in their blood."

I remembered what Nawusi had said about me: *Murder is in that child's blood.*

"Nobody has to hurt people if they don't want to," I snapped. "Nobody. They can't make us."

"Of course they can," Sanjeet said evenly. "If we're anointed, we serve at the pleasure of Prince Ekundayo. It's the council vow: *We shine as moonlight; we reflect the morning star.*"

I frowned. "Why would anyone want to be moonlight? It's white and cold. I'd much rather be sunshine."

For the first time, Sanjeet's lips twitched in a smile. His eyes, I noticed, were the color of long-steeped almond tea. Curiosity crept into his gaze, and I returned it.

"Kirah says you've lived here for ages. Can you find us food? Can't you break that chain on your arm?"

"If I could," he said dourly, "then I wouldn't be here, sunshine girl. I'm not *that* strong." He gestured to the shadowy ground. "The candidates tossed the key down there."

Thinking quickly, I dropped to my knees and pressed my ear to the floor. Memories echoed across the stone. Children's feet. The clink of a key skipping across the floor's surface and stopping beneath a sleeping mat. I groped in the dark until my fingers closed around something metal.

"Got it."

I rose and took Sanjeet's arm. He stiffened beneath my touch, then relaxed, watching me closely as I unlocked the iron cuff.

"Come on," I said, feeling suddenly shy. I turned and headed for the door. "I saw a room with dining tables. There might be food left."

He followed, hunching his towering shoulders. He looked uncomfortable with the space he consumed, as if his presence were a greedy imposition.

"So if you're not that strong," I asked, "what *is* your Hallow?"

Sanjeet stared down at me through long, thick lashes. "Now would be a good time for me to lie."

"Why?"

"Because friends can't be afraid of each other," he said bluntly. "And I want to be your friend."

I assessed him. "I don't think you'd be very good at lying."

"I'm not." He smiled. "And you'd find out my Hallow anyway; there are no secrets in the Children's Palace." He sighed, scanned my body, and rattled off a list in a monotone. "You twisted your ankle months ago. It healed stiffly, so you're easy to trip. There's a knot between your neck and your left shoulder. Your reflexes will be slower on that side. When you blink, your right eye closes faster. It causes a blind spot . . ." He trailed off, shifting his feet. "I see weakness. Bones, muscles, ruptures. They sing to me, tell me all their secrets. That's why Father put me in death matches. With my Hallow, I never lost a fight." His face hardened, and then grew soft. "Amah . . . my mother made me come here. She thought if I joined the council, I could help people. Become a doctor, or a priest. I'd like that."

"Then why did you say no when Dayo offered to anoint you?"

He swallowed. "Because if I join, I can never see Amah again." His expression grew hunted. "She would be stuck with Father forever."

Before we left the chamber, I looked back at the serene rows of sleeping mats, dappled with sconce light. Had Mbali slept here once too, like Olugbade? And Thaddace, and Nawusi? In this room, how many future rulers had dreamed away their childhood?

"Friends for life," I murmured, remembering Dayo's promise. I glanced again at Sanjeet. "Do you really think that will happen? If we're anointed, do you think we'll— love each other?"

"Of course, sunshine girl." Sanjeet stared quietly at the window, where the moon glowed through whispering curtains. "We won't have any choice."

CHAPTER 7

AT BHEKINA HOUSE, THERE HAD BEEN NO rhythm to waiting.

No pulse made the hours pass faster, like the thrum of rain on a mud-thatch roof. Questions trickled into the ground: *Will I be touched today? Will I be loved today? Will Mother come? Why . . . why doesn't she come?*

But at the Children's Palace, there was no time for questions. Routine oiled the wheels of every hour, so that before I could blink, years had passed. My body had changed. Muscles curved where timid limbs used to be, and my wide, love-starved eyes had grown hooded, hiding their hunger. I learned to drawl with an Oluwani accent, rehearsing my smiles and frowns in the mirrored palace ceilings. I donned masks until they felt like my face. The Lady's voice grew faint in my mind. I burrowed into the love of my friends—the love of Dayo, Kirah, and Sanjeet— and I almost forgot that I was made to be a killer.

My fifteenth birthday dawned with the pounding of drums, echoing through the cavernous Hall of Dreams:

pa-pa-gun-gao, gun-gao. Like all Dayo's candidates, I had learned to interpret the countless drum pitches. By the fifth *gun-gao*—*wake for prayers*—I had disentangled from my mosquito net, ripped the sleeping scarf from my neatly twisted hair, and stood erect on my mat. I waited, hands clasped over my black tunic and Swanian candidate sash, with dozens of other candidates on the girls' side of the hall.

Servants with leatherbound books pushed the partition screen aside and took their stations, accounting for children on mats, ensuring that none were missing. Then the drumming stopped, and Mbali swept through the carved double doors, joining a yawning Dayo on his dais.

"Good morning, candidates," she cried, and we bowed in response, touching our brows and hearts.

"*Good morning, Anointed Honor,*" we replied.

"Why do you rise? Why did you not die in your sleep?"

"*Because the Storyteller has granted me to live another day.*"

"Why did the Storyteller allow you to live?"

"*So that I can serve the prince, the Chosen Raybearer of Aritsar, and aspire to be one of his anointed.*"

"Why must you serve the prince?"

"*Because I love him more than life itself.*"

Mbali smiled over us, as she always did, with a mysterious blend of serenity and deep-seated sadness. "Very good, children."

Then the drums sounded again, releasing us for breakfast. Dayo exited first, of course, followed by his

Anointed Ones. It was the least favorite part of my day.

My pain at Dayo's growing council festered like an ulcer. As individuals, I liked them; but I envied their intimacy. After Sanjeet, Kirah had been first to connect with Dayo's Ray. Joyfully, she had accepted his hand in councilhood, and so every other candidate from the Blessid Valley had been expelled from the Children's Palace. I danced with Kirah at her celebration feast, grinning to suppress my tears. I knew that I could not be anointed, and now, if I ever left the Children's Palace, I could not take Kirah with me.

Other council members followed soon after: a stern girl from Biraslov, a blind boy from Nyamba, a girl from Quetzala with a wicked sense of humor—until candidates had been anointed from all of the realms except Djbanti, Swana, and Dhyrma.

Sanjeet, even after four more years as Dayo's protective shadow, still refused to be anointed. The remaining Dhyrmish candidates vied for his spot, though they feared Sanjeet almost as much as the Swana candidates resented me.

I could hardly blame them for hating me. I refused to join the council, and yet Dayo rarely left my side. Even now, he grinned from the hall doors, gesturing for Sanjeet and me to join his Anointed Ones for breakfast.

Hot-faced, I slunk past the other candidates, feeling dozens of jealous eyes bore into me. They would be released for breakfast by the location of their sleeping mats.

The last to reach the banquet chamber had the skimpiest pick of food, and shortest time in which to eat it before the day's tests began.

As I neared the door, I squared my shoulders, preparing myself for the question Dayo asked, without fail, every dawn.

"Do you love me now, Tarisai of Swana?"

And as always, I closed my heart to the warmth of his smile.

"Of course not," I snorted, gesturing back at the Hall. "Not when you've got every child prodigy from Swana plotting to murder me."

He raised an eyebrow, half playful, half serious. "We could send them all home tomorrow, you know. All you have to do is say yes." I had once towered over Dayo, but now he dwarfed me. He might have been imposing, if not for that gangly frame, and those relentlessly naive black eyes. Dayo's dense, coily hair was flattened on one side from sleep. He probably wouldn't even notice until halfway through breakfast.

"I'm not ready to try the Ray again," I muttered. "You know that."

"The only thing I know," he said, "is that you belong."

The words stuck like darts as I followed his council to breakfast, and they continued to burn as we marched to the northern palace courtyard for weapon drills and wrestling. I beat out my anger with poles and practice spears.

Every day, I had waited for a reason to fulfill The Lady's command. I had tried to believe that Dayo was a monster in disguise, like me. A demon destined to hurt Aritsar, to be a nightmare of an emperor. Why else, I had reasoned, would The Lady want me to hurt him?

But in the four years I had passed by Dayo's side, I had seen no monster. Only a boy with a big, fragile heart, and hope that could fill an ocean.

I had refused to try Dayo's Ray test again, assuming that The Lady would come retrieve me, impatient with my inaction. But as months bled into years, I could come to only one conclusion: The Lady had forgotten me entirely.

Years ago, this reality would have hurt me. But I had different ambitions now, grander dreams than earning The Lady's love. I wanted to help Aritsar, like Kirah and the other Anointed Ones. I wanted to join the faces of heroes on the Watching Wall. I longed to deserve the way that Dayo looked at me each morning.

But I was half-ehru. And as far as I could tell, there was no rewriting that cursed story.

Crack. The blunt end of Kirah's practice spear connected with my gut, and I gasped, doubling over.

"You're distracted," she observed. Sweat beaded on her brow beneath her prayer scarf, trickling down her face as she dimpled.

"Sorry," I mumbled, brandishing my practice spear to try the defense again.

"Let me guess." Kirah gestured with her head across the courtyard. "You've developed a sudden . . . *appetite* for wrestling?"

I glanced past her, and my heart gave an involuntary spasm. Kirah nudged my shoulder and I shoved her back, grinning sheepishly.

"Are you going to finish the set or not?" I demanded, knocking my spear into hers. But my gaze still drifted to the other side of the courtyard.

Sanjeet was assisting the drill masters, training candidates in a lethal grappling maneuver. Impossibly, he had grown even taller in four years. Stubble shadowed his jaw, and he stood erect now, no longer hunched with shame. Dust caked the hollow of his back, earth the same rich copper as his skin. He hooked ankles with a stocky candidate, forcing both of them to the ground. Sanjeet let his opponent scramble on top of him, and then thrust a club-like thigh over the boy's shoulder. Before the boy could escape, Sanjeet had seized his own ankle, trapping the boy's neck and arm in a chokehold. It was over in seconds: His opponent gasped, tapping Sanjeet's forearm, and Sanjeet released him.

"That wasn't fair," puffed the burly candidate, who was also from Dhyrma. "His Hallow exposed my weak spots. He should have told me where they were. Evened the odds."

The muscles in Sanjeet's back rippled as he stood, staring down at his opponent with passive, tea-colored eyes. "If you don't know your own weaknesses," he said, "it will take less than a Hallow to kill you in battle."

The candidate snorted. "What do you know of battle?

80

Back home, you were only a slum brat. I'm the son of a lord."

"When an assassin comes at you in the night," Sanjeet retorted, "will you be calling your parents?"

The candidate bristled.

"I don't know anything about battle either," Dayo said, stepping into the ring to break the tension. "You'd better throw me too, Jeet. I have more to learn than Kamal." He smiled at the Dhyrmish candidate, who bowed sullenly and left the ring. Dayo spread his narrow feet, hunching into an awkward fighting stance. "Ready when you are, Bear."

The corners of Sanjeet's mouth lifted. "Your worst weakness, little brother," he said, sweeping the prince's leg and depositing him firmly on the ground, "is seeing the good in everyone." He smiled, helping the prince up. "And I'd rather have your weakness than my Hallow."

As he dusted himself off and left the ring, Sanjeet's gaze locked on mine. I looked away, flushing to the tips of my sandals.

Most of the candidates still feared the Prince's Bear. He rarely talked to anyone except Dayo, whom he shadowed like a grim archangel. But when the others had gone to sleep, I would hear the gender partition screen shift aside. Footsteps padded to my sleeping mat, and a pair of pleading eyes would burn down on mine.

"Please," Sanjeet rasped. "Take them. Make the memories disappear."

Every night since the first, we had stolen away to the old playroom, ghosts of colorful carved animals looming around us in the dark. I touched his face, feeling his pulse race as I pressed each temple. Gruesome images barraged us both.

Ribs cracking. Limbs bruising, bones shattering beneath Sanjeet's bare hands as betting crowds egged him on to fight. His father's voice was always the loudest of them all. *"Is this hell? I'll teach you hell. I'll teach you what I taught your mother if you don't get back in the pit, boy."*

With practice, I could make Sanjeet's memories disappear for an hour, sometimes a day. But the violent images always returned by nightfall, seeping into Sanjeet's sunless thoughts.

Sometimes, brighter memories stole through. I saw visions of a young, happier Sanjeet: dancing in time with the bells on his amah's feet. Balancing with his amah on the back of an elephant as it lumbered through the dusty Dhyrmish streets. His amah taking him to visit the lame in the slums, bandaging sores and resetting bones, encouraging Sanjeet to use his Hallow to diagnose their ailments. His amah letting Sanjeet use his hands to heal . . . until his father forced them to kill again.

One night, Sanjeet had asked me a different question. "Can you *give* someone memories?"

I had crossed my arms, unnerved. "You mean make things up? Create memories that never happened? I wouldn't do that."

"No." He rubbed the back of his neck, looking uncharacteristically shy. "It's just . . . you see my story all the time. And I've never seen yours."

I stared, taken aback. "No one's ever asked me for mine before." I fidgeted. "Demons aren't supposed to have nice stories."

Sanjeet's thick eyebrows crinkled with laughter. "Trust me, sunshine girl. You're no demon. I've seen too many real monsters to be mistaken."

I swallowed hard, suppressing The Lady's voice in my head. *I command you to kill . . . kill— No. That story isn't mine anymore*, I thought fiercely. *It's unwritten.*

I took Sanjeet's broad, russet hand and held it to my cheek. Carefully, I showed him the orchard at Bhekina House, boughs red with sun-kissed mangoes. I showed him my overbearing tutors, hovering as I solved puzzles. I showed him the elephants outside my Bhekina House window, bush sprites teasing their large, silly ears. I showed him Woo In and Kathleen, bickering over my head as we crossed the deserts and mountains into Oluwan.

I did not show him ehrus, or mothers, or wishes.

The more I shared my story, the longer Sanjeet's unhappy memories stayed away. Some days, he didn't ask me to erase his stories. He just asked for more of mine.

"I'll run out of memories to show you," I warned him, and he shrugged.

"Then I guess we'll have to make more, sunshine girl."

After weapons training was over, a palace courier sprinted into the courtyard and bowed curtly, handing a message to one of the drill masters. The master glanced over it, then gestured, stone-faced, at Sanjeet. "It's for you." The master hesitated. "Maybe read it in private, son."

When we returned to the Children's Palace for our next barrage of lessons and testing, Sanjeet was nowhere to be found. His face remained on my mind as I solved the day's allotted riddles and logic puzzles. Thanks to Bhekina House, the tasks had never been difficult, and rarely required my full attention.

"What do you think happened to Sanjeet?" I whispered to Kirah as drums pounded through the Children's Palace. We were returning to the Hall of Dreams, lining up for the afternoon catechism.

She shook her head, looking worried. "He wasn't at lunch. Jeet would never leave Dayo unattended this long—not unless something bad happened."

Before we could speculate more, a pair of griot priests with oiled beards entered the Hall. They took their usual place on the dais, and we candidates stood on our mats, Kirah leaving me to take her place by Dayo's side. Drums beat out the introduction for the day's catechism: *T-dak-a, t-dak-a. Gun, bow-bow-bow. Hear the sacred story of creation.* I struggled to keep my thoughts off Sanjeet as the griots performed, pausing for the traditional call-and-response.

"Queen Earth and King Water are lovers," sang one priest as the other kept time on an hourglass-shaped talking drum. "Their children are many. Trees. Rivers. Creatures that creep, *ke-du, ke-du*, and swim, *shwe, shwe*. They are weak and dumb of speech. But are Earth and Water lonely? Tell me." *No*, we chorused around the room, *they have a friend*. "Aheh!" the priest continued. "The Pelican glides from star to star, shaking stories from its wings—*whoom, whoom*, to fill a thousand worlds. The Pelican is older than Earth and Water, older even than the sun. It does not always have wings and a bill. Sometimes it has hooves and a tail, or paws and a mane, or no body at all. Who is the Pelican?" *Am the Storyteller*. "Yes, Am, called Was, called Will Be. Watch, now: The Pelican moves through time like wind, with as many names as it has feathers. What name shall you call it? Choose wisely, for names have power.

"High above Earth and Water floats Empress Sky. She gazes below and teems—*gnatche, gnatche*, with jealousy. Before Earth gave her heart to Water, she was Sky's beloved sister. Now Sky is lonely in her airy realm, and bitter. What does she do? Tell me." *She challenges King Water*. "Yes, to a duel. The heavens howl—*hawawa, hawawa*, and oceans churn, *bushe, bushe*. The war of Empress Sky and King Water rages for seven thousand years. Earth feels neglected by both husband and sister. See her take on a new lover: the handsome Warlord Fire.

"The children of Earth and Fire multiply throughout

the realm, fierce and strong. Volcanoes! Dragons! Rubies and mountains of coal. Water realizes the children are not his own. He abandons Earth in anger, and her lakes dry up, *hasse, hasse*. Her fields turn to desert. See Earth begin to die. Who shall come to aid her?" *The Pelican.* "Yes, the Pelican hovers over Earth. See it pierce its own breast to nourish her! *Shaa, shaa*—watch the Pelican's blood fall, filling the parched places. And what now? New children are born. Fashioned from the clay of Earth, and brought to life by the blood of the Pelican." *Humankind.* "Yes, the first living people. Water reconciles with Earth, promising to raise her new children as his own. Are the children strong?" *Yes, and clever.* "Aheh. But Fire is jealous. He is angered by Earth's union with Water and her friendship with the Pelican. So he curses humankind with thirteen ways to die. Once gods, they are mortals now, weak as beasts. What shall they do? Who will lead them? Tell me." *The Raybearer!* "Aheh! See the Pelican steal Rays from the sun, blessing the first emperor with wisdom and compassion. 'You must choose eleven brothers and sisters,' it tells the emperor, shaking oil from its wings. 'For every brow you anoint, you will gain immunity to one of the thirteen deaths. Choose well, Emperor—for to the world, you will be as a god, but to your council, you will yet be a mortal man.' Aheh, aheh." *It is done.*

The myth was ancient—except for the Raybearer part, which had been added only five hundred years ago, when the Kunleos formed the empire. After finishing the story, the priests made us recite the thirteen causes of mortal death. *Poison, contagion, gluttony,* we chanted. *Burning, drowning, suffocation. Bleeding, beast mauling, disaster. Organ-death, witches' hexes. Battery, old age.* Raybearers were blessed with only one immunity at birth. But after anointing a full council of eleven, only old age could kill them—unless, of course, one of their council members turned traitor.

"Hear the duties of the future emperor's sacred council," intoned the male priest after the lesson. My fingers drummed the side of my thigh: I had been made to hear these words hundreds of times before. "The Eleven must wield their titles of power fairly and without bias. The Eleven must serve the emperor first, then the empire, and then their realms of origin. Outside the council, they must form no attachments. Inside the council, no attachment may outweigh their loyalty to the future emperor. Carnal relations are prohibited, except with the future emperor." Titters rippled across the room. Involuntarily, I remembered the hollow of a russet back, glistening with sweat and clay. I shook my head to clear it, grateful, for the first time that afternoon, that Sanjeet was absent.

"Hear the duties of the future emperor," the priest continued, bowing to Dayo. "His Highness is not permitted to marry. Instead, His Highness must anoint and protect a trusted council, through which he shall serve the empire. His Highness must select his council sisters with special care"—the priest leered over the female candidates—"for they will birth all future Raybearers."

I grimaced. The priest made us sound more like a harem than a sacred council. I raised my hand and blurted, "What happens when there's an empress?"

Several lines wrinkled the priest's protruding brow. "As I have said: Arit emperors do not marry. Such a union would interfere with the balance of council power—"

"No," I cut in. "I meant, what about when the Raybearer's a girl?"

The priest inhaled, summoning patience, then smiled. "There are no female Raybearers, child. Am has always chosen a man. That does not mean, of course, that female council members have no value. After all, you might *bear* a Raybearer." He winked at me. "The empire would be forever in your debt."

CHAPTER 8

BEFORE I COULD RESPOND, MY CHEST BEGAN to burn.

Someone had heaped coals over my heart. The heat came from inside, a dragon, a demon throbbing to get out. I gasped, clutching at my heart and sweating, glancing around and hoping no one noticed.

The moment the priest looked away, I ran from the Hall of Dreams, sandals pounding the stone until I reached the banquet chamber. Pitchers of water and cordial from our last meal still rested on the long, low tables. I seized one and poured out the water, careful to keep the ice in the pitcher. Then I lay on the floor and dumped the cubes onto my chest. The cold stung viciously; I gritted my teeth to keep from howling.

This had happened before. The surges of heat had tripled in frequency once I moved to the Children's Palace. They had first begun at Bhekina House, when I was prone to tantrums. Now the burning in my chest was unpredictable, though it often flared during catechism. Sometimes I woke from dreams I didn't understand, from memories that seeped from the Children's Palace floor, with the ghosts of girls who had features eerily similar to my own.

I shivered, willing away tears as I stared at the muraled ceiling. Did these attacks have something to do with The Lady? With the ugly truth of who—of *what*—I was?

Footsteps echoed in the hallway outside, and I sat up, cubes spilling into my lap. A face appeared in the banquet chamber doorway.

"Am's Story, Tar," exclaimed Kirah. "Did it happen *again*?"

I nodded sheepishly. She came to help me up, brushing ice chips from my tunic. "You should talk to the healers. Maybe they can—"

"There's nothing they can do," I said shortly, avoiding her gaze. The last thing I needed were palace physicians, poking around in my half-ehru insides.

Kirah pressed her lips together. "Well, you can't keep missing catechism," she warned. "The testmakers will start to talk. Next time, try to wait until sunset. I could sing to you then."

It was our ritual: Every dusk, we stole away from the tests and prying eyes of the Children's Palace, away to the An-Ileyoba rooftops, where we watched the sky turn shades of fire.

I only shrugged, and Kirah sighed as we left the banquet chamber. Before we could escape, one more trial awaited us: the daily Prince's Court.

No place made me feel more distant from Dayo than the Children's Palace throne room. I stood, invisible among the other candidates in the chamber of mirrored ceiling tiles and wax-dyed tapestry. A platform of twelve wooden thrones rose before the candidates. As Dayo, Kirah, and the other Anointed Ones took their elevated seats, I scanned the room for Sanjeet, but the towering pillar of his head and shoulders did not appear.

"By the power of Ray within me," Dayo began, tapping a plain wooden scepter on the ground, "I declare this court in session. Approach the throne." He smiled over the crowd, pulling uncertainly at the rings on his fingers. The Children's Palace acted as a microcosm of An-Ileyoba's true court, preparing Dayo to make decisions as emperor.

After a murmuring pause, a Djbanti candidate named Zyong'o stepped forward. "I have a complaint, Your Imperial Highness." Dayo nodded, and Zyong'o bowed, then crossed his arms. "When Djbanti are paired with candidates from Dhyrma, we always lose the timed logic puzzles. They slow us down. I think"—he continued over enraged objections from the Dhyrmish candidates—"I think every member on a team should be from the same realm. Why mix figs with mangoes? Why should we Djbanti, hunters and scholars, be dragged down by empty-headed merchants?"

Dayo winced at the now-unruly crowd. Djbanti and Dhyrmish candidates stood at opposite sides of the throne room, yelling and cursing each other, while Swanian candidates jeered at them both. "Silence?" Dayo said. "Order?" He sounded like a nervous farm boy, tossing seed to quell chickens. Surprisingly, the crowd quieted, though venomous looks still volleyed across the room.

"I am grieved by your complaint, Zyong'o," Dayo said, choosing each word with care. "I am sure it's hard to feel that your strengths are compromised. But I doubt your problems are the other candidates' fault. I'm sure Dhyrmish people are just as smart as anyone."

I shook my head in admiration of Dayo's patience. I would have snapped at Zyong'o to either work with his Dhyrmish teammates, or take his haughty rear end all the way back to Djbanti.

Imperial testmakers, the passive men and women who administered most of the candidate trials, stood in crimson robes along the wall. Brightening with an idea, Dayo gestured for a testmaker to approach.

"Lady Adesanya," he addressed her, "you help keep track of test results, don't you? Please share how Dhyrmish candidates perform compared to others."

The testmaker nodded, producing a thick tome from beneath her arm and opening it to the middle. "According to my records," she droned, "on average, candidates from Dhyrma consistently underperform behind their peers in logic, weapons, and science. They show equal capabilities, however, in god-studies, griotcraft, and statecraft."

Dayo's face went slack, and Zyong'o smirked and shrugged as though to say, *What did I tell you?*

The room erupted again. Djbanti candidates crowed with triumph as Dhyrmish candidates seethed, some barking that the records were rigged, while others left the room in anger and shame. Despite his good intentions, Dayo had made the problem infinitely worse.

Heat fluttered in my chest again, though this time it was invigorating, coursing through my limbs as the wheels in my head began to turn. Like the mortars and pestles of village women pounding cassava into *fufu*, the levers in my mind began to beat, binding sounds and facts and images.

People from Dhyrma were not stupid. Zyong'o was wrong. But Lady Adesanya had no reason to lie.

Pound, pound.

The Dhyrmish candidates failed at logic, but excelled in statecraft. That made no sense. Something was off: a rent in the pattern.

Pound, pound.

I closed my eyes. The Bhekina House tutors had shaped my brain to see puzzles everywhere. Every person, every place was a series of riddles, stories within stories, a system so plainly connected that to see the entire mural, I need only step back . . . and look. My eyes flew open.

"Silence," Dayo was saying again, yelling over the crowd in desperation. "The Council of Eleven reflects all realms and social classes. When the Eleven fall, so does the Arit empire. We aren't just being tested on our skills. We're supposed to learn how to work together."

It was the sleeping mats. It had to be.

Candidates from Swana and Djbanti were likely to have names later in the Arit alphabet, while Dhyrmish names occurred earlier. The sleeping mats were arranged by name. Candidates with names that came earlier slept farthest from the doors in the Hall of Dreams, making them last to reach the banquet hall. Running on virtually no food, those candidates would be exhausted for every trial administered before lunch: logic, weapons, and science. God-studies, griotcraft, and statecraft occurred after lunch and dinner—so in those trials, they performed well. The solution was so simple, it almost felt silly. I felt guilty for not noticing earlier. Dayo always invited me to eat with his Anointed Ones, and so I had never been affected.

Dayo cleared his throat, squirming beneath the unsatisfied glowers of the crowd. "I will not grant the request for unmixed teams."

I smiled, and my shoulders relaxed. *Good.* Dayo knew better than to humor the Djbanti candidate's prejudices.

"However," he continued, "I decree that from this day forward, Dhyrmish candidates will receive additional tutoring in their failing subjects. The special treatment will continue until performance rises."

Wrong. My pulse quickened. Dayo's ruling would only make the Dhyrmish candidates more exhausted than they already were. It wouldn't solve the problem at all. But as I opened my mouth to challenge his ruling . . . heat slammed my chest again.

It was worse than during the griots' lesson. A poker

seared beneath my ribs, burning for release. I struggled for breath with dawning horror.

Of course. The pounding, the puzzle-solving . . . it wasn't a *gift*.

It was a trick. My intelligence was just another part of my ehru curse: a ploy to make me doubt Dayo's right to rule. A way to bring me closer to betraying him. To hurting him.

I shuddered and brushed my thumb across my chin, the sacred sign of the Pelican. Then I banished any idea of sleeping mats from my thoughts. The throne room roiled with discontent, but I smiled up at the platform, making sure Dayo saw my support for his ruling. I had beat the evil inside me. I had submitted, and remained silent.

In the allotted free time before supper, Kirah and I slipped away to the back corridors of the Children's Palace, as we had every evening since we were small. Using a curtain cord as rope, we wriggled through a window and climbed to An-Ileyoba's gilded battlements. The wind whipped Kirah's red prayer scarf as we held hands for balance, then we sat and dangled our feet over the edge, watching the sun melt beneath the Oluwan horizon. Usually we tossed figs to peacocks in the courtyard below, laughing when haughty courtiers peered up in confusion. But today, we were quiet.

"What did you think of Dayo's ruling?" Kirah asked.

"What does it matter?" I stared over the golden domes of An-Ileyoba. In the city beyond, Oluwan's orange harvest festival was beginning to gain revelers. "The priests made it clear what council sisters are for. We should focus on protecting Dayo, not changing his rulings."

"Priests don't know everything."

"Now, now." I nudged Kirah's shoulder, teasing. "Is that what Mama would say?"

She smirked. Kirah had long ceased to quote her mother's prim truisms. When we were younger, the other candidates had mocked her—*Mama says, Mama says*—until she turned pink with anger, and sealed her mouth shut. "They're spoiled rich brats," she had complained to me in private. "They've never seen a desert, or herded goats, or worked a farm. They were raised to be tested at the palace. They've never had a *real* family."

"Neither have I," I'd pointed out. Kirah knew about my lonely childhood at Bhekina House, though I had kept ehrus and wishes out of it. "Do you think I'm spoiled?"

"Well . . . yes." Kirah had flushed, straightening her prayer scarf. "No one made you change soiled nappies. Or chase vultures for miles to find water. Or dry camel dung to fuel the cook fires." She'd paused, considering me. "But your mother never sang to you, or made you cinnamon milk, or stroked your hair when you were sick. I guess there are different ways of being spoiled."

Now, from the rooftop, we could see men and women dancing in the Oluwan City markets, paint shining on their glistening bodies as drums gave a low, infectious heartbeat.

"Mama believes what the priests say," Kirah said,

answering my question. "That people are like rocks stacked in a totem: men over women, women over children. We accept our roles, or the whole tower falls apart." She watched the palace's sun-and-moon banners twist in the wind. "A songbird was not meant to soar as an eagle."

I frowned, remembering The Lady's words on the day I had last seen her. *You caged me like a bird, but you could not make me sing.*

"What about Empress Aiyetoro?" I asked. She had surfaced out of the genealogies drummed into me by tutors. Her name was old Arit, and I faintly remembered what it meant: *peace from shore to shore.* "Aiyetoro ruled Aritsar for decades. She's the reason women can join the Imperial Guard. She founded the Imperial College, and abolished the interrealm slave trade, and—"

"Wait." Kirah held up a hand, cocking her head to listen. "Dayo's wondering where we are. I'm telling him we'll be down in a few minutes. Sorry—what were you saying?"

"Never mind." I looked away, trying not feel resentful. Kirah was my best friend. The roof had always been our space, away from the spying walls of the Children's Palace. But Kirah wasn't mine anymore. She belonged to Dayo and her council siblings now, with their minds connected through the Ray.

My gaze fell on the Watching Wall, which cut through Oluwan City below. In a muraled parade of conquerors, rainbow plaster enshrined every Kunleo emperor and council. Someday, Dayo's face would join that parade. And Kirah's, and perhaps Sanjeet's as well.

My brow furrowed as I counted the painted emperors, comparing them to the genealogies in my head. *Edebayo the First, Oluwatoyin the Vanquisher, Edunrobo Imperion, Abiyola the Third, Adeyinka the Mighty . . .*

"Empress Aiyetoro isn't there," I said at last, blinking with confusion. "They didn't paint her."

"Aiyetoro was an exception," Kirah said. "I asked the priests about her. They say she was a fluke: Am only gave Aiyetoro the Ray because her father died without male heirs. An exception does not negate the rule." She flicked a pebble over the edge of the roof, fidgeting with the tasseled edges of her prayer scarf. "You know—when I left home, I believed no place would ever be quite as beautiful, quite as *right* as the Blessid Valley."

"I remember." I grinned, imitating Kirah at age twelve. *"Mama says the Blessid Valley sky was woven by the Pelican itself. A tapestry with no snags, floating over honey-colored mountains."*

The corner of Kirah's mouth lifted. "Beauty and order were our idols. To Blessids, a pot is not finished until every lump is smooth. Our parties are always the same: the same songs, the same food. Stories we tell over and over again." She sighed. "Don't laugh, but when I first came to the Children's Palace, I used to fantasize about talking to Mama. In my dreams I'd tell her, 'Today, I learned how to use a spear!' Or, 'Today, I solved a logic puzzle faster than anyone else!' And Dream Mama would say, 'My wise and disciplined girl! See how my Kirah takes her good home training into the big wild world.' But now when I dream of Mama . . . I say things that make her frown." Kirah paused, watching a flock of synchronized swallows soar across the red-streaked sky. "I say, 'Why don't Blessids ever let women lead the caravans? They do just as much work as the men.' Or, 'Why do Blessids wash their hands after trading with other realms? Those people are no dirtier than we are.' And Mama cries and says, 'Where did my Kirah go? Who is this sneering girl who spits on her home, who questions her elders? Does the world love you better than your family? Does it swaddle you at night, and fill your belly with goat's milk? Where is my Kirah?'

"And I say, 'I'm here, Mama'—but I'm not." Kirah bit back a sob. "I'm far away, Tarisai. From all of them. And the more I learn, the farther I feel. I don't know where home is anymore."

I took her hand in mine. We sat in silence, watching the clouds fade to purple, and the torches flickering for miles across the city, like golden prayers in the dark.

I was not an Anointed One, and so my sleeping mat was far away from Dayo's platform and the pallets encircling it. But every night—after the candidate-minders had retired to bed, leaving the Hall of Dreams unattended—I embraced my popular role as Dream Giver to the Prince's Council.

"I want *steamy* dreams this time," said Mayazatyl, propping herself up on her pallet with one hand. She grinned at me, wrinkling the red bar tattooed across her nose. "Can you manage that?" Mayazatyl was Dayo's council sister from the rainforest realm of Quetzala. She was a prodigy of architecture and weapon design . . . and equally skilled at amassing love notes from tormented candidates.

I rolled my eyes. "Fine. But I'm not putting in anyone we know."

She winked. "Once Dayo completes his council and they send us to Yorua Keep, we'll be locked in that castle a *long* time, you know. When you finally let Dayo anoint you, you'll have to be less of a prude."

I looked away, wincing at *finally*. I was still cursed by The Lady, and until I found a way to break it—to protect Dayo—there would be no anointing. "Go to sleep, Maya."

She hastened her slumber by chewing *kuso-kuso* leaves, and when her chest rose in snores, I touched the top of her silky black hair. I gave her a silly, made-up memory of a handsome warrior stumbling upon her bathing. She subdued him with a crossbow she had designed herself, then seduced him as she nursed his wound. Mayazatyl snuggled into the pallet, sighing contentedly.

To Kirah, I gave dreams of her mama and baba, who kissed her cheeks and stroked her hair, and said they weren't angry about her leaving them. For Kameron, Dayo's rugged council brother from Mewe, I fabricated a pack of hunting dogs, nipping cheerfully at his ankles as he tracked a boar in the forest. Dreams of blooming roses were for Thérèse from Nontes. Adoring crowds were for Ai Ling from Moreyao, and handsome swains for Theo from Sparti. To Umansa, a blind weaver boy from Nyamba, I gave new patterns for his tapestries, swirling them around him in a brilliant prism. Finally, to hard-faced Emeronya from Biraslov, I gave flurries of sweet-tasting snow and a wizened woman who wrapped her in wool, humming a dissonant lullaby.

Dayo's sleeping platform was empty. I stared at the satin pillows and panther coverlets, remembering my first day in the Children's Palace, when Dayo had let me sleep there. For weeks afterward, he had insisted I share the platform with him, and I had pressed my head against his, feeding dreams into his brow.

Sighing, I made my way through the maze of mats to a window alcove in the corner: the same place I had found him hiding years before. The curtain was drawn, and a shadow sprawled on the broad sill behind it.

"It's weird how often you go back here," I told the shadow, poking it through the curtain. "Aren't you afraid you'll fall off the ledge?"

The damask screen pushed back an inch. I passed inside, climbing onto the cushioned ledge. The window was unglazed, and so we were exposed on one side to balmy night air.

Dayo didn't look up when I sat across from him. His

hair stuck out in locs. The laces of his nightshirt lay undone, exposing his collarbone as he cupped an object in his hands.

"You shouldn't have that out, you know," I whispered. "It's dangerous."

The mask was slightly smaller than his palm, and carved to resemble a young lion. A word in the tongue of old Oluwan was engraved on its brow: *Oloye*. Crown Prince. I shuddered, remembering my first day at An-Ileyoba, when Olugbade taunted me to kill him. Olugbade's mask was identical to Dayo's, except that his was marked *Oba* for emperor, and its mane boasted all twelve colorful stripes.

"This is the only place I can look at it," Dayo said, then stared over the window ledge at the blackness below. "It's hard to believe, sometimes. I could slip over the edge— fall ten stories down to the courtyard—and nothing would happen. I wonder if other princes have ever tried."

"Don't talk like that," I said, eyeing the mask warily. Nine stripes colored the obsidian mane, jewel tones glittering in the moonlight. For each person Dayo anointed, a new color would appear, representing the immunity that Dayo had gained, in addition to the one with which he was born. Raybearer princes wore the mask around their necks, hiding it always beneath their clothes. They showed it to no one, lest an assassin discover the kinds of death to which they were not yet immune. Only when a Raybearer's council was complete did he wear the mask openly, displaying his deathless power to all the world.

Three colors were missing from Dayo's mask—one for a Djbanti candidate, one for Sanjeet, and one for me.

"Orange, purple, and red," Dayo murmured. "Gluttony, contagion, burning."

"*Shh!*" I hissed, slapping his knee. "You want all of Oluwan hearing how to kill you?"

Dayo didn't answer; instead he stared longer at the mask before replacing it on a gold chain that hung around his neck and slipped it beneath his tunic to rest with his vial of pelican oil. "Why won't you let me anoint you?"

I shrugged, avoiding his gaze. "The Ray doesn't work on me. It gave me a headache. You know that."

"That was four years ago. Before you knew me. Before you—" He broke off and stared hard at the moon. The words he did not say, *loved me*, hung between us. "I was a wreck in court today. I had no idea what to tell Zyong'o . . . But you did."

I flinched. He crossed his arms, raising an eyebrow. "You had a better ruling," he said. "I could tell. You were scowling into space, like you do when you've solved one of the testmaker's hardest riddles. Am's Story, Tar—why didn't you say something? Why didn't you correct me, like you did when we were little?"

I shrugged. "You're the Raybearer. It's not my place to make rulings."

"Even if I'm a buffoon at making them?"

The question made me squirm, but I set my jaw and said, "*Oloye.*" When nothing happened, I waited for emphasis and repeated, "*Oloye.*" Still nothing. "Now you say it," I pressed him.

He frowned. "You've made your point, Tar."

"Say it," I insisted.

"*Oloye,*" he sighed, and through his tunic, the eyes of the mask flashed.

"See?" I said, once the stars stopped spiraling in my vision. "It's like the stories say. The mask only responds to its rightful owner: a Raybearer of Aritsar. Am chose you for this, Dayo. You don't need me."

"But I do—"

"Well, you shouldn't," I snapped, then winced, regretting it. It wasn't Dayo's fault he trusted me so blindly. For four years I had protected him, resisting Mother's wish by refusing his anointing. But if I'd had any shred of a spine, I would have left him years ago. I would have found a way to escape the Children's Palace, keeping him safe forever, instead of staying to bask in his affection.

As if reading my thoughts, Dayo said, "Promise me you won't leave." His voice was quiet. But his gaze was dilated, volatile with fear. "Promise you won't abandon Aritsar."

I tried to laugh. "Don't be dramatic."

"I can't explain it, Tar," he whispered. "But the moment I first saw you, I knew we were linked. We're beans in a pod, you and I. I think it's both of us . . . or neither."

My blood ran cold. I didn't understand. They were words a lover would say, but that was not how Dayo meant them. All I wanted was to be gone from that alcove, away from the raw vulnerability in those dark eyes.

"Fine. I promise," I said, wriggling off the ledge and opening the curtain. "Get some sleep, Dayo. And for Am's sake—stop taking out that mask."

I returned to my mat on the girls' side of the hall, carefully wrapping my hair in its sleeping scarf. Then I lay on the ground, hands folded stiffly beneath my cheek. For what felt like hours, I fought sleep—until at last, heavy footfalls crept to my side, and a shadow fell across my mat.

"I was afraid you wouldn't come," I whispered. "Where in Am's name have you been?"

He looked haunted as he stared down at me, and faint, as though he hadn't slept or eaten all day. He swallowed hard, holding out a hand to help me up. "Please," he said.

"Did the emperor ask to speak with you? It's all right. If it was scary, I can take the memories away—"

"My amah is dead," Sanjeet whispered. "Father was taken to prison."

CHAPTER 9

I LET SANJEET PULL ME UP, AND WE WALKED silently to the abandoned palace playroom. Sheet-covered toys rose in white mountains around us. We sat on a dusty divan, Sanjeet's head in his hands. My insides twisted in knots. I rubbed his broad shoulder as he shook with sobs. After a moment I reached for his face, removing my sleeping scarf to swab at his tears.

"Should we—" I paused. "Should we burn something for her shade?"

I had only seen a funeral twice before. The first was in Swana, when a deafening procession had passed Bhekina House: adults and children wailing, rattling seed-filled *hosho* gourds, and beating bruises into their chests.

The other time had been here at the Children's Palace, when Dayo had anointed Theo of Sparti to his council. The moment Dayo had touched Theo's brow, a Sparti candidate named Ianthe had risen from the banquet hall, walked calmly to the Hall of Dreams, and thrown herself from a window.

After retrieving the girl's body, the Children's Palace attendants had wailed and beat themselves, just like the mourners from Swana. But their eyes, I noticed, were dry. Their wailing was merely a ritual: It was unlucky to bury an unmourned body, and the Sparti girl had no family to cry for her. Ianthe had crossed two thousand miles to reach Oluwan and try for the council. Many Children's Palace rejects, I would later learn, had traveled alone, and could not afford the lodestone journey home.

Once the mourners had left and the Hall of Dreams hushed with sleep, the High Priestess of Aritsar crept to the window from which Ianthe had jumped. Of all the Emperor's Eleven, Mbali visited us most often. At night, she would drift between the lines of pallets, soothing younger candidates who had wet their sheets, and coaxing thrashing children from nightmares.

Pretending to sleep, I watched as Mbali placed a palm oil lamp in the windowsill and drew a gauzy cloth from her pocket: Ianthe's candidate sash. She wept—real tears, not the shrieking performance of the earlier mourners—and held a corner of Ianthe's sash to the lamp. As the cloth burned, the air in the hall suddenly turned cold. I froze in horror as a translucent girl floated into the hall, shadows clinging to her body like a shroud. She headed straight for Mbali.

I leapt to my feet to warn the priestess, but she held out a hand to stop me. "Don't," she said. "It's the only time she has left. Shades can only appear once after death. They often don't come at all . . . if they died at peace."

Carefully, the High Priestess held out her arms. Ianthe's shade rushed into them, and to my surprise, she embraced Mbali with arms as solid as a living child's.

"I'll miss you," Ianthe said.

"Not for long," whispered Mbali, kissing the girl's translucent head and seeming to suppress a shiver. "You won't miss a thing where you're going. Go, child. You're free at last." Then she murmured a blessing, and Ianthe vanished.

"We should burn something of your mother's," I told Sanjeet, retrieving an oil lamp from a sconce in the playroom. "Then you can see her again."

Hope flickered across Sanjeet's face. He hesitated, and then pulled a golden anklet from his pocket. "It's all I have."

"It doesn't have to be the whole thing," I said, removing a tiny bell from the chain. A memory passed into me—a woman's foot beating rhythmically on a dust floor, and the ring of throaty laughter. I cast the bell into the lamp, watching as the metal curved and smoldered.

Nothing happened; the air in the playroom was stagnant. Sanjeet's expression fell.

"Mbali said shades only visit if they aren't at peace," I said. "Or if they have to tell you something. So maybe it's a good sign."

He nodded woodenly. Desperate to feel useful, I taught him the blessing that Mbali had spoken over Ianthe. We stared into the dwindling lamp and spoke it together: *You are immortal now. Immoveable, a thousand hills rolled into one. May you join Egungun's Parade and pass into paradise at Core.*

The lamp went out. When Sanjeet spoke again, his voice was chillingly calm.

"I've been planning to kill him," he said. "All day, I've been trying to find a way to escape An-Ileyoba, leave the Children's Palace, and infiltrate Father's prison." He gave a tight-lipped smile. "Then I realized, that's the kind of stunt that would make him *proud* of me. I hope you never win the pride of a monster, Tarisai. It's worse than their contempt."

I rejoined him on the divan, and ran a thumb over his tear-stained cheek. "So make him ashamed of you. Stay here. Get anointed and be a protector instead of a killer. Dayo needs you, Jeet. He loves you, and you love him too. You passed his Ray test before any of us. That must mean something, right?"

Sanjeet grew very still. "Do you know why I was able to connect with Dayo's Ray?" He gripped the edge of the divan, knuckles growing pale. "It's because I had a younger brother just like him. I see people as a butcher marks an animal. Strength, weakness. Bones and flesh. But my brother, Sendhil . . . his Hallow was different. He saw weakness too, but in souls instead of bodies. He knew why people were hurting. Like Dayo, he knew just the right thing to say."

I nodded, remembering how kindly Dayo had spoken to Zyong'o in court.

"Father thought my brother was too soft. He put Sendhil in pit fights, like me. Said it would 'make a man out of him.' But Sendhil lost every fight. He felt bad for his opponents, understood their pain too well. So Father sold him as a recruit to desert mercenaries. He was nine. *Nine*, Tarisai. And before the mercenaries came for him, Sendhil asked me to help him run away. But I . . . I refused. Scared of what Father would do if he caught us. And—" His face contorted with guilt. "I wanted Sendhil to enlist. I thought the mercenaries would make him stronger. He was too kind, I thought. Too naive. If he stayed that way, the world would eat him alive. I hated my father . . . But deep down, I was just like him."

"You were just a child, Jeet. You did what you thought was best."

"I betrayed my brother." Sanjeet's expression was hard. "And when Sendhil returned on leave a year later, he was different. He used to cry when Father beat Amah. Now he just watched, like . . . like he respected Father for it. And instead of using his Hallow to comfort, now he used it to destroy. He never lied, Sendhil, not ever. He didn't need to. He could look at a stranger on the street and know the exact combination of words to reduce him to tears. Even Father was scared of him. So he returned Sendhil to the mercenaries, and soon after, Amah sent me away here. I never saw my brother again."

"I'm sorry," I whispered, placing my hand in his.

He stared into space, absently crushing my fingers.

"Amah's shade didn't come," he murmured. "Not even to give me advice. Maybe that means she's at peace. That my place is here. You're right, Tar; I can't let Dayo turn into Sendhil. I won't let him lose faith in the people he loves. I won't let him know betrayal." A chill chased up my now-numb fingers. He looked at me as though waking from a trance, expression softening. "You've helped me see my duty, sunshine girl." His lips brushed the back of my hand. "Once you're anointed, I know you'll keep Dayo safe too."

I extracted my hand, smiling at him nervously. "You can be more than the Prince's Bear. You could use your Hallow to teach people how to heal. Kirah said you have theories on how to start someone's heart again—pumping their chest with your hands. That's amazing, Jeet. It could save lives."

He nodded, but continued to smile at me with that restless, unsettling warmth. "I never let myself get attached to staying here, you know. While Amah was still alive, I couldn't commit to any person, any place forever. But now . . ." He leaned toward me unconsciously, and my pulse quickened at his scent, earth and polished leather. His face glowed with an expression I had never seen on him before: joy.

"Let's get anointed," he murmured, breath tickling my face. "Right now. We'll wake Dayo and connect with his Ray. Then—"

The door flap to the playroom burst open. "Unscheduled trial," a crimson-robed testmaker said, brusquely beckoning us to the door. "All candidates are to report to the northern courtyard."

"Courtyard?" Sanjeet raised an eyebrow. "But it's the middle of the night. What test could we have out—"

"The trial is timed," the testmaker snapped, herding us out of the playroom. Once we were in the corridor, streams of sleepy, confused children filed past, all headed for stairs leading out of the Children's Palace. Sanjeet followed them, but to my surprise the testmaker held me back.

"The prince is being kept in a different location. He has requested your presence specially. You are to come with me." Her hand closed around my wrist with surprising strength, and we charged in the opposite direction of the mass exodus, marching until we reached the abandoned back halls of the Children's Palace. We turned the corner— and my heart stopped dead in my chest.

On the ground crouched a beast I had only ever seen in books. A spotted coat of black and orange shone lividly against the sandstone corridor walls, and heat radiated from its massive body.

Leopard, my mind's library murmured.

Yet how could it be? Leopards were surely no taller than a man. This beast was the size of a horse, with wily yellow eyes that gleamed from yards away.

I screamed, but the testmaker's hand clapped around my mouth. She leaned close to my ear, and when she hissed, she no longer sounded like a lady from Oluwan. "That's enough from you, little demon."

A lilting Mewish accent laced every word. I swung around and looked up: The testmaker's face shimmered and melted away, leaving another one in its place.

"Kathleen," I gasped.

In front of us, a man emerged from the shadows to stroke the beast's enormous head. Shimmering amethyst birthmarks covered the man's golden, sinewy frame.

"I see your years at An-Ileyoba haven't taught you any manners," Woo In droned. "Meet my friend, Lady's Daughter. Hyung is my *emi-ehran*." Woo In scratched the crest of the animal's massive head, and it purred with pleasure, vanishing and reappearing repeatedly. "Am sends spirit-beasts to comfort Redemptors in their last moments of life," Woo In explained. "But I refused to die in the Underworld, and when I escaped, Hyung came with me."

"How did you get in here?" I faltered.

Kathleen smirked. "Woo In flew through a window. I became that boring Lady Adesanya, and then I made Hyung look like a lapcat." She scowled at the beast. "It was a pain, throwing a glamor around something that big. But Woo In *insisted* . . ."

"You could have made Hyung invisible," Woo In retorted.

Kathleen rolled her eyes. "Do you know how hard it would have been to convince thirty Imperial Guard warriors that they were seeing *nothing*? I'm Hallowed, but I'm not a god. Leave your pet at home next time."

I had not seen Woo In and Kathleen in so long, I

had half convinced myself that I'd made them up. For a disorienting moment, I wanted to hug them and cry. They were my sole connection to home, to Bhekina House and Swana. But their faces served as chilling reminders of who—of *what*—I was. Reminders of what The Lady had sent me to do.

"Have you been here the whole time?" I asked. "In the Children's Palace—spying on me?"

"We visit often enough." Kathleen sniffed and continued. "Enough to know you have neglected your duties."

"You left for years," I sputtered. "And you didn't tell me anything. Not that Mother used to live here, or that the Emperor's Council would try to *poison* me, or that . . ." I swallowed. "Or that the boy in Mother's portrait was Dayo."

Kathleen waved a dismissive hand. "If you had known more, the Emperor's Council would never have let you near Dayo. Especially not Mbali. Her Hallow is discerning the truth, and so ignorance was your only shield. All in all, I'd say things have actually gone rather well. Barring the obvious."

My mouth went dry.

"The Lady wishes to know," Woo In said, "why the prince has not yet been eliminated."

"The Ray doesn't work on me. I can't hurt him without it—and I'm glad," I added sharply.

Kathleen's emerald eyes narrowed. "It's no good resisting, you know. You are half-ehru. You will grant

The Lady's wish no matter how much you love the Kunleo brat, and the longer you wait, the harder it will be."

"Why do you hate Dayo so much?" I demanded. "Why can't you just leave him alone? What's he ever done to you?"

"It is not what he has done," said Woo In, "but what he will do." His usual sardonic tone had fallen away, leaving a raw hostility I had never heard before. "The Kunleo emperors have the power to change the Redemptor Treaty. They can make it fair, so Redemptors are born everywhere, instead of only in Songland."

"That can't be true," I said. "Dayo's never said anything like that."

"Perhaps your prince is not as open as you think."

I snorted. "Dayo couldn't keep a secret to save his life. Besides, emperors aren't gods. How could they decide where Redemptors are born?"

Woo In's lips pressed into a thin line. "I don't know," he admitted. "But The Lady does. And she has promised to save the children of Songland. But first, she must rid the world of Kunleos." I took an involuntary step back when Woo In's voice dropped to a snarl. "Her patience is wearing thin, and so is mine. Dayo's death is the reason you were born."

"I don't care," I said. "I won't hurt him. Not ever."

Beside Woo In, a growl brewed in Hyung's throat. "I thought you might say that," Woo In murmured. "And so you left us with no choice. I have fulfilled your destiny for you, Lady's Daughter." He gave a tight smile. "Your prince and his mask should know better than to whisper at windows. You never know who might be listening."

From behind me, the smell of burning timber assaulted my nostrils.

"No," I breathed. "No!" I tore away from Kathleen and sprinted back down the corridor. Servants were running, shrieking, and barking unintelligible orders as they herded children down the hall. Above the din of screams and footfalls, I heard someone rasp, *"Fire."*

Gluttony, contagion, burning.

"Where's Dayo?" I demanded of passersby. "Where's the prince?" My questions were met with wild stares and wagging heads. I shoved against the exodus, heading for the bedroom where I had last left Dayo. Billowing clouds of smoke obscured the hallway, and I choked but pressed on.

Then a burly arm wrapped around my waist, and a palace manservant hoisted me over his shoulder. "You're going the wrong way, candidate." I clawed against his solid grip, but until we burst through the double doors of the Children's Palace antechamber, he did not put me down.

A wave of clean air washed over us. The outer hallway teemed with guards and mewling children. We stood by the grand spiral staircase I had climbed my first day at An-Ileyoba. The landing had a marble railing overlooking the vast hall below, where frazzled servants formed a chain to pass up buckets of water.

Immediately, healers took me aside to examine me beside other candidates, giving us carafes of water and checking our skin for heat blisters.

"I'm fine," I said, batting them away and catching the sleeve of a testmaker. "Is Prince Ekundayo with the emperor?" I had spotted Sanjeet, as well as Dayo's council: Kirah, Mayazatyl, and the rest. But Dayo was nowhere in sight.

"I don't know, candidate," the testmaker replied.

"The palace is burning, and you don't know where the crown prince of Aritsar is?"

The testmaker fidgeted, fraying the embroidered red braid on his kaftan. "Lady Adesanya said he was accounted for. I went to double-check the Hall of Dreams, and his sleeping platform was empty, so—"

I froze, my stomach turning to lead.

Dayo had not been sleeping on his platform. And the woman with Lady Adesanya's face had been Kathleen.

Suddenly, Dayo's council siblings began to yell and shriek, shaking with tears. "He's still in there," Kirah gasped. "We can hear him through the Ray. *He's still inside.*"

I shoved through the press of bodies. Something tugged on my candidate sash; Sanjeet had made a swipe for me. But I wrenched away, letting the rich cloth tear in two as I plunged back through the double doors of the Children's Palace.

Black clouds filled the dome of the playroom, obscuring

the air and stinging my eyes. I kept moving, staggering around corners as I coughed, lurching through crumbling doorframes. Dayo was immune to suffocating. That bought me time. But it also meant he would be able to breathe as the flames consumed him, denied even the mercy of unconsciousness.

My lungs screamed. I turned in a circle, hunting in vain for a pocket of fresh air. Charred toys and fallen beams smoldered around my feet, and my head swam with a falling sensation. The sound of crackling flames surged in my ears . . . and then I doubled over, stumbling to my knees. A note too high for hearing penetrated my mind, like a hot poker, or . . .

Or a ray of sunlight.

I had felt this before. The power was painful, but the feeling of vulnerability was even worse, my every thought laid bare. Yet something inside me reached for this invader, like a vine creeping toward the sky. I swallowed, and then stopped resisting.

The pain vanished as quickly as it came. Clear as a copper bell, a voice sounded in my mind: *Help me.*

"Dayo," I croaked.

Tar. The answering voice sounded frantic. *Did the Ray work? Can you hear me?*

I'm coming, I thought fiercely. *Where are you?*

In the window, came the weak reply. *I was sleeping . . . Then everything was hot . . . Smoke . . . Tried to get out . . . Man stood in front of the door; couldn't see his face . . .*

You have to jump, I told him. *Remember your mask. Remember what the priests said. You won't die, Dayo.*

It . . . it's so far. I can't do it, Tar. I don't believe the priests. I don't believe my mask, I don't believe in my Ray. I can't do it.

"I'm coming," I repeated aloud, using the voice in my head as a compass. Soot covered the looming murals of past council members, sullying their benevolent smiles. As Dayo's voice grew stronger, so too did the roar of flames. I turned a corner and squinted. Before me rose a viciously bright wall of fire.

The bedroom doors.

They crackled and spat, heat searing me from several paces away. My heart beat wildly. Suddenly my heroism seemed ludicrous. I was only a girl. What in Am's name was I doing?

A beam tumbled from the doorway, landing in a spray of sparks, and I yelped as embers assaulted my face. I turned, spun on my heel, and ran back down the corridor. I couldn't do it. I couldn't save Dayo, and I didn't need to; he had the Ray. He would jump.

Wouldn't he?

My sandals slapped in retreat across the stone and charred carpet . . . and then a voice sounded in my head again. It wasn't the invading spirit, not this time. It was a memory from the day Dayo and I had first met.

You're going to be another one, aren't you? A person I like.

My steps faltered, knees weakening as sweat and grit poured down my back. I stopped, exhaled sharply . . . and then my feet were racing back toward the flaming doors. My arms whistled as they pumped.

"*I won't burn, I won't burn, I won't burn,*" I chanted. "*I—won't—burn.*"

But I didn't believe it. I had emerged from the firepit at Bhekina House unscathed, yes, but that didn't mean I was special. Bhekina House had been enchanted for my protection, and the shield had probably dissipated the moment I had left. Yet still I was running, hurtling toward those flames.

Scorching, unbearable pain—and then I was through. My clothes were alight with fire. I cried out and dropped to the bedroom floor, rolling on the tiles. Once extinguished, I didn't stop to check for burns, but crept along the ground where the smoke was thinnest.

"Tarisai?" The voice was hoarse. Dayo stood backlit by the moon in the window alcove. The curtain had been torn down, snickering beneath him in flames.

"I'm here." I scrambled over and reached for him. He coughed, his eyes glassy and listless. "Come on," I rasped. "You have to jump."

"I can't," he mumbled. His face and neck were blistered from the heat. "I'm scared. And . . . you'll be alone. I won't leave you, Tar."

For a long moment, I considered pushing him. But I couldn't bring my arms to do it, even knowing he wouldn't die. Even knowing it was for his own good . . . the action too closely resembled murder. What if pushing Dayo awoke that *something* inside me? The part of me I hated and feared?

So I helped him down instead. He swooned, legs buckling. "Sorry," he breathed. "It's just . . . the smoke—"

"I'll carry you."

"You can't. The door's burning."

"I can walk through fire." I swallowed hard, trying to believe it. "I'm not normal, Dayo. I'm not natural, or safe, or good. But I can protect you." I held out my hand, shaking. *I can choose. I can write my own story.* "All you have to do is trust me."

Dayo swallowed, nodded, and leaned against me. I pulled him up and onto my back, hiding my face in what was left of my tunic. Then I charged the doors.

Dayo screamed, but my body took the brunt of the heat, shielding him from the inferno. We collapsed on the other side, rolling, then I seized his hand again and we lurched down the inky corridor. Gasping, coughing, retching, we stumbled at last through the Children's Palace antechamber, where frenzied courtiers swarmed to claim us.

"His Imperial Highness—his *skin*, oh gods—the Storyteller will never forgive us—"

A low, throbbing voice chanted through the hubbub, and the voices gasped as the disfiguring burns across Dayo's skin began to smooth and heal. The melodic chanting continued as Kirah and Sanjeet parted the crowd, Kirah's hand outstretched as she sang, tears streaming down her face. Dayo's marred skin knit itself together, leaving nothing but a raised pale scar along his jaw and collarbone.

"Don't leave us again," she said, touching his cheek. Then she turned and seized me into a hug. Sanjeet scooped up all three of us, crushing the air from our lungs, and we laughed until the army of fretting attendants broke us apart.

"Wait," Dayo croaked, before the healers could whisk us away to the infirmary. "There's something I have to do. Something . . . I have to ask." He turned to me and grinned that impossibly bright smile.

I squirmed, feeling awkward as everyone stared at us. "You almost died, Dayo," I muttered. "Go with the healers. Anything else can wait."

"No, it can't." Dayo drew a chain from beneath his ruined shirt, and on the end dangled a gold-encrusted vial. "Do you love me now, Tarisai of Swana?"

My heart raced. "Dayo," I whispered.

"Your mind connected with the Ray," he said. "You passed the test. You heard me . . . saved me." Shakily, he knelt on the marble floor and uncorked the vial of pelican oil. He smiled and said the scripted words so many emperors had before him: "Shall you be moon to the morning star? Are you willing, Tarisai of Swana? Do you accept my hand in councilhood?"

The room burst into excited murmurs. I blocked them out.

Say yes, screamed every cell in my body. *Rule the world. Have a family. Think of Dayo. Think of Kirah, and Sanjeet, and the castle by the sea.*

But I couldn't. The Lady's wish had been clear: The moment he anointed me, I would become a monster. My cursed hands . . . they would fly around his neck, here, in front of everyone, and they would never let go. I was not normal, try as I might. I was broken. And The Lady's words were carved into my mind, a permanent scar, unless—

Unless they weren't.

Slowly, my gaze found Sanjeet, who watched me anxiously among the whispering throng of candidates. I remembered how he had looked when we first met: haunted. Hunched with nightmares and shadows, the Prince's Bear. But now his back was straight, and his brow was grim but clear. I had helped him. I had healed the scars on his mind. I had made him forget his story. Why couldn't I do the same for myself?

Inhaling deeply, I dug my fingers into my temples and laid waste to my own memories.

I was an invader, kicking down the doors of my mind's palace, and setting flame to every room. First I burned Kathleen and Woo In, letting their faces and voices smolder into hazy smoke. My mind fought back, desperate to fill in the new gaps. Who had brought me to Oluwan? A man and a woman. Or . . . had it been two women? I didn't know. What had they talked about? The Lady—Hallows—a mission . . . The words turned rapidly to mush, like fallen mangoes decaying in dry season. I knew nothing of my journey to Oluwan, and the people who had brought me were ghosts. My head swam, but ruthlessly I pressed on.

Next room.

Now the flames engulfed Bhekina House, and Melu's savannah, and the memory of Mother's first two wishes. My body began to swelter and shake. Distantly, I heard Dayo and the other children murmur in concern. Someone brought a stool and I sat, Dayo kneeling before me worriedly.

"Just a moment," I croaked. "I just—need a moment."

Most of my memories were located in just a few areas of my mind, but Melu was all over, a virus in every vein, bending me to The Lady's will. His spirit was living, reaching with difficulty from his savannah to speak into my mind.

Stop, he bellowed.

"No," I rasped.

Stop! No good can come of this. You are half-ehru, and your destiny is—

NO, my mind roared back at him, and with a wave of snickering flames, Melu's face and voice turned to ash. I knew him no more.

The last room was the hardest. I held my head between my knees, rocking and whimpering with the pain.

"We need a healer," Dayo cried, and Kirah began to sing a soothing chant, but I covered my ears. Now was not the time for distractions.

The Lady's face resisted the flames, as though she were encased in adamant. I threw embers and blazing torches, I sent rivers of fire; still she smiled, unscathed. *Give up*, the smile said. *Your mind protects me with the same ferocity with which it defends your own name.*

But I'm not you, I whispered back.

Are you sure?

My brow beaded with sweat. *My name is my own. My name is my own. My—name. My—own—*

And at last, the shield of adamant shattered.

Gone was the glow of her brilliant black eyes. Gone was the jasmine scent of her arms around me. Gone was the music of her throaty voice, the chant of *me* and *mine.*

And concealed in impenetrable smoke were those lethal words, spoken over me like an incantation: *I command you to kill him.*

I opened my eyes. The whole room stared at me, eerily still, as though turned to stone. What had I just been thinking about? I had been anxious about . . . something. I had been unhappy. Was it the fire? Bad people . . . Someone I knew had tried to kill Dayo. I had been so worried. Terrified. I couldn't bear to lose the prince, because . . . because . . .

I stared down at the scarred face below mine, the mop of black locs, the gangly features I'd come to know as well as my own. *I love him.* My feelings were certain, like the sun rising over the palace turrets, or the grasslands rolling beneath the Swanian sky.

I left the stool, knelt, and touched my brow to his. "I am willing," I said. "I accept your hand in councilhood."

Tears glistened on Dayo's cheeks. The smell of sea salt and burnt feathers filled the air as he drew a star on my forehead with pelican oil. Then he produced a small knife and made a shallow cut in his hand, then mine. "Now you're mine," he breathed, pressing our palms so the blood ran together, and heat burned through me.

I froze. Something bad was supposed to happen now. Something horrible I couldn't remember . . .

But nothing did.

Dayo stood and pulled me up into an embrace, and I shivered with relief. His touch was more than a comfort. I needed to be near him, now; needed Kirah, and Kameron, and Umansa, and all my other council siblings. My body ached for their warmth, with the same fervor that it longed for food and water. Council sickness: the permanent hunger of Anointed Ones.

Sanjeet knelt for his anointing afterward. "I never needed a sacred title to protect you, brother," he told Dayo, and smiled at the new cut in his palm. "But to stay by your side, I'll take whatever name you give me."

Then Dayo presented us to the crowd of courtiers and candidates, and they sank to the floor in respect.

I blinked. "They shouldn't be bowing. Not to me."

"Of course they should," Dayo replied, linking his fingers through mine. "Anointed Honor."

PART 2

CHAPTER 10

THE WORLD OUTSIDE WAS CHANTING MY name, but all I wanted was a nap.

"Thank you for visiting Ebujo, Anointed Honor. Look, it's you!"

"Sorry," I mumbled. How long had the child been kneeling there? From my gilded stool in the temple, I squinted down at a gap-toothed boy. "What did you say?"

Beside me, my council siblings smiled as commoners approached their stools. How my siblings managed to stay in such a good mood—accepting gifts and congratulations, kissing every infant thrust at their faces—I had no idea. We had barely eaten for hours, and had traveled nonstop for a year. After Dayo anointed our last council member, kindhearted Zathulu of Djbanti, we had taken a goodwill tour of the empire. We had crossed sand, snow, and savannah, and been greeted in each city by the people we would one day rule. Our journey had culminated here, in the holy city of Ebujo, where all council members received their official titles.

Platforms drawn by tamed lions with braided manes had

paraded us through the streets. The cheers and drumming drowned out even my own thoughts.

"Don't stop waving," Mbali had ordered us before the ceremony. "Don't stop smiling. They will pass your faces down to their children and grandchildren. You are not human beings—not anymore. You are nations. You are history walking."

The road winding to the temple teemed with commoners in their best festival wrappers. Perfume thickened the air, and children tossed petals from the battlements, a flurry of gold, red, and white. Griots beat shakers and drums, and to the rhythm, the townspeople of Ebujo sang a new version of Aritsar's well-known folk rhyme:

> *Tarisai brings his drum; nse*
> *Sanjeet and Umansa bring his plow; gpopo*
> *Kameron and Theo watch our older brother dance—*
> *Black and gold: Ekundayo!*

> *Mayazatyl sharpens his spear; nse*
> *Kirah weaves his wrapper; gpopo*
> *Thérèse and Emeronya watch our older brother dance—*
> *Black and gold: Ekundayo!*

> *Zathulu braids his hair; nse*
> *Ai Ling brings his gourd; gpopo*
> *Eleven moons watch the sun dance:*
> *Black and gold: Ekundayo!*

But all I could think of was my blistering headache.

"Are you all right, Anointed Honor?" the boy in the temple asked, shifting his feet.

My vision swam, but I forced a smile and nodded. "What do you have there?"

The boy held up a rag doll and dropped it shyly in my hand. "It's you. I made her from my best tunic. It was too small for me, and Ma wanted to sell it for scraps, but I wouldn't let her."

The doll's body was sewn from dark brown linen, matched carefully to my complexion. Cheerful button eyes shone over a seam smile, and black yarn braids burst from its brow.

My heart twinged. Memories of the boy's fingers, shakily wielding a needle and pricking himself by accident, leeched from the doll into my palm. I made the tiny Tarisai bow to him, and the boy giggled.

"Thank you," I told him. "How did you know what I looked like?"

"There's a portrait in our family inn, Anointed Honor. A merchant brought it all the way from the capital. It has you, and Prince Ekundayo, and the Prince's Bear, and the other Prince's Eleven. Sometimes we leave maize under the portrait. Or cassava, and palm wine."

I raised an eyebrow. "Why?"

"Offerings," he said, blinking as though it were obvious. "So the town will have a good harvest."

I opened my mouth, then closed it. Commoners and

nobility from all over the continent were lined up before our elevated stools in the temple. Their eyes devoured the jeweled weave of my wax-dyed wrapper, the stacks of rainbow beads on my wrists and neck, and the golden cuffs on my biceps. I squirmed. They knew I was only mortal . . . didn't they?

"You're my favorite, you know," the boy chattered. "My sister thinks Anointed Honor Ai Ling is prettier, but you can read *minds*. Or is it memories? Sis and I couldn't decide. Auntie says it's suspicious how no one knows who your mother and father are, but Papa says that doesn't matter because you saved Prince Ekundayo's life, and I think . . ."

His voice faded away as the pain between my temples surged. Those words: *mother and father.*

Ever since my anointing, headaches had plagued me. I remembered only two things from my life before the Children's Palace: a mango orchard and a name—*Lady.* I had obeyed Mbali in my years as a candidate, never speaking of my mother, and now I couldn't even if I wanted to. But as I slept, a song echoed on the edge of my dreams: *Me, mine. She's me and she is mine.*

"Are your parents poor?" the boy whispered conspiratorially. "Will you visit them when you go back to Swana?"

My temples throbbed. Air ceased to travel through my lungs. "I—I don't know. I—"

"That's enough questions for Her Anointed Honor." Dayo had risen from his stool.

The child froze and blanched. "Your . . . Your Imperial Highness."

Dayo smiled and crouched so the child's face was level with his burn scar. The thick, raised skin crept down Dayo's cheek in an intricate lattice, ending in several branches on his collarbone. It had been the best Kirah's healing song could do after the fire, and the sight of it always made my headaches worse.

Dayo's obsidian *oloye* mask dangled from his neck; there was no need to hide it now. The twelve stripes of his immunities glittered, reflecting rainbows across the little boy's face.

"Your mother must be proud of you," Dayo said gently. "I bet you're the best dollmaker in Ebujo."

The boy nodded woodenly, and Dayo ruffled his hair. Then the child bowed and retreated into the crowd, dazed with shock.

Dayo placed a hand on my shoulder. "Still no memories?" he asked.

I shook my head. "It's horrible. I'm supposed to be the Imperial Delegate of Swana. But how can I represent a realm I don't even remem—"

"Forget Swana," Dayo cut in, and I blinked in surprise. Dayo rarely interrupted anyone. "I mean . . . ," he faltered. "You're one of us now. That's all that matters, right? And you won't be Delegate of Swana anytime soon. Until Father di— That is, until Father goes to the village, we'll just be running campaigns and throwing parties at

Yorua Keep. That could last for years. Decades, even."

In Aritsar, it was bad luck to refer to the death of an emperor. Instead, we said that a deceased emperor had "gone to the village, and would not be returning soon." Most emperors did not go to the village sooner than eighty years of age, which meant that Dayo could be well into his forties before our council rose to the throne. Until then, we would live at Yorua Keep, the sleepy fortress in coastal Oluwan where all crown princes lived after completing their council. Once the goodwill tour ended, we would move straight there, only returning to the Children's Palace on rare visits to the capital.

"It *will* be nice to run our own home," I conceded. "I won't miss the trials. Or getting woken up by drums."

Dayo peered at me curiously. "You're sweating. Is the Breach making you nervous? Nothing's come out of it for years, you know."

I grimaced. "Nothing needs to come out of that hole for it to stink. How do the priests stand it?"

The heart of the Ebujo Temple was a vast chamber with high walls and no roof. Centuries ago, monsters had decimated the domed ceiling. Pillars of translucent limestone shot through with purple veins rose around us, supporting nothing but the sky. One side of the chamber held a marble altar, our semicircle of gilded stools, and standing room for onlookers. On the other side, hedged by a low spiked wall and guarded by shaman warriors, lay the Oruku Breach: an entrance to the underworld.

The rift sunk into the ground, a smirking, sulfurous mouth that steamed with blue miasma. The temple had originally been built as a fortress around the Breach, guarding civilians against undead monsters. But after Enoba's treaty, Redemptor children were forced to enter the Breach regularly, and so the impenetrable fortress had been converted into a temple. Every hundred years, the Breach chamber hosted the Peace Ritual between the Arit crown prince and the continent's ambassadors. The ritual was preliminary, a less grand version of the continent-wide Treaty Renewal, which took place one year later in Oluwan City between the emperor and all the continent's rulers. This century, the preliminary ritual happened to coincide with our council's ensealment ceremony, in which we learned the titles we would inherit from the Emperor's Eleven.

I glanced over at Kirah, who sat a few stools down from me. We had been encouraged to wear clothes representing our home realms, and she looked resplendent in the billowing tunic and trousers of Blessid chieftains. Though our titles had not yet been announced, everyone knew she would replace Mbali as High Priestess of Aritsar. Aside from Dayo's, Kirah's receiving line was longest: commoners and nobility alike, desperate for a taste of her healing Hallow. A balding old man knelt weeping at Kirah's feet, bobbing with gratitude as she chanted over him.

I summoned Dayo's Ray. When warm pressure pulsed at the center of my head, I directed the heat toward Kirah.

Don't tire yourself, I thought. *You can't help anyone if your voice gives out.*

Kirah looked up, sneaking me an exhausted smile. *I don't have the energy to heal any of them fully*, she thought. *But they still look at me like I'm a god. I don't know if that's funny or tragic.*

I frowned, sending a pulse of sympathy through the bond. When she responded, rejuvenation coursed through me. Nothing satiated council sickness like Ray-speaking.

These days, I barely remembered what it had been like to love *without* the Ray. The freedom to speak into my friends' minds—to share pictures, even feelings if we wished—was an intimacy unlike any I had ever felt.

At least, any that I could remember. Sometimes when I slept with my anointed siblings, our bodies tangled on the Children's Palace floor like a litter of lion cubs . . . familiarity twinged inside me. I had belonged to someone before, in a way just as intimate and consuming as the Ray bond. Before the Children's Palace, someone had *owned* me.

Like an island obscured by fog, a corner of my identity floated out of reach. I could build a raft and row to it—fight through the waves of my mind's resistance, reclaiming the shores of my past—but I was too much of a coward to try.

"So don't," Dayo always said when I worried. "You're home now. Why would you need anywhere else?"

That man and woman, another voice Ray-spoke in my mind. *Tarisai, you've seen them before.*

The voice caressed the center of my spine, a velvet bass

thickened by a plosive Dhyrmish accent. I suppressed my pleasure, hoping it did not travel through the Ray as I met Sanjeet's eye.

He sat one stool to my left, resplendent in the pearl-studded black kaftan of Dhyrmish generals. With his head, he gestured to the next group of well-wishers in my receiving line. *Don't you know them?*

An isoken woman in a hooded green cloak and a man whose full-body birthmarks betrayed him to be a Redemptor stood before my platform. Most well-wishers were bashful, staring at their feet as they stammered congratulations and handed me a gift. In contrast, these visitors stared directly at me . . . and smirked.

I shook my head at Sanjeet. *I've never seen them before. Have you?*

He looked uncertain. *Once, I think. In the stories you used to show me from your memories, before you forgot your childhood. But that was years ago. I could be mistaken.*

The Redemptor man stepped forward and bowed, mocking the gesture by prolonging it. "Anointed Honor."

"Thank you for coming," I responded politely. "Songland is very far from Ebujo. Were your travels difficult, sir . . . ?"

When I waited for his name, the man gave me a sardonic look, as though I had asked a question to which we both knew the answer.

"My name is Woo In," he said with a taut smile. "And the most harrowing journey of my life began in this room."

My face heated as he looked past me toward the steaming Oruku Breach. "Of course," I murmured, ashamed at my insensitivity. "This temple must hold terrible memories. I'm honored you would return here on my behalf. Please accept my deepest gratitude."

Woo In swept a dark blue cloak over his birthmarked shoulder, and bent to plant an icy kiss on my seal ring. "I have no need of gratitude," he said. "But I will accept justice: your assurance that my story never happens to any Songland child again."

I withdrew my hand sharply. "What are you talking about?"

Instead of responding, Woo In beckoned to his companion. The cloaked isoken held the hand of a young Redemptor girl. The child curtsied, looking at me with strong, inquisitive features, her skin completely covered in geometric patterns. I noted the difference between her marks and Woo In's—his were purple and glittering, and hers blue and soft. The marks of a Redemptor who had not yet crossed the Underworld.

"I'm Ye Eun," she piped up. "It's nice to meet you, Anointed Honor." On her short dark hair, she wore a lily-of-the-valley flower crown. Shyly, she offered a matching crown to me. I bowed my head, allowing her to lay it atop my twisted coils.

"Thank you," I said.

She grinned as though we shared a secret. "You're as pretty as your mother."

I froze. "I . . . What did you say?"

"You're going to save us," she said cheerily. "The Lady promised it would happen any day now, but first, you've got to get your memories back. I hope it's soon. I don't have long before . . ." Her gaze traveled to the Breach beyond me.

The child was delusional. Was that a side effect of being a Redemptor? Poor thing; her parents had likely abandoned her at birth. "Ye Eun," I said. "How old are you?"

"Almost eleven," she chirped.

My stomach turned to knots. Redemptor children were supposed to be surrendered to the Breach at age ten. Failure to comply, according to the histories, meant retaliation from the Underworld.

But surely the old stories weren't all true. How could the abiku—the spirits with whom Enoba had forged the Redemptor Treaty—resent the loss of one tiny girl? My heart lightened. The Emperor's Council had the power to help Ye Eun. They could make an exception to the Treaty, certainly. I just needed to buy her time.

I leaned forward, grasping Ye Eun's shoulders. "Listen, I need you to hide. Here in the temple, out of sight of the priests. I'll send for you once the ceremonies are over. Then you can come visit me in Yorua Keep. How does that sound?"

Ye Eun's grin broadened, but she looked at Woo In and the isoken woman for permission. They shrugged, and so the girl giggled with excitement and disappeared into the crowd.

"Are you her guardians?" I asked the strangers.

Woo In's expression hardened. "All Redemptors are my brothers and sisters. And any person who would hinder their freedom is my enemy."

The isoken woman came forward then, smirking as she presented me with a talking drum. "My name is Kathleen, oh *great* Anointed One. Please accept this humble gift. If rumors are to be believed, it once belonged to the Empress Aiyetoro. Such an artifact must contain priceless stories, and only a Hallow such as yours could retrieve them. Perhaps such stories will remind you of your own."

I examined the gift with reverent fingers. The gourd was shaped like an hourglass, strung head-to-head with strips of taut goatskin that determined the pitch. A beating stick was nestled in the skins for safekeeping. Emblazoned around the drum's face was a pattern of discs and interlinking hands, and a line in the script of ancient Oluwan. Squinting, I struggled to translate it: *The truth will never die, as long as griots keep beating their drums.*

"Where did you find this?" I asked.

Woo In smiled crisply. "There are those who would preserve history, instead of choosing to forget it."

I plunged into the drum's memories, but when my mind stole into the gourd, only dust and moist darkness teased my senses, along with the skittering of spiders on my skin. I grimaced and withdrew.

"It's been kept in storage too long," I said. "My Hallow can only go back a few decades. I could never reach

Aiyetoro. But thank you. The gift is precious all the same."

Woo In and Kathleen looked disappointed.

"I *told* The Lady that drum wouldn't work," the woman complained to Woo In, not bothering to lower her voice. "It's too indirect. She'll never remember who she is through ancient artifacts. We need to awaken the ehru inside her."

"Only The Lady can communicate with Melu," Woo In muttered. "So she'll have to solve this problem herself."

Their words made my veins prickle with cold. Had Sanjeet been right? Did these people know me? More important, why had I chosen to forget them?

But before I could question them further, drums hiccupped through the temple. A palace secretary bearing calfskin scrolls bustled into the chamber, and Woo In and Kathleen vanished into the crowd.

Amid excited murmurs, Dayo received the scroll from the secretary. "Citizens of Aritsar, and honored guests from Songland," he announced, bowing to each of the groups surrounding us. "My father's council has long deliberated over the imperial positions my council will inherit. Today, it is my sincerest pleasure to read their decisions." Silently, he sent each of us a pulse of affection through the Ray.

Ready? Kirah Ray-spoke, and eleven voices echoed in my head. *You're kidding, right? . . . Don't care which one I get . . . Can't wait . . . As long as we finally get to move out of that cramped Children's Palace . . .*

Dayo cleared his throat and unfurled the scroll. A grin

split his face, and so I knew the first name on the list was no surprise. "As her heir apparent to the title of High Priestess," Dayo said, "Anointed Honor Mbali of Swana has selected Kirah of Blessid Valley."

The temple rang with cheers, and Kirah stood, hazel eyes shining. "I accept my title as High Priestess Apparent," she croaked, and glowed as the imperial secretary came forward to place a gold circlet on her brow.

The next declaration was also no surprise. "As heir apparent to the title of High Lord General," Dayo said, "Anointed Honor Wagundu of Djbanti has selected Sanjeet of Dhyrma."

Sanjeet stood, accepting his title and circlet without expression. My heart twinged; Sanjeet hated using his Hallow for violence, and he had hoped for a more peaceful appointment. But Aritsar hadn't had a civil war in decades, and foreign continents rarely attacked. Perhaps, I hoped naively, he would never have to hurt anyone.

I didn't know what title to expect for myself. While most of Olugbade's council had grown used to me, Nawusi still considered me a sin against nature. With her influence, I anticipated that my title would be less than glamorous— High Lady Treasurer, perhaps, responsible for collecting the empire's taxes. Or High Lady Archdean, tasked with supervising the empire's stuffy academies and scholar guilds.

Dayo paused before the next reading, taking a moment to face me and beam. "As his heir apparent to the title of

High Lord Judge," he said, "Anointed Honor Thaddace of Mewe has selected Tarisai of Swana."

My stomach dropped to my sandals.

Judge?

High Lady Judge of Aritsar?

Deciding the fate of Aritsar's worst traitors and criminals? A sixteen-year-old girl who couldn't remember her own past beyond five years ago, when she first came to the Children's Palace? What in Am's name had Thaddace been thinking?

I could refuse to accept. But the Emperor's Council had deliberated for months, and my rejection would start the process all over again. After getting their hopes up for Yorua Keep, my council would have to return to the Children's Palace—and even then, the results might be the same.

So I rose from my stool, clasped my hands to hide their shaking, and rasped, "I accept my title as High Judge Apparent." Then I bent my head for the heavy gold circlet.

"You'll have to take off the flowers first, Anointed Honor," murmured the secretary.

I had forgotten Ye Eun's lily-of-the-valley crown. As I removed them and the delegate crowned me, the Redemptor girl's trusting, inquisitive features flashed in my mind. As High Lady Judge, I could influence the terms of the Redemptor Treaty. If I could help children like Ye Eun . . . maybe being High Lady Judge wouldn't be that bad.

The rest of the ceremony passed in a blur. A smug Mayazatyl was appointed future High Lady of Castles, head of defense and civil engineering. Ai Ling, Hallowed with formidable powers of persuasion, was appointed future High Lady Ambassador, in charge of interrealm trade. Umansa, who could read vague fortunes in the stars, would be High Lord Treasurer, and Zathulu, with his bookish head for facts, would be a competent High Lord Archdean. Thérèse, our Hallowed green thumb, was destined to be High Lady of Harvests; and Kameron, who had routinely snuck dubious animal rescues into the Children's Palace, happily accepted his future as High Lord of Husbandry. Mysterious Emeronya would regulate sorcery as High Lady Magus, and as future High Lord Laureate, bleeding-heart poet Theo would curate the art and music of all twelve realms.

When all of us were crowned, I allowed myself to relax. Our exhausting journey of diplomacy was almost over. Dayo would conduct the Peace Ritual with the continent ambassadors. Then our council would whisk away via lodestone to Yorua Keep, with nothing to do but study scrolls, play house, and throw sumptuous parties for decades to come.

Priests swept the four corners of the temple, ritually cleansing the chamber. Dayo, the eleven Arit ambassadors, and a royal emissary from Songland came to stand at the altar. A child choir of acolytes sprinkled myrrh around the marble platform and harmonized in rounds:

Sharp and cold the world received you
Warm with blood it sends you home
Back to earth, to holy black
Dark to dark:
Beginning and beginning.

On the altar rested a gourd flask and an ancient oval shield, which had once belonged to Enoba the Perfect. In one year, the thirteen continent rulers would travel to the capital and spill their blood into the shield's basin, renewing humankind's vow with the Underworld to uphold the Redemptor Treaty. In today's ceremony, the Peace Ritual, Dayo, the ambassadors, and the emissary would spill water instead of blood, a good-faith promise that their realms would participate in the official renewal.

"To beginnings," cheered the ambassadors as one by one they spilled water into the shield, sealing their commitment. First to approach were the ambassadors from the center realms—Djbanti, Nyamba, and Swana— then those from the north—Mewe, Nontes, and Biraslov. Ambassadors from the south, Blessid Valley, Quetzala, and Sparti, and from the east, Moreyao and Dhyrma, were next in line. Then came the emissary from Songland.

He was a bent old man in a sweeping, high-waisted robe who grimaced as he poured into the shield. "To beginnings," he wheezed. "Songland shall participate in the Treaty Renewal. May it bring peace to our world. And may the parents of the lost children be comforted."

The onlookers squirmed uncomfortably. The last words had not been scripted into the ritual, though no one dared chastise the emissary.

We all knew that Redemptors had once been born at equal rates throughout the continent. It was horrible that Redemptor children were now born exclusively in Songland, but for the most part, the continent rulers accepted this phenomenon as fate.

Why had Ye Eun thought I could change that?

Songland had tried to boycott the Treaty several times. But the Underworld would not be pacified unless every realm participated in the Treaty ritual. Whenever Songland resisted, the continent crawled with deadly plagues and monsters until at last Songland complied, grimly sending three hundred Redemptors into the Breach each year.

Dayo was last to pour water, representing both Oluwan and the empire of Aritsar. Then one of the choir children gave him a handful of myrrh, which he dropped into the shield. As a sign of the Underworld's acceptance, the water was supposed to turn brown, the color of earth and fertility. I fidgeted, wishing for the ceremony to end, and for the chance to rest at last.

But the water bubbled and turned white: the color of bones and ash. The color of death.

The priests gasped, murmuring as the sulfuric stench intensified throughout the temple. The blue miasma thickened over the Breach, and up from the shadowy chasm rose two small figures, walking hand in hand.

CHAPTER 11

I HAD SEEN DRAWINGS OF THE ABIKU before—demons that took the form of sickly children, a mocking tribute to Redemptors. But nothing could have prepared me for the creatures who approached the altar.

The courtiers and townspeople shrieked, and my palms broke into a cold sweat. They looked like twins, no older than five or six, with pallid gray skin and eyes made completely of red pupils. They stopped at the barrier of myrrh spread by the priests, unable or unwilling to come closer. Then they tilted their heads in unison, flashing tiny smiles of yellow, pointed teeth.

"Good health to you, Prince," one of the abiku said. "Don't you know it's rude to withhold gifts at a party?"

Dayo swallowed hard. "What do you want, spirits? Why didn't the water turn brown?"

The other abiku gave a grating peal of giggles. "Does a treasurer loan gold before the previous debt is repaid? You swear to honor the Treaty. But as we stand here, you break it."

"That's a lie," Dayo said. "The shamans promised that

every Redemptor of age has been paid to you."

"They miscounted," sighed the first abiku, its irisless gaze landing briefly on mine. "Every Redemptor has been sent except one."

My blood turned to ice. The abiku were here for Ye Eun.

It wasn't fair. How could the demons miss one little girl out of three hundred? What use could they possibly have for her? I set my jaw. If the abiku thought I could be bullied into giving Ye Eun up, they were wrong. Before the Treaty, during the War of Twelve Armies, the Underworld had suffered losses as well as humankind. Surely they would not give up peace for the sake of a single child.

"You spirits speak of debts? Of fairness?" sputtered the emissary from Songland. "How dare you!" The old man stood dangerously close to the myrrh barrier, eyes bulging with anger. "Shades haunt the halls of Eunsan-do Palace, the shades of child Redemptors, wailing day and night. If the abiku cared anything for fairness, they would cease to rip babes from the arms of their mothers, from the same poor realm, year after year!"

The abiku cocked their heads again, blinking as though surprised at the emissary's outburst. "When it comes to the birthplace of Redemptors," one of them purred, "it is the blood, not us, who decides."

I frowned. What in Am's name was that supposed to mean?

As the abiku spoke, two young Breach warriors had

crept up behind them, expressions fearful and manic.

"You—you aren't authorized to be here," the young warrior stammered, gripping his weapon halter. "You're in violation of the Treaty of Enoba. Back away from the prince."

"There is no Treaty," the abiku hissed, "until humanity's debt is paid."

The creatures took a step toward the warrior . . . and the Breach warrior spooked. He staggered back, scooped a handful of myrrh from the floor, and thrust it at the abiku.

"Die, spirits!" he cried.

The creatures screamed . . . then exploded in a cloud of noxious, biting flies.

"To the prince," Sanjeet bellowed as the temple descended into chaos. Ambassadors, priests, and laypeople dove for cover. At Sanjeet's command my council siblings leapt to their feet, and we retrieved our weapons from behind the stools. Sanjeet fit his pair of black-hilted scimitars in a snug halter on his back, and I brandished my steel-headed spear, shaft carved with the Kunleo sun and moons. Our eleven surrounded Dayo in tight formation, and the Ray synchronized our movements with inhuman speed.

The deep-throated howl of temple warning horns cut through the air. Feathered clumps were rising from the Oruku Breach, obscured by the miasma. They emerged as winged beasts, ugly as hyenas, diving for their victims with outstretched talons.

"I'll be fine," Dayo yelled at us. "Help the commoners."

We tensed, but kept formation. The order of our priorities, drummed into us by the palace priests, had been clear: *Serve the prince, then the empire.*

Defending commoners was the job of the Imperial Guard, to whom Sanjeet and Mayazatyl now barked commands. "Fall into cohorts! Man the war machines! Ammunition lines, up!"

Mayazatyl had recently designed the weapons outfitting the temple walls. The sleek cannons were powered by fire, but armed with balls of ice—frozen holy water, stored in chambers deep beneath the temple grounds. The Imperial Guard warriors, burly recruits from all over the empire, formed a chain, passing up ammunition to the warriors manning the cannons. With a crack, the first round ignited, and orbs of splintering ice collided with the flying beasts and hurled six to the ground.

Mayazatyl cheered and warriors roared in response, loading the second round. Then the ammunition line broke as clouds of flies dove for the warriors on the ground. My council tried to escort Dayo to safety, but crowds of screaming courtiers stampeded for the exits, creating a lethal jam. A Djbanti woman cried out in her native language as she was trampled on the ground, causing a Djbanti cannon warrior to turn and look. The cannon misfired, and the ball of ice sailed into a crowd of Nontish emissaries. One fell and did not get up.

"Fool," screeched a Nontish cannon warrior, seizing the Djbanti warrior by the lapels. "You killed the ambassador!"

"I didn't mean to," hyperventilated the other. "I'm sorry, I—"

"Typical of you Djbanti! Lazy head in the clouds, never at your post—"

"Leave my people out of it," another Djbanti warrior snarled, punching the Nontish man in the jaw.

"No," Mayazatyl rasped. "No, no. This is not the time . . ."

"Man your stations," Sanjeet boomed up at the fisticuffing warriors as they teetered precariously on the wall. "We're in the middle of a battle! People are dying, you idiots; I said man your—"

Both warriors fell two stories to the ground. Then another swarm of beasts rose from the Breach.

The Imperial Guard warriors broke ranks. Instead of manning the cannons that might have saved us all, the panicked men and women scrambled to protect their own kinspeople. Warriors from Nyamba ignored shrieking wounded Spartians to help Nyamban courtiers. Moreyaoese warriors stepped over a bleeding child from Djabanti, ignoring him to help a woman dressed in Moreyao silks. Oluwani commoners, who had found cramped shelter behind upended chairs and tables, hissed away people from Nontes and Dhyrma seeking refuge. As the cannon fire stopped, the beasts wheeled overhead, and then dove.

I shrieked, adrenaline coursing through my veins as talons scooped up bodies and sunk into backs. Blood soaked through festival robes. I choked back bile, then spotted a small figure crouched beneath a stone table, flower crown drooping over eyes like forlorn moons.

Ye Eun.

"Leave me and find shelter," Dayo hollered at our council, and then pointed at the mask on his chest. "For Am's sake, *I can't die*, remember? Protect yourselves!"

It was enough to break my trance. Pulling out of formation, I dove across the hellscape of bodies, beasts, and flies to join Ye Eun beneath her table. I pressed an arm around her trembling shoulders, and used the other to brandish my spear.

"It's all right," I rasped, trying to shield her from view of the Underworld beasts. "Don't worry. We're getting out of here."

She did not move, limbs turned to stone as she watched a beast rip a man to pieces.

She said, "It's because of me, isn't it?"

"No," I lied, gritting my teeth against the unfairness of it all. "Don't think that, Ye Eun."

Her tear-stained, intelligent features fixed slowly on mine. "You're right," she whispered. "None of this is my fault. It's yours."

My heart missed a beat.

"You were supposed to stop it." Her bottom lip trembled, then hardened. "The Redemptors believed in you. You were supposed to change everything."

"I don't understand."

"There's no such thing as heroes, is there?" The girl spoke

tonelessly to herself. She watched the teeming battleground, all at once, looking four times her years: innocence lost in the space of a breath. "Outcasts only have ourselves."

Then she wrenched my arm off her shoulders and sprinted from beneath the table.

"Don't—" I grabbed for her and missed, heart pounding with dread. "No. *No*. Ye Eun—"

But she had already cleared the length of the chamber, standing over the yawning blue mouth. The force of the miasma blew her hair around her face as she balled her small hands into fists. She looked back only once—a reproachful stare that shook my bones—before closing her eyes and stepping over the ledge.

The temple went quiet. A cry echoed across the stone, and I would later realize it was mine. The abiku beasts had vanished. The debt was satiated.

Afternoon light shone on the limestone with terrible serenity, and over tiles strewed with corpses. I crossed the chamber, moving as though through water to the Breach's edge, deaf to the yells of my council siblings.

My chest racked with sobs as I crumpled in a pile of petals. Ye Eun's lily-of-the-valley crown remained at the lip of the Breach. The buds, barely opened, lay soiled in pieces.

CHAPTER 12

SIX MONTHS PASSED.

The freedom of Yorua Keep paralyzed me at first. The old fortress, located on a perennially sunny cliff at the coastal tip of Oluwan, had no trials or testmakers. No drums to make us dance from prayers to meals to lessons. No painted facades, hiding eyes that watched our every failing. Strangely, I missed those eyes. In the weeks after the disaster at Ebujo, freedom had lost its romance for my council.

We crept through the airy, salt-scented halls of Yorua Keep in a whispering huddle, ghosts of our own castle. Shyly, we asked for schedules from our new servants: peasants from the village below our cliff, along with a chef and steward from the palace.

"When should we report to dinner?" Dayo asked the head steward.

The man blinked in confusion. "Your council . . . reports . . . to no one, Your Imperial Highness. Meals are at the times you schedule them to be."

And so week by week, the ghosts of Ebujo began to fade, making way for the numbing addiction of running our own household. Our council reserved mornings for prayer and meditation, and then trained on the beach, conducting drills on sand shaded by palm trees. We bathed in the sea and returned to lunches of roasted fish and palm wine. Then we scattered to our favorite crannies of the keep—always in pairs, to stave off council sickness. We studied for hours, anxious to practice the imperial roles we would someday fill.

Ai Ling and Umansa usually took to the fortress turrets. She yelled diplomacy speeches at the clouds while he wove tapestries on his loom, charting prophetic constellations that only his sightless eyes could see. In the courtyard far below, Kameron kept a caterwauling menagerie, treating beasts for rare diseases as Mayazatyl drew diagrams for weapons and defense towers in the dirt beside him. Thérèse tended her sprawling orchard while Theo plucked chords on his zither, coaxing her plants to grow with griot stories and love poems. Emeronya and Zathulu sealed themselves in one of the keep's dusty studies, murmuring over scrying glasses and essays by budding Imperial Academy scholars.

I spent most of my days on a shady balcony with Kirah, fretting over my court cases, while she scowled at her theology scrolls. To my disappointment, Sanjeet was often called away, and Dayo joined him, leaving the keep to lead the Imperial Guard on its peace campaigns. When

Dayo was home, he had the formidable task of learning all our disciplines. He shadowed us for hours, taking voracious notes during the day and informing his father of his progress with long, formal letters at night. I began to wonder if he ever truly slept. Then again, none of us slept well after Ebujo.

Our favorite distraction came once a month, when peddlers were permitted in the heavily guarded keep courtyard. A glut of luxuries—embroidered wrappers, jewel-studded bangles, roasted kola nuts, and pots of flavored cream—were spread before us in a maze of stalls and blankets. The miniature market was for council members only, and musicians and tumblers entertained us as we shopped and made sizable dents in our generous imperial allowance.

The fortress had twenty pristine bedchambers, and we used every single one for storage. Sleeping separately, after all, meant eight hours apart, and the resulting nausea of council sickness was too steep a price. Instead we slept on the floor of the keep banquet hall, rolling out pallets as we had in the Children's Palace and snoring together in a sweaty pile.

The banquet hall floor was a mosaic of the Kunleo sun and moons. Dayo lay in the golden center, with the rest of us scattered among the eleven pale orbs. Sheer curtains hung from floor-length, unglazed windows, screening us from the warm night air. As moonlight glowed across the tiles, we could hear the Imperial Guard warriors changing watch and the crash of the Obasi Ocean, churning on rocks hundreds of feet below.

The lullaby was almost enough to chase away the screams of commoners speared by talons. The jeers of citizens who had refused each other shelter. The scent of Ye Eun's lily-of-the-valley crown, marking where her birthmarked feet had leapt into the breach. Almost, but not enough.

Some demons could not be soothed by any lullaby.

I was fast asleep on my pallet. Thaddace routinely sent me cases from the capital, and today's collection had been particularly exhausting: everything from village disputes over cattle to housemaids reporting their masters for rape. I frowned into my pallet, burying deeper into the down pillows as a hand jostled my shoulder.

"Go'sleep, Dayo," I mumbled. He woke me often these days, requesting dreams to help him sleep. "I'm tired." The hand was insistent, so I grimaced and sat up.

It wasn't Dayo. Sanjeet knelt over me, shirtless and disheveled. "He's gone," he said tersely. "Don't wake the others."

"What?" I whirled around. Dayo's pallet was empty.

"He's sleepwalking." Sanjeet held a finger to his lips. "If the guards hear a commotion, they'll come running. We don't need rumors that the crown prince is unstable. I saw where he went, but we'll need to use your Hallow."

All of us suffered from night terrors, but Dayo had it worst. Once a terror took him, only one thing woke him up: removing the most grotesque of his memories. I sighed and pulled off my satin sleep scarf as Sanjeet woke Kirah. Then the three of us wove through the sleeping bodies of our council siblings, stealing out onto the banquet hall balcony. A steep whitewashed stairway led down to the garden, and far beyond it, the pale gold beach.

I swore. "Did he really take these stairs? He could have broken his neck. Why didn't the guards stop him?"

"He wouldn't have died, even with a broken neck," Kirah pointed out. "And the guards probably don't know he's sleeping. Don't tell them. Try to look calm."

We nodded at the guards at the foot of the stairs, as if midnight strolls in our underclothes were nothing out of the ordinary. The armed warriors bowed. After an awkward pause, one of them ventured, "Will Your Anointed Honors also require a shovel?"

I blinked. "Shovel?"

"It is what His Imperial Highness asked for, Your Anointed Honor. We did not ask what for."

"Oh." Kirah cleared her throat. "No. I'm sure one shovel is sufficient for the prince's business." *Whatever that is*, she Ray-spoke dryly.

Sanjeet addressed the guards in a smooth, low voice that made me shiver. "There is no need to mention Prince Ekundayo's activity to anyone."

"Yes, Anointed General." The warriors nodded curtly, and then one of them lifted a flaming brand from its niche on the wall. "Will you take a torch, Anointed Honors?"

The torch's heat murmured across my face, crackling

and wicked. Every bone in my body turned to jelly. For a moment I was melting, and the flame grew louder; the blazing doors of the Children's Palace rose in my vision, opening their mouths to devour . . .

"Anointed Honor," the guard began, peering at me as my breath came in shallow gasps. "Are you—"

"She's fine," Sanjeet replied curtly. "As you were." He and Kirah led me down the path, gripping my petrified hands. We passed through an arbor of hanging wisteria into the keep garden, lit on either side with more bright torches.

"Don't look at them," Sanjeet advised me.

"Still?" asked Kirah. "After almost two years?"

I nodded mutely, staring at my bare feet. My arms prickled with goose bumps, free of the burn scars I should have received the day of my anointing. The day Dayo had almost died in the Children's Palace.

Burn scars marked his face, but mine were all inside. For years, the heat of fire—the sound and smell of it—had turned my knees to water. The flames mocked me, hinting at secrets, summoning demons from the pit of my memories. With practice, I had learned to light candles without trembling, but bonfires—and torches—were still out of the question.

"It's strange how that fire took your memories," Kirah said with a frown. "Maybe it's time we found a healer from the capital—"

"I'm fine," I said, avoiding her gaze.

The garden gate opened to a sandy incline, tumbling down to the Obasi Ocean. At first, I thought Dayo had disappeared. Then a loc-covered head of hair popped up behind a ledge and vanished again. What was Dayo doing in a *hole*?

We padded across the beach and stopped at a shallow pit, yards from the churning tide. His nightshirt damp with sweat, Dayo hurled shovelfuls of sand over his shoulder, muttering. The obsidian mask dangled precariously from his neck.

"Dayo," I panted. "Dayo, you're not well. Wake up."

He continued digging, bloodshot eyes glassy and unfocused. After exchanging a look, Kirah and I climbed into the pit. Sanjeet ducked to avoid the arc of Dayo's shovel, then wrestled the tool away. Dayo paused, staring blankly at his now empty hands. They were bleeding.

My stomach knotted. "Dayo, you idiot." I cleaned his fingers with the hem of my nightshift. "What in Am's name are you dreaming about?"

"Bring them back," he mumbled. In the moonlight, the burn scars shone pale against his dark skin. Sand clung to his sweat.

"Bring them back? Bring who?"

"Children," he said. "Redemptors. I'm the future emperor. I should—I should save them."

"This year's Redemptors are gone, Dayo," Kirah said softly. "Most of them are already dead, or lost." She grasped his arms. "This has to stop. You have to accept things you can't change. You can't keep scaring us like—"

"Underworld," Dayo repeated.

I stared, realization slowly sinking in. "You asked for a shovel so you could *dig* to the Underworld?"

Sanjeet, Kirah, and I looked at each other. Then we began to laugh, a breathless, wheezing noise that sounded suspiciously close to sobbing. Our shoulders shook, and we held each other up for support. Dayo stood quietly, watching us with those vacant black eyes.

Sanjeet hoisted him from the pit, and I pressed Dayo's temples with both hands. Heat pulsed through my fingertips as I silenced his memories. I erased the shrill of wounded villagers, the shrieking hyena-beasts, the cries for help, the ghosts of vanished children.

Dayo sagged in Sanjeet's arms. Then he revived and stood, looking about dazedly. "Tar . . . Kirah. Jeet." He took in our beach surroundings, and his face shaded with understanding. "Twelve realms, not again. I'm so sorry."

"Do me a favor, little brother." Sanjeet dusted sand from Dayo's hair and clapped him gently on the back. "Next time you're digging to the Underworld, bring a bigger shovel. Thérèse could weed her dahlias with this one."

"And be more careful with this," I added, securing the obsidian mask back around Dayo's neck. His immunities to death were not affected by whether or not he wore the mask. Still, the thought of him damaging it made me shiver.

"What would happen, I wonder?" Kirah asked, frowning at him. "If you lost it?"

Dayo shrugged. "Not much. There are only two Raybearer masks, mine and Father's. And according to legend, they always find their way back to their rightful owners."

When we returned to the garden, I grimaced and touched my wrist—I'd hurt myself helping Dayo from the pit. Sanjeet noticed, scanning me immediately with his Hallow.

"You pulled a tendon," he said. "We'll need to stop by the medicine shed."

"I can fix it," Kirah piped up.

I shook my head. "Save your Hallow to help Dayo get back to sleep."

"We won't be long," Sanjeet put in. "Go on. We'll catch up."

Dayo nodded, giving me an apologetic smile before Kirah helped him climb the banquet hall steps. Sanjeet and I stood in the garden alone.

I raised an eyebrow. "We don't have to do this. My wrist can wait till morning."

"Do you feel like sleeping right now?"

"No."

"Me either."

Night had aged into the indigo hours before dawn. Our feet crunched on white gravel as we passed beneath the wisteria again. Sanjeet was too tall for the arbor; violet petals tumbled down his bare russet shoulders. Somewhere in the dark, an owl cooed. I let my fingers pass over the wisteria vines, and my ears rang with lisps and giggles:

the whispered conversations of council siblings long ago. Generations of Anointed Ones had frolicked where I stood, unaware of the eavesdropping branches overhead.

Nestled between orange trees, a wooden shed stood in the shadows, and Thérèse's herb garden sprawled around it. When healers were unavailable from Yorua Village, Sanjeet, Kirah, and I practiced medicine here, using our Hallows to treat our guards and servants. Sanjeet would scan a patient's body for ailments, and if the problem was physical, Kirah would attempt poultices or a healing chant. But if the problem was mental, I extracted memories and reshaped them, setting old demons to rest.

I had never tried to heal myself. For reasons I couldn't explain, I sensed that Ye Eun's fate had been my fault. The day after the disaster at Ebujo, I had tried to invoke Ye Eun's shade, burning the remains of her flower crown and sitting up all night. But she didn't appear, not even to reprimand me, which somehow felt more damning. I dared not hope she had survived. So I allowed her reproachful stare to haunt my memories, hoping guilt would make me a better Anointed One than I had been at Ebujo.

Sanjeet unbarred the shed door and ducked inside, lighting palm oil lamps from the garden torches. The medicine shed was long and narrow, lined with shelves of bottles and bundled herbs. I waited on a crumbling stone bench until Sanjeet emerged, armed with bandages and a stoppered vial. I winced as his calloused fingers bathed my wrist in primrose oil.

"Keeps down swelling," he said. His touch was clinical, precise, sensing the tendons beneath my skin as he bandaged. "You've hurt this hand before. You were thirteen, training in spearwork in the palace courtyard."

"Your Hallow showed you all that?"

He looked sheepish. "No. I just remember when it happened." He tied the bandage and cut the excess with a knife. "Keep it dry. Kirah can fix you up properly tomorrow."

"You're good at this." I turned my wrist, admiring his handiwork. "Do you ever wish you could be a healer full-time? Instead of training to be High Lord General?"

Sanjeet gripped the edge of the damp stone bench. "Dayo will inherit the Imperial Guard and the entire Army of Twelve Realms. He will need help commanding a force that large." In the hollow of his chest, sweat glistened from when he had wrestled the shovel from Dayo. "I will be what he needs me to be."

A moment passed in silence. "Do you think Kirah's right? That nothing can be done about the Songland Redemptors?"

"I don't know," he replied. "But we need that Treaty with the Underworld. Without one, Aritsar will never have peace."

"But we could change the Treaty," I suggested. The renewal ceremony was in six months. After the continent's rulers accepted the Treaty's terms, they would be forced to uphold them for another hundred years. Nothing would change. The Breach would devour thousands more children like Ye Eun. "I don't know why all Redemptors come from Songland. But if we made a new deal—if we started over—we could make it fairer."

Sanjeet shook his head. "The Arit rulers would never allow it. Redemptors used to be born in every realm. No one knows why it stopped, but I doubt anyone's eager to go back to the way things were."

I chewed my lip, scowling into the darkness. For just a moment, the old heat flashed in my chest, a demon restricting my lungs, roaring to get out. "Why does everyone hate change so much?" I demanded.

"Because things could get worse."

"Maybe. But do you know what I think?" My chest throbbed. "I think deep down, we're afraid that things could get better. Afraid to find out that all the evil—all the suffering we ignore—could have been prevented. If only we had cared enough to try."

"That's a grim prognosis."

I shrugged, then crossed my arms over my chest, coaxing the burning to rest.

Sanjeet's profile was tense in the garden shadows. I remembered the night we had first met. His features had still been boyish then; awkward and round. That was gone now—replaced by an angular, protruding brow, and the shadow of a dense curly beard. His ears were the only whimsical thing about him, sticking out from his head like conch shells. I had always liked those ears.

"If Dayo didn't need your protection," I asked, "if he didn't remind you of Sendhil—would you still have joined the council?"

"Yes," he said slowly. "I think so. On my campaigns, I've seen the scars of what this continent was like before. Back when the abiku did whatever they chose. Burning towns and demanding sacrifices, causing floods and plagues, setting realms against each other. If the Kunleos hadn't made us work together, united us in a common goal . . . I don't think the realms would have survived. Still, I doubt Enoba Kunleo was as perfect or peaceful as the history scrolls say. No one conquers an empire with charisma alone."

"What about the councils?" I asked. "Do you think they're perfect?"

He didn't answer. Instead, his fingers brushed the top of my unbandaged hand, sliding in meditative circles down my wrist. "There she goes again," he said. "Asking illegal questions. Even when we were small, a word, a small suggestion from Tarisai of Swana . . . and every candidate in the Children's Palace would be buzzing about systems they would topple. Rules they would break." He smiled at me, and my breath shortened. "You're infectious, sunshine girl." Then suddenly he withdrew his hand, balling it into a fist.

"What's wrong?" My skin chilled where his fingers had been. He shook his head, but I pressed him. "Tell me."

He sighed. "When I promised to protect Dayo, I didn't just mean his life. I meant his heart too."

"It's not like you to be cryptic, Jeet."

"Now is another one of those times," he said, "that I would like to tell a lie."

I laughed in spite of myself. It was an old joke now: Sanjeet's crippling inability to sugarcoat. His honesty was his tribute to Sendhil—the lost brother with a Hallowed tongue that never lied.

Sanjeet inhaled, and then spoke as if battling his own nerve. "Dayo will need to sire a Raybearer someday. He has to choose a partner from our council. And it's going to be you. Everyone knows it, and I'm not going to get in the way. I shouldn't make things—complicated."

I practically fell off the bench. "Oh, *everyone*, is it?" I stood and planted my hands on my hips. "All of Aritsar is just waiting around for Dayo to impregnate me?"

"Yes." Sanjeet's tone was unnervingly matter-of-fact. "Some courtiers thought it might happen before we left the Children's Palace."

"What the—" I gaped with disgust. People had been gabbing about Dayo bedding me since we were kids?

Sanjeet stood too, running agitated fingers through his dark curls. "Look, I'm not saying it's right, it's just . . . when you and Dayo are together . . . Tar, you've no idea how it looks. I can't explain it. The two of you are like planets. Orbiting. Two sides of a coin."

Beans in a pod. I shivered, remembering Dayo's words from that night in the Children's Palace.

"It won't be long before Dayo stops seeing you as a

sister." Sanjeet's jaw hardened. "And it's time I accept that some things are set in stone."

"Stone?" I snorted. "Don't I have any say in this?"

Sanjeet's expression remained carefully blank. "I assumed you felt the same way about him."

"Well, stop assuming."

"Because it's none of my business?" Sanjeet fixed me with those tea-colored eyes. "Or because I'm wrong?"

"Uh, both?"

He swore softly and shifted his feet, shaking his head. "Sorry. I'm being stupid. Just . . . forget I said it."

A long moment passed. "I've never wanted Dayo that way," I said quietly. "All right? I'd kill for him. Die, even. But I've never wanted . . . more." I considered. "Not like that."

Several emotions crossed Sanjeet's face. Most of them I couldn't read—but one was unmistakable, spreading across his features like the shy halo of dawn.

Relief.

Dragonflies spun circles in my stomach. I turned on my heel, needing to be back with the others, anywhere but there, beneath the heat of those searching eyes.

"Going to bed," I mumbled, tucking my bandaged hand beneath my arm and fleeing back through the wisteria arbor.

Sanjeet did not follow me. But the Ray fluttered at the back of my neck, and a deep, warm voice floated above my ear.

Sleep well, sunshine girl. I will take whatever dreams you give me.

CHAPTER 13

"YOUR COUNCIL IS HEINOUSLY BEHIND IN ITS studies."

"Glad to see you too, Uncle Thaddace," Dayo quipped. "Feeling refreshed after your trip from the capital?"

It was early morning, mere hours after my talk with Sanjeet in the garden. Pigeons cooed from the window of my keep study, where I sat shoulder to shoulder with Dayo. Thaddace sat across from us at my kneeling desk, rolling his sharp green eyes at Dayo's attempt at a joke.

Two of the Emperor's Eleven visited Yorua Keep every month, overseeing the studies of the heirs who would replace them. The High Lord Judge and High Priestess had arrived from Oluwan City only an hour ago. The idea of meeting with High Lord Judge Thaddace had made me nervous, but I had been excited to meet with Mbali. I felt horribly underprepared to assume her position as Swana Delegate, and so Mbali had scheduled time this morning, offering to tutor me in Swanian economy and customs. But when I had arrived at my study, she wasn't there.

"Oh—forgot to tell you," Dayo had said, yawning and patting the cushion next to him. "I rescheduled your meeting with Aunt Mbali. You don't want to discuss stuffy Swanian politics this early, do you? Besides, I want to hear what you have in mind for your First Ruling. I've invited Uncle Thaddace to consult."

Surprised, I had put away my notes on Swana, pulling a stack of court cases from beneath the desk instead.

As Crown Prince, Dayo had the authority to dictate our schedules at the keep, though it was unlike him to wield it. This was the second time Dayo had rescheduled my lessons with Mbali. Strangely, when she had visited months ago, Dayo suddenly needed my assistance on a trip to Yorua Village.

I shook my head, dismissing my annoyance. Dayo was right. The years leading up to my First Ruling would pass quickly, and I needed all the preparation with Thaddace I could get.

High Judge Apparents were granted a coming-of-age ceremony called the First Ruling: a way to foster the empire's confidence in the young new judge. In the palace Imperial Hall, the High Judge Apparent would hear a controversial case, weigh the evidence, and bestow an official ruling. By imperial law, a High Judge Apparent's First Ruling was irreversible—even by the emperor. Thaddace had written to Yorua Keep, asking that I review court cases backing up the pipeline and pick one to consider for my ruling.

"I see," the High Lord Judge intoned, shrugging off his

tartan-lined council cloak, "that the goodwill tour hasn't made you children less incorrigible." He looked wan; traveling by lodestone had probably wreaked havoc on his stomach. I was surprised he could sit upright at all.

"I'm sorry I'm behind in my studies, Anointed Honor," I said, stifling a yawn. "We've had some trouble sleeping."

"Yes. Well." Thaddace adjusted the red mourning sash he wore around his neck for the lost citizens of Ebujo. "I can only imagine, after what happened in the temple. Your council made quite a mess, though it has also done an impressive cleanup. When Ai Ling gave her speech last month, she made Arit citizens feel safe again. Riots are at a minimum. You could learn from your council sister's methods."

I frowned. "How would Ai Ling's speeches help me solve cases? Beg your pardon, Anointed Honor, but I'm not trying to make people happy. I'm trying to be fair."

"Fair." The overhang of Thaddace's brow deepened. "I often find that term . . . short-sighted. But you will learn in time. Have you selected a case for your First Ruling?"

I produced a dog-eared stack of pages. I had spent weeks looking for a case that didn't bore me, and once I had found one, I had worked into the small hours of every morning, determined to come up with a flawless ruling. I might have failed Ye Eun, but this was my chance to change something, to help people. At last I would shake off this deep, ugly feeling that for reasons I could not remember . . . I was a threat to everyone who trusted me.

Thaddace frowned over my chosen case, then made an incredulous noise as he read the title. "'Bipo of Nyamba versus the Imperial Council of Aritsar'?"

I nodded. "I thought it was a joke at first. But I checked the laws. If a citizen can prove that anyone—including the council—has hurt them unjustly, then they can submit a case to the Imperial Court."

Thaddace's brow wrinkled with amusement as he leafed through the pages. "I would be lying," he said at last, "if I said I wasn't impressed."

"As you can see, Bipo is a beggar. He's accusing our councils of being responsible for his life on the streets. When his parents died, he was kept at an orphanage workhouse, and never had a chance of learning a trade, or having a family."

Thaddace's eyebrows rose into his hairline. "And what exactly," he asked, "do you propose we do about it?"

I sucked in a breath. "Rule in his favor," I said, producing another stack of paper. My heart beat with excitement as I pushed the stack toward Thaddace. "We're the wealthiest empire in five oceans, so why do we still have children wandering the streets? I call it the Lonesome Child Edict. Think: If we give Arit families silver for adopting orphans and teaching them a trade, then orphanages would empty overnight. We'll send Imperial Guard warriors to check on each family, making sure the adopted children aren't harmed. The reward would be higher for older children and misfits . . . I've written out all the details here."

"Am's story, Tar," Dayo exclaimed, flipping through the pages. "This is brilliant. Uncle Thad, why didn't we think of it sooner?"

A deep V had formed on Thaddace's brow as he glanced over my edict and shook his head. He sighed, making a tent with his hands. "It is an admirable notion," he said at last. "But ultimately, a foolhardy one. Do you know how many millions of greedy hovel-dwellers would swarm the orphanages in hopes of silver? Do you think they'd care a whit about a child's well-being?"

"That's what the guards are for," I countered. "They could check."

"How often? Every month until the child is grown? Every week? How much would that cost the crown? Would Imperial Guard warriors travel to every smallest hut in every farthest village, to check if a farm boy is too thin?"

"We could just . . . ," I began, but stopped, biting my lip in embarrassment. I hadn't actually calculated the cost of sending warriors to every village in Aritsar. The lodestone fare alone could vastly outweigh the price of running orphanages.

"But we have so much money," Dayo blurted. "Surely the crown can do something."

"I understand your objection," Thaddace murmured. "Believe me, I do. When given the power of a High Judge, one wants to heal every wound in the empire's body. But authority is not power. Not completely. It takes resources, sustainability. Popular support."

"What about what's fair?" I demanded. "For the children? For everyone?" I crossed my arms, staring at the notes I had worked on for weeks.

Adopted children must be permitted to call their carers "Mother" and "Father." No caretaker shall be absent for more than one week, unless the child is informed of the caretaker's whereabouts.

The child's room must have a window, never to be boarded up.

The kindness did not leave Thaddace's gaze, though the lines around his mouth deepened. "It took me many, many years to learn this, Tarisai. But justice is not about being fair. It is about keeping order."

Wrong. Immediately, fire blazed in my chest, and I winced in surprise. The mysterious heat had rarely assaulted me since we left the Children's Palace. What was wrong with me? I struggled to maintain my posture, breathing evenly. "If my ruling is impractical," I asked, "what would you suggest instead, Anointed Honor?"

Thaddace considered for several moments, then sat up and rapped the table. "I have it," he said, brightening. "You'll rule in favor of Bipo, and win the hearts of every Arit noble in An-Ileyoba. But instead of the Lonesome Child Edict . . ." He took a new leaf from my desk, and a faint burning smell hung in the air as words appeared rapidly on the paper. I had never seen Thaddace use his heat-precision Hallow in person, though I'd received plenty of his calfskin letters before, inkless script tanned neatly into the hide. "You will introduce the Edict of Orphan Day," Thaddace announced, and a new title smoldered at the top of my case notes. "A festival for family dreams. Decree a holiday in which all nobles take orphans into their homes for a day and a night. The nobility won't require payment. They'll do it because it's fashionable, and to curry favor with the crown." He snorted. "Hell, they'll probably compete with each other. Who can lavish their orphan with the most luxury? It's neat. Decorous."

Useless, I thought glumly.

He put down the quill, wiping the ink from his fingers. "Children like your Bipo get a temporary family. A night in a villa, and a cartful of sweets. And no family is stuck with a child they won't care for. Who knows? Maybe the nobles will get attached. They can be very sentimental."

The ruling barely solved anything. But he had made my plan feel like fishing for the moon, while his looked so . . . plausible. Was it better to have a perfect solution that I couldn't enforce? Or a weak solution that everyone loved?

Slowly, I gathered my draft of the Lonesome Child Edict and closed the papers in a drawer. "It certainly sounds orderly, Anointed Honor."

"Good." Thaddace smiled and then frowned, noticing my deflation. He produced a document from his robes. "I was going to wait before announcing this. But I see now that the sooner you are accustomed to the realities of running an empire, the better. This edict is just in from the capital. In time, His Imperial Highness would like your assistance in promoting it. Another goodwill campaign, perhaps."

He laid the imperial calfskin on the desk, and Dayo and I leaned forward to read it.

---

*B*y decree of His Anointed Honor, High Judge Thaddace of Mewe, in the name of His Imperial Highness Emperor Olugbade of Oluwan, descendant of Enoba the Perfect:

All griot drums, stories, and history scrolls of individual realms must be surrendered to the emperor's forces. In exchange, citizens will receive gifts: new drums, scrolls, and songs, compliments of the crown.

These gifts will reflect the new stories of our beloved empire. The story of assimilation, of realms growing together instead of apart.

Families are encouraged to forgo realm names for their children, choosing instead names that reflect virtues of a united Aritsar. While this request is not mandatory, children with empire names will be rewarded with additional food for their families, as well as clothing cut from Empire Cloth: the new favored style of the capital.

The emperor thanks his subjects for ushering in this new era of unity and peace. Residences will be searched, and griots will be watched. Failure to comply will be met with discipline.

"I proposed the Unity Edict to Emperor Olugbade after the disaster at Ebujo," Thaddace explained. "The realm loyalties displayed by Arit citizens on that day resulted in the loss of human life." His pale hands clenched into fists. "Rewarding families for birthing isokens was a step in the right direction, but it clearly wasn't enough. If the twelve realms continue to see themselves as separate entities instead of as one Aritsar . . . we will never survive another attack by the abiku."

Dayo reached for my hands, which were clasped over my heart. The words of the edict had made the dragon in my chest return with full force, and I gasped, trying to fight it. But before I could respond, Thaddace's sharp gaze drifted toward the woven study door flap. The severity melted from his features like butter, and without looking, I knew who had entered the room.

"We have never quite agreed on that point, Thaddace." The High Priestess of Aritsar leaned against the doorframe, light grazing the threads of her pale yellow wrapper.

"Good morning, Aunt," Dayo greeted. For just a moment, he winced nervously, glancing between me and Mbali. "You're not here to give Tarisai Swana lessons, are you? We still have a lot to cover with Uncle Thad."

"Let me guess." Mbali's voice was like thrush song, bright and clear. "The High Lord Judge has been impressing you with his unique definition of justice?"

"He said there's no such thing," I muttered, finally managing to cool the heat in my chest. "That there's only order."

Mbali's soft, round nose flared with distaste. Bangles winked on her toned black arms as she challenged

Thaddace. "You are perfectly aware," she said, "that in the Storyteller's eyes, justice begets order."

Thaddace flushed. "I'm just trying to keep our world from falling apart."

"But when the cause is right, we have risked chaos before." Mbali smiled at him inscrutably. "Haven't we?"

The air shivered above me: the crisp energy of council members speaking through the Ray. Thaddace and Mbali were having a private conversation, and judging from the way their gazes roved over each other . . . I was grateful I couldn't hear it.

When the silent exchange was over, Mbali entered the study. But her steps faltered—like Thaddace, she was still recovering from their lodestone journey.

Mbali laughed when Dayo and I rose to steady her. The sweet scent of cocoa butter washed over me as she embraced us. When my cheek touched hers, Mbali purposely showed me a memory: Dayo and I, age eleven, giggling with stolen sweets as we ran hand in hand from the Children's Palace kitchens, unaware of Mbali's gaze, watching us through a hidden door in the wall.

She winked at me, then touched her pelican pendant and tapped my and Dayo's chins, a blessing. "Am's Story, Thaddace. Only yesterday, these two were lisping the Candidate's Prayer in the Hall of Dreams. Are these the same troublemakers?"

"Yes, they are," Thaddace said shortly, and Mbali smirked at him over our heads.

"You know you've missed them. And I've come to take your star pupil away; she's needed in the gardens."

Thaddace frowned. "She is eons behind in study. We've barely begun—"

"Twelve realms, Thad; it's a holiday." She gestured out to the hallway, where Yorua Keep servants bustled with palm wreaths, sides of uncooked goat, and platters of peeled plantain.

Today was Nu'ina Eve: a festival observing when Am the Pelican fed its blood to Queen Earth, nursing her back to health and creating humankind. It was the only shared holiday of the four major religious sects of Aritsar. That evening, our council would ride in a processional to Yorua Village, where revels would last till dawn.

"The children will need to prepare," said Mbali. "The braiders have already arrived; that's why Tarisai is wanted in the garden. She had better go. I'm sure her council sisters cannot gossip properly without her."

"Not so fast," Thaddace barked before I could escape through the door. He thrust a pile of cases into my arms. "Solve these while you're out there sitting pretty. Find me if you get stuck. And for Am's sake—stop trying to be *fair*."

CHAPTER 14

"LOOK WHO FINALLY ESCAPED," KIRAH GREETED me when I arrived in the garden. She patted the cushion next to her and scooted me a chalice of palm wine. The grass was littered with pillows and cosmetic bottles, and the smell of olive oil hung in the air. My council sisters chattered in a circle as braiders sat above them on stools, working fastidiously.

"We thought Thunderbrow Thad would keep you forever," Mayazatyl put in. "Wait—are those *court cases*?"

"I had to bring them." I clutched Thaddace's assignments sheepishly as I sank onto a cushion. "He thinks I'm behind. I know, I know—" I shielded my face as Kirah, Mayazatyl, Thérèse, Ai Ling, and Emeronya pelted me with figs.

Braiding parties were sacred: No studying was allowed. Once a month, the strict security of Yorua Keep lifted for beauty artisans to visit from the palace. Their deft fingers would comb away our weeks' worth of tangles, styling our hair in the Oluwan court fashion: hundreds of braids, interwoven with soft wool yarn and burned at the ends so the plaits wouldn't unravel. The style took hours to complete and lasted for weeks. I sat submissively as my braider tugged and raked my coils with a wide-toothed wooden comb, laying out lengths of richly dyed dark yarn that matched my hair.

"Besides the figs, we've got fried *chin chin* dough. And palm wine," Ai Ling said, pointing to each platter and smiling mischievously. "I managed to smooth talk the cook. He was saving it for the festival tonight."

"I do not think the revelers will miss it," Thérèse said with mock gravity as an artisan braided white yarn into her pale tresses. "Some treats are more intoxicating than palm wine."

Mayazatyl spit out her drink, chortling. "Twelve realms, Reesy! I'd never expect to hear that from *you*—"

"I may have been sheltered," Thérèse said mildly, "but I was not born yesterday. In Nontes, we have Nu'ina Eve festivals too, though we call it Fête du Feu there. I knew what happened when a lady found a rosebud in her wine."

"In Oluwan, it's not a rosebud," said Kirah. "It's a cowrie shell. Am's Story, I hope *I* don't find one." She wrinkled her nose. "What would I trade it for?"

"A kiss." Mayazatyl grinned. "Or something *naughty*. It's up to you, priestess."

Kirah turned pink. Emeronya's features bent in a confused frown. "You are talking of sex," she said in her blunt, deadpan way. She was the youngest of our council, barely thirteen. "Is that what Nu'ina Eve is like in Oluwan?

A night for being drunk and making babies?"

Ai Ling laughed, patting Emeronya's knee. "Not *just* that. Poor Em. Don't they have holy festivals in Biraslov?"

Emeronya scowled, as she always did at the slightest hint of condescension. "In Biraslov," she said with a sniff, "People of the Wing celebrate Nu'ina Eve with fasting and a vigil. Am's gift to Queen Earth was a sacrifice, not a party."

"Then I'm glad I was born in Quetzala," snorted Mayazatyl. "People of the Well know how to relax."

"So do People of the Wing," retorted Kirah, who belonged to the same religious sect as Emeronya. She added, turning an even deeper shade of pink, "Though I'm *not* going to kiss anyone." Which of course made Ai Ling and Mayazatyl tease her more.

"The wine at the festival is filled with tokens," I told Emeronya, knowing what it was like to feel left out. Catching up to the countless opulent traditions of Oluwan life had taken me years. "The tokens are shells, bits of bone, things like that. Some are bad, some are good. If you find a good token, you can trade it. A cowrie shell is worth . . . a favor."

"From a lover?" Emeronya asked.

"From anyone you like." I matched her deadpan tone, wiggling my eyebrows. In spite of herself, Emeronya laughed.

"I wouldn't trade with a boy," she said. "Girls are prettier. Except maybe Theo."

"Theo wouldn't kiss you," Ai Ling informed her. "Last

time I checked, he was still writing sappy love poems to farm boys in Yorua Village. Besides, council members can't trade our cowrie shells. We're not allowed to fall in love."

"Speak for yourself," crowed Mayazatyl. "Though what Kameron and I did last Nu'ina Eve wasn't *love* exactly . . ."

"Maya," I hissed in warning, glancing up at the braiders.

Their expressions remained placid, and hardened yellow wax glistened on their earlobes. Any commoner who waited on the Prince's Eleven was required to seal their ears so our affairs would remain private.

"They can't hear us," said Mayazatyl. "Besides, everyone knows council members aren't actually celibate. They've dallied for centuries. Have you read some of the messages scrawled in the sleeping chambers of Yorua?" She smirked. "Then, of course, there's Enitawa's Quiver." Mayazatyl waited as we watched her, taking a languid sip from her chalice and filing her nails with a small knife.

Ai Ling rolled her eyes. "Fine, Maya, I'll bite. What's Enitawa's Quiver?"

Mayazatyl batted her lashes innocently. "Why, it's only a tree. With smooth waxy branches that grow straight up, like arms twisting around each other. Warriors used to make their quivers from the wood, because it's flexible and it sings." She took another long sip from her chalice, relishing our anticipation. "When the wind blows, the branches hum like flutes. Loud enough to cover up any noises that a pair might make in Enitawa's shadow." My sisters giggled nervously. "The tree grows beneath a cliff north of Yorua, barely a mile away. Rocks block the spot from view. Council members have been meeting there for centuries."

Kirah's face went blank, as it always did when she was trying to weigh the moral weight of something. "I know most of you have had dalliances," she said slowly. "But what about imperial law? People who represent realms can't be making calf eyes at each other. We're supposed to be impartial, or our subjects will suspect our rulings of favoritism."

"Only if they find out," said Ai Ling. "The point of councils is to prevent war. So if we maintain the empire's *sense* of equality, it shouldn't matter what we do in private." She flashed a rueful smile—her real one, not the charming dimples she used when giving speeches. "We're not the saints people think we are."

"You're the High Judge Apparent," Emeronya said, turning to me. "Will you throw us in prison if we have lovers?"

I laughed, but wasn't sure how to answer. Enforcing the law would be my job, after all. Or at least, I had thought it would be, before my tutoring session with Thaddace. His words colored my vision, making everything murky.

Justice is not about being fair. It is about keeping order.

"Ai Ling's right, I guess." I shrugged. "The purpose of councils is to prevent war. So as long as we protect Aritsar during the day . . ." My gaze drifted to the garden bench where I had sat with Sanjeet the evening before. "It shouldn't matter what we do at night."

Thérèse hummed in warning. "If I learned anything

from the Nontish court, it is this: What happens in the shadows always comes to light."

Hours later, the smell of burnt yarn filled my nostrils. My braider held a candle to the tips of my finished plaits, searing the ropelike ends shut one by one. I held my breath, sitting on my hands to keep them from shaking. *It's just a candle flame. Don't be stupid. It can't hurt you.*

She handed me a mirror. Hundreds of braids spilled over my shoulders, shining with oil and winking with tiny gold accents. I felt beautiful, but—

I tapped the artisan's ear, asking her to remove the wax. "It's very tight," I told her. "My scalp aches."

The braider raised an eyebrow. "With respect, Anointed Honor, that's how ladies prefer it in the capital. Not like those unruly edges they sport in the countryside! Think of your title. Oluwan ladies rein every strand into place. Complete control."

I gazed at myself again, remembering how I had trembled over a candle. A *candle*. Perhaps I could use some control. "It's perfect," I told the braider, smiling, and she bowed smugly.

As my council sisters made admiring noises over each other, I guiltily collected my assignments. I had barely touched them, and I cringed at the thought of facing Thaddace again. But he *had* offered help. Maybe I could find him before the festival tonight. Scalp aching and bottom numb from sitting, I left my cushion to find the High Lord Judge.

The study was empty when I arrived. That was no

surprise; after having his body jumbled by lodestone travel, Thaddace would have needed to recover in his rooms. I turned a corner, mounting the broad stairs that led to the guest chambers. Then I stopped. From a dim corridor leading to salons we never used, I heard a muffled growl that sounded strangely like Thaddace.

I frowned and turned down the corridor. What was the High Judge doing in there? One of the salon's woven door flaps hung slightly askew, as though it had been closed improperly. From its opening, a narrow beam of light cut across the floor. I approached slowly, raising my arm to knock on the door. My hand froze midair.

On a dust-covered divan, Mbali straddled Thaddace, clasped to his lean chest. Clothing littered the floor. He buried his face in her neck while their bodies entwined beneath the slanted light of shuttered windows.

I did not blink. If my eyes stayed open, I told myself, what I had seen would evaporate, like water from stones. I spun on my heel and swept back down the corridor. I was going to my room. I had always been going to my room. The salons had been empty, and I had seen no one.

My slippers were mercifully noiseless on the rough tiles. I stepped from the corridor, nearly escaping the secret— and collided with a scullery man.

"Anointed Honor." Bobbing, the servant gathered up the rags and bucket I had made him drop.

"Where are you going with those?" I asked. The question came out shriller than I had intended.

"Dusting, Anointed Honor. Sorry. I'll just—"

I stood in his way and asked loudly, "Are you looking for Anointed Honor Thaddace?"

"No, Anointed Honor. I was going to—"

"Anointed Honor Thaddace is in his chambers," I continued, my voice carrying down the corridor. "On the other side of the keep. He told me to take a message to Anointed Honor Mbali. Return to the kitchens and take each of them some palm wine. In fifteen minutes," I finished slowly, "I am sure you will find Anointed Honor Thaddace in the *western guest chambers*, and Mbali in the *eastern garden*."

Behind me, I heard a faint scuffle from the salon. I smiled manically at the servant. "Off you go."

He bobbed again and retreated the way he had come. The smile remained on my face as my feet carried me back to the study. I laid the court cases neatly on the desk, sank onto the divan, and plopped face-first into the cushions.

My sleeping chamber in Yorua Keep scarcely deserved the name. It was used only to store my possessions: my spear, piles of handmade gifts from commoners, and a daunting collection of tunics and wrappers. I stood naked as I sorted through piles of memory-soaked fabric. The musical din of markets rang in my ears, and my skin pricked with the acrid heat of dye vats. My body was suddenly made of fibers, letting the skillful hands of weavers press me together. Inanimate object memories were bewildering, and I usually avoided them—but today I welcomed the distraction.

It had been hours since I'd walked in on Thaddace and Mbali. Water still beaded on my skin from the keep bathhouse, where my council had freshened up for Nu'ina Eve. In a marble chamber partitioned by gender, we had scrubbed with cocoa ash soap and swum in orchid-scented pools, careful to keep our yarn braids dry. Over a wall, I had heard my council brothers splashing and roughhousing. My ear had tuned to a voice deeper than the others: a laugh that rumbled like thunder across the echoing marble tiles.

I ran agitated fingers over gowns and wrappers. I told myself I wanted to impress villagers at the festival. A future High Lady Judge should be seen at her finest. My indecision had nothing to do with a pair of broad shoulders and tea-colored eyes, nothing at all.

I rubbed my skin with shea until it glowed. Rainbow beads stacked in towers on my arms and neck, in the Swana style. Most Arit fashion mixed elements from all over the empire, but Anointed Ones were encouraged to represent their home realms through their clothing. I wondered if this would change after Thaddace's Unity Edict.

The Nu'ina Eve festivities would be conducted by priests of all four Arit religious sects—including priests of the Ember. I shuddered, steeling myself in advance for copious displays of fire. Unable to extinguish the thought of flames from my mind, I held up a wrapper of red and cardamom yellow. I had designed the pattern myself; the Yorua village women had taught me how to make my own wax-dyed cloth. In the keep courtyard, my council sisters and I spent hours using beeswax to draw patterns on yards of fabric. Once we finished, we plunged the cloth into vats of dye, and then into boiling water. The wax would melt away, leaving our intricate designs behind.

I wound the garment around my body. Across my hips, a huntress and heavy-maned beast repeated in a pattern, silhouetted in ochre and crimson. The figures connected at tail and spear, so that the woman and monster blended together. Even when my eyes crossed from gazing, I could not tell which would devour the other.

CHAPTER 15

"YOU'RE SQUIRMING," KIRAH YELLED AT ME over the music, elbowing my arm. "You should join in."

"I don't dance," I said uncomfortably. "Leave me alone."

My council had arrived at Yorua Village in a parade of palanquins, guards, and liveried servants. The villagers had welcomed us with drums and palm leaves, flinging the branches across our path as they sang that ancient folk rhyme:

> *Eleven danced around the throne,*
> *Eleven moons in glory shone,*
> *They shone around the sun.*

In return, we had brought food enough to feed the village for a week. We held the festival in an oceanside valley, beneath the glittering black quilt of the Oluwan night sky. The air smelled of cayenne and thrummed with talking drums. Spilled goat's milk and honeywine ran ruts in the red earth. Rice and pepper stew rose in savory mountains on each table, and children's faces glowed with grease and cream. My council watched the revelry from cushions on a narrow dais, piled high with the villagers' gifts of herbs and good-luck carvings. Thaddace and Mbali had their own dais, and after Mbali blessed the Nu'ina festival, acolytes from the temples of Clay, Well, Ember, and Wing began their holy dances.

All four religious sects in Aritsar worshipped the Storyteller, and believed in the basic catechism of creation. But People of the Clay revered Queen Earth above all else. Many lived in rural realms like Swana, Mewe, and Moreyao, and they refused to eat meat and opposed the clearing of jungles and development of cities. In contrast, People of the Well criticized Earth for her fabled infidelity to Water. Many of these believers lived in coastal realms, like Sparti, Nontes, and Djbanti, seafaring people who discovered islands and continents beyond Aritsar. But the most devoted inhabited the rainforests of Quetzala, praying at lakes and underground rivers. People of the Ember—the most popular religious sect in both Oluwan and Dhyrma— credited Warlord Fire with Earth's wealth, and showed their gratitude by mining jewels and precious metals, and forging tools and weaponry. Finally, fastidious realms like Biraslov and Blessid Valley appealed to People of the Wing, who worshipped only the Pelican Storyteller. They covered their heads, spurned other gods as distractions, and embraced a life of simplicity, piety, and sacrifice.

The festival drumming tripled in speed, and the acolytes

united to dance the irubo: a pantomime of the sacred Pelican flying down to save Queen Earth, piercing its own breast to nurse her. The dancers' bodies rippled with sweat, chests glistening with crimson paint as they pulsed to the music. They leapt and spun, stretching mantles of feathers across their backs as wings.

Kirah nudged me again. She looked stunning in the tunic and billowing trousers of her home realm. A gauzy green prayer scarf nestled around her face, and belts of silver coins dangled at her waist and brow. "I'm going to learn it," she said. "The irubo."

I groaned. "Why do you always have to memorize everything?"

Kirah's features were round and bright. I suspected that she'd had too much honeywine, though her hazel eyes were hard and clear. "Because I'm tired of limits on what I'm supposed to know."

I was quiet for several moments, letting the downbeat of strings, talking drums, and shaker gourds braid themselves together in my ears. Faintly, I had a vision of standing at a window, watching children as they sang beneath me on a rolling grassland.

But traitors rise and empires fall,
And Sun-Ray-Sun will rule them all,
When all is said-o, all is said
And done-heh, done-heh, done.

"Wherever I came from," I told Kirah as irubo dancers whirled around us, "I think music was forbidden. Whenever I hear a song, it feels like I'm stealing something."

In the center of the festival, a vast pit gleamed with ominous red light. From within, firebrands and white coals made heat ripples in the crisp night air. Villages dug the pit to represent Am's journey to the Underworld. If a reveler found an unlucky token in their honeywine, they were considered cursed until the next Nu'ina festival . . . unless a champion crossed the pit on their behalf. A single wooden slab lay across the pit's mouth, making a laughably narrow bridge. It was only for show. Most festivalgoers would sooner brave a year of bad luck than have a friend cross that deadly oven.

My palms sweated every time a dancer whirled too close to the edge. I wanted to scream when village children peered into the pit, throwing bits of goat fat and giggling when the flames crackled and popped. Didn't they know how dangerous fire was? How evil and treacherous?

No. Those children are normal. You're the crazy one. I stuffed my mouth with fried plantain, wishing for more honeywine to dull my frayed nerves. My scalp still ached from the tight yarn-plaits, throbbing every time I moved my head.

As the irubo ended to cheers and applause, the musicians struck up a mischievous tune on bells and shaker gourds. Children flocked to the festival clearing and took turns doing the worst dances they could imagine. They pursed their lips and pulled faces as they chanted, *Brother-sister do as I do; don't laugh as I do; don't laugh as I do* . . . Each child had to copy the leader's dance without smiling or falling out of step, or else lose the game. My council tried to keep dignified faces, but within minutes our cheeks smarted from laughing. Dayo jumped off the front of our dais, dancing into the circle of children. With mock gravity, he pulsed his hips to the beat, shaping his arms in a tangle of poses.

The village watched, speechless. Then a little boy dared to giggle. Then, an old woman—and in a tidal wave, the crowd was copying their future emperor's ridiculous dance, helpless with laughter.

Dayo grinned. He reminded me of a pool in a savannah, drawing creatures of every stripe to quench their thirst. He made people love him: naturally, permanently. And the brighter he glowed, the more fragile he seemed to me. He was everything our empire hoped for, and everything we had to lose.

I jumped as the pit flared up again. Someone had tossed a bowl of perfumed oil onto the flames, signaling that it was time for the choosing of tokens. Village elders disguised by large wooden masks chanted over vessels of honeywine. The vessels' tapered necks shielded the tokens inside from sight. One by one, the masked elders called us to dip smooth-handled drinking gourds into the vessels. We were each to drink until we found a token.

Dayo went first, fishing a smooth cocoa bean from his

gourd. The token had a well-known meaning: a future bitter and sweet. "That is a token you may trade," intoned one of the elders. "Shall you keep it, Imperial Highness?"

Dayo's slender fingers closed around the bean. "Of course," he said, raising the token above his head and making the traditional speech. "I will swallow bitterness so the lives of my people may be sweet." The villagers cheered as Dayo chewed the raw bean, and my stomach churned for reasons I could not name. A young village girl crowned Dayo with a wreath of woven grass, and then trembled before him with an unspoken request. He knelt to hear it, and the girl pointed shyly to his mask.

"Make it sparkle," she lisped.

Dayo grinned, then cried the word emblazoned on the mask in old Arit, calling its power as only true Raybearers could. "*Oloye!*"

The mask's eyes burst into scintillating light, making all who watched gasp and shield their faces. Then the villagers whooped and burst into applause: To be touched by the divine light of a Raybearer, many believed, meant a year of splendid luck.

Thaddace and Mbali claimed their tokens and festival crowns next, then my council siblings, until only Sanjeet and I remained. When I drank from the gourd, something hard clicked against my teeth. I spat the object into my palm.

It was a small sunstone, erupting with fiery light. A small hole had been bored into the gem, as if meant for a chain. The heat of skin seared deep in its memory, along with the *pound–pound-pound* of a strong, stubborn heart.

The elders seemed confused for a moment, their immense wooden masks bobbing in conference. "Dominance," one of them intoned at last. "That is the traditional meaning of such a token, as sunstones rest on the brows of Arit emperors. But you are a girl, and so the meaning refers to your proximity to greatness. You shall, perhaps," said the elder, bowing his head coyly, "bear the fruit of dominance."

My face burned. A murmur rippled through the village crowd, peppered with stifled giggles. Apparently the rumors about me and Dayo had spread farther than Oluwan City.

Kirah gave an irreverent snort. My gaze met hers. She rolled her eyes so hard, laughter bubbled in my throat, and my shame fell away.

I held up the sunstone. "I will bear fruit for Aritsar," I said sharply, "with my imperial scepter. As your High Lady Judge, equality and justice will be my children. Perhaps," I added coolly, "my only children. Long live the sun and moons." The crowd fell silent. Without rushing, I pocketed the sunstone, collected my crown of grass, and returned to my seat. As I passed, the villagers who had snickered lowered their eyes in fear. Good.

Then it was Sanjeet's turn. He looked resplendent in black as he approached the vessels, decked in the long embroidered tunic and linen trousers of Dhyrma princes. When the elders saw his token, they were silent for even longer than they had been for me. From a distance away, Sanjeet seemed to hold an ivory stone. Then he turned the object toward the firelight.

It was a small carved skull.

"Your hands were made for death," a masked elder said simply. "There is no other interpretation. You may not trade this token."

An indignant murmur rose from my council's dais. "That's not fair," I sputtered.

But Sanjeet only shrugged. "It's nothing I don't already know." He rolled the skull around in his wide palm. "I hoped once that Am would use my hands to heal instead of kill. But I am overruled. A High Lord General protects the innocent. I will dirty my hands to keep my prince clean." Then he knelt to accept his festival crown.

The village girl who held the wreaths didn't move. When Sanjeet glanced up at her, the whites of her eyes flashed in terror.

"Rude girl," one of the village mothers scolded, looking embarrassed. "You must crown His Anointed Honor."

The child did not move, staring at Sanjeet like a cornered deer. "I don't want to," she mewled. "I don't want to."

Sanjeet paled. "Please." He held out his hand to the child and smiled. "Don't be afraid."

She leapt as though Sanjeet had tried to strike her. "No, Prince's Bear, don't hurt me—" She burst into tears and bolted back into the crowd, abandoning Sanjeet's grass crown in the dirt.

Sanjeet knelt for a long time, staring at the crown in silence. Then he stood, face hardening into its usual mask. A few brave villagers came to dust the crown off, flocking around Sanjeet and bobbing with apologies, as Dayo and the others made a fuss, demanding the elders supply another interpretation.

I said nothing, though my feet carried me from the dais. The scene around me faded to white noise, and my vision tunneled. I had to keep moving—I could not back down, not now. As my skin poured with cold sweat, a panicked cry cut through the air.

"Anointed Honor Tarisai is crossing the pit!"

My bare soles chafed on the hot wooden grain. I had left my sandals on the pit's edge. The board was barely wide enough for both my feet; I had to place one in front of the other, forcing me to look down.

The inferno grinned at me.

I choked back a cry as the coals shifted, sending up a cloud of embers. The pit was gone, and I was running again toward the Children's Palace bedroom doors. The air was blistering, and I couldn't breathe, couldn't see, and Dayo was going to die all over again and it would all be my fault . . .

My vision swirled in red and white, blind as my feet continued to cross that flimsy board. My eyes stung and wept from the smoke. A sea of forked tongues rose with the heat and light, roaring in my ears: *ours, ours, ours.* And in that moment, I realized the true reason I feared fire.

It knew.

Fire recognized me for what I was. It claimed me as a daughter; it crackled and commanded that I burn and destroy. Fire would not hurt me, because fire had made me.

And someday, Made-of-Me, murmured a voice as my nostrils filled with a musky floral smell, *I will have you once again.*

"No," I whispered, and stumbled. Then my soles met cool, dark earth. Arms reached to steady me as my guards and council siblings babbled with relief. They checked me for burns and dusted the embers from my wrapper, stamping the sparks in the dirt. I shook all over but ignored the fuss, pushing through the crowd to where Sanjeet stood frozen.

Water pooled in his eyes. The mask had fallen from his face, replaced with shock, disbelief, and a simmering passion that made my knees weak.

I took the skull from him and held it above my head. "I have broken Sanjeet of Dhyrma's curse," I croaked, voice still parched from the smoke. "His hands were made for life, not death. Bear witness." Then I hurled the skull into the flames. The village cheered, and the drummers pounded a deafening beat. I retrieved the last wreath crown and placed it in his combed curls, and Sanjeet caught my hands and held them against his face. My heart slammed in my chest, but just as abruptly he relinquished me, striding over to the elders.

Sanjeet held out his hand, demanding the drinking gourd without a word.

"Yes," an elder said, handing over the gourd hesitantly. "Since your last token has been revoked, you may choose again."

Sanjeet plunged the gourd into the vessel, tossed back some honeywine, and spat out a glittering ruby.

"Ah," the elders crowed. "An excellent token. Am has smiled on you—"

The revelers gasped as Sanjeet threw the ruby in the dirt. He submerged the gourd into the vessel again, and this time he fished out an emerald the size of a plum pit: twice as valuable as the token before. He tossed that aside too.

Speechless, the entire village watched as Sanjeet drank and plunged, over and over, discarding a small mound of treasures in the dirt. At last, he stopped and smiled. A small round token winked in his palm.

A cowrie shell.

CHAPTER 16

SANJEET POCKETED THE TOKEN AND LEFT THE festival grounds without a word. His back melted into the shadows beyond the pit's glow. I stared after him even when the musicians began another song and revelers gyrated around me to the tonal beat of talking drums.

From her dais across the grounds, High Priestess Mbali waved me toward her. She stood and began to descend from her dais, but before she could, an arm pulled me into the crowd. I jumped, prepared to rebuke an impertinent villager . . . and found myself scowling up at Dayo's grinning face. Why did he always spirit me away when I tried to speak with Mbali?

"I don't dance," I reminded him.

"But you *can*," he said. The obsidian mask glittered on his chest as he moved in a rhythmic circle around me. "I saw you. Years ago at the Children's Palace. You snuck up to the roof with Kirah to watch the festivals in the city. And you danced."

"You followed me?"

He placed a hand on my waist, coaxing it to sway instinctively. "I followed you."

Oluwan dancing relied almost entirely on hips. The drums pulsed fast and high, like the heartbeat of a wild hare. I lacked the natural grace of Oluwan women. I was awkward and stilted in places they were fluid and sultry. My steps faltered, and my face heated with embarrassment. "Everyone's watching," I muttered.

"Don't look at them," Dayo said. "Look at me."

I did. His broad Kunleo features were radiant. He winked, teeth bright against his skin, which was beautiful even with the burn scar. I remembered how cheerfully Dayo had mocked himself in the earlier game, and I envied his childlike freedom. My hips began to roll to the beat, and I mirrored Dayo's arms.

"Don't look," he reminded me as my gaze slid to the crowd of villagers around us. The Ray hummed in my ears and I heard him add, *Do you love me now, Tarisai of Swana?*

The music's tempo increased. My muscles loosened; we revolved like moths in firelight. Dayo's long, lean form grew suddenly unfamiliar as I tried to imagine it near mine, closer than we'd ever been: a promise beyond council vows. I heard the question buried beneath his words. *Look at me.*

I had always felt close to Dayo in a way I couldn't explain. We knew the rumors surrounding us, the public expectation that I would bear Dayo's heir. But the intimacy we shared had never invoked the heat between our legs. I loved him—would die for him—but this new language, the message we sent with our bodies as we danced, felt . . . insincere. Staged. As though we were acting out parts that the world expected us to perform.

I found my mind slipping away, gone to those shadows beyond the festival grounds, where another man waited in the welcoming darkness.

When the song finished, I backed away from Dayo, letting the revelers form a river between us. He looked on, confused, craning his neck to find me. But I turned and ran from the festival.

Like hurling a stone into a well, I sent the Ray into the darkness. After several moments I found Sanjeet; he had walked half a mile from the village, to where the Obasi Ocean lapped at the mouth of the valley.

When I arrived, the tide was low, revealing a patchwork of pools that winked with shells and sand dollars. The waves crashed like soft cymbals. Blue sprites hummed in the balmy night, winking in Sanjeet's shadow.

He didn't look up when I approached. He was leaning against a boulder jeweled with barnacles, his hands busy with something I couldn't see.

"You sure made a lot of villagers happy," I said. "They lunged for those jewels you threw away."

"Good for them." He still did not look up.

I swallowed and changed the subject. "Why do we give village elders so much power, anyway? What right do they have to say who you are—who anyone is? It's a dumb tradition." I scowled at my reflection in a tide pool.

"When I'm High Lady Judge, I'm going to change it. Don't let me forget."

"And off she goes," Sanjeet murmured. His voice was cavernous, even against the roar of the waves. "Bent on winning freedom for the entire world. Tarisai of Swana." He laughed, a gentle growl that made my insides restless. "She would have us be masters of our own fates, whether we like it or not."

"You think I'm naive."

"No. I think you're Aritsar's best hope. I think there are people in power who see what I see, and they are scared witless. And I think I've loved you," he said, "since that night you pulled a shackle off my arm."

Sanjeet crossed the dappled mirror of tide pools, and my heart raced, but not with shame or fear. I reached for his cheek, and he leaned into my hand, lips brushing my palm.

"Which laws would you break for me?" I asked.

"Your pick." His jaw ticked with humor. "You're the High Lady Judge."

I flushed. "I want to be responsible."

"We'll be careful."

"No, I meant . . . I want to be responsible for you. For your good dreams. Your nightmares, Jeet. I want to know them all." My hands fell to his chest, where solid muscle warmed through black linen. "I won't always know how to help. But I want to be there for all of it."

"As my council sister?"

My nose wrinkled with distaste, and he chuckled. "I've

come," I said, gripping the front of his tunic, "to claim that cowrie shell."

Suddenly I was airborne; Sanjeet had swept me up, and I laughed as his burly arms wrapped around me. He placed me on the barnacle-covered boulder, and revealed what he had been working on when I arrived: an anklet of tiny gold bells, the same one he had shown me that night his mother died. Sanjeet had linked the cowrie shell onto the chain.

"I kept Amah's anklet with me to remember. But it's yours now." He insisted when I hesitated: "You let me carry your story. I trust you to carry mine." His hands cupped my foot, dusting off sand and red earth from the festival grounds. The cream-colored shell winked against my ankle as he clasped the chain. The faint sensation of another woman's fingers pricked in my thoughts. I heard her laugh, bells shivering against her heels as she danced and sang.

"I want to give you something too." I fumbled with the folds of my wrapper and held out the fiery sunstone.

"You shouldn't," he said. "That's special."

I snorted. "I have no plans to 'bear the fruit of dominance.'"

He chuckled and accepted the stone. "But this isn't a token for trading."

"No. But the cowrie shell is," I intoned in my best impression of the solemn village elders. "You must take something in return."

Warmth spread like butter over Sanjeet's face. He pulled me to the boulder's edge, bracing my hands on his shoulders. "I choose the girl who walks through fire," he said. "I choose sunshine."

I had kissed boys before. We all had, at the Children's Palace, in the games children play when they're bored. Every touch had been a dare, a cheap thrill, a way to flaunt our developing bodies and to sample adulthood.

This kiss was different. As his mouth pressed into mine, there were no games or experiments. Just a silent pledge that shook the earth beneath me.

When his tongue grazed my bottom lip, the kiss deepened. I ran my fingers through his hair, and his hands tightened on my waist. He still tasted of honeywine, heady and sweet. When we parted, his face remained close, lashes brushing mine.

"There's a tree," I said after a moment. "Enitawa's Quiver. Mayazatyl . . . she told me it's where . . ."

"I've heard of it." He raised an eyebrow, searching my face with surprise and amusement.

"I've never been before," I said quickly, feeling flustered. "But maybe that's where we can go later. To talk. And . . . be like this."

The stubble on his jaw tickled my neck. I shivered. "When?" he asked.

"Tonight," I said. "Tonight."

We both stiffened. A barrage of distant voices echoed in our minds, vying for attention. The Ray.

Sanjeet groaned. "Our council's worried."

I nodded, resting my head against his. "We'd better go back. You don't suppose they've guessed?"

"They can't read our thoughts unless we let our mental guards down," Sanjeet said. "I've got nothing to hide if you don't." Dayo's forlorn expression after the dance flashed in my head. Sanjeet read my features, guessing correctly where my thoughts had gone. "We'll keep it between us, then."

"For now," I said.

"For now," he agreed.

We held hands until the festival grounds were in sight, then reluctantly walked side by side, keeping space between us. We fooled no one, of course. Once our council siblings saw we were safe, they nudged each other and threw knowing smirks in our direction.

Well, well, if it isn't the Judge and the Bear! Found a better party than this one, eh?

I avoided looking at Dayo. He could never hide pain, and never had the pride to try. But when I gave in and peeked, his face merely shone with relief. We grinned at each other, sheepish. Dayo had not wanted to be my lover any more than I had wanted to be his. I wondered, then, about the bond between us, different than what I felt for my council siblings. In some ways, it was even stronger than the spark between me and Sanjeet.

Before I could return to the Prince's Council dais, an Imperial Guard warrior stepped into my path. She bowed to me, then pointed at Thaddace and Mbali's dais across the festival grounds.

"Their High Anointed Honors have summoned you," the warrior said.

I gulped. Had they disapproved of my disappearance from the festival? I sighed and slunk obediently to the far dais, bracing for a reprimand.

Mbali and Thaddace stared down at me from their tasseled cushions, looking resplendent in their festival wear. Mbali represented Swana, like me, and wore stacks of rainbow bangles on her willowy arms and neck. Thaddace was swathed in green Mewish tartan. I knelt on the dais steps, staring nervously at their gold-trimmed sandals.

"I'm sorry I left the festival," I babbled after an unnerving silence. "I know it's unseemly for Prince's Council members to travel alone. But we're so close to the keep. And I was worried about Sanjeet, and—"

"We've put you in a difficult position," interrupted Mbali.

I opened my mouth to bleat out another apology, then closed it. "Anointed Honors?"

"We know what you saw in the keep, Tarisai." Mbali waited until I could have no doubt about what she meant. My face heated.

"I assume," Thaddace intoned, "that you have told your council." He stared over my head, and I realized that he was embarrassed. Poor Thaddace. I had seen him naked, and he still had to be my law tutor.

"It's only natural if you told them," Mbali added kindly. "They're your council siblings. But our secret is very dangerous, Tarisai. It could threaten Aritsar's stability. Your discretion is essential." I nodded, but she continued in a neutral tone. "In his letters to the emperor, I hope you will encourage Dayo to be discreet as well."

I gaped like a fish out of a stream. Mbali and Thaddace wanted me to keep a secret.

From the *emperor*.

But why would Olugbade be worried about his council members having a dalliance? What threat could it pose to him, except the mild scandal of court gossip? Still, I nodded again, fidgeting with the beads on my wrists. "May I be excused, Anointed Honors?"

Mbali learned forward to peck me on the cheek. "I think you will make a wise Delegate to Swana," she said. "And an excellent High Lady Judge."

I tried to return to my council's dais, where my siblings were busy accepting gifts and blessing the village children. But as I turned toward them, my head swam, as though struck with a sleep dart. I swayed on my feet, and a sweet musk filled my nostrils.

I heard myself mumble an excuse, though no one was close enough to hear: "Going to relieve myself." Woodenly, I glided away from the firelit festival, where that familiar musk drew me, growing stronger with every step.

Several minutes outside Yorua Village, a masked elder stood in a crop of acacia trees. The brush was still, and the moon bathed us in deathly white. The elder's mask was female: a round face of ivory bone with red slits for eyes. Its brow had an edge of jagged points, as if to imply a queen's crown.

"Do . . . do I know you?" I whispered.

For some reason, I found it difficult to form words. I wished I could identify that smell—its name danced out of reach, like warning bells too faint for hearing.

The elder tilted her mask and bowed. A vessel rested in the crook of her strong, shapely arm. With her other hand, she held out a smooth-handled drinking gourd.

With effort, I shook my head. "I've already selected a token. We're not allowed more than one."

But my muscles relaxed as another fragrant wave rolled over me. I'd felt this way before. Small. Submissive. My fingers closed around the drinking gourd's handle, and I dipped into the vessel when she offered it. The liquid was clear amber—not golden, like honeywine.

"What is this?" I asked.

The elder tensed impatiently, pantomiming for me to drink. The longer I stood in her presence, the hazier my thoughts grew. I could think of no objection, no reason to disobey. I brought the gourd to my lips and drank. It was then that I remembered the name of that smell.

Jasmine.

Fire burned over my skin, waking sounds and images that had slept for five years. *This will be the day—The Lady will be so pleased—Melu, won't you come out and play?—When you love him the most, and when he anoints you as his own, I command you . . . to kill him.*

I stumbled back and the gourd fell from my grasp. As the liquid splashed on my open sandals, a sob caught in my throat.

I remembered everything.

The third wish. Our mango orchard. The tutors. The journey from Swana. Kathleen's warning. Woo In setting the Children's Palace on fire.

"What have you done?" I gasped at the elder. "What have you given me?"

"Water from Melu's pool," she said with a laughing, melodious voice that made my veins run cold. "You wanted to forget. But the ehru inside you knows who you are, daughter. It knows what you were made for." Then the figure removed her mask, and I was staring into a mirror. A face chillingly like my own: the first face I had ever loved.

The Lady smiled, her brilliant dark eyes glittering with tears. "I have missed you, Made-of-Me."

She kissed my forehead, and my heart grew as hollow as the drinking gourd. The Lady took my hand. Her wish draped around me like a mantle, and I sighed with horrified relief, like a warrior who had cheated death too many times—a fugitive tired of running.

"I was so hurt when you chose to forget me," The Lady whispered. "Your own mother. But I forgave you, once I realized the truth. You rebelled because you *are* me." She laughed softly. "Strong-minded. Independent. I cannot fault you for mirroring my strengths."

She smiled, and lay a small silver dagger across my palm. Obediently, my fingers closed around the hilt.

"It is time," The Lady said, and I nodded. I walked as if through water back to the village. Back to my council siblings—to warmth and innocence and light. *You don't belong here*, whispered the pit flames, shadows dancing on my siblings' faces. *And you never did.*

CHAPTER 17

WHEN THE PALANQUINS RETURNED TO YORUA Keep, my council siblings were clumsy with honeywine. They slept fully clothed on their pallets, snoring in heaps of jewelry and wax-dyed mantles.

I lay among their sweaty bodies, watching their chests rise and fall. Dayo's breaths tickled my neck. I listened to the guards change watch as the night grew old.

I waited.

I had promised to wake Sanjeet once the others were asleep. He lay on the edge of the sun-and-stars floor mosaic, backlit by the arched windows. All night, his fingers had searched for mine at the festival, restless and tender. I had teased him into chalice after chalice of honeywine, pretending to drink with him. Now, as he lay across from me in the banquet hall, he Ray-spoke drowsy messages through the dark: *Promise you'll wake me up when it's time.*

I will, I replied.

Sanjeet fell asleep, his mental guard down, and I stole into his thoughts. He was dreaming of Enitawa's Quiver.

I tried to make myself crawl over to his pallet. I tried to feel something. Anything.

But cold emptiness spread like fog through my mind, and I shook Dayo awake instead.

My lips caressed the burn scar on his jaw. He roused, confused, and I held a finger to my lips. I pulled him up, and hand in hand we wove around the sleeping bodies, slipping from the banquet hall. We stole through keep corridors, bare feet pounding on stone.

"Tar, what's going on?" Dayo yawned. I didn't reply, snatching a torch from its sconce and hurrying down a staircase. He puffed to keep up. "Are you all right? Is someone hurt?"

He sounded distant, an echo in my head. "Enitawa's Quiver," I told him, rounding a corner. After several drinks at the Nu'ina festival, Mayazatyl had revealed the tree's hiding place. A passage ran through the bowels of the keep, circumventing the guards and leading outside Yorua.

Dayo stopped dead in his tracks.

I glanced back at him impatiently. His pupils were dilated from sleep and disbelief. He wore nothing but trousers and a linen shirt, undone to reveal his collarbone.

"Tar," he whispered.

"What?" I asked. "Isn't this what you want?"

His gaze searched mine, shy and vulnerable. "I—I don't know. It's what's expected of us. But then I saw you with Sanjeet, and I thought—"

"You thought wrong," I said, seizing his hand and

sweeping down a narrow staircase. We passed through a heavily barred door into a passage beneath Yorua Keep.

As we charged into the damp darkness, Dayo noticed my torch. "Aren't you afraid of fire anymore?"

"No, Dayo." The flames snickered in my ears. "Not anymore."

According to Mayazatyl, the passage let out onto a mossy plateau, shielded from outside view by an outcrop of brush and sharp boulders. Before long, a breeze teased my face in the passage. I hung the torch in a niche and stepped out into the open.

A single tree grew in the plateau's center. It had a slippery pale trunk with branches like twisting arms, tinted purple as they reached for the sky. A soft, high moan shivered in the air as Enitawa's branches sang, heavy with the secrets of lovers who had rolled beneath its shadow. The ground was spongy beneath my feet, damp with a bed of ochre leaves.

"Come," I said. *Run, Dayo.* A dim voice struggled to rise in my thoughts, like a seabird keeping abreast in a storm. "Come here."

Run, Dayo. Run, please.

"I don't understand," he said, but drew near anyway. When I stroked the raised scar on his jaw, he relaxed into my touch. Words seemed to escape him as my fingers traced the veins in his neck. I explored the bones beneath his warm skin, admiring their weakness. Marveling at how easily they could break.

Dayo, get away. Run as far as you can. The voice was

wheeling, drowned out by waves and crashing thunder. My fingers were steady and cold as they peeled off Dayo's shirt, caressed the obsidian mask, and danced across his bare chest. He stiffened.

"Tar," he whispered. "There's something I should tell you. I don't . . . I don't think I want sex. Ever. And I don't mean with you, I mean—with anyone. Girls, boys. Anyone." He stared at the leaves on the ground, smooth brow furrowing. "I mean, I've had crushes before. On you, on Jeet, and some of the others. I've just . . . never been interested in the sex part. Sometimes I wonder if I'm broken."

You aren't broken, protested the voice inside me. *You're the kindest, most loving person I know. Run. Live.*

"But I'm crown prince," he continued, grimacing, "and I have to have heirs someday, so . . . I guess—if I could choose anyone—"

"There is no choosing," I intoned. There were only suns and moons. Demons and wishes. Curses written into the stars.

He sighed. "Do you love me now, Tarisai of Swana?"

"She did love you," I whispered. "But she wasn't strong enough."

Then the girl under the tree, the one who shared my face and voice, plunged the silver knife into Dayo's stomach.

"Don't look."

We are twelve years old, sitting side by side in a palanquin as it ambles through the Oluwan City Imperial Square. Dayo peers through the embroidered window flap. I wrestle him away, ignoring his protests as I clap my hands over his eyes.

"Don't look," I tell him again.

"Why?" Dayo's head nestles against my neck, tickling me with his soft curly hair. He thinks I'm playing a game. He laughs, a warm, gurgling sound.

Through the window flap, guards lead an old woman in white rags through the square. Her hair hangs in matted clumps. Onlookers spit and hiss as she is forced to climb a platform. Traitor. Traitor. Her bruised knees shake.

"Let me go, Tar," Dayo whines. "I never get to see the city."

"It's not good. It's an execution."

"Well, I've got to see one someday," he retorts.

"Please, Dayo." My throat is dry. The woman on the platform kneels, forced to lay her head on a wooden block. "Please don't."

"Why?" The hollow thud of imperial drums fills our ears, pulsing beneath the crowd's roar. "You think I'm weak, don't you, Tar? Just like everyone else does."

"No. I think you're too good." I hold Dayo close as hazy noontime light glints on the executioner's ax. "You think people are kind and soft and pretty." The ax falls, and blood runs from the platform to pool on the paved square. "I'll make it true, Dayo. When I'm grown-up, I'll make the world better, just for you. But for now, close your eyes."

He sighs into my chest, and I bury my face in his hair.

"I'll keep you safe, Dayo."

He gasped as my knife slid into his side. We fell together to the leaf-carpeted earth, like the lovers for whom Enitawa's Quiver was intended. He gaped up at my unseeing eyes, his features contorted in agony. "Tar."

"Will you come home now, Mother?" My voice was a monotone. "It's so lonely in Bhekina House. The servants won't touch me and I don't have any friends and I hate it when you leave; please come back . . ." I blinked, suddenly very, very tired. "Mother?"

Where was I? And why was it so cold?

Bhekina House wasn't drafty. The tutors had boarded up my windows . . . No. I didn't live there anymore. Mother had sent me away to Oluwan with Kathleen and Woo In. Then the fire happened, and it was all my fault. I had been responsible for protecting Dayo. He had trusted me, everyone trusted me, but they shouldn't, because I was a demon and Mother had sent me here to—

To—

Every hair on my neck rose as I registered the person in my arms.

"No," I said. A scream worked its way up my throat, but came out as a croak. "No. It's not—you're not— Stay awake, Dayo! It's over now. I'm back. I'd never let anything hurt you; I wouldn't— Damn it, *damn it*." I sobbed, pawing his face. I didn't dare touch the knife.

He watched me hyperventilate. "You remembered," he said.

"Don't talk. Rest, I'll get help." His words didn't make sense. My tears were a torrent; my ribs shuddered with each breath.

"You missed my heart." He smiled, voice gurgling with blood. "That means you're stronger than her, Tar."

"What's that supposed to mean?" I breathed. "Dayo, stay—"

His eyes fluttered closed.

"No." I wagged my head, baring my teeth at the sky. "Am, *no*. I don't care if you're the Storyteller; I *hate* your stories. Kill me instead. Doesn't that make more sense? Write something better. I'll give up anything. Anything." Tears ran into my open mouth as I pressed my ear to Dayo's bare chest. The dimmest of heartbeats pounded against my cheek. "Anything," I said, and felt the uneasy sensation of a sealed promise.

A footstep crunched behind me. Then I turned and locked eyes with a stiff, horrified face. Sanjeet stood over me in his wrinkled black festival clothes.

"Thank Am," I said. "Jeet, we have to get help; Dayo, he—"

Sanjeet's hand clamped my shoulder hard enough to leave a bruise. He wrenched me away from the tree, and I toppled, stunned.

He knelt, shielding Dayo's body with his broad back. "Little brother," he said, "don't sleep. Don't you dare sleep." Avoiding the knife's hilt, Sanjeet's fingers ran precise patterns across Dayo's side, assessing the failing organs.

I began, "We need help. I'll—"

"You shut up," Sanjeet rasped. "Just shut up and stay back."

"Jeet," I whispered. "It's not . . . It's not what you think."

"Who are you?" Sanjeet asked. His quiet voice was more ominous than any roar. When he looked at me at last, his eyes were wet and savage. "*What* are you?"

"I don't know," I sobbed. "I don't know, I don't know." Dayo needed help. My mind raced; he couldn't be moved without making it worse. We needed a miracle-worker.

I flung the Ray back toward Yorua Keep. With difficulty it traveled through the stone; my temples pounded with pain by the time I found Kirah. *Dayo's hurt*, I said as her mind woke up groggily. *We need you. Don't wake the others. Hurry.*

"Kirah's coming," I told Sanjeet as my mind guided her to Enitawa's Quiver. I could feel Kirah's panic through the Ray; she barraged me with questions. *Just come*, I begged, adding to myself, *Come and don't hate me.*

At last, Kirah stumbled from the murky passage into the clearing. "Where?" she panted.

I pointed at Dayo and said, "Please."

The color drained from Kirah's face. "Am have mercy," she wailed. "An assassin infiltrated the keep? How? Why didn't the Ray protect him?"

"Stay close to me," Sanjeet snapped. He reached for Kirah, casting a searing glance my way. I nodded, keeping my distance. Kirah wasn't mine anymore—demons didn't have best friends.

Kirah coaxed Dayo's head onto her lap, muttering prayers. Her hands trembled as they clutched the tassels of her prayer scarf. Sanjeet found Dayo's shirt and bunched the fabric into a tourniquet.

"On three," Sanjeet said curtly, and Kirah looked sick but nodded. He counted and pulled out the knife. As Dayo's blood soaked the tourniquet, Kirah raised her veiled head to the moon and sang.

Blessid chants resonated in the throat, packed with power to cross miles of desert sand. Kirah's song soared into the night, so strident I could see the notes winding around the stars. She sang lullabies to slow the rush of blood, high-pitched trills to scare away infection, basket-weaving rhymes to knit the flesh together. But her last and longest chant was a mother's plea to a restless daughter: a song to keep a soul in its body.

No rubies for my baby's head, no satin for her feet
No castles can I offer her, no princes dark and tall
But wandering girl, come find your bed,
sheets pressed with purple flowers
For castles have no camel's milk; my kiss is baby's crown.

Kirah crooned the song over and over, her homesickness

pouring into each note until blue tinged the predawn sky. Sanjeet pressed his hands on Dayo's side, repeatedly searching for weaknesses and telling Kirah where to direct her healing song. At long last, they sagged with exhaustion.

"The organs are intact again," Sanjeet said. "Still weak, but getting stronger. He needs rest, lots of it. But you pulled him out of danger, Kirah." He clapped her shoulder, his eyes glistening. "Thank you."

"We'll have to carry him back to the keep," she said hoarsely. "We have to be careful, but between the three of us—"

"She will not touch him," snapped Sanjeet.

"Why not?" Kirah blinked, still disoriented from hours of chanting. She glanced at me, then up at the tree. "What happened here? Tar, were you having a dalliance with Dayo? But I thought you liked . . ." She trailed off, noticing the tension between me and Sanjeet. "Great *Am*. Jeet . . . did you stab Dayo because . . . because you were jealous?"

"Jealous?" Sanjeet barked a laugh, and the sound pierced my stomach like a spear. "What for? The love of a monster?"

"Tell me what's going on right now," Kirah demanded. "Don't make me call the others—"

"I tried to kill Dayo," I said.

For the first time, Kirah noticed Sanjeet's dry, clean hands and my shaking, bloody ones. She took in the tears and mucus streaking my face. "You didn't," she said. "You couldn't."

I said nothing.

"You're scaring me, Tar. This isn't funny. Am's Story, say something—"

"You should tie me up." I held out my wrists. "The cellar beneath the keep kitchens has a lock; put me there. Tell the others I'm sick. That I need to be quarantined. When it's properly morning, I'll have a guard smuggle me to the nearest lodestone port. I'll go . . . somewhere far. A place I can never hurt him again."

Kirah's face contorted with horror.

"I'm half-ehru, Kirah." The words came out as mangled as Enitawa's branches. "Mother had three wishes; she gave one to me. I had to obey. I've resisted all this time, but she found me and I had to give in . . ." I shook my head. I sounded like a madwoman. But I had to make her understand. I couldn't lose her, not Kirah.

And as for Sanjeet—

The phantom of his lips brushed against mine. How could that same mouth call me *monster*?

"I can explain," I said, stretching out my hands again. "Please. Let me show you."

Both of them were still. Sanjeet's jaw hardened, and he placed a protective arm around Kirah.

"If we touch you, you could steal our memories," he said. "Like you used to steal mine in the Children's Palace."

For a moment I floated above my body, watching the scene from above. The Crown Prince of Aritsar, barely breathing. Sanjeet and Kirah huddled together, shielding

Dayo from the demon. The girl sniveling and stammering excuses. Even now, she was pretending to love them. Pretending to be sorry, to know what it meant to have a family. Looking in from the outside, I would have banished that girl to the traitor's block in a heartbeat. My palms beaded with sweat. But I *wasn't* pretending.

Was I?

Every mask, every Tarisai I had ever been scattered in the dark, puzzle pieces on a vast floor. The recluse of Bhekina House, willing to kill for her mother's touch. The Prince's Favorite, meddling in the minds of other candidates. The protector, carrying Dayo from the burning Children's Palace. The High Lady Judge, making empty promises to Ye Eun. The lover, crossing a fiery pit for a brown-eyed boy.

They were all true. All of them. How could I pick which one to believe? I was a monster, yes—but I could not let that be all that I was. Not now.

I dried my hands on my wrapper. "I never stole your memories," I corrected Sanjeet. "I only took your bad dreams."

"You should have let me keep them," he said. "You are the only nightmare."

Kirah left Sanjeet's side. She searched my face, looking for the Tarisai she knew: the girl who had giggled with her on the Children's Palace rooftop. The girl who had cornrowed stories into her hair.

I'm still here, I Ray-spoke.

Kirah placed her cool, soft palm over my bloody one. She seized Sanjeet's hand too, so he was forced to listen. My story poured into them both like rain, making up for lost time in rivers and floods. When they had seen all my memories—the ehru, The Lady's murderous wish, my self-inflicted amnesia—Kirah was still frowning. But she didn't stop holding my hand.

"Can you control it?" she asked. Bags puffed under her eyes, and her face was wan in the morning light. "Be honest, Tar. Can you keep yourself from making The Lady's wish come true?"

"I'm not sure," I admitted. "I could make myself forget again. But that only worked until Mother found me." And she would find me again. She would always find me. My temples grew clammy as Melu's voice echoed in the air: *Until you grant her third wish, neither you nor I will be free.*

Melu's name jarred in my thoughts, awakening after so many years. My father, the ehru. Bound to that savannah until I killed Dayo.

"I have to go back to Swana," I gasped.

"Why?" Kirah asked, frowning. "Won't your mother find you there? Isn't that where she lives?"

"Yes. But only Melu would know how to break the curse. He can't free himself; he can't leave that grassland. But maybe I could free us both."

Kirah's lips pressed together. "I'll come with you."

"You can't. What if Dayo needs you to sing? He barely made it through the night."

"Swana's four lodestones away," Kirah countered, "not including the time you'll have to rest in between. You'll be feverish with council sickness by then. Suppose you don't make it back?"

"Then our problem's solved."

Kirah glared at me, bottom lip trembling. "Don't you dare. Don't you dare take the easy way out, Tar. What would Dayo do if you died?"

"Live," I spat. "He would live!"

"No. You'd just be killing him another way."

"I'll go," said Sanjeet.

Kirah and I turned to stare at him. He was expressionless, a soldier volunteering for a thankless duty. I could no longer envision the tenderness with which he had fastened a gift around my ankle. The cowrie shell still dangled against my foot, cold as bone.

"You don't have to," I said.

"I know," he growled. "But I will. For his sake."

He lifted Dayo onto his shoulders and disappeared down the passageway. Before they vanished, I memorized the curl of Dayo's hair, the breadth of his nose, the slope of his narrow back.

"I may never see him again," I whispered.

"Maybe not," Kirah said. "But you aren't a monster, Tarisai. No matter what Sanjeet says."

I sobbed as she stroked my back, rearranging the heavy yarn braids that hid my face. "I don't deserve you," I said.

"Too bad." Kirah gave a tired smile. "Because none of us

will give you up without a fight. Dayo's probably forgiven you already. He doesn't know how to hate anyone. Not even a murderer."

"But do you think the rest of our council will?"

She chewed her lip. "I think it would be best if they didn't know. Not right away, anyway. But they'll understand. Well, everyone except . . ." She looked wearily in the direction Sanjeet had gone. "You know what happened to Sendhil."

I nodded, swallowing hard. Sanjeet had almost lost his little brother for good, again.

And it was all my fault.

PART 3

CHAPTER 18

DAWN BROKE, AND WE WASHED THE BLOOD from our clothes.

Dayo rested, feverish and delirious, in one of the keep's rarely used bedrooms. "He was sleepwalking," Kirah told our council siblings. "He took a fall."

The keep servants fussed, bringing tea and poultices from the kitchens. Thaddace and Mbali did not send word to the emperor, because no one was afraid that Dayo would die. Raybearers were immune, after all, to everything.

Everything except me.

Kirah prevented servants from fetching healers from the capital. "We have it all under control," she told them, smiling a little too brightly. A bandage hid the stab wound on Dayo's side, which could not yet pass as a bruise from an innocent tumble.

I knew Kirah and Dayo would keep my secret, though Sanjeet was unpredictable. If the rest of my council siblings found out what I had done, I would lose everything.

The council would side against me, and Kirah and Dayo would join them. They would have no choice.

I stayed far away from Dayo's sleeping body, memorizing the silhouettes of my council brothers and sisters as they huddled together, lighting incense to Am for Dayo's recovery. Without seeing them, I could summon their voices, their tics and mannerisms. Kameron's tongue, lolling thoughtfully in his cheek. Ai Ling's jaded, strident laughter. Umansa's sleepy smile. Thérèse's pale eyebrows, furrowed in meditation.

Why do you hate them so much, Mother? How could you take away the person they love most?

Melu was my only hope. But even if he broke my ehru curse, I might never earn my council's trust back. Perhaps it was best if I never returned.

Unable to say goodbye, I stole away to my chamber. Clothes lay in piles from last evening, when my only anxiety had been impressing Sanjeet on Nu'ina Eve. None of my possessions seemed appropriate to pack for the journey ahead: rainbow wax-dyed wrappers, jeweled council regalia, High Judge case scrolls. I especially avoided touching the piles of handmade gifts from villagers. Every item held a story of sweat and sacrifice, of love I did not deserve. Biting my lip, I remembered the last gift I received.

"I'm sorry, Amah," I whispered, and slipped the cowrie shell anklet from my foot.

The pallet in my chamber was dusty from neglect, since our council always slept together in the banquet hall. But

I had not rested for two days, and sank gratefully onto the mudcloth blankets. The coarse cotton, dyed with earth-toned patterns of brown, black, and white, chafed my face. I counted them feverishly until sleep fell like a shadow. When I woke, I was still clutching the anklet.

"Time to go," Sanjeet said. He stood in my doorframe and tossed a pile of leathery items on the floor. "Get dressed."

I rubbed my stiff face and squinted at the pile. "Imperial Guard uniforms?" Sanjeet already wore the dark draping pants and protective padding strapped across his bare chest and arms. An oval shield leaned beside him in the doorway. I frowned. "Wouldn't peasant clothes draw less attention?"

"Imperial Guard warriors patrol the valley, changing shifts every three hours. If The Lady is watching the keep, Guard uniforms allow us to leave undetected. We must conceal your absence from Yorua for as long as possible. If The Lady knows her weapon has been compromised, she may try to reclaim it."

"Weapon," I repeated. "Is that my name now?"

"It has always been your name," he said, and shut the door flap.

I changed into the black-red-and-gold armor. I had already cried every tear my body could spare, and so my face was dry when I looked in the mirror. A dark silk turban bound my telltale yarn braids. A dust mask would conceal the lower half of my face, helping me blend in with the guards leaving and entering the keep. I strapped a pack of supplies to my back, and as an afterthought, added Aiyetoro's drum.

I had barely touched the empress's artifact since Woo In and Kathleen had brought it to me in the temple. They had thought it would restore my memories; perhaps it held a clue to breaking my curse as well.

When I was finished, I presented myself to Sanjeet, holding out my arms like a spear dummy. "Search me," I said. He balked. I reminded him coolly, "I'm a weapon, remember? If you're traveling alone with me, you'd better make sure I'm not armed."

He paused, and then felt down my arms, breast, and thighs. Surgical and efficient. Never meeting my gaze. "Clean," he grunted.

"Good. Now you can be sure I won't run off. Or stab you while you sleep." I was being unkind. None of this was Sanjeet's fault, and I had no right to be petty about his coldness. But I couldn't bear it. I needed—just once—for him to look at me.

"We should go," he said, staring hard at my sandals.

I swallowed hard and tossed him a small woven pouch. "You'll need these."

He shook the pouch's contents into his palm. The first item was my council ring. The sun-and-moon emblem was still sticky, mottled from court cases I had signed with wax. I could not identify myself without my seal. No guard would let me darken the door of an imperial building. As long as Sanjeet had that ring, I could never return to Yorua

Keep or An–Ileyoba Palace. Dayo would be safe forever.

The second item was his mother's anklet. When he saw it, Sanjeet's stone expression shifted. For the first time, his tea-colored eyes met mine.

I kept my tone light. "You can't trust a monster with your story, right? Better save that for someone who's human."

I hated this. He did too. I could see it in the lines of his face, rigid with pain. But we were griots in a pantomime, forced to sing every line in this grim story, dancing to a beat my mother drummed.

Sanjeet put away the items and hung the pouch around his neck, tucking it beneath his leather chest brace. "We should get moving," he said. "The nearest lodestone is a day's journey as the pelican flies, but two days by the main road. We'll spend a night at the village."

"We can't," I said. "Yorua Village is where I saw The Lady last. And we can't camp on the road; there are lions this time of year. We need to travel to the lodestone directly."

Sanjeet stiffened, instinctively touching the curved blade in his halter. "So. We go . . ."

"We go through the Bush."

Every Arit realm had a place like the Oluwan Bush. Nyamban people called theirs *Shida-Shida*. Nontish people, *Trou-du-Fae*.

The Mewish name was most direct: *Lost-Soul-Land*.

Enoba the Perfect had created the Bushlands by accident. When he united our realms as one continent, the magic had grown new earth. These enchanted lands, scholars theorized, tempered the climate of our vast continent, allowing for fertile ground in landlocked areas that would otherwise be rendered arid. But the land had also plowed over ancient ocean passages to the Underworld, trapping malevolent spirits between this world and the next.

To mortals, Bushland appeared no different than any other savannah or forest. A goatherd could wander from pasture to Bush-pasture without knowing it. Animals were better at sensing the difference, though plenty of cattle, lured by the smell of seductively sweet grass, had vanished overnight. The poor beasts emerged from the Bush several days later, half-starved and eyes white with madness, with fewer limbs—or sometimes *more*—than they had entered with. At present, however, no monster frightened me more than my own reflection. If it meant avoiding The Lady, I would cross every Bush in Aritsar.

Disguised in our uniforms, Sanjeet and I left Yorua Keep with a cohort of Imperial Guard warriors. We traveled on foot; mules would have been no faster. They would have stumbled on the winding dirt path from the Yorua Cliffs and gone half-mad once we neared the Bush.

The Lady did not appear to steal me away. Our Imperial Guard disguises seemed to have worked, but I remained skittish. Sometimes I saw her, a mirage lounging under a cliff, grinning like a lion at an antelope. She could so easily transform me into her lethal puppet: a sip from Melu's pool, and I would turn on Sanjeet and the Guard warriors, racing back to the keep to finish the bloody job I had started.

When Sanjeet had announced our plan to cross the Bush, the guards had inhaled sharply, blessing themselves with the sign of the Pelican. But Arit law forbade them from contradicting Anointed Ones directly, so they told stories among themselves instead.

"Captain Bunmi," said one of the warriors as we marched, "have you heard of Oro-ko, the Bush-spirit with no stomach?"

"I have not, Yinka." The captain was a tall old woman with a gold septum ring and a necklace of imperial sun-and-moon tattoos. She cocked her head at the warrior in feigned fascination. "Is Oro-ko as bad as the Bush-Wife, the spirit that lures infants into lakes?"

"Much worse, Captain. Oro-ko is a spirit that cannot eat, so he forces travelers to eat for him!"

"I do not believe it."

"It's true, aheh! Once, Oro-ko lured a peasant and his son into the Bush, beguiling them with smells of saltfish and honeyed garri cakes. The son saw a great feast, and began to eat. But when he awoke from the trance, was it garri? I am not a liar: The son had eaten his father!"

The warriors traded macabre stories for hours as we traveled, speaking loudly to ensure we would hear.

"At least take a spear, Anointed Honor," one of the warriors pleaded, noticing my empty halter. "You must protect yourself."

I smiled ruefully, glancing at Sanjeet. A weapon would make me more dangerous than any ghost-creature of the Bush.

We stopped at a field thinly dotted with corkwood trees. Wind whistled through gnarled, long-reaching branches. Wood posts etched with skulls marked the edge of the otherwise serene meadow. The air hung faintly with kiriwi: Someone had planted the fragrant herb across the border, hoping to ward off evil. The downy plants had spread into the plain, marking an informal path.

"Stay by the kiriwi," Captain Bunmi said, doing her best to hide her anxiety. We had forbidden the warriors from accompanying us through the Bush. "And I beg, Anointed Honors: No matter what happens, stay together." She considered us. "Perhaps you should hold hands—"

"No need for that," Sanjeet said. "We'll be fine."

He tried to cross into the Bush, but I stopped him. "Me first," I said. "If I'm behind you, how can you make sure I don't run off?"

The grass crunched beneath my feet as I entered the crop of trees, Sanjeet close behind. "Am be with your Anointed Honors," the warriors yelled. We waved goodbye and moved farther in. Except for our footsteps, the meadow was pristinely quiet. A breeze tickled my face, teasing the strings of my dust mask. Within minutes the mask came loose, fluttering away. I stumbled after it.

"*Stay by the kiriwi!*" Captain Bunmi shrilled from across the meadow. I could barely hear her.

My fist closed around the mask. "It's all right," I called, turning to wave. "I've got . . ." My voice died in my throat.

The warriors were gone.

All around was an empty plain, corkwood trees snickering in the wind. My heart hammered, but to my relief, Sanjeet still stood behind me.

"You're here," I breathed.

"I'm here," he echoed.

"How did that happen? The warriors just disappeared. Maybe they're still there, but we've been blinded or . . ." I trailed off as I noticed the meadow. "Oh no."

The kiriwi had vanished too.

Sanjeet's hand closed around mine. "We'll be fine," he said.

I blinked up at him in surprise. Sanjeet's tea-tinted eyes were calm, and his jaw free of its recent tension.

"We should find the kiriwi," I said. My stomach fluttered with unease. I had almost forgotten what Sanjeet's gaze felt like when he wasn't angry. Had it only been two sunsets since he kissed me by the ocean?

"This way," he said, still holding my hand. "We saw the plants over there."

The area to which he gestured didn't strike me as familiar. But now, neither did any part of the meadow.

I followed him through the grass, which grew taller and thicker with every yard. "Jeet, do you think—"

"As long as we go in a consistent direction, we'll reach the other side."

"Are you . . . feeling all right?" I asked.

"Are you?" He glanced back, running his thumb over the top of my hand. "Please keep up, Tarisai. I wouldn't want to lose you."

My head swam in confusion. Had Sanjeet . . . forgiven me? Did he trust me again? No. He was only being kind so I would calm down and we could escape the Bush. I let him tow me over the meadow, which thickened with hills and trees.

We walked for what felt like an hour. I admired the back of Sanjeet's neck, where loose curls grazed the top of his weapon halter. He hummed a song in his cavernous bass: an old lullaby I had heard from a maid at Bhekina House. I remembered the moon streaming through my window, and the evasive scent of mangoes as I drifted to sleep.

"That's from Swana," I mumbled, feeling warm and sluggish. "I didn't know you knew Swana songs."

Sanjeet did not reply. We had stopped in front of a cave, sunken into the face of a brush-covered hill. Corkwood trees surrounded us on every side.

"Do you need to rest?" he murmured, touching my arm. His expression, soft and earnest, made my knees buckle. I resisted the urge to trace his slanted brows, his ridged nose, the deep creases beneath each eye.

I asked, "Why are you being so nice to me?"

"You're tired, sunshine girl," he sighed into my turban. His embrace was sudden, catching the air in my throat. "I'm sorry for taking you so far. The sun's too high for walking. But it's cool in that cave. We could rest for a while. Sleep." He pulled back and smiled, his tone gently suggestive. "Or not."

"I—" I shook my head, as if to clear it. "I don't understand."

"What happened last night wasn't your fault." His lips brushed my forehead. "I see that now. Your mother forced you to hurt Dayo; you had no say in it. I'm sorry for saying those cruel things. You're nothing like The Lady."

"Nothing you said was wrong," I faltered. "I *am* The Lady's daughter. And I chose to join the council. Even though I knew it would put Dayo in danger—"

"It wasn't your fault," he insisted. Slowly, my muscles relaxed. He unwound the turban of my disguise, letting my braids spill heavily over my back as his fingers grazed my neck. "You did nothing wrong. There is no reason to feel guilty."

It was more soothing than his lullaby. More potent than any of Kirah's chants. It was all I needed to feel blameless and beloved, and everything I wanted to hear.

"Tarisai," said Sanjeet. "Come into the cave."

My blood cooled. In a daze, I extracted myself from his arms and backed away.

"What's wrong?" Sanjeet's face was a perfect portrait of

243

concern. "I need you, Tar. I trust you more than anyone. I never should have doubted—"

"Stop," I rasped.

"Tar? I don't understand."

"Sanjeet of Dhyrma would never lie to make me feel better." I snapped a slim branch from a tree and brandished it in front of me. "What are you?"

The person froze. Then he—*it*—smiled with Sanjeet's face. The Bush-spirit distorted, body rippling as it melted into acrid fog that billowed around me. I couldn't move—couldn't *see*. Ghostly laughter shook the corkwood trees.

My feet began to advance, laboriously, as though a powerful weight pressed behind each heel. I realized with horror that I was heading toward the cave. I was sure it led to the Underworld, or some horrible limbo like it. If I entered, would I become like *it*? A malicious Bush-spirit, trapped for all eternity?

I pulled against the weight, fighting, thrusting myself in the other direction. For a moment, it worked. But I was aimless; the fog muddled all direction. Before long that push, push, *push* toward the cave returned. I threw myself again. I was tiring. I would never keep this up for long, and then the only thing left would be to—

"Give in," the spirit murmured, still using Sanjeet's voice. "You would be safer with us. Dayo would be safer. Don't be selfish, killer-girl."

"Shut up," I growled. But already my muscles were

weakening. My feet began their advance again. One step. Two. Three . . .

And then a new voice echoed from the ground, vibrating in my limbs, as though it had traveled through thick layers of dust and leather. But it wasn't someone. It was Aiyetoro's drum, strapped to my back, pounding of its own accord: *pum-bow, pum-bow, gigin, go-dun-go-dun-bow.*

The meaning of each pitch came together in my mind: *Stone. Stone. Vine-covered stone.*

I peered wildly through the mist. There, beyond two trees, a rock lay covered in vines . . . and in its shadow, a kiriwi bush.

I lurched for it, scaling the ground as the Bush-spirit howled, doubling its efforts. But the closer I got to the kiriwi, the thinner the fog became. I saw through illusions everywhere—trees grew transparent, and a path previously concealed sprung into view. The kiriwi bush was one of many, dotting the way I had lost earlier. When I reached the path, the pull on my limbs melted away. I looked back. The circle of trees and Bush-spirit were gone . . . but the cave remained. That ominous place had *not* been an illusion.

I shivered in a heap on the ground, wanting to vomit. But I couldn't rest. Not now.

"Sanjeet," I whispered. "Where are you?"

CHAPTER 19

I WOULD NOT DISOBEY CAPTAIN BUNMI AGAIN.

Stay by the kiriwi. I walked so close to the fragrant bushes, their branches scraped my sore legs. The Bush had transported me away from the border the moment I left the path. Sanjeet—the real Sanjeet—must have watched me disappear. Had he made it through to the other side?

At least I didn't have to worry about human adversaries. Most bandits and thieves valued their lives too dearly to risk the Bush.

With each step, my head throbbed; the afternoon heat stifled me. I had not eaten before I left Yorua, unwilling to face my council siblings at breakfast. Kirah had lied to them and said Thaddace had sent me to officiate a court case. Far, far away. If I died in this wilderness, my only friends would never know what had happened to me.

Phantom murmurs seeped from the shadows of the corkwood trees. I heard the voices of my council siblings, sweet and forgiving.

"Tar? Is that you?"

"It is! It's Tarisai!"

"Thank Am . . ."

"We've been looking ever since you left the keep. We don't blame you about Dayo, Tar. We know it wasn't your fault. Come home—"

"Stop trying so hard," I snapped at the shadows. "I'm not leaving this path, so you might as well shut up!" Then I summoned the last of my strength and flung the Ray's heat into the Bush, searching. I felt him. Sanjeet was still alive.

Hope buoyed my footsteps, though when I tried to Ray-speak, he didn't respond. His mind felt submerged in water; the normal guard around it was gone. A snippet of his thoughts bled through the fog.

Look at you, brother. I can't believe you're so strong.

Sanjeet was happy. *Delighted.* Who on earth was he talking to? I searched with the Ray again, and sensed him farther up the path. I heard young voices, and a sound like the *clack* of wooden practice weapons.

"What in Am's name?" I muttered. Then, with a single step, the landscape changed.

I spun and blinked rapidly. Tents dotted the previously empty grass, and smoke rose from campfires. Scruffy uniformed youths drilled with their captains, each bearing the sigil of a cobra. From their accents, the warriors appeared to be Dhyrmish mercenaries. Cautiously, I stepped back.

The camp disappeared.

I crept forward, and the mercenaries blossomed again into view.

The scene was staggeringly lifelike. I could even smell

the cooking spices wafting from each fire. But when I hunted for mistakes in the illusion, I found them. Tents that failed to cast a shadow. Warriors wrestling on the ground without making an imprint in the mud. "Am's Story," I muttered. Why would the spirits make such an elaborate pantomime?

Then I saw him: the only living person in a camp full of ghosts.

"Jeet," I cried out.

He was facing away, laughing. That rare, thunderous sound gave me so much joy, I wondered if the Bush had conjured it to seduce me. But it was real. *He* was real, the solid center around which the transparent illusion shifted. Sanjeet was sparring with one of the mercenaries, a clean-shaven young man with a scimitar.

"Jeet," I repeated, grinning and waving at him.

He turned at my voice. But his deep brown eyes were glassy: He couldn't see me.

"Follow my voice," I said. "It's all an illusion. You'll see when you—"

"Careful of ghosts, brother." The young mercenary stepped between me and Sanjeet. "We lose rookies every time we cross the Bush. Spirits always imitate people you know."

My jaw dropped. This spirit had the audacity to pretend that I was one of *them*? I noticed then the resemblance between Sanjeet and the mercenary. The same copper complexion, heavy jaw, and protruding ears. But the spirit's hair was straight, unlike Sanjeet's loose curls. His face was soft and shy, a dramatic contrast to Sanjeet's own.

"Sorry, Sendhil," Sanjeet replied, shaking his head. "I just . . . I thought I heard someone."

The spirit grinned. "An old sweetheart? *Sanjeet, come find me.*" The spirit mercenary mimicked my voice in a girlish falsetto. "*You're in danger . . .*"

"Don't listen to him," I snarled. "He's not real. None of this is real. Jeet—"

"Afternoon heat's making us delusional," said the spirit with a convincing shudder. "There's a place we can cool off over the hill. Beat you there." It grinned at Sanjeet boyishly. "I'm as tall as you now, big brother."

Sanjeet hesitated, but when the spirit beckoned, he jogged after him. Soon I heard him laugh again, that warm, incredulous sound.

"Oh, Jeet," I sighed. "You and your damned guilt complex."

Of course he would leave the path for Sendhil. Sanjeet had longed for his brother's forgiveness, just as I had longed for his. The Bush had lured him with his deepest torment—and now I couldn't save him. If I left the path, the Bush would simply bewitch me too.

I paced, a panther in a cage. Then I dropped to my knees and tore up the fragrant purple flowers. I rubbed the downy leaves on my skin and stuffed them in the crevices of my Guard uniform. The blossoms tickled in my throat as I swallowed a mouthful. I didn't know if the protection would work, or for how long. But it was Sanjeet's only chance . . . and so I lunged off the path, and into the illusion.

When at last I spotted him, Sanjeet was standing at the mouth of a murky brown pool. He had taken off his sword halter. The spirit-Sendhil was treading water, whooping and laughing. Even from a distance, I could hear the spirit's taunts.

"What's taking so long, big brother? Did you forget how to swim in that fancy Children's Palace?"

"I can't see the bottom," said Sanjeet. His words sounded slurred, suspended between wake and sleep. I reached the pool just as his foot hovered at the water's edge.

"No!" I grabbed his arm and yanked, toppling him backward. He landed with a confused grunt. I threw myself on top of him, snarling territorially at the Bush-spirit. "You can't have him."

"Tar?" Sanjeet blinked up at me, dazed. The kiriwi had enabled him to see me. "Where . . . ?"

"Careful, brother," the spirit-Sendhil cried. "It appeared out of nowhere; it must be a ghost. Don't let it touch you." Obediently Sanjeet pushed me off him and stood, backing away.

I leapt to my feet, brandishing fistfuls of kiriwi. "I'm not a ghost, Jeet. And if you go into that pool, you'll never come out."

The spirit laughed. "Too good for watering holes, brother?" It paused, carefully arranging its face to look sad. "Of course. Anointed Ones have fancy bathhouses. Must be nice. It's no wonder you didn't come find me after Father sent me away."

"I didn't want to stay away," Sanjeet protested. Unconsciously, he moved toward the pool again. "Don't ever think that, Sendhil. I'll never stop being your brother."

It was then I noticed an item on the ground, nestled with Sanjeet's abandoned clothing: the pouch containing my imperial seal.

I stared for a moment, transfixed. The voices from the shadows returned, honeyed and pleading. *Take it. Take it and return to the keep.*

The spirit held Sanjeet's gaze. "I called for you, and you didn't come. But don't feel bad, brother. It wasn't your fault."

"Sendhil." Sanjeet's voice was broken. He took another step.

You can't save Sanjeet, the voices told me. *Besides, he'll never forgive what you did to Dayo. Take the pouch. Go back to your friends; this quest is too dangerous for a girl. You'll find Melu another way, a safer way . . .*

"There's nothing to forgive, brother," said the spirit as Sanjeet grew closer. "I know you didn't really abandon me. You're nothing like Father; you would never leave me to fend for my—" Then the spirit ducked beneath the water, and the pool was unnervingly still.

"Sendhil?" Sanjeet cried out, teetering over the water.

My trance broke. "Stop," I barked, and seized his arm.

The spirit resurfaced, coughing and sputtering. "Something—it's below—help me, brother—"

"It's a trick," I gasped, tightening my grip as Sanjeet grew frantic. "Jeet, why would Dhyrmish mercenaries be camping in the Oluwan Bush? Why would Sendhil just happen to find you?"

Sanjeet's gaze snapped from me to the spirit, who screamed and flailed again. He freed himself easily from my grasp, preparing to jump.

"You once told me that Sendhil never lies," I said in a rush. I didn't want to continue; I hated to be cruel. But I had no choice. "Your brother wouldn't deny that you abandoned him, Jeet. Because you *did*. You agreed with your father. Mercenaries took Sendhil because you didn't protect him."

Sanjeet froze. Firmly, I cupped his face and searched his mind for memories of the real Sendhil, drawing them painfully to the surface. Sanjeet gazed down at me, eyes clear and wet with shock.

"Lies will never set us free, Jeet." Then I tossed a handful of kiriwi into the pool.

The spirit shrieked, and the pool turned chalky white. The water rippled, and in its place yawned a fathomless pit. Immediately I felt that *pull*, that malevolent hunger for souls and living blood.

"Run," I said.

Hand in hand, Sanjeet and I barely managed to retrieve the pouch and weapon halter before sprinting across the

Bush. Maybe the kiriwi gave us strength—or perhaps together, we were harder to overcome. Either way we somehow reached the path, collapsing in a pile among the leaves and purple blossoms.

As we caught our breath, I checked his skin for scrapes and bruises. He had sparred with spirit-Sendhil and could have sustained wounds that the Bush concealed.

"You stayed," he said.

I peered up at him, puzzled.

"You stayed," he repeated, staring at me. "Instead of going back to the keep. You had your seal. You could have gone back to Dayo and left me to die in the Bush."

I paused my search, hands lingering on his chest. Then I stood and turned away, shrugging. "Even monsters can surprise you."

He inhaled through his teeth. "Don't—don't call yourself that."

"Why not?" I dusted off my Guard uniform. "You did."

"I'm sorry." When I didn't turn around he said, "I mean it. Am's Story, Tar—when I saw Dayo all bloody like that, and you standing over him, I lost my head. I couldn't help it. But you didn't deserve that. You . . . you aren't The Lady."

I stiffened, remembering spirit-Sanjeet's caressing voice. "That isn't true."

"She isn't you," he countered. "You didn't want to kill Dayo."

"That's the problem, Jeet. Part of me did." I faced him

so he knew I was serious. "When I attacked him I felt numb, but I also felt *right*. Like I was fixing a mistake that shouldn't have been made. There was an . . . anger in my blood that had to be satisfied."

"You didn't choose to feel that way."

"Does that matter? It's still me." I was pacing now, determined to have it out at last. "For years, I told myself that I was nothing like The Lady. That I would *never* be her. But my mother is part of me, Jeet. Just like your father is part of you. No, it isn't fair. No, we don't deserve the burdens that our parents gave us. But we can't defeat monsters that we won't face." I thought for a moment, listening to the rustling grass, where illusions hid to steal our souls. "I thought I could forget. That if I buried it deep enough, The Lady's wish would disappear. But if I'd been honest with myself, Dayo would have been safe. I never would have joined the council."

"And I would have stayed chained to that pillar in the Children's Palace," said Sanjeet. "I would be the Prince's Bear, with a rat's skull as a token instead of a cowrie shell." His voice was soft, and he appeared to consider taking my hand, just like spirit-Sanjeet had.

But instead we remained apart, staring at each other as if scouring mire from glass. A clear and cold reflection of our truest selves: the good and the monstrous.

"You had enough faith in me to cross a firepit," Sanjeet said. "For everyone's sake, Tar, have that faith in yourself."

CHAPTER 20

WE STUMBLED THROUGH THREE MORE FALSE landscapes before we reached the end of the Bush. The illusions had been made for Captain Bunmi and her four warriors, who had leapt into the Bush impulsively after seeing me disappear.

"We can't leave them," I said grimly. Sanjeet nodded and we swallowed kiriwi until we felt sick.

We found Captain Bunmi in a quiet field, surrounded by the bodies of dead imperial warriors. None of the corpses were real, of course—I could tell from the blood, which was too lurid, and from the way each body flickered when Bunmi wasn't looking.

The captain sobbed on her knees, screaming the names of her comrades. I picked through the corpses and put a hand on her shoulder. She stared up at me, blankly.

"I . . . killed them," Bunmi said. "They looked like enemies at first and then they . . . changed. The Bush tricked me, *it tricked me*—" She clawed at her head, desperate to expel the images lodged there.

Sanjeet restrained her arms. "It's all right," I said. "Come with us. Come back to the path."

She shook her head slowly. "I can never go back. A captain does not abandon—I should stay with them, in the Bush—I can never go back."

"Your warriors are not here. They're fine," I said firmly, and prayed to Am I was right.

We rescued three more warriors. The third we found brandishing a spear over a lifeless body.

A real one.

The beguiled warrior had pierced the fourth remaining warrior, a woman named Awofeso, through the heart. The Bush had tricked him into seeing a wild beast. When his vision cleared, he began to tremble, yelling, then whispering her name. He continued to ask for Awofeso even when we reached the end of the path, crossing out of the Bush into a rural village.

"Sometimes, the Bush wants to keep you," Bunmi told us as we put the warrior to bed at the village inn. "Other times, it only wants to steal your joy, so instead you carry the Bush with you, always." The warrior's lips continued to shape that name, over and over, until at last I brushed his temples, plucking the memory of his comrade's mangled body from his mind. He stilled, sighed, and fell fitfully asleep.

Sanjeet and I spent the night side by side on straw mats in the inn's best room. The floor was packed dirt, strewn with fresh hay. More than once, I wanted to touch him. He twitched often, as if he wrestled with the same temptation. But our arms stayed by our sides, and I stared up at the wattle-and-daub ceiling, knowing we couldn't go back.

The children who had kissed by the sea were gone. We were different people now, more jaded and honest. If I touched him that way again, I would be making a promise that I had no power to keep. How could I swear to love anyone when The Lady still held my puppet strings?

I turned away from Sanjeet so he wouldn't see my features contort with anger. "It's my story. Mine, you hear me?" I hissed at a woman only I could see. "And I'll get it back. You'll see."

When we said our goodbyes to the Imperial Guard warriors the next morning, their faces shone with grave new respect. This time, they did not challenge us when we kept our destination secret and nodded when we insisted on going alone.

"If you had left the Bush without rescuing my warriors," said Bunmi, "no one would have blamed you. You are Aritsar's future. Your lives must be preserved. But you came back." She squinted and locked her jaw, restraining tears. "I will never forget what you did, and neither will any of my comrades. The Imperial Guard shall always be loyal to Tarisai of Swana and Sanjeet of Dhyrma. For the first time in many moons . . . I smile for the future of Aritsar."

As Sanjeet and I walked away, her last words rang strangely in my ears. *For the first time in many moons.* The Imperial Guard was more loyal to the empire than anyone. Why would a captain have doubts about Aritsar's future?

A three-hour walk from the village, a bustling town guarded a lodestone port to Nyamba, the realm northeast of Oluwan. Sanjeet and I had planned the journey with a map the night before. Each lodestone could transport travelers to only one place. Nyamba was the opposite direction from where we needed to go, but from there, another port could take us directly to Swana. Going the wrong way via lodestone was faster than going the right way on mule or on foot.

"Names and reason for travel," barked a scowling old man when we arrived at the port. The lodestone, a smooth bed of black rock ten men wide, was nestled in a copse of trees at the edge of town. A palisade fence surrounded the port, with openings on either side, flanked by guards. I could feel the power pulsing in the stone from several feet away. My stomach gurgled, anticipating the nausea. The last time I had taken a lodestone had been when my council moved to Yorua Keep. We had taken two days to recover, lying on our pallets and clutching our middles.

Sanjeet flashed our council seals at the guard, and the man's eyes widened. "Your Anointed—"

"Keep your voice down," muttered Sanjeet, and paid our fare.

"Of course, Anointed Honors. You're free to cross . . . No. Wait." The man peered at the lodestone's surface, from which lines of ghostly black script began to rise. "Someone's coming."

With a thunderous crack, a cohort of imperial militia burst into view from thin air. "No time to waste," the captain shouted to his comrades, stepping off the lodestone and shrugging off the nausea. He flashed his identification at the guards. "We may have captured the abomination, but her servants still lurk in the empire. They were last spotted not far from . . ." His voice trailed off as the cohort left the port, running in formation.

"Who knows what all that was about?" said the old man, smiling at us with nervous courtesy, then waving us on. "It's safest if you hold hands," he called after us.

I looked at Sanjeet askance, but he held out his calloused palm. I stared at our clasped hands as we stepped onto the lodestone. Warmth pulsed into my soles, and vibrations traveled up my legs, belly, and chest until my eardrums rang. We stepped again. The scene around us shimmered, and I could no longer see our hands. We continued to walk, blinded by a growing whirl of heat and wind, until at lasted we jolted to a stop.

"Names and reason for travel," a reedy voice said.

My vision was still blurry. Now we stood atop a new lodestone, slightly smaller than the last. This port rested inside a city; I could hear the bustle of carts and street criers outside the palisade wall. Shaking his head to clear it, Sanjeet produced our council seals.

"Welcome to Kofi-on-River," said the guard, stepping aside. "Enjoy your stay in Nyamba, Anointed Honors."

I smiled at him shakily and stepped off the stone. The world tilted, but Sanjeet caught my elbow. "Inn," he said, clutching his stomach, and I nodded.

"The best accommodations are toward the city center," the guard called after us. "I'd be wary today though, Anointed Honors. The streets are rowdy."

When we reached the city square, indignant roars echoed off the stone high-rises. Smoke rose to the sky, and Nyambans shrieked objections from every direction, crowded around something I couldn't see.

"That's not fair—"

". . . older than the empire—"

"How dare you erase our griots' legacy—"

I gasped as an imperial crier yelled above the din, reciting words I recognized: Thaddace's Unity Edict. I hadn't known it would be enforced so soon. Sanjeet stood head and shoulders above the crowd, and grew rigid as he watched the square.

"What do you see?" I demanded. When he didn't answer, I elbowed my way through the angry citizens.

A towering bonfire burned in the square. Imperial Guard warriors wrestled drums and scrolls from a trembling line of griots. The stories—some no doubt hundreds, thousands of years old—were cast into the flames. The imperial crier thanked each griot curtly, and handed them new drums and crisp imperial scrolls.

My face grew wet with tears, and I stepped back into the crowd, back, back, until strong hands found my shoulders.

"We should go," grunted Sanjeet.

"Why take their drums?" I asked dazedly. "Isn't taking their stories enough?"

"The drums carry their own stories," Sanjeet reminded me grimly. "I guess Thaddace and the emperor didn't want to risk it."

We found an inn several streets away. When night came I tossed and turned, though this time our room had wood floors, and sweet-smelling down pallets instead of straw mats.

Thaddace had made the Unity Edict sound so reasonable. He had been right—the disunity at Ebujo had been disastrous. If the realms had only put aside their differences and worked together, fewer people would have died. But . . .

I remembered a griot from the town square, an old woman with sad, sunken eyes, wailing as her drum was wrenched away.

"That can't be right," I mumbled. Could it?

We were supposed to wait a month before traveling via lodestone again. We waited only a week. I was eager to find Melu . . . and to leave Kofi-on-River. When at last we left the town, the smoke of griot drums still stained the horizon.

The lodestone to Swana was ten miles west of the city, in a lush Nyamban valley. My stomach lurched as we crossed into Swana. When we came to a stop, I crawled across the lodestone and vomited over the edge.

"Names and reason for travel," came the expected demand.

An eerie feeling crept over my spine as I took in the lodestone port. I had been here only once before: when strangers had taken me from Bhekina House. My palms began to sweat. This was *her* turf. Her domain of power. Already I could see the walls of Bhekina House rising around me. I was a child again, friendless, windowless, trapped—

"Tar." Sanjeet was crouching beside me with a hand on my trembling back. "Your home realm is beautiful."

I blinked, staring dumbly at him, and then looked around.

"It's just like the memories you used to show me," said Sanjeet, sounding almost shy.

A copse of slender acacia trees and vibrant green grass surrounded us. The air was sweet with honeysuckle, and winked with whorls of lavender light. "Tutsu sprites," I whispered. "I haven't seen them since I was small."

"Those only exist where the land is especially fertile," said the Swana port guard, standing straighter with pride. I smiled weakly—even while trapped in his grassland, a little of Melu's blessing still remained in Swana. I wondered how much longer that magic would last.

The port was located in a secluded crossroads. As we left, our stomachs still sloshing from the lodestone, the sound of singing and plodding donkeys greeted us.

Oluwan and Swana bring his drum; nse, nse.
Dhyrma and Nyamba bring his plow; gpopo, gpopo.

"It's market day," I observed.

"Good," said Sanjeet, heading toward one of the caravans, which rocked with goods and gleeful children hanging off the sides. "We can ask for directions to Melu's pool. If they don't know, they can guide us to a town where someone does. Maybe they'll even give us a lift." When I didn't follow him, he glanced back quizzically.

"I used to watch them," I said quietly. "From my window. I used to dream about joining them and having a family. About being . . . normal."

The corner of Sanjeet's mouth lifted. "You can be a market girl today, if you like, I won't tell. Imperial Guard gear might give you away, though."

When Sanjeet and I approached the caravan, the family's singing died. They eyed our uniforms, stiffening.

"We don't have any griot drums," said a bearded man in hoop earrings. "No scrolls either."

My eyes widened. "Oh, we aren't—"

"Check if you must," said the man, uncovering the cart's load. "We were already stopped twice in Pikwe Village."

Wrappers in starry patterns shone from the cart: wax-dyed cloth of blue and maize yellow, beet purple and fuchsia. Rainbow-beaded bangles winked in the sunlight, waiting to be stacked on the arms of Swana lords and ladies. Thankfully, native clothing was not illegal under Thaddace's edict. But how long until this merchant's sales dwindled? How long until villagers and townspeople bowed to the pressure of empire cloth?

"We'd like to buy your whole stock," I blurted.

Everyone, including Sanjeet, gaped at me.

"I'll need my purse," I told Sanjeet. "Just for now." Puzzled, he retrieved my coin purse from the pouch around his neck. I selected three gold coins and offered them to the merchant.

"I am an honest man, lady warrior," the apparel merchant stammered. "That is twice what I profit in a year. One gold and some coppers would more than suffice."

"Two golds for the stock. The rest for you to finish your journey, and give the clothes away for free at the market. Color the whole town in your beautiful fabric."

Sanjeet and I gave false names, and learned the merchant was called Tegoso. We traveled in his mule-drawn cart for eight miles, and he introduced us to his four daughters and one son, the latter of whom had not yet been born. His wife and fellow merchant, Keeya, pressed my hand to her belly.

"I know it is a boy," she told me. Keeya was a plump, frank-voiced woman with cornrowed braids that fell to her hips. "I always know. I want to name him Bopelo, after his grandfather. But Tegoso thinks Overcomer or Peacemaker would be best. Good Arit names, he says. Meanings that everyone can understand. I tell him Swana people understand Bopelo just fine." She laughed, then sighed and said, "My husband will have his way, in the end. We need the reward money for our daughters' schooling."

I grimaced, remembering the edict's incentives for

giving children empire names. Rashly, I slipped another coin from my purse and pressed it into Keeya's palm. "For Bopelo," I said. When she gasped, I winked and added, "I think Tegoso will come around."

Keeya fussed maternally over my yarn-plaited hair, admiring the gold accents but gasping at the roots. "So tight, ah-ah! This is how fancy ladies are wearing braids in Oluwan? Cutting off the air to their brains?"

I shrugged. "I don't mind."

"Doesn't it hurt?"

"Only when I think about it. It's better this way," I explained. "Everything under control."

I asked about Melu's pool. Keeya told us that only one kind of creature could help us find an ehru: tutsu sprites. A blind hermit was said to have control over the tutsu, and she lived several miles north of the nearest market town. When we reached a dirt compound with a high, broken gate, Tegoso stopped the cart.

"Old Mongwe lives in there," he said, helping Sanjeet and me down. We wobbled, still queasy from the lodestone. "She helps travelers. It's the duty of her holy order, the priests of the Clay. If she cannot find Melu, she can at least settle your stomachs." He dimpled. "I suspect most imperial warriors do not have such refined accents, nor do they carry purses full of gold coins. But I will not ask your true names. Go well. If ever you pass through Pikwe Village, know you have a friend in Tegoso."

He gave me three bangles, and a cobalt blue blouse

and wrapper dyed with yellow stars. Sanjeet received a flowing tunic in the same fabric. We waved until the melodic chants of Tegoso's daughters—*Black and gold, isn't he perfect?*—faded in the distance. Then we turned to a tiny thatch farmhouse. Beyond the gate, tendrils of acrid smoke rose from the overgrown courtyard.

"Are you just going to stand there?" called out a nasal voice. "The sprites said you two would be late, but they did not mention that you were dawdlers."

CHAPTER 21

WE CREPT UP THE SHORT DIRT PATH, through a broken gate, and into the courtyard. At first, I thought the mud-thatch house was covered in bits of glass. But every minute or so the clusters of bright specks moved, adjusting themselves in the sun. Tutsu. *Hives* of them.

A green mound rested by a cookfire. No, not a mound: a woman, barely four feet tall, wearing a cloak woven from fresh leaves and rushes. A wizened arm stuck out from the cloak, stirring a pot of bubbling brown slime.

"You have come on soap day," she complained. "If you had waited a week, I would have had solid bars. Eh! You will have to wash with mash. Beggars cannot be choosers. Not even fancy beggars in imperial armor."

A mud-and-stick mural of a woman's face splayed across the ground. Her nose was soft and broad, and her lips dark and full. Round stones swirled to form a crown of hair. I had not been brought up in a religious sect, but I had seen this sacred mural before. Mbali had tried to teach me how to make one, since Swana belonged to People of the Clay. The believers often meditated by assembling portraits of Queen Earth, made from natural or living materials.

Beyond the mural, a rough linen screen flapped on a clothesline. Behind it sat two washtubs, towels folded neatly over each rim. Waiting.

The woman turned her ear toward us when we didn't move, rustling the leaves on her hood. Her eyes were milky glass.

"Are you Old Mongwe?" I asked.

"No," said the Clay priestess with a straight face. "I am Mongwe the Newborn Babe. Old Mongwe is in the *other* sprite-covered earth shrine in the middle of the wilderness. Sit down and drink your tea, you tiresome child."

A kettle and two cups of golden liquid rested on mats beside her. We hesitated, then sat obediently and claimed the clay mugs. The tea didn't smell enchanted or poisoned, and the steam relieved my lodestone nausea instantly. Sanjeet frowned at Mongwe before taking a sip. "How did you know we were coming?"

Mongwe rolled her sightless eyes. "How could I not know? Those chatter-mouths love stray adventurers." She gestured toward her house, where tutsu hovered sleepily in the eaves. "All day they whine, '*Mongwe, a boy is on the road taking a magic cow to market. Mongwe, a dairy maid is running away to be with her true love. Mongwe, a wuraola and her friend have come to seek an ehru.*' You are all the same, young people. Full of questions and deaf to ugly answers.

268

Leaving your safe homes, your warm beds because—let me guess—you want to follow your heart." She laughed, a dry, wheezing sound. Then she turned back to her pot, stirring as she muttered. "Should a fool follow his heart? A thief? A murderer? Your heart is not your friend unless you know who you truly are."

"Thank you for the tea," I said after a confused pause. "What's a wuraola?"

"How should I know?" She sniffed the pot, then dumped it in a vat of ashes. "You will have a hard time convincing them to take you to Melu. Protective of alagbatos, the tutsu. Especially when it comes to *him*. The last time they helped someone find Melu . . . Well. He suffered."

I stared at the bottom of my teacup, heart sinking. If the tutsu knew that my mother had enslaved Melu, they would never help me.

"Name your price," Sanjeet told Mongwe. "The tutsu will listen to you. We'll pay anything."

She snorted. "Haven't the two of you slung gold around the savannah enough today? You will be robbed and toothless before the evening is out."

"Please," I begged. "Dayo's life depends—"

"What am I supposed to do? I am a priestess, not a sprite whisperer. You need a bath, a cure for the common cold, I'll help you. But tutsu?" She sucked her teeth. "I just let them nest on my home. In return, they keep beetles away from my yams. They also guide me to honeycomb, if they are feeling grateful. But other than that, I ask them no favors. You will just have to convince them that you are someone worth listening to."

I sighed, glancing at the roof. "At least they look calm."

Mongwe's cracked lips spread in a grin. "Those are only spritelings. It is their parents you will have to persuade." She cocked her head and sniffed the air, grimacing. "You smell like a frightened hare. Perhaps you should bathe first—"

"We don't have time," I said, standing. "Tell us where to go."

She pointed beyond the house, where knee-high grass rustled in an airy field. I realized then that the constant, high-pitched humming in the compound was not wind.

"Let me go alone," I told Sanjeet. "We wouldn't want to spook them."

When I crept into the soft, dense grass, the air throbbed with silvery voices, an army of mouths and wings I could not see. Specks of lavender light danced in intricate patterns above me. Some of them hovered close to my face, investigating my heavy braids, ash-covered arms, and borrowed imperial uniform. The tutsu whined and tittered, flying in circles until I felt dizzy.

I was being mocked.

"Understood," I muttered. "I'm a mess. But I'm guessing you know why I'm here. Please, I just need to find Melu. Don't you want Aritsar to be safe? I'm tired of being dangerous; help me be normal."

The tittering increased in pitch, drowning out my voice.

I bit my lip in frustration.

I tried again, struggling to be heard above the whining. "If I can break The Lady's hold on me, then Melu will be free too. Don't you care about him?"

The tutsu did not break their lazy patterns, continuing to swoop and dart as though I had not spoken. Even the few that hovered around me lost interest, going to join their brethren in the dance above my head.

I yelled and pleaded. I insulted. I even threatened to trap them in jars, like the merchants who sold sprites in markets. "You could be night lamps for all I care," I said. But nothing worked. The tutsu ignored me.

Hot-faced, I stomped back to Sanjeet. "It was worth a try," he said. "We can find Melu's pool another way."

I nodded grimly. "We'll visit every puddle in Swana if we have to." But my heart sank. Swana was the second-largest realm, bigger than Djbanti and Nyamba combined. It could take us weeks to find Melu's pool on our own. Months. And if The Lady had as many spies as I feared . . . she would find me long before then.

"Back already?" said Mongwe when we returned to the courtyard.

"They didn't care," I said. "Not about Melu's curse, or keeping Dayo safe—none of it. They don't care about anyone but themselves."

Mongwe laughed that dry, wheezy sound again. "Of course they don't."

"Then why did you let me try?"

Mongwe hummed, savoring the harsh, nutty smell wafting from her soap pot. "First lesson of growing tall," she said. "People never listen to what you want. They listen to who you are." She paused and cocked her head toward the house. "The tutsu are chanting about you, girl. They say there's someone you are desperate not to hurt."

I straightened, alert. "Yes, there is. Do they know how I can protect him?"

She listened. "No. They think your case is hopeless, for the most part, though the gem that he carries"—she pointed to Sanjeet—"will help."

Sanjeet blinked in surprise, then shyly drew a small, fiery object from his pocket. The sunstone I had given him on Nu'ina Eve; he had kept it. Even after calling me a monster.

"Maybe that's it," I whispered. "Maybe the stone can cure me."

"Of course it can't," Mongwe snorted. "I don't know what ails you, girl, but I know a sparkly bauble isn't medicine." She frowned, considering. "Sunstones *are* known to strengthen the will, however. In some. If you are tempted to do harm, a sunstone will not protect you. But it may make it easier, just a whit, to resist."

My heart sank, but when Sanjeet insisted, I took the stone, threading it through a leather tie meant for my hair and suspending it from my throat.

Mongwe smiled. "Now. Doesn't a bath sound nice?"

She had arranged the washtubs on opposite sides of

the linen screen. Still scowling, I stalked to one side and peeled off my grubby uniform, but I kept the sunstone on. Miles of dirt and dust chafed my skin, and when I lifted myself into the tub, my scowl melted away. The water was cool, and fragrant rosemary and neem leaves floated on the surface, clinging to my legs. I scrubbed with a lump of soap mash, still warm from Mongwe's pot. At first, I held my braids atop my head, craning my neck at awkward angles to protect each yarn plait from the water. The roots throbbed, and my scalp itched with sweat and grime. I paused then, noticing my shadow on the linen screen. My shape was contorted and stiff, like a rooster perched in a barnyard. I felt ridiculous.

So I plunged my head in.

A bubbled sigh escaped my lips as my roots soaked up the water. I could feel the yarn frizz, curls escaping from the tightly coiffed edges. *Unruly*, the palace braider fretted in my ear. *Shameful. Think of your title. Ladies rein every strand into place.*

But what title would ever describe me?

Assassin? High Judge Apparent? Puppet demon? Vanquisher of Bush-spirits? I had betrayed Dayo. I had saved his life. No yarn, no matter how tight, could hold back the jumble of contradictions that was Tarisai of Swana. I lathered my scalp and dunked the braids again, letting the suds froth around my ears.

When I emerged from the water, I gasped, braids streaming in a sopping mantle down my back. My limbs felt oddly light. I hummed as I wrung the plaits over the sweet-smelling water. After, I reached for my dusty Imperial Guard uniform, and then thought better of it. Instead I opened my travel pack, pulling out the starry blue garments from Tegoso.

What title can contain me?

The cotton chemise was soft, with sleeves that hung loosely to my elbows. Over the chemise I wound the wrapper, tying it snugly at my waist. I smiled, admiring the woven pattern as it clung to my hips.

Sanjeet was quiet for a moment when I stepped out from behind the screen. Then he said, "It suits you."

He had bathed and changed too. The kaftan from Tegoso looked imperious on his towering form, and droplets sparkled in his hair. "Ready to go?"

"Not until I've said goodbye," I said.

He followed me, puzzled, as I marched behind Mongwe's house and strode into the field of tutsu. They whined and tittered again, but I spoke louder, chin high.

"You don't have to help me," I told them, shaking my head of gloriously clean, wet hair. "But you will listen when I speak. You will listen, because there is no history I cannot see." My chest was burning, but this time it didn't hurt. Instead, the sunstone warmed over my heart, soaking up the heat, and sending it in pleasant tingles down my collarbone. I reached with my Hallow into the ground, consuming the births, deaths, and dances of a million sprites, drinking the tiny stories of power seeping into every blade and flower, every tree and anthill in the vast savannah.

"I am Tarisai of Swana," I murmured, "and I've seen your stories now. They belong to me, as mine belong to you. You don't have to help me change the world. But you mark my words; when I get going, this world will change. And you can be a part of that . . . or you can stand back and watch."

The field went quiet. The specks of light grew still, hovering like stars in the daytime. My heart thrummed in my ears.

Then the tutsu swarmed.

The specks of light dove at me with a deafening hum, surrounding me in a tunnel. I held up my hands in defense and heard Sanjeet cry out . . . but no pain came. Instead, warmth radiated over my skin as the tutsu streamed beneath my arms, over my shoulders, through my hair: a living breeze.

"They aren't attacking me," I yelled.

"No," Sanjeet yelled back, laughing incredulously. "They're choosing you."

My feet left the ground. As the tutsu continued to swirl, something fell into the grass. A length of yarn. Then another, and another. The tutsu unbraided my hair, removing the hundreds of plaits with blurring speed, until there was nothing left but my midnight cloud of hair, unbound and unyielding, bursting from my scalp in a dark halo.

The tutsu set me down at last, and then hovered at a distance. Waiting for orders.

I glanced back at Sanjeet. Mongwe had joined him at the field's edge, arms crossed.

"Well now," she said placidly. "Didn't I tell you a bath would help?"

CHAPTER 22

SANJEET AND I FOLLOWED THE TUTSU FOR what must have been several hours, though it seemed like minutes. My head floated on my shoulders. I realized then that I had suffered from a headache for days, and only now had it vanished.

As the tutsu swarmed above us, a low, rippling cloud across the savannah, I found myself babbling to Sanjeet: a side effect of my new, weightless freedom. I told him the stories I had made up when I lived in Swana, as a child forced to watch the world through a window.

"This savannah might as well have been Biraslov," I said, catching a jewel-toned dragonfly as it hummed past. I cupped the annoyed creature in my hands, drinking in its memories of sparkling ponds and seas of grass. "I'd never gone farther than the Bhekina compound. I forced my tutors to describe things I couldn't see—villages, markets, weddings. I'd make a picture in my mind, and put myself inside. My favorite story was called *school*. I made up six brothers and sisters, and an evil school mistress who paddled us. I'd never been spanked before. I thought it sounded exciting." Sanjeet laughed, and I let the dragonfly escape. "My tutors wouldn't dare touch me. They were too afraid I'd steal their memories. I would have been spoiled rotten, if The Lady hadn't sent me away." I glanced dubiously at Sanjeet. "Were you *ever* naughty as a boy? I can't imagine it." Sanjeet had more self-control than anyone I knew. Even now, as we walked, he was shortening his stride to match mine, every movement a conscious decision.

Sanjeet looked thoughtful. "I was taller than my mother at eight years old," he said after a pause. "By eleven, I'd passed Father. They forgot that I was still a child, and so I stopped being one. Mistakes were expensive. I broke things all the time, awkward with my own strength. And once I figured out my Hallow, well." He grimaced, then shrugged. "Emotions were expensive too. I could see any person's weakness, and so revenge was . . . easy for me. Effortless. I realized it was safer not to feel. If I was never too happy, then no one could make me sad. And if I was never sad or angry, then I would never hurt someone. Except in the fighting pits, of course. When Father made me."

He spoke casually, as though recounting someone else's life instead of his own. Sadness welled in my stomach as I examined him anew, remembering every time I had watched that face smooth into passive stone. I had always assumed he was shutting the world out . . . not shutting himself in.

I slipped my hand in his. "We were both of us raised in cages."

His fingers curled slowly around mine. "I guess that's how we survived the Children's Palace."

The sun was low in the sky, dyeing the savannah in red and gold. The tutsu were slowing down, congregating over a scatter of trees in the distance.

"That's it," I muttered. Then I laughed, breaking into a run. "We did it! That's it—that's Melu's pool."

When we arrived, the clearing was just as I remembered. The sighing brush, the purple and white river lilies, bobbing on their tall, slender stems. The amber pool was mirror glass, reflecting the tutsu, who hung like stars against the reddening sky. Far off, the rooftops of Bhekina House smoldered in the setting sun. I shivered. Did The Lady know I was here?

I remembered the man with cobalt-fire wings, bending over me with those warm, slanted eyes, placing a finger on my brow: *I bargained with The Lady for the privilege of naming you.*

I had missed Melu, I realized with a pang. I had never craved a father, at least, not as I had craved The Lady. But that night in the savannah, the ehru had made me feel . . . seen. Had he missed me too?

I scanned the clearing eagerly—but instead of a blazing man, a dark, narrow form rested on its side by the pool. It did not move as we approached. Blue wings lay dormant in the dust, smoldering like a waning fire.

"Melu," I breathed. I rushed to his side, not daring to touch the long, shimmering limbs. "No. Don't be dead. Please don't be dead."

Silence. Then a dry chuckle. "Alas," Melu said, "death is a wish I may not grant. No matter how deeply I long for it."

I blinked, taken aback. Laboriously, the ehru roused his pole-like body and stood, wings twitching as they shook off dirt. The Lady's emerald cuff still glinted on his forearm, and the whole savannah seemed to shudder as Melu gazed down and sighed.

"Oh, daughter. Why did you have to come back?"

It was not the greeting I had imagined.

I stammered after a pause, "You know why, Melu. To break The Lady's bond. To free us from the curse."

"And how do you propose to do that here? The Kunleo boy is miles, leagues away."

I glared. "You know I refuse to hurt him."

He turned away. "As long as you keep running from him, you will always be The Lady's plaything. And I will always be her caged bird."

My hands clenched into fists. Sanjeet, who stared up at the ehru with horror and wonder, placed a restraining hand on my arm. "Tar."

I had heard once that alagbatos were difficult to persuade. They were wary of sharing secrets with mortals, even in the direst of circumstances. But I had seen deep into Melu's gold-flecked eyes, gazing at a spark identical to one in myself. Melu had given me his pride: a trait as old as the Swana sky, and as deeply rooted as the grasslands.

"Are you telling me," I said coolly, "that the mighty, all-knowing guardian of Swana has *no idea* how to free himself?" Sanjeet's grasp tightened, but I shook him off and stalked after Melu, refusing to let the ehru turn his back on me. The sunstone warmed on my chest. "Are you telling me that hurting an innocent person—*killing* Dayo—is the only way for an alagbato to be free of a human's whim?"

Melu stiffened.

"You're too strong to let a mortal decide your fate," I told him. "And you sure as hell aren't going to decide mine."

Sanjeet swore and fumbled for his weapon halter as Melu began to glow, radiating blue heat like a smoldering coal. The ehru hovered closer, closer, bending down until his shimmering face was level with mine.

Then he smiled, giving a deep-throated chuckle.

"Put away your sword, Dhyrma boy," the ehru said. "My daughter has nothing to fear from me." He touched my brow with a long, slender finger. "You were well-named, *Behold-What-is-Coming*."

"Then tell me," I demanded. "How do I break The Lady's hold on me?"

Melu considered. "Only one thing is more powerful than a wish, and that is a purpose."

"You'll have to be more specific than that."

Melu's wings stirred with agitation, as if he struggled

for the right words. "Every creature has a purpose. A place in a grand story, a tale as old and pure as life, and stronger than any mortal's wish. To diverge from the path your mother has set, you must find your place in that grand story. Otherwise, The Lady will decide your place for you. That is all I know." Melu paused, looking ashamed. "Killing the Kunleo boy was a simpler solution, and that is why I urged you to do it. But I see now that your fate will never be simple, and if you are ever to find your purpose, then you must know who you really are. You must know who The Lady is."

My pulse quickened. "Tell me everything."

Melu rose again, ascending until he hovered over the smooth amber pool. "I will tell you, and show you." The pool's surface rippled, and from its depths a young face appeared.

It was Dayo. No—a boy who looked like him, playing with wooden spears in the Children's Palace. The pool rippled again, showing a council woman who had just given birth, cradling a baby girl. A barrage of moving pictures illustrated Melu's words as he spoke.

"An emperor sires many children in his lifetime. But you only ever hear of one: the Raybearer. Any other heirs are considered irrelevant. As a result, Kunleo daughters— and Rayless sons—are born without fanfare, sent away after weaning, adopted by nobles who raise them away from court.

"By custom, Kunleo girls are not christened. But when

a daughter was born to Olugbade's father, the young crown prince took a liking to her. Prince Olugbade's sister was so beautiful, clever, and precocious, he gave her a nickname: The Lady."

Cold washed through my veins and froze, rooting me in place. I shook my head, slowly, and did not stop shaking it until the story was done.

"The Lady worshipped her older brother. At night she would steal away from her nursery to Olugbade's bed, lisping his name. The prince was flattered. Breaking centuries of custom, he brought The Lady to the Children's Palace, where he kept her as his pet. For many moons, Olugbade showered The Lady with trinkets. He taught her at his knee, and for as long as The Lady was young and ignorant, Olugbade loved her.

"But one day, The Lady began to interrupt Olugbade's lectures. She started to talk circles around him in history and philosophy, stumping him with riddles and beating him at chess. Olugbade had suffered from a stutter in his youth, and had a tendency to ramble. But when The Lady opened her mouth, entire rooms hushed to listen.

"The prince began to shun The Lady. Confused by her brother's growing coldness, the girl threw herself into her studies even more. Surely, she thought, being useful would win her brother's love again. She haunted the halls of the Children's Palace like a charming ghost. She befriended the candidates who vied for Olugbade's council, slipping them hints on how to pass each trial. Olugbade had tried the Ray on many children. But the test always failed.

"Prince Olugbade was an intelligent boy, thoughtful and quiet. But behind his gentle manner, he had one weakness: a crippling fear of intimacy. With inferiors, Prince Olugbade was kind and generous. But with equals, he was closed and paranoid. He required constant proof of their love and loyalty, recoiling at the slightest hint of criticism. All but the most patient children found him exhausting. The Lady understood Olugbade better than anyone, and would have loved him, if he had let her. But for reasons that Olugbade could not put into words, The Lady's effortless charisma filled him with rage.

"Months passed, and The Lady's friends tripled. From her divan in the playroom corner, always crowded with giggling candidates, she watched her lonely brother with pity. If only he would look at her. If only he would see her: the *real* Lady, a partner, not a pet. She could make up for all his weaknesses. They would be a team, a family, and everything would go back to the way it was before.

"So The Lady plotted. A spark had nestled in her breast from the moment she was born, an ember she had never dared coax into flame. According to the priests, her spark should not exist. Its presence was impossible; an arrogance, an abomination, and so for years she had suppressed the ember out of shame. But now, she thought, perhaps that spark was just what she needed.

" 'I want to show you something,' she told Olugbade at supper. The Lady was ten years old, and her brother, fifteen. Around them, candidates laughed and chattered. She sat at his side as he reclined in the Children's Palace banquet hall, letting servants feed him grapes and plantain.

"'Another of your dolly plays?' Olugbade smiled down at his sister. 'I've told you, Lady. Princes don't have time for toys.'

"'I don't write dolly plays,' The Lady snapped. Then she exhaled, determined to keep her temper. 'I write debates. About the empire. I do act them out with my dolls, sometimes, but I wouldn't need to if you read them, brother—'

"'Don't call me brother,' Olugbade chided patiently. 'Raybearers have no blood kin, only council. Remember that, Lady.'

"'I wasn't going to show you dolls.'

"'What, then?' Olugbade sighed. 'Will it take long?'

"The Lady knelt close to him, heart pounding with excitement. The banquet spread out before them at a long, low table. 'Tell me what you want to eat. Anything you see. Whisper it in my ear.'

"Olugbade rolled his eyes . . . but his expression grew soft. He liked his sister this way: anxious, desperate for his attention. It felt much better than when she beat him at chess. 'Very well,' he said, patting her beaded braids. 'Bring me some *moi moi* pudding.'

"She focused for a moment, then looked up, grinning. A child at the far end of the dinner table rose and came over, offering the prince a wobbling cake of *moi moi* bean pudding.

"Olugbade blinked. 'How did you . . .'

" 'Ask for something else,' The Lady said, clapping her hands.

"Olugbade's jaw ticked. 'Saltfish. Yam stew. Fried *chin chin.*' He barely spoke above a breath. But around the room, two more children shot up and hurried over with the dishes.

"By now, the other candidates were watching, curious. The Lady gathered her courage. She drew herself up and announced, 'I told them with my mind.'

"The room fell deathly still.

" 'These three candidates'—she gestured at the food-bearing children—'are my friends. *More* than friends, brother. They can be yours too.'

" 'Impossible,' rasped Olugbade.

" 'Don't you see?' The Lady said. 'I can do it again—'

" 'You can't have that power. You don't. It's not the will of Am.'

" 'I don't know what Am wants,' said The Lady. 'But I know my friends can hear me. Maybe they could hear you too.' The Lady swallowed hard. 'Maybe we could share a council.'

"Dishes crashed in every direction as Olugbade leapt to his feet. His nostrils flared—and then he inhaled, arranging his features in a fatherly smile. 'I am disappointed in you, Lady. Your vain little games have gone too far. You should not play at usurping a crown prince of the empire.'

" 'Usurping?' stammered The Lady. 'No. I just— I thought we could be partners.'

"Olugbade laughed quietly. 'You? Partners with a Raybearer?'

" 'But I have the Ray too,' she blurted.

"The dining hall went completely silent.

"The Lady gulped, clutching her linen wrapper to keep her hands from shaking. 'I stole pelican oil from the temple. I anointed my friends because you needed a council, and because . . . I'm *good* at ruling people, brother. You've had trouble with the Ray. But I haven't. We could join forces. We could rule as Kunleos. Together.'

"Olugbade's pupils dilated, and muscles tensed beneath his gold-encrusted tunic. 'The priests were right,' he whispered. 'I should never have kept a girl as a pet. Spoiled her. Let her *play* at statecraft, humored her . . .' He stopped, fists shaking, staring at The Lady with cold determination. 'You will leave Oluwan by tomorrow morning. You and your traitor friends.'

"The Lady trembled, eyes pooling with disbelief. 'Leave the realm? But where will we go?'

" '*Out*,' Olugbade snarled in a rare loss of temper, upending the banquet table. The children whom The Lady had anointed flocked to her protection.

"The Lady reached for a child who still lingered behind the table. 'Come with me, Mbali,' she said. 'I can anoint you too. You're better than this place. Leave him.'

"Young Mbali gazed at The Lady with tortured indecision. 'I want to help Aritsar,' she whispered at last. 'But . . . I can do better work here, with the prince.

Still . . .' She glanced nervously back at Olugbade. *I believe you*, she mouthed at The Lady. *You have the Ray too.* Then she turned away, going to stand by Olugbade's side.

"The Lady's lower lip trembled. 'You will regret choosing him over me.'

" 'Guards,' roared Olugbade.

"The Lady and her friends fled from the banquet hall, and were never seen by the palace again. Where The Lady went, or how she survived all these years, is a tale too long for one night. Suffice it to say: The world is not kind to a girl it wishes dead. Years of cruelty soured her own kindness. Her heart calcified to a self-preserving stone. And soon, Arits would trade tales of a strange new cult traveling across the empire: a bandit ring of abandoned, Hallowed children, led by a nameless child queen.

"Eventually, Olugbade's fear of intimacy lightened. He successfully anointed a council of his own, and in every courtier home, the tale of The Lady was silenced or forgotten.

"But every night, ever since that banquet at the Children's Palace, the emperor has paced the An-Ileyoba halls, blind and deaf to any who try to comfort him.

" 'She was nothing,' he repeats, long into the night. 'Nothing. There is only one.' He grips the lion mask that hangs around his neck. 'There is only one.' "

CHAPTER 23

THE POOL RIPPLED, AND OLUGBADE'S TWISTED face disappeared into its depths. I collapsed to my knees, as though only Melu's voice had kept me upright. The sun had dipped below the horizon, and the living constellations of tutsu provided the only light.

"My mother is a Raybearer." I said the words, but did not believe them. Craving normalcy, I looked up at Sanjeet. "There are no female Raybearers." I expected him to nod in agreement. Instead he was frozen, staring at me in wonder.

"I knew it," he said.

"What in Am's name is that supposed to mean?"

"I wasn't sure for a while," he said, his gaze distant. "That spark, that . . . *heat* I saw around you when we first met . . . it disappeared when you made yourself forget your past. Still, the spark came back, sometimes. When you were very happy, or very angry. I had doubts, but never quite stopped believing . . ." He laughed, shaking his head. "I was right."

"I don't understand."

"You glow like Dayo," he said. "The heat that draws people, that makes them want to trust him, follow him . . . I felt it the first day I met you."

I staggered to my feet, shaking my head. "That's treason. Stop it. Believing in folktales won't do us any—"

"The fire in the Children's Palace," he interrupted, pacing. "I thought I was going crazy, or that my eyes were playing tricks on me. You didn't have a single burn, not one. But it makes sense now," he said. "You're immune to fire. You were born that way, just like Dayo was born immune to poison."

"That's because The Lady was protecting me. Or because I'm half-ehru," I insisted, but Melu shook his head while still hovering above the pool.

"The Lady has no special ability to protect anyone. And while your alagbato blood provided your ability to see memories, the rest of you is human."

"There are no female Raybearers," I repeated, and Sanjeet crossed his arms.

"What about Aiyetoro?"

"She was an exception," I said, parroting the priests from Oluwan. "Am only chose her because the emperor's son died, and Aritsar needed a leader . . ." My voice trailed off. Who could prove that Aiyetoro had not been born with the Ray? She had been sent away at birth, just like every other Kunleo girl. Doubt wormed its way into my mind, but I resisted it, stubbornly. "The Lady couldn't be a Raybearer, because Olugbade already has the Ray. There can only be one per generation."

"Why?"

"Because—because—" I quailed, trying to remember the careful lines of reasoning the priests had taught in our catechism. "Because that would mean war. A man and a woman couldn't *share* rights to the crown. How would they rule?"

"Together," Melu replied, and the answer's simplicity unnerved me.

I scowled at the ehru. This was all wrong. There could not be two Raybearers. The empire could not have been mistaken for dozens, for *hundreds* of years.

"And if the two rulers disagree?" I shot back. "What then?"

The ehru shrugged. "Defer to their council. Flip a coin. Divide tasks according to their strengths. Compromise." He sighed. "I've never understood why mortals make things so complicated. Am's story for men and women has always been simple: You are equals, built to work side by side. But when it comes to power, mortals have always loathed simplicity."

"Olugbade and The Lady could never rule together," I insisted.

"On that point," Melu conceded, "I'm afraid you are correct. Olugbade's fear of The Lady has festered for too long, as has The Lady's anger at him. She means to erase Olugbade's entire legacy, including Ekundayo. But the prince's story is yet unwritten—as is yours." He descended, pool rippling in his wake. "You have seen the mask of the emperor, and the mask of your prince. They were forged by Warlord Fire himself, and the story of their creation is etched in the crypts of An-Ileyoba. Should a mortal translate those ancient words, she would see Warlord Fire created not two masks, but four. Four Raybearers. Emperor and empress. Prince and princess."

"Then we can prove it," said Sanjeet. "We can prove that Tarisai's a Raybearer. If we present the masks to the priests, they'll have to admit it."

"For that very reason," said Melu, "the other two masks have been lost. Aiyetoro was the last to see them. And as they were forged beyond this realm, I cannot track them through the earth. But you must find them, I think. I do not know Tarisai's purpose, but she shall never obtain it without first claiming her name."

"My purpose is Dayo," I said. The world was spinning. Mbali's voice in the Children's Palace, the words I had repeated every day for five years, roared in my ears. *Why do I live? So that I can serve the Prince, the Chosen Raybearer of Aritsar, and aspire to be one of his anointed. Because I love him more than life itself . . .*

"Stories are meant to be shared," Melu said gently, "but no one was *made* for another person, Tarisai."

"No." I remembered the moment I had pierced Dayo in the gut. I purposely resurrected my old panic, my armor of fear and self-loathing. *You are dangerous*, I told myself. *Freedom for you will always mean harm for Dayo.*

But the harder I tried to remember my treachery, the more I saw the tutsu. I saw them whirl around me, lifting the weight from my scalp and humming their choice.

"What's a wuraola?" I asked Melu.

"Ah . . . I have not heard that name in many years." He cocked his head. "A wuraola is a girl made of gold. A girl . . . full of sunshine."

Sanjeet grinned. "Of course it is," he said. "Tar, it all makes sense. This is what's wrong with Aritsar. Why the Imperial Guard's attempts at unity have always failed. This is why the empire never truly came together. Don't you see? We were never meant to be ruled by one man. If you and Dayo—"

"I'm not ruling anyone," I snapped. "I never said I wanted to be empress."

"You've never said it," he retorted. "But . . . I think you've always known."

I tried to deny it . . . But memories made my throat close up. The restless nights I had spent in the Children's Palace and in Yorua Keep, heaping piles of ice on my chest so the burning, the flame I kept hidden, would disappear. The countless times I had blinded myself to Dayo's faults, white-knuckling my intellect into submission. Pretending that his decisions were best. Pretending I couldn't have done it better.

"I don't know what I am," I said. "But believing in me could be dangerous, Jeet. And I'm tired of hurting you. I'm tired of hurting everyone."

"I swore to serve the Raybearers of Aritsar, Tarisai," he said. "I intend to keep my vows."

I pressed my lips together. "We should find shelter," I muttered. "It's not safe this close to Bhekina House."

"You have nothing to fear from The Lady," said Melu. "Not here."

I huffed in disbelief. "How can you be sure?"

"The Lady is not here. She was captured by Olugbade's forces shortly after you left her on Nu'ina Eve."

My veins ran cold. "What?"

"The emperor has never stopped looking for The Lady. Not once in thirty years," Melu explained. "And you ended up being just the bait that Olugbade needed. Your public appearance on Nu'ina Eve was The Lady's only chance to make you her weapon again. So she returned to Oluwan for the first time since her banishment, not knowing that the emperor's spies were waiting."

"What will he do to her?"

"I do not know. But death will not be enough for Olugbade. He has something to prove—to himself, as well as to the world."

Sanjeet pointed out, "If The Lady is a Raybearer, then the emperor can't kill her. Not if she has a council."

"During her banishment, she succeeded in anointing only ten council members." Melu shrugged. "This means she lacks an immunity. It will not take Olugbade long to discover which one."

"We can reach her before he finds out," I said. "Tell us

The Lady's weakness—we'll fool the emperor somehow. Make sure he doesn't use it."

The ehru was silent. Slowly, I read the coldness in Melu's face.

"You want her to die," I whispered. "You're *glad* Olugbade caught her."

"Her death will free us both," Melu replied. "If Olugbade wins, you will not have to kill Ekundayo. You need not claim your title as Raybearer, nor struggle to find your purpose. It is by far the simplest solution, and much faster than waiting for old age to claim her."

I reeled, wanting to shake him . . . but my limbs were numb. Melu's indifference was justified. The Lady had made him an ehru, and me a slave.

So why did my stomach turn at the thought of her suffering?

A battle festered inside me. The Lady was my mother: She had treasured me. The Lady was my enemy: She had created me to hurt people. But The Lady had been hurt as well. And though I still felt loyal to the emperor, I had begun to doubt his righteousness. Whatever he planned for The Lady, I suspected, would look nothing like justice.

"We'll save her without your help," I told Melu.

The ehru smiled. "Olugbade's strongholds are too strong even for you, daughter. The Lady's Hallowed council is her only chance of escape. One council member is here, at Bhekina House. She plots to free The Lady even as we speak."

"Good," I shot back. "Then we'll help her. Come on, Jeet. We'll spend the night at Bhekina House and leave at first light."

Melu frowned. "That house was not a happy chapter of your story. Are you sure you want to return?"

"That's none of your business."

Melu considered, and then made a smooth gesture. Several yards away, a canopy appeared in the clearing. Creamy draped linen billowed in the night breeze, tinted gold by lamps in the grass.

"I will not bother you any longer," he intoned. "But sleep here, and visit Bhekina House in the morning. The magic of that place is not gentle on one's mind. Remember this, Tarisai: No matter what happens, I will always be glad that I named you." Then he vanished in a cloud of dust.

"Let's go," I told Sanjeet, nudging him toward Bhekina House, but he looked uncertain.

"You could use the rest," he countered. "And the house is still far off. We can't see it from here."

"It's right there." I pointed. "We can ask The Lady's friends about Aiyetoro's masks. There might even be clues in the manor; we can search . . ." I trailed off as Sanjeet squinted at Bhekina House, his expression blank. "Oh. Right." My stomach sank. "The Lady wished for 'a stronghold that no one may see or hear.' Not unless she desires it." And if I could see those red rooftops, then The Lady wanted me to return. She wanted to keep me, as she had for years, in that windowless study. Her caged bird. Her Made-of-Me. I swallowed, stepping back.

"I'll go in the morning," I told Sanjeet. "It's . . . easier to search by daylight."

Melu's canopy arched over downy bedrolls on raised pallets. He had summoned satin pillows and baskets of dates and kola nuts. They were scattered on straw mats so fine, sprites must have woven them. Somehow, the canopy shielded us from mosquitoes and gadflies, and probably beasts as well, though Sanjeet still kept a scimitar by his pillow as we slept. I woke the next morning with my head on his shoulder, and his arm across my torso.

Mortifying, I thought, and did not move an inch.

Sanjeet's lashes twitched. Like me, I realized, he was too still to be truly sleeping. Mutually caught, we fumbled apart.

"Don't be shy on our account," called a familiar cheeky voice. "It's nice to see you two have made up."

Sanjeet's scimitar leapt into his hand, and we were both on our feet in seconds. Two figures, one tall and sullen, and one short and merry-faced, approached our canopy.

"Kirah!" I cried at the short figure, delighted. "And . . . *Woo In?*"

They rode a catlike beast that sent thrills up my spine. The luridly bright leopard was the size of a horse, each paw the width of two human hands. Its wily yellow eyes glowed even in daylight. I exhaled through my teeth. I had not seen Woo In's emi-ehran since the day the Children's

Palace had burned. It was no wonder Woo In had survived the Underworld with *that* as his protector.

Sanjeet tightened his grip on his scimitar, lowering into combat stance. "Wait," I said, touching his arm. "I know that beast."

Kirah waved and hopped down from the emi-ehran's back. A bandage covered one of her hands. Along with her gauzy prayer scarf, she wore the clothes of a Blessid priestess: a sand-colored tunic and pantaloons. They blew about her in a strangely sudden wind as she ran toward us. Sanjeet lowered his blade in confusion.

"You're all right," she gushed, suffocating us both in a hug. I inhaled her scent of cinnamon, dizzy with surprise and happiness. I had wondered if I would ever see Kirah again. Her cheek was hot against mine, and her lips were chapped and swollen.

"You're sick," I fretted. "Kirah, you're burning up."

Better by the second, she Ray-spoke, and Sanjeet and I replied in our minds, coaxing the jaundice of council sickness from her skin.

"I can't tell you," she whispered, "how good that feels."

"Your fever's going down," said Sanjeet, scanning her with his Hallow. "Thank Am you're no worse. How long have you gone without the Ray?"

"Only two weeks."

"*Only* two?" I scolded. "You could have gone mad!"

"That doesn't happen for a month. At least, that's what he says." She tossed her head back at Woo In. "And he would know. But never mind that. Tar, I've never seen you wear your hair loose; it's glorious."

Sleep had flattened my puffy coils. I pulled at the hair in fistfuls, restoring its cloud shape, then crossed my arms. "You won't change the subject that easily," I said. "Why are you traveling with *Woo In*? Why are you here at all? How did you find us?" My fingers rose, itching to seize the answers from her memories. "Is Dayo—"

"Dayo's fine," she said, laughing and batting my hand away. "Only a scar left. And our whole council was summoned to An-Ileyoba, so I had to come fetch you and Jeet. As for Woo In—" Acid flashed in Kirah's large hazel eyes. "Well. He's using me. At least, that's what he's been telling himself." She added in a stage whisper, "It's not working out very well."

Woo In descended from his mount, haughtily graceful as always, but he winced at Kirah's words. He looked . . . guilt-ridden.

"What in Am's name is going on?" I snapped at him. "What are you doing with my council sister?"

He bowed, using that gossamer voice I had once known so well. "It has been too long, Lady's Daughter." He looked much sicker than Kirah, with sunken cheeks and dry, wan lips. Along with the purple veins of the Underworld, fever sweat shimmered on his bare chest. Coughing, he patted the emi-ehran's flank. "You remember Hyung."

"Of course," I said. "We met the night you tried to burn down a palace full of children."

Woo In stiffened, growing even more ashen. "We took measures to ensure none would die," he replied. "No one except—"

"An innocent boy who had never hurt anyone," snarled Kirah.

My brows shot into my hairline. "Wait. You know about Woo In setting the fire? Who told you?"

"He did. He told me a lot of things. And for someone so determined to be free, he acts an awful lot like a puppet."

"I have nothing against your prince," Woo In murmured. "Kirah, please. I was just following orders. I was trying to prevent *more* deaths—"

"How do you even know Woo In?" I blurted, head swiveling back and forth between them. The tenderness in his tone, as well as the flush in Kirah's cheeks, was beginning to make me uneasy. "I haven't seen him since our council was crowned at Ebujo. And even then, I didn't remember who he was."

"I met him on the road," she replied. "He was following me—and he's been spying on us! Remember how we used to sit on the Children's Palace roof? He was there, all last year. Listening."

"Following orders," he repeated wearily.

If Kirah was right, then Woo In had heard my most vulnerable secrets: my dreams, lusts, worries. And by eavesdropping on us . . . I stiffened as Woo In stammered excuses at Kirah. In the last year, he had gotten to know her, as well. He had grown . . . *fond* of her.

Sanjeet came to stand between them, scrutinizing Kirah's right hand, which was heavily bandaged.

"This is fractured," Sanjeet growled, rounding on Woo In. "If you laid a hand on my council sister— If you threatened—"

"Actually," Kirah said calmly, "I threatened *him*. I first met Woo In on my way from Yorua. He stopped me in the road, so I pulled a knife. It didn't come to blows then. He only wanted to know where Tarisai had gone, thinking the emperor might have taken her, like he took—" She broke off and gasped. "Oh, Tar. I'm so sorry—"

"It's all right," I said. "We know what happened to The Lady."

"If he didn't fight you, then what happened to your hand?" asked Sanjeet.

"Oh—" Kirah winced at her fingers. "This happened yesterday. His face was denser than I thought."

Only then I noticed the bruise on Woo In's cheek. "You punched him," I said in shock. "Did he . . . Did he try to—"

"Of course not," Woo In rasped. "I would never disrespect a woman that way. I would never hurt Kirah in *any* way. I was just—"

"He confessed about trying to kill Dayo," Kirah said. "That's why I hit him. Before that . . ." She frayed the edge of her prayer scarf. "We were getting along, actually."

Why would Woo In tell Kirah the worst thing he'd ever done? "Why are you traveling together?" I asked, shaking my head to clear it. "And how did you get here so quickly?"

"Besides riding Hyung? We flew." She paused. "I didn't know anyone could fly until Woo In showed me. In Nyamba, we flew up a mountain at sunset. I'd never seen anything so—" She stopped, turning pink. "Anyway. He knew the way to Bhekina House, and I would never have found it without him. He didn't have to bring me along, but he needed a way to influence you. At least, that's what he said. So here I am: his leverage." She beamed at me. "Is it working?"

I laughed and Kirah smiled, though her expression hardened. For the first time, she rounded on Woo In.

"You're a fool to serve The Lady, you know," she said. "So what if she promised to free the Redemptors? You don't even know how she plans to do it—and you've served her for years! She doesn't care about innocent Songland children, Woo In. For Am's sake—she tried to kill Dayo. Her own nephew!"

"She cares," Woo In insisted. "You don't know her."

"And you do?" Kirah snorted. "Is The Lady your lover or something?"

"Don't be absurd," Woo In spat. Then he sighed, collecting his temper. "The Lady found me when I was a boy, Kirah. I had only just escaped from the Underworld. Everyone else saw a cursed child, but The Lady saw a son. She was a mother to me, and a friend." He paused, staring hard at Kirah's sandals. "I should not have tried to kill your prince," he whispered. "I was young, and desperate, and I'm sorry. The Lady told me it was the only way. That to free the Redemptors, Olugbade and his line must be vanquished, and The Lady crowned—" He broke off, glancing at me in alarm.

"Crowned empress," I finished for him. "I know who The Lady is, Woo In."

Kirah peered at me, reading the surprise and guilt on my face. "Tar . . . How long have you known that you're a Kunleo?"

"How long have *you*?"

Kirah exchanged a glance with Sanjeet over my head. "Years," she admitted. "I mean, I didn't know for sure until Woo In told me. But Jeet and I always suspected you had the Ray. Some clues were small: tics, mannerisms you share with Dayo. But there was something else. A *haze* around you sometimes, when you're angry, or happy. Or sad."

I shifted my feet. "You shouldn't have come looking for me. It isn't safe."

"I didn't have a choice." Kirah searched her pockets and produced a calfskin scroll. The seal had been broken. "I had to make sure it was urgent," she said. "Jeet, there's one for you too. Our whole council has been summoned to the capital."

I scanned the familiar burnt script of Thaddace's Hallow-writing.

IMPERIAL SUMMONS

*His Anointed Honor, High Judge Thaddace the Just, in the name of
His Imperial Highness, Olugbade of Aritsar*

Bids Tarisai, Apprentice Delegate of Swana and High Judge Apparent

To present herself at An-Ileyoba Palace

In preparation for her First Ruling Ceremony

Which shall take place

On the 75th day of Dry Season.

CHAPTER 24

"THE SEVENTY-FIFTH?" I SAID. "BUT THAT'S . . ."
I counted in my head. "Four months from now. I've barely
trained for *six*. Thaddace said my First Ruling wouldn't
happen for years."

Kirah looked suspicious. "What ruling does he expect
you to pass?"

I shrugged. "It's stupid. 'Orphan Day': a holiday for rich
people to spoil poor children before tossing them back on
the streets."

"Sounds like a move to please the nobles," Sanjeet said.
"Maybe Thaddace needed a distraction from The Lady's
arrest. Something to amuse the court, so they don't gossip
about a second Raybearer."

"But why summon our whole council?"

Sanjeet frowned at his scroll. "Looks like we all have duties.
High General Wagundu wants me to drill with the emperor's
personal guard. Later this year, I'm to help lead a campaign."

Kirah cocked her head. "Against who? No one has
attacked the continent in decades."

"Against our own people," Sanjeet said grimly. "We're to lay siege to any city that fails to comply with the Unity Edict."

Kirah shuddered. "The emperor summoned me to help Mbali write new chants of prayer," she said. "All priests and priestesses are encouraged to adopt a Book of Common Song, faith traditions no longer separated by Clay, Well, Ember, and Wing."

"That sounds like a disaster. How could the emperor—" I began, but stopped when I remembered Woo In. It didn't feel right to criticize Olugbade in front of someone determined to bring him down. I hated how the emperor had treated my mother, but the candidate catechism still echoed in my ears. "I'm sure the emperor and his council don't mean to harm anyone," I mumbled, correcting myself. "They only want peace."

"Peace," Woo In said, "is different than silence." His face had grown paler. Hyung's yellow eyes flashed, and Sanjeet's hand went again to his scimitar. But the beast only bent its massive head, licking Woo In's cheek.

When Woo In succumbed to a violent round of coughs, I gestured to Melu's canopy. "You should lie down." I still hadn't forgiven Woo In for setting the palace fire, but we shared an uneasy kinship. We both had loved The Lady, and tried to kill for her.

He nodded and staggered over to a pile of cushions, smiling. "Don't worry, Lady's Daughter," he said. "Help is on the way."

Sanjeet's head snapped up, locking on a figure approaching from Bhekina House: a rippling smudge of green. Energy crackled faintly in the air, almost like someone was . . . Ray-speaking.

"Don't have a conniption," Woo In said aloud, in apparent response to a voice I could not hear. "Am's Story, you're almost as bad as my *real* big sister."

The stranger's cloak blew around her as she stormed under the canopy, doffing her deep green hood. "Honestly, it's no wonder Crown Princess Min Ja disowned you," the woman sniffed.

"Kathleen," I breathed.

She ignored me, placed her hands on Woo In's chest, and shut her eyes. The crackling energy intensified, and healthy color flooded Woo In's lips. Kathleen examined him, and when it was clear his strength had returned, she slapped him.

He only laughed. "I've missed you too, Kat."

"Really?" Kathleen demanded. "Really? First The Lady gets captured, then you disappear for *three weeks* without contacting a single council member? I was worried sick, Woo In. We thought you were dead."

"You're the one who ignored orders," he retorted. "Fleeing to the safehouse the moment there was trouble—"

"It was standard procedure," she hissed. "If The Lady is taken, her council returns to Bhekina and regroups. That was the plan."

"Not for us," Woo In said. "You and me, we protect

307

the heir." He pointed at me, making me flinch. "Those were The Lady's orders, Kat. Protect the heir, no matter what. And if you hadn't left your post at the keep, we never would have lost track of her."

"It hardly matters now," Kathleen sputtered. "She's safe, isn't she? And you can't follow any orders if you're dead."

"I wasn't alone," Woo In responded after a pause. "I . . . I had a song-healer." For the first time, Kathleen noticed Kirah, who stiffened.

"I'm thirsty," Kirah announced, and turned on her heel, marching off toward Melu's pool. Sanjeet and I followed her, grateful to distance ourselves from the foreign energy surrounding Woo In and Kathleen.

"It's proof," Sanjeet said as the three of us knelt in the grass. I had brought one of Melu's baskets, and we breakfasted on dates and kola nuts by the sparkling amber pool. "The Lady anointed her own council," Sanjeet insisted. "They're using The Lady's Ray."

"Or it's witchcraft," I shot back. "Or—I don't know, we've been out in the wilderness too long and we're going insane."

"Am's Story, Tar," Kirah snorted. "How many more signs is it going to take? Why can't you believe that your mother has the Ray, and that you have a gift, just like her?"

"Because—" I bit my lip, hard. "Because the Ray is supposed to pick good people, all right? My mother forced an enslaved being to bed her on this very spot! One sip of that"—I pointed to Melu's pool—"and I become some soulless monster who lies to her friends and stabs them! The Lady and I aren't gifted, Kirah. We're cursed."

"The Ray," Sanjeet said, "doesn't pick good people. The Ray picks leaders. And if I've learned anything from serving on the Imperial Guard, it's that leadership isn't good or evil. It's what you choose to do with it."

"You didn't call me a leader when Dayo was bleeding under that tree," I said, and immediately regretted it. Sanjeet's and Kirah's faces crumpled with pain, and the clearing fell into silence.

"He forgives you, you know," Kirah muttered after a moment. "Dayo. He made me promise to tell you. Once you've broken your curse, he wants you back as a council member."

Tears of relief flooded my throat. I forced them back down. "Then Dayo's a fool," I said.

Sanjeet shook his head. "That's all you have to say? Am's Story, Tar, give him a break. After everything you both have gone through—"

"That's the problem," I sputtered. "After everything we've gone through, he shouldn't want me back! He shouldn't want anything to do with me! But he was raised in a gilded hothouse where everyone adored him, and so he'll never see the world for what it is: cruel and stupid and full of monsters. Monsters that look like me."

Kirah pressed her lips together. "I wasn't born in a gilded hothouse," she pointed out. "And neither was Sanjeet. But we're still here, in the middle of nowhere, doing everything

309

we can to help you. What does that make us? Just more fools in your cruel, stupid world?"

"No," I said after a sheepish pause. "I'm sorry." I sighed, fidgeting with the sunstone. It had grown cold and dim at the base of my throat. "I'm just . . . tired, Kirah. And I don't know what to do. Melu says the only way to get rid of my curse is to find a purpose. A place in some big, grand story."

She brightened and sat up. "Of course. A bellysong: the cure for any soul in bondage. I should have thought of that."

"A belly what?"

"That's what we Blessids call it, back home."

Home. What a foreign concept. The chilly white walls of Bhekina House loomed in the distance, reminding me that I had never been part of anything—not until I joined Dayo's council.

"The place closest to your soul isn't your heart," Kirah explained. "It's your stomach. Anger, love, and sorrow simmer together there, like bubbles in a cauldron. People of the Wing believe that when the Pelican breathed each soul into being, it wrote two secrets on a burning coal: your greatest good and your best desire. You swallowed the coal before being born, and it burned in your belly. That's why we wail as newborns, Mama would say."

Kirah smiled into the tall grass, as if seeing her parents there, and the many infants for whom she had helped to care. She had real siblings somewhere, blood brothers and sisters that she had left behind for this. Being priestess to the world, and sitting with a monster in the wilderness. I wondered if she ever regretted it.

"High Priestess Mbali says that people have many gifts," Kirah continued. "But our greatest good is the one we can't contain: compassion, loyalty, softness, fierceness. The ability to win hearts, or recognize beauty, or weather a storm . . . Our gift could be anything, really. And when we use our greatest good for something beyond ourselves, that's our best desire. Our purpose." She paused. "But the coal inside us gradually grows colder. We forget our cry as newborns, our bellysong. We forget our knowledge of why Am made us, and our frustration at being too small and weak to fulfill it. We grow old and content, and unless we try very, very hard—we never wail our bellysong again."

I broke off a stalk of grass. "Why Am made us," I repeated, ripping the stalk into pieces until my fingers were stained lurid green. "Why Am made us."

Sanjeet blinked at me. "Are you all right?"

"I guess I'd better be," I said, standing and throwing the grass into the pool. "Because if Kirah and Melu are right, then we're all djinns. Just lines in the poem of an almighty griot." I flopped my arms like a puppet, then dug my nails into my fists. "If Kirah's right, then the Storyteller is no different than The Lady."

Kirah recoiled, making the sacred sign of Am on her chin. "That isn't true," she said.

"You have to believe that. You're a priestess."

"What, so I don't have a brain?" Kirah retorted. "The Storyteller isn't a djinn-master, Tarisai. Singing your bellysong is a choice."

"Not for me! If I don't find a purpose, then Dayo dies, and The Lady wins, and the whole empire falls apart. What kind of a choice is that?"

"You have a choice," Kirah said slowly, "because there's another way. After you left Yorua Keep, I had to come up with a plan and . . ." She avoided my gaze, grinding her sandal soles into the dirt. "Look, it's not what I want. Dayo refused to even consider it. But it's a good plan, all right? He won't be emperor for years, so there's time to train a new Swana delegate. The rest of us could split your duties as High Judge, and . . ."

Sanjeet's expression sickened. "You're talking about Tar leaving the Eleven. You think she could stop being an Anointed One."

She nodded grimly. "A living one, anyway. We would make up an accident. Find a body and say it's her. Hold an empire-wide funeral. She would be muraled on the Watching Wall, and of course"—she added gently—"we would place a likeness on her throne."

The title of an Anointed One lasted beyond their grave. Council members who died prematurely could not legally be replaced, even if their duties were assigned to someone new. The emperor fashioned a bust from the council member's ashes and placed it on one of the twelve great thrones of An-Ileyoba. There, legend rumored, the ghost of the lost Anointed One would remain until the emperor died, releasing the deceased council member from their duty.

"Council sickness will be bad, in hiding," Kirah admitted. "But we would visit you. It would have to be a place no one could find, ever. A realm close enough to Oluwan that Sanjeet and I could slip away. Somewhere like . . ." Her gaze drifted down the plain, where she knew The Lady's fortress shimmered invisibly.

Bile stung the back of my tongue. "Bhekina House," I whispered. Back to watching the world from a window. Back to those four mudbrick walls, rising like night around me. "Forever."

"Or not," Kirah said hurriedly. "We could disguise you. You could live in Oluwan City, in an outer district, far away from the palace. The risk would be greater, but not impossible." She chewed her lip. "Some people don't believe in bellysongs, you know. To them, Am is just a concept, and Am's Story is no story at all. It's simply the essence of being alive: the soup in which we all live. I don't know if I believe that, but those people find happiness, and you can too. What I'm trying to say is: You have choices, Tar. And you always will."

I nodded slowly. "And I'd go anywhere to keep Dayo safe." Overhead, the tutsu from last night had dimmed, and they drifted in aimless patterns against the clouds. "But so much of my life has been a lie. I . . . I don't think I want my death to be one too."

Sanjeet's features flooded with relief. "Then choose life,"

he said. He locked his fingers through mine, as though I were in danger of vanishing. "Your greatest good, your best desire—whatever it takes, we'll find it. All we need is time."

After a long moment, I let my hand curl around his. "If we're not going to fake my death, then I have to answer the emperor's summons. I can't afford for him to get suspicious and come looking for me."

Kirah beamed. "So we'll go to An-Ileyoba. Who knows? Maybe you'll find your purpose there. There's also a good chance Aiyetoro's masks will be at the palace. Woo In told me that The Lady has searched for them everywhere except there."

"Dayo will be at An-Ileyoba," I pointed out.

"We'll be careful—"

"I won't see him," I said firmly. "Don't you dare let me. At the palace, I'm staying far away from him until I've found my cure. And thanks to Melu . . ." The ehru's words curled around me like smoke. *If you are ever to find your purpose, then you must know who you really are.* Grimly, I set off toward Bhekina House. "I know just where to start looking."

"You shouldn't go in there alone," Sanjeet countered as he and Kirah hurried after me.

"She won't," said Kathleen. She and Woo In were waiting by the gates of Bhekina House, leaning against a wall that Sanjeet and Kirah could not see.

Sanjeet shuddered, then scoffed. "You expect us to trust you?"

"We expect you," Woo In droned, "to consider that we've protected her for six years."

"You should have protected her from The Lady," Kirah retorted, crossing her arms. Then she winced and uncrossed them, having clearly forgotten about her sprain.

"Can't you fix that?" Woo In asked, eyeing her wrist with concern.

She scowled at him. "Soul-singers can't heal themselves. That's like—like trying to exhale and inhale at the same time. My Hallow doesn't work that way."

"Then I'll help with the pain," Woo In insisted, and before Kirah could protest, a whirlwind materialized in the savannah. The whipping air condensed into a shimmering ball, which Woo In directed toward her. "Your hand," he said. "Please, Kirah."

Slowly, she placed her bandaged hand into the levitating ball of wind. The ball attached itself to her arm, making it float, and her features relaxed instantly. "It isn't throbbing anymore," she muttered.

Woo In made an effort not to look pleased. "It's the same airstream we used to fly. It doesn't heal, but wounds tend to stabilize."

I considered him suspiciously. "You never fully explained your Hallow to me," I said. "It's more than flight, isn't it?"

"Much more," Kathleen said, smirking at Woo In. "In a way, it's really not even a Hallow, is it, princey?"

He sighed, rolling his eyes. "What you Arits call my Hallow," he explained, "Songlanders call *sowanhada*: the language of nature. Unlike your Hallows, sowanhada can be taught, though some forces respond only to certain bloodlines. The silent language of wind and air, for example, may only be spoken by the royal family. Our military exclusively recruits fire-speakers. That's why The Lady wants Songland's army," he added. "Sowanhada warriors can do a formidable amount of damage, even against Olugbade's vast Imperial Guard." He nodded at Kirah's hand. "That ball of air should last a few hours. Enough time to search the house for clues about a certain person's bellysong."

My eyebrows shot to my hairline. "How did you know about—" Then I remembered a breeze whisking around Melu's pool as I had spoken to Kirah and Sanjeet. "You were eavesdropping. Again."

"Old habits, Lady's Daughter." Woo In bowed. "Shall we?"

Sanjeet bristled, but I only sighed. I didn't feel like going anywhere with Woo In, but I knew he wouldn't hurt me. He was too loyal to The Lady for that. Still, I crossed my arms at him. "Why would you want to help break my curse? Don't you *want* Dayo dead?"

"I never wanted anyone dead," Woo In said. "I just wanted The Lady crowned so she could save the Redemptors. But I have long felt . . ." He rubbed the bruise on his cheek and shot a furtive glance at Kirah. "More suffering is not the answer. There must be another way to crown The Lady."

"We could exile Prince Ekundayo instead of killing

him," Kathleen suggested brightly. "Off to some island where he can never threaten The Lady's claim—"

"Dayo's not going to an island," Kirah snapped at her. "Once we find Aiyetoro's masks, Dayo and Tar can rule together. That's how it's supposed to be."

I sputtered with exasperation. "Can we forget about my supposed Ray for a second and focus on protecting Dayo?"

Kirah ignored me, narrowing her eyes at Woo In and Kathleen. "You're the ones who gave Tarisai that drum. So you have access to Aiyetoro's possessions. Where do *you* think the masks are?"

"If we knew where to find Aiyetoro's masks," Kathleen replied, "then we would be breaking The Lady out of prison right now, not babysitting you in this backwater savannah. The empress and princess masks are the only remaining proof of The Lady's right to rule. She has spent decades searching, and has never come closer to finding them."

"What about the drum?" I asked.

"The Lady stole it from the palace as a child. When she found out that you had erased your memories, she made us deliver the drum to you in Ebujo, hoping your shared lineage with Aiyetoro would awaken your true identity. Clearly," she added dryly, "it didn't work."

"We'll help you search Bhekina House," Woo In told me. "The Lady stored most of her records there. She likely has leads on where to look for the masks."

I frowned. "If she did, wouldn't she have told you?"

Woo In and Kathleen exchanged an uneasy look.

"The Lady told us what we needed to know for the tasks we were assigned," Kathleen said at last, her tone defensive. "Not all Raybearers are as naive as your prince, spilling secrets left and right. The Lady likes her privacy."

The insult to Dayo angered me, but the feeling melted to pity. Kathleen and Woo In had given their lives to my mother, and still she held them at a distance. Where they could not hurt her, I realized. As her brother had, as the world had. I pitied The Lady too.

We turned toward the shimmering red rooftops of Bhekina House. The compound was smaller than I remembered. As a child, the palisade gates had towered over my head, an impossible-to-cross barrier to the whole world.

"Is anyone still living here?" I asked, my lungs constricting.

"The Lady dismissed most of her servants after sending you to the capital," Kathleen replied. "But some of your tutors were my anointed siblings. They're traveling to Songland as we speak, hoping to convince Queen Hye Sun's army to break The Lady out of An-Ileyoba. A few servants still live here to open the gate and look after the chickens. But the compound never needed farmhands." Kathleen looked unsettled. "The orchard has always cared for itself."

The perfume of mangoes washed over me as Woo In called a password, and the palisade gates creaked open. A rheumy-eyed guard peered at us, then gasped when he recognized my features.

"She is not here," he wailed. "The Lady is gone, gone." Wrinkled, leathery skin covered his arms as he operated the heavy gate crank. I recognized him. The man had guarded the gate when I small. He had been just as old then as he was now. How could such a frail man survive for so long? Then again . . .

How could an orchard of mangoes bloom year-round with no one to care for them?

"What are you looking at?" Kirah asked me, squinting up at the guard, and I realized that she and Sanjeet could not see or hear him. They could not sense the towering gates, or even smell the ripe orchard yards away.

I shivered, bid them goodbye, and entered the compound with Woo In and Kathleen. When I turned back to wave, Sanjeet and Kirah stared straight through me, looking unnerved, as though I had vanished into thin air.

The courtyard, manor, huts, and fruit trees of Bhekina House were eerily still. The heat of Melu's enchantment seeped through every wax-coated leaf, every brick and cobblestone. How could I not have noticed, before, how the walls hummed quietly with power? This place had once seemed so ordinary. Then again . . . it had been all I'd known.

I remembered Melu's words about Bhekina House: *The magic of that place is not easy on one's mind.* I pitied my former tutors and servants. No wonder they had been so stiff and paranoid. It was a mercy they had not gone mad.

We passed through the manor's smooth plaster halls,

searching for clues about Aiyetoro. "This house felt like a prison," I murmured, "but it's still beautiful. I wonder why The Lady didn't stay here."

Woo In was quiet for a moment. "She did," he said.

Kathleen shot him a warning look, and I shook my head.

"She would vanish for months," I countered. "I would lie awake at night, wondering where she was. Wondering—" I swallowed. "Why she never missed me as much as I missed her."

Kathleen nudged Woo In, scowling, but he pushed her away. "She deserves to know," he told her, and turned back to me. "The Lady watched you to the point of obsession. She did leave a few times, to anoint more council members. But she always came straight back. She took notes on your first steps. Your first words. Your progress in all your lessons."

I snorted. "*A few times?*" Woo In's adoration of The Lady must have mottled his memories. I had been lucky to see my mother more than once a year.

Woo In winced. "I . . . did not always agree with The Lady's methods regarding your upbringing," he muttered. "But I'm sure she wanted the best for you. For all of us."

My forehead wrinkled with doubt.

"Come," he said. "There is something you should see." We climbed a staircase carved into the plaster, and my heart pounded with recognition. Before us hung the thick, embroidered door flaps of my old study.

"I can't go in there," I said.

"Why not?"

"Because—" I bit my lip. Because in that room, I hadn't been one of Aritsar's anointed. I hadn't been the wuraola who commanded tutsu, or even the friend in whom Sanjeet and Kirah put their trust.

In that room, I had been an ehru. The Lady had been all I knew of love, and I would have killed for her. I had always been her puppet, even before she bound me with a wish.

"I tried to scrub them off, you know," Woo In said then.

"What?"

"The maps," he explained. "After I escaped the Underworld, I covered my skin with clay. Dressed in layers up to my chin. But I was always checking under my clothes. Fearing that the lines had grown. Hoping that they had faded. I checked so often, it became easier just to dress like this." He gestured to his bare, pattern-covered chest. "I saw my past in the mirror every day. I grew accustomed to it. And then—" He drew aside the heavy door flaps. "I stopped being afraid."

I hesitated, then passed into the dim room. The smell of musty scrolls washed over me. Dust motes twinkled in sharp slats of light, which fell from boarded-up windows. My tutors had shut them so I would not hear the songs of other children. I could still feel the splinters in my hands, the arms gripping my waist, restraining me as I tried to rip the boards away.

"The Lady and the emperor have more in common than they think," I murmured. "They're both terrified by stories they can't control."

Kathleen sniffed. "The Lady only wants what's best. For all of us."

My old stepping stool lay on its side beneath a window, covered in spiderwebs. Just like when I was little, the long, high study table was piled with books and censored history papers. From its pedestal, the carving of The Lady still watched over the study, its onyx eyes gleaming. Woo In picked up the carving, blowing dust from the wooden crevices.

"Stop," I stammered. "Be careful with that."

He smiled and handed me the heavy bust. "Notice anything unusual?"

I squinted at the shapely face, so cold, and so like my own. I had studied beside the carving every day, and noticed nothing different about it now. Except—I held it to my ear and gasped quietly. "It hums," I said. "Like the walls, and the orchard. I think it's enchanted."

Woo In took the carving back. "I'm guessing the servants didn't let you touch it."

"How did you know?"

He hesitated. "Because you would have taken its memories. You would have seen." He beckoned, and I followed him to a narrow corridor I remembered as the entrance to the servants' wing.

That place is very haunted, the servants had told me. *Ghosts live there. Bad spirits, who take little girls away.*

What if I want to go away? I had retorted.

Spirits who eat little girls, the servants had amended quickly. *And first they take them far away, where The Lady can never find them. It is a very bad part of the house. You are lucky we live there instead of you.*

I had not been sure I believed them, but the idea of being forever parted from The Lady had dampened my curiosity. I had never lingered near the servants' wing again.

Woo In led us down the plain corridor, and after several yards—just far enough to be out of earshot of the main house—the hall turned sharply, and my feet passed from stone tile onto lush carpet.

The perfume hit me first. My heart reacted to the smell of jasmine as it always had, with terror and longing. Expensive mudcloths dyed with indigo patterns swathed the walls. Woo In fumbled with a shimmering lock, on a wooden door inlaid with mother-of-pearl. "It takes a singing password," he said, scowling as he tried to remember. "You know the one. '*Me . . . mine . . .*'"

"She's me and she is mine," I finished, my voice a whisper, and the door clicked open.

We entered a small apartment of rooms. Jasmine seeped from every futon, every wax-dyed drape and tasseled pillow. A creeping sense of betrayal quickened my pulse, but I smothered it.

"Is this where she slept when . . . when she visited?"

"The Lady did not visit, Tarisai." Woo In's tone was patient. "She lived here."

"No." I shook my head. "She knew how much I missed her. How I cried for her every single night. She couldn't have been here. She wouldn't. She—"

A hand mirror glinted on a kneeling desk, making the words die in my throat. The reflection wasn't right—it should have shown the smooth plaster ceiling of the apartment. Instead it showed a moving face. Knees suddenly weak, I sank down to the desk and grasped the bone-handled mirror.

Woo In's reflection stared back at me. "I'm sorry," it said.

I whirled around. Woo In was holding the carving, looking bleakly into its face. He turned the carving toward the desk—and then the mirror displayed me, seated on the floor cushions in The Lady's apartment.

"The whole time," I breathed. "She was watching."

Paper covered the desk: notes in an even, elegant hand. The first I picked up was dated a year prior.

Sometimes I still look in the enchanted glass. It is folly, I know. She will not appear. But seeing that empty study, the table where she used to sit frowning over her genealogy scrolls . . . It reminds me of the old days, when I was her world. My sweet, adoring girl! When I pretended to come home after a long journey, her face would glow. Such joy. Such longing.

I am sure Olugbade's brat never looks at him like that.

Was hiding my presence cruel? But suppose I had commanded her by accident? Threw away my last wish—our only chance at victory? No. Regret is folly. The guilt will pass. It always does.

Bile rose in my throat. I swallowed and seized another paper. This one was dated only a month ago.

Still no word of her progress. She has chosen to forget me. The festival on Nu'ina Eve is my best chance. I shall make her remember. I shall make us one again.

Older notes had been bound into a calfskin journal. I stole a moment of its story, and shivered. The calloused grip of my mother's hands pressed into the leather spine. The first page was dated almost sixteen years ago, on my first birthday.

She's walking. My girl—my Made-of-Me—is walking! A tutor said her name, and she stumbled toward him. Clever, wondrous creature. Just like her mother.

I wish that she had walked to me instead, but I was afraid of commanding her.

Would "Come here, daughter" count as my third wish? Melu refuses to tell me.

I visited her tonight, as I always do. I kiss her brow as she sleeps, and sing our special song. I tell her all the realms we shall rule together. My girl smells of violets, of honey and grass.

She smells—to be honest—too much of the wild, sun-soaked savannah. I tried to give her my smell, to bathe her in jasmine oil, but she sprouted a rash. Ah, well. I will see she grows out of it.

I could not resist picking her up tonight. She woke and fussed, but quieted when I pressed her to my breast. Such a bright child— already she knows that all objects have names. Genius simmered in her large dark eyes as she tried to remember the word for me.

"Lady," she said.

"No," I told her, kissing that bed of soft, perfect curls. "Not Lady. To you, I am—I will always be—Mother."

The ink blotched and ran as I sobbed, shoulders quaking as I turned the pages. Woo In and Kathleen searched the rest of the apartment for clues, tactfully allowing me privacy.

I read for over an hour. All the attention, all the affection I had craved from The Lady was here, written in clear, generous script. I could even feel her love, wafting from the memories of each page. But from the years of notes, one thing was missing. The journal called me *my daughter. My girl. Darling. Made-of-Me.*

But never, ever Tarisai.

Kathleen and Woo In returned, and wordlessly, he offered me a silk handkerchief.

"Did The Lady mention Aiyetoro's masks in there?" Kathleen asked.

I shrugged, letting Woo In take the journal as I swabbed my runny nose. The handkerchief was so heavily scented it must have been from The Lady's wardrobe. I sneezed.

Woo In scanned the journal voraciously. "Sometimes," he murmured. "She references previous searches, so maybe there's more in the other journals. There's plenty in here about us, though." He chuckled at a page. "My, my, Kat, The Lady doesn't think much of your singing voice."

Kathleen huffed in offense and tried to wrestle the journal from him.

"Be careful with that," I ordered, and the two of them jumped, staring at me.

"Am's Story," Kathleen muttered. "For a moment, you sounded just like The Lady." She relinquished the journal to Woo In.

I asked him warily, "How many of you are there, again?"

"You mean of The Lady's council? Ten, so far," he replied. "Three came with The Lady as children from An-Ileyoba. The rest of us were found after her exile."

"Where did she hide after leaving Oluwan?" I asked. "And why did she anoint you? Council members only represent Arit realms. Songland isn't part of the empire."

"The Lady had a new kind of empire in mind," said Woo In, his voice soft with reverence. "She's different from your ancestor Enoba. He barred Songland from trading with the rest of the continent as punishment for our refusal to join his empire. But The Lady wants to change everything. That is why she anointed me. When she is empress, Songland can be represented on the Arit council, regardless of whether we choose to join the empire. Before I was your nursemaid, I campaigned for The Lady in Songland, convincing my family to trust her, and lend her aid when necessary."

It was hard to remember that Woo In was a prince. Most Redemptors grew up in orphanages, abandoned at birth by families who could not bear the pain of sacrificing them later.

"What's it like?" I asked. "Being a prince who wasn't

supposed to survive? I'm sure you and Mother had a lot in common."

"We did, and do." He smiled tightly. "But I had better luck than The Lady when it came to older siblings. My sister Min Ja has always been protective of me, though . . . critical of my alliance with The Lady."

"I still don't understand why you think Mother can help you. No one can control where Redemptors are born."

"As I told you long ago," he replied, "only a Raybearer may unlock the secret of the Redemptor Treaty. Enoba made sure of it. The Lady knows how to save the Songland Redemptors, but she couldn't share the process with me: She said it's too intuitive for the Rayless to understand." He pressed his lips together, as if trying not to let the secret chafe at him. "It's the only way. If The Lady becomes empress and succeeds in freeing Songland, then my mother, Queen Hye Sun, will recognize me as Prince Ambassador: the first Songlander to have a seat on the Arit Imperial Councils."

I frowned. The abiku had implied that the selection of Redemptors was random. They had said, "The blood decides." Had they been lying? Could The Lady really control where Redemptors were born?

"Maybe she explains it in here," Woo In murmured, flipping fervently through the journal. I watched him with pity. How could The Lady keep secrets from a follower as devoted as Woo In? And how could he love her so much, that he trusted her anyway?

Then I laughed at my own hypocrisy. Of course Woo In trusted The Lady. Just like a touch-starved little girl, gazing from her study window, had trusted that her mother was away on important business.

Together, Woo In and I collected several other volumes of The Lady's journals and papers. I hunted for evidence of her Ray and read of her failed attempts to locate the fabled lost masks of female Raybearers. In the meantime, Woo In devoured any book that mentioned Songland, even if only for a page. Hours passed. I grew irritable and hungry, and went to forage with Kathleen in the enchanted orchard. Woo In remained in the apartment, lips moving silently as he pored over The Lady's documents.

When Kathleen and I returned, arms full of mangoes, Woo In was sitting frozen against The Lady's desk, a journal open on his lap. He stared straight ahead, his face drained of color.

"Am's Story, Woo In. What's the matter?" Kathleen asked, kneeling to read over his shoulder.

He jerked away, and hurled The Lady's journal against a wall with a cry.

I gasped, then retrieved the journal and checked the spine for damage. When I looked up, Woo In had fled the apartment. Kathleen chased after him in confusion.

The book fell open to the page he had been reading, calfskin still wrinkled from his viselike grip. The entry was undated, as though The Lady had been scattered in her thoughts.

Will he forgive me, I wonder?

He ought to. It would be unfair, at least, for him to hate me. Songland will trade with Aritsar, just as I promised. He shall have his seat as ambassador. These are gifts of which he could never have dreamed when I found him, a sullen Redemptor princeling, still licking his wounds from the Underworld.

Am I not kind?

Am I not as faithful as prudence allows?

The entry broke off, then began again in slightly different ink, as though The Lady had attempted to abandon the entry, and returned to it days later.

Their markets will prosper, she had written in hurried, restless script. *Songland families will have me to thank when their bellies are full of Arit maize and their purses are lined in Arit silver.*

What better balm for the loss of a child?

Besides—if I let the Underworld take Arit children, the empire would never let me rule. What good is a fallen empress to anyone?

Another break. Then the entry resumed, and this time The Lady's handwriting was calm and even.

I will pay the price of peace, as my ancestors have before me. But I am better than Enoba. I did not take without giving in return.

The words were a puzzle, and cold crept across my skin as the riddle came together, a picture I understood only in pieces.

The Lady had known—or pretended to know—a way to prevent Songlanders from being chosen as Redemptors.

Then she had made a promise, one she had no intention of keeping.

I will pay the price of peace, as my ancestors have before me.

Under her rule—despite her promise—Songland children would continue to be sent to the Underworld. The Lady had lied to Woo In, using him to gain control of Songland's army. And judging from the white rage that had crumpled his features, he would not soon forgive her.

CHAPTER 25

"HE'S GONE," KIRAH SAID WHEN I RETURNED to Melu's canopy. "Woo In just left with Hyung. Didn't even say goodbye." She tried to sound nonchalant. "Kathleen left too. What happened?"

Too stunned to explain, I touched Kirah's and Sanjeet's brows and let them explore my memories of Bhekina House. Then I showed them the journal, as well as the small hand mirror and enchanted carving, which I had taken with me.

"The Lady is wise to reinstate trade with Songland," Sanjeet observed grimly. "If she succeeds in overthrowing the emperor, she will need forces to control the capital."

"Unless Woo In changes his family's mind," I pointed out.

"He could have said goodbye," murmured Kirah.

We left for An-Ileyoba that afternoon. We took a different sequence of lodestones this time, traveling through the heart of Swana. We continued to avoid towns, partly because of the Unity Edict riots, but also because a conspicuous cloud of sprites persisted in following wherever I went. Only when we left Swana did they disperse, and on a balmy evening several weeks later, we arrived in Oluwan City.

I had expected An-Ileyoba Palace to look different now—for the outside to somehow match my insides, swathed in shadow and uncertainty. But ten-story empire flags still fell proudly over the sandstone walls. The music of griots wafted from the gardens. Peacocks strode around the courtyard, getting in the way of servants and sentries. Even the air smelled the same, of palm oil and citrus flowers. The Children's Palace had been repaired after Woo In's fire, no longer marred by soot and splintering timbers. The red domes shimmered in the setting sun, and a pennant flew from the highest balustrade: The crown prince and his council were in residence.

"They're here," I breathed.

"The emperor summoned them from Yorua. They would have wasted no time," Sanjeet said. "After all the riots, he'll want the Prince's and Emperor's Councils to show a united front."

It had now been over two months since I had seen Dayo and my other council siblings. Sanjeet's and Kirah's presence had slowed the symptoms of council sickness: As long as I had at least one anointed sibling with me, the illness was mild, and I would never go completely mad. But the Ray still bound me to the remaining members of our family. I ached, like a body functioning without all its parts.

But if they knew what I had done to Dayo, would they

still love me? Mayazatyl, and Ai Ling, and Umansa, and the rest? Would they even want to see me? My stomach churned as Sanjeet and Kirah flashed our seals, and the palace guards hurried us through the gates.

"It's good to have you back, Anointed Honors," sang a palace attendant as she led us through the polished stone halls. I remembered her well—Bimbola, one of many Children's Palace maids who had cared for us as candidates. She could not be more than ten years my senior. When she took my hand to kiss it, a memory passed into me: her plump, gentle fingers weaving my hair into neat cornrows. She had been kinder than the other maids, who would smack my head with the comb when I squirmed. "The palace has been so lonely since the trials ended," she sighed. Bangles rang on her arms as she walked. "I have a child of my own now. Sometimes I take him to the playroom and say, 'See? That is where the crown prince played tag with Anointed Honor Tarisai. Yes! She was small once, just like you. And look, this was Anointed Honor Sanjeet's favorite playsword. Shall you grow big and defend the prince, just like him?'" Bimbola smiled warmly. "The chambers are just as you left them—before the fire, anyway. His Young Highness and council have just sat down for luncheon. They will be so excited to see . . ."

Kirah noticed my wooden steps and sweaty palms. *They'll understand if you explain*, she Ray-spoke, guessing my fears. *They'll forgive you. I'm sure of it.*

But she could not be sure. My council could shun me

forever. They could want me killed. Besides—how was I to explain The Lady's actions? *It's not my fault I stabbed Dayo,* I imagined saying. *The Lady thinks I'm a Kunleo and that I deserve Dayo's throne.* My shoulders hunched around my ears. That explanation was worse than none at all.

I stopped in the middle of the hall, and Bimbola paused in surprise. "Is something the matter, Anointed Honor Tarisai?"

"I'm not coming," I said.

Kirah smiled briskly at the attendant and took my elbow, turning us away and lowering her voice. "Our council needs to see you," she said firmly. "If you keep hiding, they'll start to wonder—"

"I won't put Dayo's life in danger again."

"Then where will you live while you're here? A locked prison tower?"

"That's not a bad idea."

Despite Kirah's and Sanjeet's protests, I asked Bimbola to prepare the farthest possible room from the Children's Palace. Bemused, she bowed and hurried away.

"Someone will have to guard me at night," I told Sanjeet. "Are you up for the job?"

He nodded reluctantly, though Kirah groaned. "Come on, Tar. You're not a wild monster."

"No," I retorted. "I'm a quiet, clever one." I handed her the bust of The Lady. "I won't miss you all terribly," I lied. "I can watch the Children's Palace through Mother's mirror. Don't let me miss too much."

An hour later, I stood alone in a chamber with close walls and a high, shadowy ceiling. Bimbola had shown me multiple bedrooms throughout the central wing of An-Ileyoba, each grandly furnished, with direct access to the courtyards. I had refused them all. The exasperated attendant had finally found a tower in the southwest wing: the farthest possible building from the Children's Palace.

The walls were round, dappled sandstone hung with mudcloth tapestry. The floor had been hastily swept and strewn with reed mats. Near the hearth lay a down-stuffed bedroll, clearly salvaged from another bedchamber. A table, two weathered chairs, and a mirror tinted with age comprised the furniture. Most important: The only entry was a wooden door that locked.

"We can remove that from its hinges," Bimbola had suggested brightly. "Put up some pretty cloth flaps, perhaps—"

"The door stays."

She tutted. "Well, we'll at least make the place presentable. I'll send for a chest, and a futon, or at *least* some cushions . . ."

I barely heard her while I stared through the single unglazed window.

It was a direct view of the Children's Palace. The domes rose far away, on the opposite end of An-Ileyoba, but I could still make out the arched windows of the Hall of Dreams. Unable to resist, I drew The Lady's mirror from my pocket.

Kirah had placed The Lady's bust on a ledge overlooking the Hall. My breath caught: My anointed siblings, my best friends, were roughhousing and laughing, mouths open in jokes I could not hear. They retraced our old haunts, giggling at our cherished games and toys, checking furniture for initials we had carved underneath.

I considered sending a pulse through the Ray, tempted to watch their expressions as my voice sounded in their minds. *Do you miss me? Do you hate me? I miss you more than you'll ever know.*

But I said nothing, and put the mirror back in my pocket. It was wrong to spoil their joy. The Lady's curse was mine to bear alone.

Bimbola had promised to return with a second bedroll, since Sanjeet would be sharing my confinement. When knuckles rapped on the tower room door, I was at the window again. The sill was deep enough to make a seat as I watched the Children's Palace. Still wearing my dusty wrapper from Tegoso, I hugged my knees as someone entered the room.

"You're early," I said without turning. "There isn't a bed for you yet."

A high voice cleared its throat. Bimbola, two palace attendants, and a female guard stood in the doorframe instead of Sanjeet.

"You've been summoned by the emperor, Anointed Honor," said Bimbola, worrying her bangles with excitement.

My stomach turned to stone. "What does he want?"

Bimbola's eyebrows shot up at my irreverent tone. "I was not told. But you can hardly meet him as you are. We shall accompany you to the bathhouse. Perhaps I can . . ." She looked askance at my hair. "Assist in your toilette."

Several minutes later, I stood in a shallow, bubbling river that wove through a tiled floor. Stone hyenas perched on walls overhead. Water gushed from the beasts' grimacing mouths, fed from a reservoir on the roof. The rainwater lapped at my bare hips, and sunlight warmed my back, streaming through unglazed windows shaped like suns and moons.

I had washed in the palace bathhouse before, a child splashing with dozens of other candidates. Now that I was anointed, the chamber had been emptied for my privacy.

My attendants had stripped to their shifts and waded in beside me, scouring my skin and coaxing tangles from my hair. "You're feverish, Your Anointed Honor," Bimbola tutted. "That's council sickness for you. The sooner you're back with your anointed siblings, the better."

After my bath, the attendants buffed my limbs with shea butter until they glowed, and then swabbed my pulse points with fragrant bergamot. I refused to let Bimbola restrain my billowing hair, but consented to a thick crown braid at my hairline. My new clothes were an ochre blouse and azure wrapper, embroidered with raised yellow patterns. As a finishing touch, the attendants dusted my jaw and collarbone with shimmering gold powder, clucking with satisfaction.

We passed through the gilded halls of An-Ileyoba, deeper and deeper into the palace's heart. My attendants grew quiet as we passed over the gleaming tiles, our faces reflected on walls of onyx marble. My feet were wedged in the latest Oluwan fashion: leather slippers with precariously high soles.

Someone rounded a corner of the corridor, nearly causing a collision. My attendants leapt to surround me, tutting with offense—then they recognized the stranger.

"Anointed Honor Mbali," Bimbola stammered, sinking with the others in a curtsy.

I tried to bow as well, but Mbali grasped my shoulders. The pelican pendant on her breast rose and fell, and her priestess robes were rumpled, as though she had sprinted across An-Ileyoba. Her fingers dug into my sleeves.

"I looked—the Children's Palace," she panted. "You weren't there. Thank Am I found you before—" She glanced behind her, where the wooden doors to Olugbade's chambers loomed. "Remember the mango tree."

I shook my head. "Anointed Honor, I don't under—"

"When you first came to the palace, you stole a story from my head." Mbali's grip on me tightened. "Remember what happened when the boy grew afraid of his tree. He cut it down. He burned the branches. But as long as the tree stays in its pot—as long the boy believes it will never grow—the boy is happy. Remember, Tarisai."

My heart hammered. She did not release me until I nodded. Then she stepped aside and let us pass, and when I looked back, Mbali was gone.

We entered the imperial antechamber, a round, gilded room leading to the personal wing of Olugbade and his council. My attendants bid me farewell, and two Imperial Guard warriors replaced them to march me into a small, warmly lit apartment. Then the door flap was shut behind me, and I was left alone with the emperor of Aritsar.

He faced away from me, stirring the chamber's small firepit with a poker. He was smaller than I remembered: broad but of short stature, with thinning gray curls, and robes that would blend easily into a crowd. The room had modest tapestries and no windows—a former servant's quarters, converted into a study. A conspicuous display of humility.

Quietly, I lifted the sunstone around my neck and concealed it beneath my blouse. Then I knelt to the man's back and murmured, "Your Imperial Majesty."

When he turned, I clasped my hands to hide their trembling. I had forgotten how strongly the emperor resembled Dayo. The same full mouth and sudden, infectious smile, though his lacked the glow of innocence. "My son's favorite," he greeted.

I remembered the mango tree.

"The Crown Prince of Aritsar has no favorites, Your Imperial Majesty," I replied, reciting the catechism I had memorized as a candidate. "A Raybearer loves his council with equal favor, and governs Aritsar with equal justice."

"You have learned well," he replied, and I glanced up just in time to see that his jaw had clenched, and a vein pulsed in his forehead. But the expression vanished, replaced by the jovial, fatherly face beloved by all the empire. "Rise, child," he said. The lion mask shone on his chest, its striped mane glittering in the firelight. "And tell me why you left Yorua Keep the day after Nu'ina Eve."

"Research, Your Imperial Majesty," I said, rising. "I felt stifled in Yorua. I wanted to see how our laws affected our people."

"A natural desire," Olugbade said, "and one that does you credit. But you must know how your actions appear. My forces arrested The Lady on Nu'ina Eve, and you left the next morning. I am not angry. I know it must have been hard to remain at the keep, knowing that your mother was in danger."

His voice was so kind with pity, I almost nodded. But Mbali's hunted gaze was too fresh in my memory. "When I left, I did not know that The Lady had been captured, Your Imperial Majesty," I said, neatly dodging the trap in his words. "Kirah brought word to me in Swana."

He cocked his head. "Your mother has many friends in that realm."

"I would imagine so, Your Imperial Majesty. She raised me there for many years. Was Swana where she was born?"

"No, she—" Olugbade stopped, and his calm facade slipped as he tried to determine how much I knew. I blinked, doing my best to look insipid. At last he asked, "Why do you think your mother is in prison, Tarisai?"

I pretended to consider. "I heard she was caught near Yorua Keep, trying to trespass. Perhaps she wanted to visit me. She should have known better," I added. "Everyone knows that members of the Prince's Council aren't allowed to see their parents. No one is above the law."

"No one indeed." Olugbade nodded. "Which is why you will condemn The Lady to death at your First Ruling, in one month's time."

The blood drained from my face. "I . . ." My mouth was dry. "Anointed Honor Thaddace means for me to give a different ruling, Your Imperial Majesty. He thought—a festival. For orphans . . ."

"Thaddace is aware of the change," said the emperor. "If Arit citizens are to accept you as their High Lady Judge, you must demonstrate that your loyalty is not compromised. That your allegiance to the empire is complete. But perhaps your love for The Lady is too strong. I would understand, Tarisai. Any parent would. You must tell me if this task is beyond your capability."

"I—" Mbali's warning gripped my throat. I must be a tree who loved her pot. I fought to keep my tone docile. "I was not aware that death was the punishment for trespassing, Your Imperial Majesty."

"You do not understand the charges." Olugbade arranged his features in a sympathetic smile. "Many years ago, The Lady committed treason. She led a coup, trying to turn my own candidates against me. I showed mercy, allowing her to escape, but her continued disregard for the law has forced my hand."

Lies, my heart pounded. *Lies, lies, lies.*

"No one at court has seen The Lady since she was a child," Olugbade continued. "Few, if any, have made the connection between the woman I have in custody and the child traitor of thirty years ago. For your protection, I would prefer to keep it that way. The court gossips know only that I have imprisoned your mother, a raving Swana woman, for crimes against the empire."

He wasn't trying to protect me. He was afraid that someone at court would recognize The Lady, and revive rumors of a second Raybearer. "If my mother is a traitor," I asked, doing my best not to snap, "then why did you allow Dayo to anoint me?"

"Because it was time to rewrite the past."

We stared at each other. I understood, then, the true reason I had survived as a child in Olugbade's palace. He had not killed me, because doing so admitted the possibility that I was a Raybearer. Killing me admitted that The Lady had been right all along.

Olugbade had watched me grow beside his son, watched my subservience, my submission in my gilded cage—and he had enjoyed a peace of mind that my death could not have brought him. My First Ruling would be his ultimate victory. The final proof that only one Ray ruled in Aritsar. Mbali had known this all along, and her message in the hall had been clear: survive.

"No one is above the law, Your Imperial Majesty," I repeated, and curtsied serenely. "I look forward to my First Ruling."

When I emerged at last from Olugbade's chambers, my attendants flocked around me in the corridor. "Was it terrifying, Anointed Honor?" Bimbola fretted. "Am's Story! Such trembling hands. Your fingers, they're cold as rocks—"

"Take me to see her. Now." My voice was hoarse. "I want to see The Lady."

PART 4

CHAPTER 26

SHE TOO LIVED IN A TOWER NOW. BUT UNLIKE me, The Lady had not chosen hers. The open-air prison of An-Ileyoba was located on a roof overlooking the north courtyard, and most children learned of it from a nursery rhyme:

Thieves will rot in hell below, hell below, hell below
But Heaven is where traitors go, traitors go, traitors go.

Ordinary convicts were kept in the palace dungeons. But Heaven—as courtiers had nicknamed the turret obscured by clouds, with no walls and a sheer, ten-story drop— was reserved for the emperor's most personal enemies. The design was effective: No guard could watch a prisoner better than a crowd of gawking courtiers. Day and night, visitors squinted from the courtyard to observe a distant, sunburnt figure sleep and eat. The giggling audience dodged out of the way when the prisoner vomited, or emptied his or her bladder over the edge.

As a child at An-Ileyoba, I had never let myself believe that the prisoners in Heaven were real. They were shadows against the sky, and their anguished cries were so faint, I could pretend to hear the call of birds instead, or the wail of wind between the turrets.

A staircase inside the tower led to a landing, from which a single door led out to Heaven. I smelled the roof long before my attendants reached it: the sickly sweet stench of feces and urine. The door was made of iron bars, and a hatch opened at the bottom. Two buckets lay on the other side: one with water, and one encrusted with filth and flies. An impassive pair of guards manned the landing, which was lit dimly by a lamp on the floor. On the roof, a stiff bundle, pressed against the landing door, attempting to shelter itself from the night wind.

Mother.

My lips felt frozen, but I must have said the word out loud. The bundle shifted, and cracked hands gripped the bars. Then a slow, elegant voice.

"My darling girl."

Three words, and sixteen years of abandonment evaporated. I was no longer Anointed Honor Tarisai, the High Judge Apparent. She was no longer The Lady, a puppet master who had forced me to attempt murder.

I was a little girl in a cold study, and she was my warmth: the only one who touched me, who loved me, who wasn't afraid.

I let the guards search me for lockpicks and weapons,

then I bribed them to stand out of earshot. When I knelt at the door, The Lady reached through the bars, touching my loose hair. "This must be recent," she observed. "My spies did not report it." The Lady's throaty voice was still musical, though her comment turned into a weak cough.

"I've missed you," I said.

She laughed and made a tutting noise. "Now, now, Made-of-Me. We both know that isn't true."

The words stung. "You pretended to leave me," I said, pulling away. "When I was small. You lied and hid at Bhekina House, even though I cried for you every night. Why?"

She sighed. "Children are always so ungrateful."

"What? Mother, I—"

"You had a lovely childhood."

She spoke with such calm certainty, I began to doubt my own memories. Perhaps I hadn't been so miserable, locked in that study with no light. Perhaps I hadn't thrown myself in firepits, or sobbed myself to sleep when she went away.

"You were perfectly happy," she continued. "I provided every comfort you needed, and you repaid me with hatred. You chose to forget your own mother."

"I don't hate you." This was not how I had imagined our reunion. I had envisioned The Lady smiling as I appeared on the landing, holding me through the bars as we cried in each other's arms. I had thought she would tell me about her days in exile, her years as a child bandit queen.

I had planned to talk about my life in return, sharing the adventures that spies could never tell her.

Instead, The Lady crossed her arms and stared over my head. Her features were stony, wounded, a queen betrayed by her vassal.

"I was scared," I protested. "You told me to kill someone. An innocent person."

"Everything I said," she replied, "everything I did, was for you. For our future together."

"You never told me anything. I didn't know—" I broke off and glanced at the guards farther down the landing, lowering my voice even more. "I didn't know you wanted to be empress. But Melu told me everything. About Aiyetoro's masks. And about . . . you."

The whites of The Lady's eyes flashed. "Then Melu is a fool," she growled, "and he has put you in grave danger. If Olugbade's brat ever finds out that you have a right to his throne . . ."

"I don't want Dayo's throne, Mother. Even if I did, I wouldn't hurt him. I can't do it. I won't."

A tarnished cup lay by The Lady's hand. She plunged it into the murky bucket of water and drank. "Did Melu show you," she asked, "what your darling prince's father did to me?"

"He shouldn't have banished you. I know that was wrong. But Dayo isn't responsible—"

"Did Melu show you what happens to a palace girl who is thrown onto the streets?"

My heart sank. I shook my head.

She continued in a cool tone. "Did Melu let you see the bruises on my body? The scars that never faded? Did he show you the starvation and the cold? Or did he shield you from those things, as I shielded you in Bhekina House, where you never felt a pang of hunger or endured a single day of suffering?"

Shame heated my face. "I didn't mean to be ungrateful," I stammered. "I'm sorry, Mother. About everything."

"And I will forgive you," she replied, "because you are mine. But your years under Olugbade's thumb have made you weak." She sighed. "I expected more of you, Made-of-Me."

I swallowed hard and said, "Say my name, Mother."

Her jaw hardened. She pressed her lips together and was silent.

"You've never done it before," I said, gripping the bars. "I . . . I just want to hear you say it."

Tears glinted on her smooth cheeks. "So Olugbade has won after all. You have let him convince you to disown me. You despise being made of me, you are ashamed."

"No. No, Mother, I just—"

"You would let him poison your mind. You would cast off your own blood, your own family."

Humiliation washed over me. I remembered just minutes earlier, bowing with a docile smile before the emperor, who had signed my mother's death warrant.

"I won't abandon you," I whispered.

"What a coincidence," murmured The Lady. "That is what Woo In said months ago, when I was captured. I told him to ensure your safety first. But here you are, safe and sound . . . and he is nowhere to be seen. So much for council vows."

"Woo In read your journal at Bhekina House," I said. "He thinks you've betrayed him."

For the first time, The Lady looked unsettled. She picked at the frayed edge of her mantle, muttering almost to herself. "He will forgive me, of course. He loves me. He is mine, just like all the others."

"What is the Redemptor curse? Why did Woo In think you could control it?"

The Lady dipped her cup again. She poured the water over her fingers, washing away the dried blood until a pale red puddle pooled on the floor. "Do you know why you are more fit to rule Aritsar than that bumbling Kunleo prince?" she asked. "Because your blood is stronger. Thanks to Melu and myself, your veins run with both mortal and immortal royalty. When you anoint a council of your own, that strength will flow into them, just as theirs flows into you. Such power comes with choices, Made-of-Me. And no matter what you say—no matter what promises you make—you must always choose to preserve yourself."

My stomach twisted. "I should go." I stood and backed away from the bars. "I'll visit—I'll help you. Don't worry."

"You have never worried me, daughter." The Lady sighed, turning away. "You have only disappointed."

When I returned to my tower, I'd hoped for solitude, a place to release the tears building with each step as I descended from Heaven.

But the room was a henhouse of attendants, bustling to arrange furniture and cushions as Sanjeet hunched awkwardly in the center. A manservant wrestled another bed pallet into the room, and nodded at me for instruction before setting it down.

"Will your Anointed Honors need . . . contact?" the head manservant asked me and Sanjeet. "We can connect the pallets."

"Of *course* she needs to touch him," said Bimbola, bangles ringing as she giggled. "Their Anointed Honors must ward off council sickness. Perhaps it would be better if they shared—"

"No," Sanjeet and I blurted in unison. We glanced at each other and reddened.

"Anointed Honor Sanjeet is here as my personal guard," I announced stiffly. "Separate pallets are fine. He just needs to sleep between me and the door."

The manservant placed the pallets side by side, gave a sidelong glance at me and Sanjeet, and then pushed the pallets together. My attendants built up the fire and laid out basins for washing. Then they stripped Sanjeet and me to our shifts, tittered to themselves, and disappeared.

We had shared a room before, of course. In various inns on our way to Swana, and beneath the canopy in Melu's savannah. On the road, conventional propriety had mattered little as we escaped death by Bush-spirits, and followed tutsu sprites to find a mystical ehru. But this was different. Here in the palace, surrounded by hidden whispers and perfumed wall hangings, the space felt . . . heated. Charged.

Mortified, I sat on one of the pallets and faced away. I busied myself with wrapping my hair in its sleeping scarf. Sanjeet cleared his throat, then retreated to the washbasin. Every sound was magnified: the swish of silk on my ears as I wrapped, the splash of water against his skin.

I slipped beneath the bedding and felt Sanjeet climb onto his pallet. The scent of rosewater wafted from his hair, mixed with his smell of leather and clay. For several minutes, we lay unnaturally still. Then a breeze whistled across the window, and I thought of The Lady, alone and exposed on the An-Ileyoba turrets. My breath caught. What I intended as an exhale came out as a long, low sob.

Sanjeet hesitated, then rolled over and touched my arm. "The attendants said you saw her," he mumbled. "I didn't know if you wanted to talk about it."

"I'm a horrible person," I whispered.

"I've met worse."

For some reason, his clinical honesty made me laugh. I turned and touched his brow, showing him my conversation with The Lady. "She was just a child when the emperor banished her," I said after the memory had finished. "She was abused and abandoned for years, and all I did was hurt her more. How could I be so ungrateful?"

Sanjeet stared at me as though I were raving. "She starved you of affection," he said. "On *purpose*. She forbade people from touching you. All so you wouldn't learn enough to ruin her plans."

"And to keep me safe," I pointed out.

"She let you make your first friend," he said slowly, "and then *ordered you to murder him*."

I frowned in the dark. "But she was trying to give me a future. She risked everything she had, and I forgot her on purpose. She thinks I hate her. That I *want* the emperor to kill—"

"She's manipulating you, like she always has. She made you ashamed of *wanting your own name*. Tar, how can you think that's what love is?"

"I . . . don't know." I wiped my nose and shrugged. "You only get one mother, Jeet. It's like your father. He hurt you, but can you imagine—truly imagine—having any other kind?"

Sanjeet was silent for a long time, then swallowed once. "No. No, I can't."

Ever since the attendants had left us alone, I had been avoiding his gaze. Now I met it and saw my own ghosts mirrored there. In that moment, the curse of our parents' legacy—the monsters we loved and feared, and the scars covering us both—tethered us together.

"I shouldn't have brought him up," I said. "I'm sorry."

"It's fine." He shook his head, smiling wanly. "I guess the only gift Father gave me was a way to understand you." His thumb brushed my tear-streaked face. "A way to share the burden."

"I don't want to share, Jeet. If I fall again, I'm not bringing anyone else with me."

"That's the problem, sunshine girl." His voice was a rumble in his throat. "When it comes to you, I will never stop falling."

He kissed me. It was the first time since Nu'ina Eve, when he held me against the spray of the Obasi Ocean. I longed to lose myself in those solid arms, to believe the promise in each caress. *You are not dangerous. You are not cursed. You will never hurt anyone; you will only be loved.*

When we parted, Sanjeet untied the pouch containing my seal from his neck. He pressed the ring into my palm, and didn't let me give it back. Then something else fell from the pouch, glinting in the dying firelight: the cowrie shell anklet. Sanjeet unhooked the anklet's clasp and Ray-spoke.

I love you.

But I knew, deep down, that love had never fixed anyone. It had only given them the strength to try over, and over, and over again. So when Sanjeet reached for my foot on the pallet's edge . . . I moved my leg away and said, "I can't offer you something I don't have."

"I don't want something. I want you."

I closed his fingers around the anklet. "And I don't belong to myself. Not while The Lady's still controlling me. I love you too, Jeet, but you can't be my savior."

"Well, I won't be your jailer," he retorted. "So what can I be?"

I held his heavy fist to my lips and caressed the scars. "My hope," I said. "For a future when kissing you isn't dangerous."

A future, I added in my head, where no child was bound by curses, and every daughter had a name.

CHAPTER 27

I LAID MY HEAD ON SANJEET'S CHEST, LULLED
to sleep by his heartbeat. I dreamed first as myself, chasing
the scent of jasmine through large, abandoned halls. Then
I was a twelve-year-old boy with limbs too long for my
body.

*A cramped balcony is my refuge on a street that smells of
cardamom. I love my sleepless city of Vhraipur, though Father
has done everything in his power to make me hate it. Pure voices
drift from the temple across the road, where child acolytes sing
on the rooftop. An Ember priestess dances before an altar, her
stained arms and legs glistening in the moonlight. With every
leap of her body, light shoots into the sky, dissolving in soft
clouds of red and purple: a visible prayer. The children worship
the Storyteller and Warlord Fire in tandem:* Give us mercy.
Give us justice. Let it burn, burn, burn.

I mimic the strong movements of the priestess, sending up a prayer of my own. Protect Amah. Punish Father. Make me brave, brave, brave.

The rustle of curtains startles me. I drop my arms and pretend to punch the air. "Practicing," I mumble. "For the fight tomorrow."

But it isn't Father. Amah laughs from the balcony door. "You were dancing," she says, reaching to stroke my cheek. I am taller than my mother, but still I hang my head, ashamed of my lie. She smells of fennel. Sheer pink muslin drapes her sturdy frame, and dark, curling hair falls to her waist in a gray-streaked braid.

I reach up to touch her fingers. Then just in time, I remember that my hands are dangerous. I pull back.

"Don't tell Father," I say.

"I won't. But you pray so beautifully. Would you like to be a temple dancer?"

I want to snort. As if Father would let me near a temple, or any building that did not exist for profit. But I shrug instead, not wanting to hurt Amah's feelings. Sometimes, when she thinks I'm sleeping after a day of pit fights, she sits on the edge of my pallet and watches me. Her hands tremble as she wraps the bruises and wipes away the blood dried on my knuckles. She curses the money that falls from my shirt. Coins thrown at me after each victory. Coins that Father missed. I am a prize bear: a hero in this city that bets on boys like horses.

"I'm fine," I say.

"No child," Amah whispers, "who has been forced to kill is fine." Sendhil's name hangs unspoken between us. "What do you want to be, my son? A blacksmith? A healer? I have seen you set bones before. You sense alignment, find bruises before they appear.

You have a gift, Jeeti. Tell Amah what you want."

Her arms wrap around my torso. I long to hug her back.

"Let go," I say, not moving an inch. "I could hurt you by accident."

"You will learn to control your strength. Prince Ekundayo is building his council, and they need candidates from Dhyrma. Your Hallow means a path to Oluwan, my son. A way out." Her eyes gleam, and I notice a dark purple mark on her shoulder.

"What's that?" There are daggers in my voice.

She pulls away, hastily covering the mark with her shawl. "An accident. Nothing."

"Father," I growl.

"Nothing," she repeats, fixing me with a gaze feral in its protection. "I will get you out. Away from this house, from this city. You will not become the man I married. I am sure of it." She stands on her tiptoes, and kisses my cheek. "You will never make your living by causing pain."

Knuckles rapping on wood roused me from Sanjeet's memory-dream. We sat up, squinting blearily as an imperial warrior marched into the bedroom and bowed. Bimbola and my other attendants scampered in after him.

"Apologies, Anointed Honors," Bimbola panted. "We told him you were still sleeping."

The warrior handed one calfskin to me and another to Sanjeet. The messages bore the emperor's seal.

My summons was from Thaddace. I was to present myself at the Imperial Library, where I would begin my research for The Lady's trial. When I read the summons aloud, Bimbola made protesting noises.

"She'll burn with fever," she pointed out, confronting the warrior with her hands on her hips. "You expect an Anointed One to spend hours without a member of her council?"

The warrior inclined his head. "The Prince's Council will be studying in the Imperial Library today. Anointed Honor Tarisai will have company."

"I'd rather study alone," I blurted, then added, "Or with Jeet."

But Sanjeet shook his head. His face had been soft with sleep just moments before, free of shadows and lines. Now, after reading his summons, the stone mask had returned. "The High General requires Dayo and me to drill with the Imperial Guard."

"Drill?" I frowned. "For what?"

"The 'suppression of dissent.'" He contained a grimace. "We'll be practicing riot control."

Remembering the boy in my dream who had feared his own hands, I stroked Sanjeet's arm. The attendants noticed and giggled, chattering behind our backs as they brought our trays of breakfast. After we ate, they dressed us in matching outfits, humming with pride when they finished. Apparently, even the Unity Edict couldn't convince palace courtiers to exchange their finery for empire cloth, though

I wondered how long until the request was mandatory. Over his sparse imperial uniform, Sanjeet wore a black robe of crisp jacquard, woven through with gold patterns. I wore a mantle of the same fabric, draped over a silk halter gown the same hue as my skin. The gown's earth-colored train whispered behind me as I walked, balancing on high-soled slippers. I continued to hide the sunstone beneath my clothes.

The Imperial Library lay just outside the An-Ileyoba gates, a castle in its own right. Orbs of captive sprites lit the cavernous, muraled ceiling, and the walls blazed with wax-dyed tapestry. Black, brown, and scarlet books towered down the aisles, titles tanned on calfskin spines. Boughs of palm fronds and pear blossoms spilled from vases, filling the air with their perfume. A griot's pure tenor floated above the hush of studious whispers.

Every family in the empire received library ribbons after paying the imperial tax. Scholar-class ribbons were black, good for five visits a week. Noble-class ribbons were blue, and good for three. Gray-ticketed merchants and peasants were allowed one visit a month. When I flashed my seal, the guards waved me in without a word. There was no limit on knowledge for an Anointed One.

The central hall ceiling was one of the oldest in Oluwan, with a mural commissioned by the first Imperial High Priestess. It was unusual: Most murals portrayed a story, usually a battle or a coronation. The Imperial Library ceiling, now heavily faded, portrayed two overlapping gold discs, bordered by a multicomplexioned circle of linking hands.

"Who painted that?" I asked the chief librarian, trying to remember where I'd seen the image before. "Do you know what it means?"

The heavily robed man frowned, scratching his graying head. "I'm afraid not, Anointed Honor. The mural was commissioned by Aiyetoro, back when the Imperial Library was first being built. Most of the relevant documents vanished over centuries ago."

"Aiyetoro?" I echoed. I remembered then where I had seen the symbol of discs and linking hands: tanned faintly into the border of Aiyetoro's drum. "She built the Imperial Library?"

The librarian frowned more deeply, nodding. "Yes. Making knowledge accessible to the public was very important to Aiyetoro Kunleo. Too important, in my frank opinion. Knowledge, after all, is dangerous in the hands of the wrong people."

"Like an empress who isn't supposed to exist?"

"Beg pardon, Anointed Honor?"

"Never mind." From somewhere in the vast building, I heard a familiar ring of voices that filled me with longing and dread. They were here: my anointed siblings, chattering and laughing. I prayed they wouldn't see me as I followed the chief librarian, who ushered me to a private study.

The cramped room was lamplit and strewn with lion pelts. In the center, a mahogany kneeling desk curved around a large red seat cushion.

"His Anointed Honor, the High Lord Judge, has been so considerate as to assist you in gathering sources," said the librarian, gesturing to the books and papers piled on the desk. "He sends his regrets that he cannot join you. Complications regarding the Unity Edict's enforcement have kept him . . . occupied." The librarian bowed smartly and instructed my attendants to wait outside my study door, and fetch more dusty tomes if I needed them. Then he left me alone.

With a sigh, I knelt behind the cold desk on the stiff tasseled cushion. The stacks of books and records had been neatly labeled. I peered at the note on the first pile: *Treason laws, Enoba era to present.* Books lay beneath with binding so thick, it had been fortified with leather string. The next pile was shorter, but the label made me uneasy: *Disorders of the mind. Case studies: madness and acts of violence. Case studies: delusions of grandeur, belief in self as god; belief in descent from royal blood.* The last stack was made entirely of scrolls and letters—and labeled with four words:

Lady X: exile years.

I tore into that pile, devouring the scrolls, hungry to fill in the gaps of my mother's story. But even after hours, it felt even more piecemeal than before. The documents were varied: half-burnt letters, spy logs, pages from decades-old diaries. One sheet appeared to be a portrait of The Lady above a manifesto in Songul, the prevalent tongue of Songland. The paper was water-damaged, and my Songul was remedial, but I recognized the Arit words *divine right* and *liberator*. When my stomach gurgled for lunch, the palm oil lamp wicks now half their original length, I had more questions than when I began.

Council sickness made my vision blur. I had not seen Sanjeet for hours, and nausea threatened to blossom into a headache. But when someone cleared their throat behind the study's woven door, the pain between my temples mysteriously faded.

"Come in," I said, and my spirits rose when a round, cheery face peered around the frame.

"Heard a rumor you were hiding in here," Kirah announced, teetering beneath the weight of several books as she burst through the door flap. She wore a gauzy priestess's kaftan, and looked well rested. Reuniting with Dayo and our council siblings had agreed with her. She dumped the books into a pile, dusted off her hands, and collapsed beside me at the desk. "Thought you could use some reinforcements."

"Thaddace gave me more than enough," I groaned, and then noticed the titles on Kirah's stack. *Arit Imperial Policies: the Aiyetoro Era. Genealogy of the Kunleos. The Peace Age: A Treatise on the Preservation of the Oluwan Economy Under the Reign of Aiyetoro.* "Oh."

"I heard about your First Ruling. Maybe proving The Lady's lineage will delay the trial. I know you weren't close with her, but . . ." Her expression grew stormy. "No one should have to kill their own mother. Am's Story, it's so cruel. How could the emperor . . ." She trailed off.

On the theater of her face, I watched Kirah's anger battle her allegiance to the throne. I had fought a similar battle in my head, ever since seeing the story in Melu's pool. Kirah flushed, surprised at her own outburst. "I'm supposed to be rewriting old sacred texts," she said, retrieving her imperial summons from her pocket. "Editing away verses that could 'threaten empire unity.' I know it's wrong to question the emperor. But every time I think about changing the old songs . . . my blood wants to boil."

"Maybe," I ventured, "it's all right to be angry."

She pressed her lips together, and we stared at the desk in silence, sharing the bond of our uncertainty. In the bittersweet moment, I realized why council members were called siblings. Kirah and I were made of different clay, but the Children's Palace testmakers had shaped us into similar vessels. Defending the Kunleos had been the carefully crafted goal of our existence. But in these last few months, that purpose had been stripped apart, leaving a hole with no stopper.

"I'm sorry you're in this mess with me," I said, throat tight with guilt. "I'm sorry you had to see Dayo bleeding. I'm sorry you had to keep secrets from our council, and cross the empire with Woo In. But—" I squeezed her hand. "I'm so happy you're in my story, Kirah."

She squeezed back. "And I'm happy you're in mine." We smiled at each other, and then a flash of mischief darted across her face. "You know," she said. "Traveling with Woo In wasn't always that bad."

My brow shot into my hairline. "How not that bad?"

"Mayazatyl was right," she observed lightly. "Kissing isn't gross after all."

I gasped, then laughed, then gasped again. "Kirah."

"Like you haven't devoured Sanjeet's face a million times by now."

"Not a million." My face heated. "More like . . . six." We both dissolved into giggles, but when we caught our breath I asked, "Why Woo In?"

"Why not? I mean, I didn't know he had tried to kill Dayo when I kissed him."

"But he's odd. And sullen. And old enough to be your . . ." I considered. "Older brother. All right, that could be worse, but still—"

"I know nothing can happen," she said abruptly. "He isn't a council member, so it wouldn't be right." Her voice grew uncharacteristically soft. "I just . . . felt we had something in common. A hunger, I guess."

"He tried to burn down the Children's Palace."

"You lured a man to a cliff and stabbed him with a knife."

"Good point," I conceded. "When it comes to friends and lovers, you have horrible taste."

"Mama would be appalled," she agreed, but she didn't sound ashamed in the slightest.

Every day, Kirah returned to the study, keeping me company at my desk while buried in studies of her own. Instead of rewriting sacred texts, she had tracked down every record in the Imperial Library about Songland. For hours she bent over the texts, scribbling notes and occasionally reading lines out loud.

"Look," she insisted one morning, showing me an etched diagram of rice fields. "Their irrigation techniques are more advanced than ours. They grow mountains of rice, but they can't trade it with the rest of the continent. So their villages remain poor. It's not fair, Tar. It's just not fair." Minutes later, she blurted, "'I crest at dawn with the world on my arms. Welcome: My heart rises and breaks. Come and stay awhile.' A shepherdess wrote that. A shepherdess! People in Songland compose poems for everyday life. Not just for rituals or histories, like Arits do. Tar, isn't it amazing?"

"I wonder if Ye Eun liked poems," I murmured. I still dreamed of the girl often, wondering if she had survived. "Did Woo In tell you what the Underworld was like?"

Kirah turned pink, as she always did when I brought up the prince of Songland. We hadn't heard from him or Kathleen since they'd left Bhekina House. Kirah considered my question. "Woo In said that every step was like dying. Not pain, exactly. Just the cold, gnawing emptiness that every creature feels before its last breath. It's something you're only supposed to feel for a moment. Then death relieves you, and you pass into the true afterlife, Core: a paradise at the center of the earth. But Redemptors aren't really dead . . . so that relief never comes."

When a living thing passed through the Breach, Kirah

went on to explain, it was only a temporary form of death. If Redemptors found their way out, they could return to the land of living. The only other escape was being killed in the Underworld: their final death. In the Underworld, abiku could not cause physical harm to a living creature, unless the creature asked of its own free will. But the feeling of cold emptiness was so unbearable, most children only lasted for a few hours before begging for the final release.

Woo In had lasted seventeen days.

"He focused on remembering every warm thing he'd ever felt," Kirah whispered. "Festival bonfires. His mother's arms. The sound of his sister's laugher. He was only ten." Her voice broke. "The only way out was via the map on his skin. The birthmarks glowed, even in the dark, so he was able to follow a path. But every step was torture. The spirits tried every trick they could. Illusions of twisting caves and pits full of snakes, meant to lure him off track. Voices of his loved ones who had died—his father, his grandparents—whispering from the shadows, pleading with him to join them. He lost track of time. His body ached with hunger and thirst, but he couldn't die. He would have given up if not for Hyung. The emi-ehran found him in the Underworld, and breathed strength into him. Step by step, they made it out together. But the nightmares still plague him. It helped when I sang." She smiled sadly. "Our families are alike, Woo In's and mine. We both had parents who kept us in bubbles. Families who feared change, even if it could mean helping our own people. Woo In and I both grew too big for our homes. So we left, and we've been lost ever since. And now—" She sighed, scowling at her imperial summons. "I wonder if we left one cage, only to find ourselves trapped in a bigger one."

CHAPTER 28

MY OWN STUDIES PROGRESSED AT A GLACIAL pace. Sources on the only empress in Kunleo history were sparse and contradictory. Like all Kunleo girls, she had been raised in obscurity, away from court. Some sources described her as fragile, weeping in secret beneath the weight of her reign, and leaning on the men around her for support. Other sources painted her as conniving, a vain and irrational shrew, caring only for her own survival. But neither of these portrayals supported the empress's legacy. No historian, no matter how begrudging, could deny that in less than twenty years, the quiet, obscure Kunleo girl had abolished the Arit slave trade, crushed the ensuing rebellion, and brought an era of peace that had lasted for centuries.

The daughter of Folu Kunleo had not been summoned to the palace until she was almost a woman. When it became clear that her father would produce no sons, the reluctant priests had acknowledged her as Raybearer. She arrived at court friendless and without protection, without even an official birth name. The nobility had rubbed their palms, expecting a puppet empress they could bend to their interests. When the short, thin-boned girl arrived in the throne room, the rulers of each realm had swarmed, insisting on the privilege of naming her.

"She will be called Ireyuwa," announced the king of Swana. "For she is half Swanian and will bring a time of great wealth for my realm."

"She will be called Cihuacoatl," demanded the king of Quetzala. "Do not my people supply gold and weapons for the throne? Her power will come from us."

"She will be called Etheldred," crowed the queen of Mewe. "For she spent her years of obscurity in my realm. She will not forget the land that raised her."

As they argued, the girl had soundlessly pushed through the crowd. She mounted the great dais, plain sandals slapping the marble, and seated herself on the gold-encrusted throne. The carved wooden staff of her father lay before her. She picked it up and beat the floor, once, with a resounding crack. The room fell silent.

"I will be called Aiyetoro," said the daughter of Folu. "For mine will be an era of peace at any price."

"I just wish we knew more about her," I told Kirah. It was two weeks before my First Ruling. We had left the library for the Imperial Theatre Garden, where we meditated daily. "When Aiyetoro died, all her journals—her letters, the books her council wrote about her—were lost in a fire. The record keepers say it was an accident. I bet it wasn't."

"Stop it," Kirah scolded. She knelt across from me on a prayer mat, eyes serenely closed. "No conspiracy talk during meditation, remember? You'll only get distracted."

I sighed, squirming on my own mat. Several yards away, Kirah's attendants sat with mine, gossiping as they watched the stage far below. The Imperial Theatre Garden was sculpted into the side of Palace Hill. Designed by master architects from Quetzala, the garden was composed of shelves of vine-covered terraces descending steeply to a stone platform. Audiences picnicked on the terraces, and when a performer stood on triangles cut into the stage, their voices echoed throughout the garden.

"The mantra," Kirah coaxed.

"I have a purpose," I intoned reluctantly. "There is music deep inside me—"

"A song," she corrected.

"A song," I muttered. "I learned the song at birth. I draw it from within . . . Kirah, is this really helping?"

"Better than nothing. You've got to find your bellysong somehow." She hummed and crossed her legs, touching the pendant on her chest. "And if you never slow down and think, how will you ever know what your greatest good is?"

Greatest good. Best desire. The phrases had plagued me every day since we left Melu's pool. Hours of meditation had not made the words clearer. What greater good could I possibly have than protecting Dayo? Out of all the things I loved—all the things I had ever cared about—his life was the purest. But if protecting Dayo was my bellysong—my purpose—how could I fulfill it while The Lady still controlled me?

I flopped onto the grass. "Why did Melu think I could do this? He's the wise immortal one. Why doesn't he just find *his* purpose and free us both?"

Kirah laughed and gave up on her meditation. "Maybe alagbato purposes don't work that way," she mused. "And alagbatos aren't immortal, not really. In Blessid Valley, we called our alagbatos *juniyas*. They all died thousands of years ago, when the rivers dried up and left a desert."

I squinted up at the cloudless sky, considering this. "Maybe Melu's purpose is to inhabit Swana," I murmured. "Swana's crops were fertile once, and that stopped once The Lady enslaved him. I guess as long as he's confined to that tiny grassland, he can't do what he was made for." I sighed and sat up, hugging Aiyetoro's drum to my chest. The more I learned about Aiyetoro, the less comfortable I was with leaving the drum unattended. So I had brought the hourglass-shaped gourd to the garden, leaning it against my thigh as we meditated.

Kirah peered at the inscription emblazoned on the instrument. "'*The truth will never die, as long griots keep beating their drums*,'" she murmured. "What an odd thing to write. Can't you take its memories?"

"I've tried." I pulled the heavy instrument onto my lap and ran my fingers across the goatskin tension cords. "Most of the memories are from spiders and beetles, and whatever else crawled across it in storage. I tried to take more of its story, but—" I shook my head. "It's just so old. Using my Hallow, I've never seen further than a few decades. I'd have to go back *two hundred years* to reach Aiyetoro." I didn't mention that sometimes, when I slept with the drum beside me, I dreamed as someone else. My body belonged to a woman with long, slender fingers and a low alto voice, beating the drum as she swayed side to side.

"Maybe it would help if you played it," Kirah suggested.

I shivered. "Isn't it bad luck to play another person's drum? Especially one belonging to a griot?"

Kirah shrugged, biting back what I knew she was thinking. *No worse luck than being born half-ehru, destined to murder a prince and forced to sentence your own mother to death.* At this point, my luck could only improve.

I slipped the drum's beating stick from where it had been tucked beneath the tension cords, then squeezed the drum against my rib cage. "Sorry," I told the gourd, then held my breath and struck.

The sound was surprisingly muted. Talking drums were known for their resonance, and were used to communicate across miles. Why did this one sound flat? Then again, it *was* two hundred years old. It was a miracle it hadn't fallen apart after I dragged it across Aritsar. I tapped again, using my Hallow this time, and several dozen spiders scuttled across my consciousness. I shuddered, withdrawing from the drum's memory.

"Still nothing," I told Kirah.

"You've only played one note," she pointed out.

"Easy for you to say," I retorted. "You're not risking the wrath of a malevolent griot spirit." I made a face and squeezed the cords for different pitches. Facetiously, I began to beat out the military sequence for *retreat*, which could also mean *the effort is going nowhere*. But instead of finishing the phrase, which ended on three high notes, the drum made a low *bong*, followed by a throaty *gun godo*. I frowned, trying the phrase again. This time, all the notes came out wrong. "Tuning must be damaged," I said.

But as I continued to play, Kirah grew very still. My mouth went dry. No matter how many phrases I tried, the drum made the same sequence of pitches, over and over. *Bong, gun, godo godo gun.*

I released the gourd, letting it tumble to the grass as a chill rushed up my spine.

Kirah croaked, "You don't think . . ."

My palms were sweating. "I think it's talking to us. It's happened before. Aiyetoro's drum saved me in the Bush."

I racked my brain for the drum phrases Mbali had taught us as children. The first *bong-gun* matched the pitches for *eternity*, which could also mean *always*. The last half, *godo-godo-gun*, sounded like the *all clear, come now* phrase miners used in quarries. "Always come here?" I guessed.

Kirah shook her head. "It's the wrong pitch for a

command. And the note goes down at the end, so it's talking about the past. Not *come here . . .* more like, *I was here. I was inside.*"

I frowned. In drum language, *I* could just as easily be *she*, or *they* or *it*. "Always . . . it . . . was inside," I said. "What's that supposed to mean?"

After a pause, I took up the drum again, half-hoping our ears had been playing tricks on us. But again the drum intoned: *It was always inside. It was always inside. Bong, gun, godo godo gun.*

"We should stop," I said, glancing down at the garden stage. "We'll distract the warriors."

We sat on the terrace farthest from the stage, shielded from view by ferns that needed trimming. From our hiding spot, I could still make out the scene below.

During festivals, griots performed in the Theatre Garden, declaiming praise poems about the emperor and his council. This afternoon, however, the lower terraces were crowded with Imperial Guard warriors. Nearly naked and glistening with sweat, they drilled in groups as Sanjeet barked orders from the stage.

"Hyena Cohort, shields up!" His voice was hoarse and joyless. "Hold. Shoulders square. Hold your position, I said. Lion Cohort, charge. Again. *Again.*"

Repeatedly, a group rushed forward as the other stood its ground. A wall of shields braced against the onslaught of shoulders and spears. The men and women were training, I realized, to contain riots.

Anointed Honor Wagundu, Olugbade's High Lord General, observed the drills with stern approval. Then a gangly young man rushed onstage, bobbing apologies for being late.

Kirah stiffened. "Tar—"

I dove behind the terrace's hanging ferns, blocking my view. My vision blurred and reddened, but before *kill, kill* began to pulse through my veins, I fumbled with the neckline of my wrapper and seized the sunstone.

The murderous lust still burned in my throat, but my mind cleared. "Hold my arms," I whispered to Kirah. "I need to see how bad it gets." She complied, and I steeled my jaw and peered through the curtain of ferns.

It was the first time I had seen Dayo since leaving him in the keep, still bleeding from my knife wound.

I drank him in, blessing his legs for standing, his side for being whole. From this distance, I couldn't tell if his torso had a scar. But he looked healthy, albeit awkward, shifting from foot to foot as he nodded at the warriors. My heart brimmed with sympathy. Dayo had always shrunk from violence. But he was required to watch the Imperial Guard with Sanjeet and help design their drills. His face looked wan and sleepless. After a day of studying with his council, he probably spent his nights helping Olugbade prepare for the Treaty Renewal, which was two days after my First Ruling.

"Get strong," I murmured, gripping the sunstone until it cut into my palm. "Stay safe from me."

Kirah helped me stand and we hurried away, leaving our confused handmaidens to fetch the prayer mats and scurry after. "He misses you," Kirah whispered, threading my arm firmly through hers until the Theatre Garden was out of sight. "He barely sleeps unless I sing, or Thérèse makes one of her teas. If you won't see him, you could at least write."

I had refused the notes Dayo sent daily to my tower, worried they would weaken my resolve to stay away. "Studying is better than writing," I said. "If I find a purpose to break the curse, I won't have to stay away."

Kirah huffed a laugh. "We'd better find your purpose quick. Rumors are getting out of control."

I turned sharply. "What rumors?"

"There aren't many reasons why two anointed council members would sleep in a tower all by themselves," she pointed out. "Even our council's getting suspicious. Mayazatyl's demanded regular reports of your belly size." When I looked blank, she wiggled her eyebrows. "She thinks you're carrying Sanjeet's *pikin*. To save you both from palace scandal, she's concocted an elaborate plan for Dayo to pass off your love child as his own."

I snorted. "She *would*. Am's Story," I groaned. "When we move to An-Ileyoba for good, Mayazatyl's gossiping rear end will fit right in."

"I hope we never move here," Kirah blurted. "I mean, I know we will. We have to. It's what we've trained for our whole lives. It's just . . ." She sighed and stopped in the tiled northern courtyard, letting the pristinely groomed peacocks explore the hem of her priestess kaftan. Beyond Palace Hill, the roofs of Oluwan City spread in a jagged sea. Smoke rose from bonfire mountains, where the stories of griots burned. "When I was in the Blessid Valley, I longed for a bigger world. I wanted to travel the empire, learn all there was to know. But the more I learn about Songland, the more suffocating Aritsar feels. I don't know what I want. I only know the world is big, and I'm sick of pretending it's smaller."

The day of my First Ruling crept closer. Crowds of dignitaries, nobility, and commoners would attend, and so the palace bustled in preparation. Many royals, I learned with chagrin, would attend as well. This was unusual: The continent's rulers typically sent a proxy to everything but the grandest imperial events. But since my First Ruling would occur so close to the Treaty Renewal, many of the empire's royals would be at the palace already.

Kirah and I searched fruitlessly for the lost masks of Aiyetoro, the only proof that empress and princess Raybearers truly existed. We combed the Imperial Library for leads every day, and searched the palace crypts at night. I continued to visit Heaven. I could not come often, in case word got back to Olugbade, and his suspicion of me grew. But after hefty bribes, the guards allowed me to bring small gifts: a lump of soap, a thin blanket, a pot of salve for The Lady's wind-whipped skin. After sliding the items through the bars of her cell door, I would sit—sometimes in silence, other times asking questions. She mostly ignored the latter, especially ones about her childhood. She only paid attention when I babbled about the inner workings of Yorua Keep, or about being tutored by Thaddace and Mbali.

"You rarely speak of the High Judge without mentioning the priestess," she observed one day, cocking her head.

I shrugged and blushed. "They're always together."

"That sounds like a story, daughter." When I hesitated, she laughed and patted my hand through the bars. "Do not worry for their reputation. I am hardly in a position to spread gossip."

I was eager to make her smile again. Shyly, I recounted the time I had stumbled on Thaddace and Mbali at the height of passion. The Lady listened intently and chuckled. I joined in, the first time I had ever shared a joke with my own mother.

I wondered if she had heard the rumors about me and Sanjeet. Mothers, according to Kirah, were protective of daughters when it came to young men. But if The Lady suspected that I had flirtations, she never asked about them. The existence of a love affair—or any aspect of my life unrelated to her master plans—never seemed to cross her mind.

Sanjeet collapsed, exhausted, into my arms every night.

He would gather me to himself, limbs rigid as amber until at last he relaxed, discarding the mask he wore for the Guard. On the worst days, the mask remained even as he slept. Frowning with worry, I would rub circles into his clenched jaw until it released.

"The drilling's over," he said one night. "We've begun our campaigns in the city." The smell of bonfires still lingered in his hair. His hands were newly bruised from when civilians had fought back, resisting when their drums and books were wrenched away. Against Sanjeet's Hallow, they would not have resisted long.

"You won't have to enforce the Unity Edict forever," I said, though the comfort sounded hollow even to me. "People will get used to it. And things could change when Dayo's emperor."

"How many nightmares will I have by then? And how many will I have caused?" He smiled grimly, turning away on the pallet. "I guess Amah was wrong. I will always earn my keep by breaking bones."

I scowled into the darkness, tracing patterns on his muscled back until he fell asleep. "This is not," I whispered, "what I crossed a coal pit for."

In the small hours of the morning, I lit a palm oil lamp and penned a calfskin letter, sealing it with my ring. Then I rapped on my tower door, which I had insisted be locked at night. I slid back the wooden hatch that hid a grate in the door's center, allowing me to peer into the antechamber where my attendants slept. A yawning Bimbola staggered to the hatch, and I stuck my hand through the grate.

"This letter must be posted at first light," I said, and dropped a hefty portion of my imperial allowance into her palm. "Divide this among the runners. They'll have to use lodestones. Spare no expense." Bimbola nodded, eyes round with curiosity. As she bustled out of the antechamber, she snuck a glance at the letter's sealed front, which was addressed in my hurried script: *KEEYA THE MERCHANT. PIKWE VILLAGE, SWANA.*

CHAPTER 29

THE NIGHT BEFORE MY FIRST RULING arrived, and the empress Raybearer masks were still nowhere to be found.

I paced my tower room, trying to drum out the parade of death in my head. *Poison, contagion, gluttony, burning.* The grit of sandstone pressed into the balls of my feet. Sanjeet watched worriedly as I tried to crush the words into the floor, pound them to dust, where they could never hurt anyone.

Drowning, suffocation, bleeding.

"The emperor doesn't know," I said aloud, shredding the hem of my sleeping scarf. "The emperor doesn't know what The Lady's weakness is." The Lady had never finished anointing her Eleven, which meant she could still be killed by someone other than her anointed. Olugbade only needed to figure out how.

Beast mauling, disaster. Organ-death, witches' hexes, battery.

"He'll probably try every one until he finds it." My voice was barely audible. By now, the edge of my sleeping scarf was a tangled mess of thread. "It will hurt her. Even if she doesn't die, it will hurt. Jeet—I don't—I don't know what to—"

He folded me into his chest, but I stood rigid as steel. "Dayo and the others will be happy to see you again," he murmured. "They're in the Children's Palace, preparing for your ruling right now. When I left them, Kameron and Theo were, ah, debating whether Kameron could smuggle a meerkat pup into the ceremony."

I laughed weakly, accepting the distraction. "Why?"

"Kam thinks you could use the emotional support."

Sanjeet fetched The Lady's enchanted glass from the window seat, and I watched as my council siblings stood like mannequins around the Hall of Dreams, swathed in jewels and finery, teasing each other as palace garment-makers hovered, attaching buttons and hemming trains.

Yesterday, the garment-makers had come to prepare my First Ruling garments, clucking over which hues suited me best. I had almost chosen a spicy green silk, embroidered with bursts of gold. Then Bimbola had cleared her throat.

"The emperor suggested you wear this, Anointed Honor." She held up a stiff ream of brocade, bleached as bone, with the Kunleo sun-and-stars glittering in a pattern across the hem.

Empire cloth. So the world would know who owned me.

I spied on the Children's Palace long into the night, even after Sanjeet had fallen asleep, and my siblings had collapsed onto their pallets. But one bed in the Hall of Dreams, I noticed with a frown, was empty.

A soft knock sounded on my tower door.

I sighed. That would be Bimbola, come to chide me for burning a lamp instead of resting. I padded across the room and opened the door hatch, peering through the grate.

My attendants had vanished from the antechamber. Only one person stood outside my door, shadowy in the dim moonlight.

"Dayo," I breathed.

My hands flew up to my throat, seizing the sunstone. His broad features were still smooth and unlined, but somehow he looked older. Wiser. He wore only his bedclothes, laces undone at the collar to reveal his obsidian mask. He had been dressed the same way my last night at Yorua, when I'd lured him to that cliff.

"I'm sorry," I said, choking through the flood of violent urges that still controlled me, and thanking Am for the locked wooden door. "I'm so sorry."

"You haven't been reading my messages."

"You shouldn't be here."

"Because you'll try to kill me again?"

His matter-of-fact tone made me shiver. As I watched his face, I realized with slow, pressing discomfort that I had no idea what Dayo was thinking. The sensation was foreign. From the moment we met, Dayo's features had been a page for me to read as I liked. Even when we stood apart in a room, the warmth of his Ray glowed at the edges of my mind, relaying his emotions and fleeting desires. His Ray did not reach for me now.

I searched his pure black eyes in the dark, smarting at the caution I saw there. His former trust had seemed like weakness to me, a folly, not a gift. Now I knew that trust was a privilege. Suddenly, I regretted burning his letters.

"I only came back because of your father's summons," I mumbled. "I didn't want to put you in danger again."

Dayo considered me, grave and guarded. "Sanjeet told me about Melu's pool. He said that The Lady's hold over you will end if you find a purpose. Or if—"

"If I sentence her to death," I finished. "But it doesn't matter if I break The Lady's curse, Dayo. You don't have to take me back. I know I've lost your trust." I shifted, wondering how he could look so calmly at someone who had slid a knife into his gut. "I'll leave after the ruling. Forever, if you like."

"Leave?" For the first time, his features gleamed with pain. "So you would break your promise again."

"What promise?"

"The night of the fire in the Children's Palace, you said you'd never abandon me or Aritsar. We made a pact."

"You should never have anointed me," I said. "We both know that. If I had told you from the beginning—what I was, what I'd been sent to do—"

"I knew, Tarisai. I knew the whole time."

Speech deserted me.

Dayo shrugged, playing with the strings of his nightshirt. "Do you remember when we used to share my pallet in the Children's Palace? When we were little—Once, after you fell asleep, you put your hand on my face. And I saw everything. The alagbato, The Lady. The day she showed you my picture, and wished for you to kill me. You didn't mean to share that memory, I think. But you wanted to. Looking back, you tried to warn me a million different ways. Even while you slept."

"'You remembered,'" I murmured. "That's what you said when I stabbed you." Suddenly I was kneeling beneath the quiver tree again, Dayo's voice rasping in my ear. *You missed my heart. That means you're stronger than her.*

"I tried to help," he said. "I thought I could keep you from remembering, so The Lady couldn't control you."

"That's why you always kept me from thinking about Swana," I said slowly. "And why you never let Mbali tutor me. You were trying to protect us both." My head spun. "If you knew what I came to do, then why not have me killed? Why anoint me?"

"Because you could have let me die so many times. When you saved me from that fire, I knew you weren't The Lady's pawn. I needed you. More importantly . . . I knew Aritsar needed you." He swallowed hard. "It's hard to explain. When I woke up after Enitawa's Quiver, and you were gone, it felt like being stabbed again. Losing you wasn't like losing a friend, Tarisai. It was like . . . being erased. Like losing half of myself."

"I tried to kill you. It didn't make sense for me to stay, not then and not now. It isn't safe."

"What if you found the empress and princess masks?"

I froze, and my throat went dry. No. He couldn't. He couldn't possibly know unless—

"Don't be angry at Kirah," he said slowly. "She confirmed it when I asked, but I've always known you had the Ray. I could feel it when we were children. And I'll admit: It scared me, Tar. I had trained my whole life to be emperor, but deep down, I knew you could do it better."

"That isn't true," I snapped. "To be as kind as you are—to see the best in everyone, the way you do every day—that takes more courage than I'll ever have. You're exactly what this empire needs, Dayo. Aritsar would be heartless without you."

"But it would be weak without you," Dayo retorted. "You see a mural where I see fractured pieces. You see systems. I only see people."

"Am didn't give you the Ray for nothing. You were meant to rule."

"We were meant to be a team. And you made a promise." Dayo reached through the grate. Shaking, I released one hand from the sunstone, and let him entwine my fingers with his. "Swear you won't break it again, Tar. This isn't our parents' story. Swear on our blood bond that you'll do whatever it takes to stay." His grip tightened, and his expression was bright, desperate. "Whatever it takes."

391

I closed my eyes. In that moment, my hours of meditation with Kirah came to a crystal clear solution.

My bellysong was to protect Dayo. And the only way to ensure his safety—the only path to my freedom—was to kill The Lady.

My heart sank to my sandals. I knew what I owed Dayo. I had failed him once already, and no matter how his father had wronged The Lady—no matter how that girl in the Bhekina House study still longed for her mother—I could not fail Dayo again.

I gripped his fingers in return. "Tomorrow," I said quietly, "I will be who the empire needs me to be." I kissed the seal of his imperial ring and added, "That's a blood promise."

I twisted the gold cuffs on my arms, rubbing the scarlet marks they had dug into my skin. The sun had barely risen over An-Ileyoba, and thousands of Arits—including the kings, queens, and chieftains of twelve realms—were filling the Imperial Hall to witness my First Ruling. From the corridor where I listened, floors above, I could hear them: a dull echoing roar.

Sanjeet stood beside me at the double woven door flaps of a dressing lounge, where our council awaited my entrance.

"Mayazatyl will be disappointed you aren't pregnant,"

Sanjeet observed. I laughed so I wouldn't cry. His hand closed around mine. He looked magnificent in the sweeping, pearl-studded black kaftan of Dhyrmish nobility. Waiting to be ceremonially dressed before our council, I wore nothing but a silk robe and the sunstone.

"I should have found a way to visit them," I said. "I should have been braver. Now I won't have time to explain."

After the dressing ritual, I would enter the Imperial Hall in a grand procession, flanked on all sides by my council siblings: a display of empire unity. The whole continent would be watching—but in this moment, I only cared about my council siblings. Would they forgive me for staying away all these months? How would I ever explain?

The double doors opened, and ten pairs of eyes turned to me. I found Dayo's, and Sanjeet's hand formed a viselike grip on mine. The sunstone burned on the bare skin of my chest, and I steeled my limbs, restraining the beast. *You can't kill him here*, I reasoned with the monster inside me, using her devilish logic against her. *Everyone in this room has a Hallow. They would kill you before you could finish the job. Wait.*

Utter silence. Then Ai Ling crowed at Mayazatyl, "You owe me seven gold coins. Tar doesn't have a *pikin,* after all."

Then everyone except Dayo engulfed me with hugs, teasing and bombarding me with questions. Kirah forced them to give me air, but I didn't want it. I wanted nothing more but to be buried in my siblings' chaos, deep within their love where I belonged.

"You look amazing," I hiccupped, swiping at tears. "All of you."

They truly did. Attendants had dressed each of them in the clothing of their home realms: individual creations of silk, wool, or wax-dyed cloth. In tribute to the emperor, however, all of them wore elements of Oluwan. My brothers looked imposing in onyx circlets emblazoned with the Kunleo seal, and my sisters towered in Oluwan *geles*, starched pieces of fabric that bloomed around their heads in bright folded patterns.

"You look like you're about to fall over," Kameron snickered at Emeronya, who scowled, adjusting the massive cloth headdress on her small head.

"Mayazatyl's just as short as me," Emeronya pointed out.

"The difference," Mayazatyl sighed, "is that I look splendid."

We laughed as she flirted with her reflection. The lounge belonged to Olugbade's council, and jewelry and sashes draped a dozen floor-length mirrors. Servants had brought oranges and cream cakes, but the baskets lay untouched; excitement must have killed my siblings' appetites. Several carafes of palm wine, however, lay open around the room.

"I'll need some of that," I said, and Sanjeet placed a goblet in my hand. Dayo lifted his cup to me from across the room, with a desperate stare that twisted my stomach. He wore an immaculate Oluwan *agbada*: a pale gold kaftan with heavily draped sleeves, winking with sunstones and raised white braid. Judging from the bags beneath his eyes, he had slept no better than I had.

I'm sorry, he Ray-spoke. *I know sentencing your mother today will be hard—*

Let's not talk about it, I replied, avoiding his gaze, then said aloud, "Can we start?" I shivered in my thin robe. "I'm tired of being naked."

Attendants signaled for a wizened griot to enter the chamber, and my dressing ritual began. The griot sang a parable about the triumph of justice, keeping time on a hand drum while, one by one, each of my council siblings handed me an item of clothing.

"As High Priestess, I will lean on you," said Kirah, handing me part of my gown. "So as High Lady Judge, you may lean on me."

"As High Lord General, I will lean on you," said Sanjeet, handing me a bangle. "So as High Lady Judge, you may lean on me."

"As High Lady of Castles," said Mayazatyl, painting a dot on my brow, "I will lean on you . . ."

Soon all eleven of my siblings had murmured the vow of support, and I stood fully dressed before the semicircle of mirrors, not recognizing my maze of reflections.

My empire-cloth gown was so white, I was surprised it did not chill my skin. The fabric wrapped snugly around my frame and stopped beneath my arms, leaving my collarbone bare. An avalanche of cloth unfurled in a train from my shoulder blades. A necklace of polished cowrie shells draped in strands across my breast. Dots of paint, Swana-style, scattered the bridge of my nose, and arched over each eye. The tall points of a spiked halo headdress gleamed in my hair, ivory spears framing my face like moonbeams.

High Judge Thaddace would escort me into the ruling. When he arrived at the lounge, I curtsied, barely able to bend beneath the stiff fabric. I noticed then that we matched; instead of the plaid wool of Mewe, he wore an empire-cloth tunic, bleached white clashing uneasily with his pale complexion.

He offered his arm. When I laid mine on top, he leaned down and murmured, "There is no justice . . ."

"There is only order," I finished tonelessly, and he nodded with approval. We left the lounge, Dayo and my council following in a silent procession.

I heard the Imperial Hall before I saw it.

The rumble of thousands: courtiers, commoners, royalty from all twelve realms, dialects colliding through the cavernous gilded chamber. Sandstone gleamed beneath the domed ceiling's skylights. Twelve onyx pillars loomed overhead. Each was chiseled in the shape of a man or a woman, one for each realm of Aritsar. Their features were hauntingly detailed, and their bodies thick as cedar trees, several stories high. Together, the giants supported the Imperial Hall dome on their stone shoulders.

Usually, the hall held twelve thrones. Today there were twenty-four raised on a multilevel dais: a united front of emperor, prince, and both imperial councils. Olugbade and his council were already seated. All of them had dressed in the ghostly white empire cloth.

The rest of the hall was standing space, with people teeming on the floor and on tiers and balconies that stacked all the way up to the ceiling. Drummers and dancers lined the hall, leading the crowds in a chant as I walked toward the dais. The song was deafening, and to understand the words, I had to read the crowd's lips. *Kwesi Idajo. Seneca Idajo. Jiao Idajo. Mawusi Idajo. Helene Idajo. Obafemi Idajo. Thaddace Idajo.* The names and title of every past Anointed High Judge, culminating at last with one phrase, over and over: *Ta-ri-sai Idajo. Ta-ri-sai Idajo. Ta-ri-sai Idajo*: Tarisai the Just.

My council took their seats. Then I climbed the great dais, my train rustling with each step. When I sank into the wood-carved throne by Dayo's side, the crowd hushed to a hiss, like the icy Obasi Ocean. I looked straight ahead, holding my ivory-crowned head high, as a thousand gazes bored into my skin.

I cleared my throat, and winced as the sound ricocheted. Quetzalan architects had fashioned the dais from the same echo-stone used on the Theatre Garden stage. Dayo reached to give my arm a reassuring squeeze . . . and then thought better of it, folding his hands in his lap. Even now, the monster inside me hungered to hurt him, scanning the dais for easily accessible weapons. Again, I convinced her to wait. *The world is watching. Too many contingencies.*

Then I swallowed and forced the rehearsed words up my throat.

"As heir to Thaddace of Mewe," I said, "High Lord Judge of Aritsar, I invoke my right to preside over this hearing. Who brings a case before this court?"

"I do," said Olugbade, also as rehearsed. He sat on a throne behind me, so I was spared seeing the pleasure on his face. "I, Olugbade, King of Oluwan and Oba of Aritsar, accuse Lady X, a Swana woman, of treason against the empire."

More whispers, then booing and jeering, as from the entrance guards marched a figure in chains down the Imperial Hall. They had cleaned her up, I noticed, which on their part was a foolish mistake. Even in a threadbare wrapper, hair matted about her head, The Lady was stunning. Her posture was perfect, muscles taut beneath her weather-scarred skin. Chains clanked as the guards shoved her, forcing her shackled legs to buckle and kneel a few hundred feet from my dais. But she held herself erect, like a warrior—or an empress.

"The accused is before you, High Judge Apparent," Olugbade intoned, barely containing the smugness in his voice. "You have reviewed the evidence. The punishment for treason is death. Shall you accept this case for your ruling?"

I stood, as he expected me to, and assessed the The Lady. She ignored my gaze, expression as blank and cold as her bust in the Bhekina House study. I heard Dayo shift in his seat next to me, and remembered my grim promise.

"No," I replied to the emperor's question. "I will hear another case today."

The crowd hummed with surprise. Before Olugbade or Thaddace could interfere, I announced hastily, "According to the ancient rites set in place by Enoba the Perfect, a High Judge Apparent may hear any case that she sees fit. I remind the court that the First Ruling, once passed, is irreversible. Who else brings a case before me?"

"I do," cried a voice from the entrance. Amid a cacophony of murmurs, Keeya the merchant marched into the hall, brandishing her new son, barely three months old. Captain Bunmi and her Imperial Guard cohort, whom I had asked to protect Keeya on her journey to court, escorted the mother and child.

She stopped at the dais beside The Lady, who turned her eyes on me with brilliant curiosity. Keeya bobbed a curtsy, her waist-length cornrowed braids sweeping the floor. She held herself with dignity before the twenty-four looming thrones, though her voice shook as she said, "Please hear my case, High Judge Apparent."

I gave her a smile of encouragement. "Whom do you accuse?"

Keeya took a deep breath, then pointed at Thaddace where he sat, speechless, on his throne. "His Anointed Honor, High Lord Judge Thaddace of Mewe."

More gasps, and an enraged scoff from Olugbade. I held up a hand for the crowd's silence. "With what do you charge him?"

Keeya held up the baby in her arms. "Causing discord between a husband and wife," she said. "I want to give our son a Swana name: Bopelo. It has been in my family for generations, and I dishonor my ancestors by failing to pass on their legacy. But my husband disagrees. He fears that unless our newborn son has an empire name, he will never become a successful merchant. Anointed Honor Thaddace's Unity Edict has caused all of this. If he had not requested that Arits give up realm names, I would not be fighting with my husband—and my son would have a name besides *Baby*."

Shocked silence. Then the crowd began to buzz with laughter. It was ludicrous for a commoner to charge a High Lord Judge with causing her marital disputes. But according to the scrolls I had dug up in the Imperial Library . . . it was perfectly legal.

"I accept your case," I said. "At this point in a ruling, a High Judge is supposed to ask for evidence. But I don't need to. The evidence is all over Aritsar." I turned my face up to the tiers of commoners and nobility, returning their wide-eyed stares. The crowds were grouped by realm, a semicircle of nations around the room.

I pointed through the hall's towering arched windows, where bonfire clouds still stained the horizon. "The sky is burning with your stories," I said. "The lives of your ancestors, the legacy of your children, vanished in smoke. Does unity cause strife between wives and husbands? Does it make an old woman weep in the streets? Does it make generals take up arms against their own people?"

Uneasy murmurs. I addressed the section of commoners and nobility from Swana, switching from Arit to their native tongue. Then I faced another part of the hall, repeating the phrase in Nyamban. Then I swallowed hard and faced another, and another, until I had addressed the crowd in Moreyaoese, Sparti, Biraslovian, Nontish, Quetzalan, Mewish, Oluwani, Djbanti, Dhyrmish, and Blessid. *"Uniformity is not unity. Silence is not peace."*

The crowd was quiet now. I could feel Olugbade's rage simmering behind me, ready to burst. I did not have much time. Quickly I switched back to Arit, bellowing so my words could not be undone. "I, Tarisai Idajo, rule in favor of Keeya of Swana. Peace comes when stories are celebrated, not erased. Henceforth, the Unity Edict shall be revoked"—I persevered over a sea of gasps—"and replaced with the Imperial Griot Games. Every twentieth moon, all realms must send their best griot to perform the stories of their people at the capital. The most talented griot shall be rewarded from the treasury, and all performers shall receive imperial titles, for their stories bring great honor to the empire. Let the record be sealed. My First Ruling is passed."

"No," Thaddace and the emperor roared in unison, leaping to their feet. But they were drowned out by a sound that made the hair stand on my arms. A sound that set my heart swelling in my chest, and my legs trembling with joy and fear.

Cheers. From every side of the Imperial Hall, people were cheering, pumping fists and stamping feet, chanting in a deafening din: *Idajo. Idajo. Tarisai Idajo.* Beside Keeya, The Lady turned in a slow circle. Her eyes widened to moons as she watched my name on the lips of thousands, and when she looked at me again, an expression that I had never seen before transformed her features.

Wonder.

A hand clamped around mine, sending a thrill to the monster inside me: Dayo. Heart pounding, I looked up at his face expecting to see disappointment. I had purposely misled him the night before. He had thought I would kill The Lady.

But he only looked worried. "You need to get out of here," he whispered. "Now."

"Let go of her," Olugbade snapped at his son. "Guards. Guards!"

Sanjeet leapt to his feet, shielding me with his arm, and in a fluid movement my council siblings joined him, surrounding me and Dayo as we hurried down from the dais. "After them," rasped the emperor, but when I looked back, Thaddace was restraining him.

"They've done nothing illegal," the High Lord Judge said, and then gestured at the crowd and hissed, "The world is watching, Olu. It is not the time for rash decisions. Let them go." He shot a sharp look my way. "We will sort this out in private."

Captain Bunmi and her cohort escorted me, Dayo, and

Keeya through a side door, our council siblings in tow. Keeya pressed her infant to her chest, protecting his ears from the noise still blaring from the hall.

"You can return to your village in a few months," I told her. By then, I hoped, no imperialist vigilantes would be searching for the commoner who had dared challenge Thaddace. "For now, I've arranged a safe house in the Swana capital. Captain Bunmi will escort you. Your family will meet you there; I've made sure they will want for nothing." I began to tell her where the house was, and then stopped, aware that palace walls had ears. I squeezed her hand instead, sending my memories of the safe house into her mind. "Thank you, Keeya."

Her face glowed. "Thank *you*," she said with a grin. "I think Tegoso will not question what I name our babies again." She winked as Bunmi's cohort led her away, raising her son's tiny hand. "Wave goodbye, Bopelo. Goodbye to the High Lady Judge."

CHAPTER 30

MY COUNCIL SIBLINGS, GIDDY WITH EXCITE-
ment, insisted on my return to the Children's Palace.

"You don't need to be alone now," Mayazatyl pointed
out. "You're done studying. Your ruling's over."

I shook my head. Nothing was over. The ground shivered
as *Idajo, Idajo* continued to echo through An-Ileyoba. Then
the sound surged, and all I heard was drumming, pounding
in my ears: *It was always inside.*

My blood ran cold as pieces of a puzzle came together in
my mind. "I have to go," I said.

Escaping from my council siblings' protective huddle,
I dashed across the palace, ripping off my ivory crown,
unhooking my train, and discarding my slippers as I ran.
Sanjeet was hard on my bare heels. "You can't be alone," he
barked. "Not now. It's not safe." I ignored him, not stopping
until we both reached my room in the north tower.

Aiyetoro's drum lay by the window, next to The Lady's
mirror. I snatched it up, then looked around wildly. "I
need something sharp."

At my own request, I had not wielded a weapon since the night I had stabbed Dayo. Puzzled, Sanjeet unsheathed a dagger from his belt and handed it to me. Then he watched as I sliced open the head of Aiyetoro's drum.

Several pieces of crumpled journal paper, thick with the rounded handwriting of Old Arit, toppled out . . . and then two objects clinked onto the stone floor.

Hands shaking, I picked up the jewel-toned masks and turned them in the light. They were shaped like the heads of lionesses, and each was carved with a word: *Obabirin. Iyaloye.* Empress. Crown Princess. Both masks roared with the memories of beating hearts, the strident voices of Kunleo girls, of Raybearers who refused to be silenced.

The obabirin mask had several stripes, representing the council members anointed by The Lady and her birth immunity. The iyaloye mask had only one stripe. Bright red, for the immunity I had been born with: burning.

"There have always been four," I whispered. "Two rulers and two heirs. Raybearers. All of them." An image flashed in my mind: the mural in the ceiling of Aiyetoro's library. Overlapping gold discs. Two suns, surrounded by linking hands—a united Aritsar.

Sanjeet's expression was calm. "After what just happened in that hall," he said, leaning down and pressing his lips to mine, "if anyone doubts you, they're a damned fool."

"You shouldn't kiss me," I giggled, manic with nerves. "I'm still cursed. Still dangerous."

"Very," he said. "Very, very dangerous. And all of

Aritsar knows it." He kissed me again, and I trembled with laughter, heart thudding in my chest.

"Thaddace will challenge my ruling," I said when we parted for air. "It'll take him a while, but he'll find a way to reverse it. I haven't accomplished anything."

"You've won the people's hearts." Sanjeet traced my brow, where my cloud of hair, unfettered by the ivory crown, now sprang around my face. "Not to mention the Imperial Guard. They remember what you did for Captain Bunmi, and they were miserable enforcing Thaddace's edict. No matter how the emperor sullies your name, Aritsar won't give up the hope you gave them today. Not without a fight." He smiled and touched the crown princess mask with its mark of iyaloye. "You should call it. Say its name."

I sucked in a breath, remembering how Dayo's mask had flashed with light. It was the last test: the ultimate proof of a Raybearer.

"All right," I murmured. "Iyalo—"

Then footsteps padded on the tower landing. Sanjeet held me close, putting a hand on his scimitar hilt—but it was Kirah who burst through the door.

"The emperor," she panted. "He's sentenced The Lady to death. He's taken her back to Heaven, where she'll be executed on the hour." Her pupils were dilated, and tears spilled on her round cheeks. "I'm sorry, Tarisai."

A warrior blocked our way at the bottom of the staircase to Heaven. "Pardon, Anointed Honors," he stammered at me, Sanjeet, and Kirah. "I have orders from the emperor. Everyone authorized to facilitate the execution is already upstairs. If you like, you can watch downstairs from the courtyard, with the rest of the court—"

Arm darting out like a snake, I clasped the warrior's neck, releasing him just as quickly. He stumbled back, brandishing his spear.

"Anointed Honor. Why did you—"

"What were your orders?"

He blinked and frowned, rubbing his head. "I . . . I'm sorry, Anointed Honors. I don't remember."

"Then let us pass," I snapped, and the three of us pushed past him and launched up the stairs. There were more guards on the landing; I took the memory of one while Sanjeet and Kirah restrained three more. "We'll hold them," Sanjeet told me. "Go." Then I charged through the iron door into the brow-beating sunshine of Heaven.

Olugbade and his Eleven stood in a semicircle around The Lady, who stood as tall and impassive as the tower itself. All except the emperor held bows, cocking arrows at The Lady's heart. A warrior beat a mallet drum, counting down.

"No," I screamed. Only the drummer flinched. Olugbade's Eleven remained perfectly still, letting the emperor's Ray unite them in focus. Hundreds of feet below, spectators filled the courtyards, squinting up to view the execution.

"You should have stayed away." When Olugbade turned to face me, his tone was maddeningly gentle. "A child should not oversee the death of her parent. I see that now. The stress of such a decision caused your misbehavior in the Imperial Hall. So tomorrow, you will revoke your ruling and express your apologies. Then I think you must be sent away for a while." He smiled in a manner so benevolent, it made my bones shiver. "A young girl must be given space to grieve."

The only space you want for me, I thought, *is the bottom of a crypt*. "You can't kill her," I shot back. "She hasn't had a trial."

"Ah." Olugbade tutted, shaking his head. "I never needed a trial to kill her, Tarisai. But I needed to test you. To unmask the monster that I raised beside my own son." The emperor sighed. "I was kind, Tarisai. Any natural child would have given me their loyalty. But I see now that an egg laid by a python, no matter how small, will always sprout fangs in the end." He turned back to his council. "Release."

I screamed again, and arrows flew through the sky. The crowds below grew still . . . and then began to rumble, agitated with wonder.

Eleven arrows hovered in the air around The Lady, inches from her skin, before falling harmlessly to the floor. The roof fell silent except for the drummer, who fainted as one who had seen a god.

His instrument fell with a resounding thud, rolled over

the edge of the tower, and splintered on the ground far below.

The Lady asked, "Am I still a fake, brother?"

"It's an illusion," Olugbade said firmly. "Enchantment. Sorcery. We'll try another way."

"We can't, Olu," Thaddace said without taking his eyes off The Lady. "I don't know what happened. But what we saw . . . *Everyone* saw." He gestured at the teeming crowds below. "You can't kill her now, not like this. People will have . . . questions."

My chest tightened with hope. Olugbade's pride had trapped him. He should have murdered The Lady in private, trying every form of mortal death until he found one that worked. No one would have seen his failed attempts. No one would have guessed at The Lady's power.

But my First Ruling had made Olugbade rash. Like a snake gripping a branch in flood season, he clung to his belief in The Lady's illegitimacy. By insisting on this public execution, he had trapped himself.

"Poison," Olugbade said, reaching beneath his agbada to produce a vial of noxious liquid. The emperor's pupils were dilated as he produced a knife from his robes, shaking the contents of his vial over the blade. The smell stung my nostrils, and Olugbade smiled. "Enchant *this* away, witch."

The Lady was immune to poison too. I had seen the empress mask, and remembered the glow of a vibrant green stripe. But to my surprise, The Lady agreed.

"Fine. I submit to you, brother." She paused. "But an

honorable emperor would allow me my last rites. Before you kill me, let the High Priestess read me the Ending."

After terse whispers from his council, Olugbade set his jaw and nodded for Mbali to step forward.

The High Priestess was shaking as she made the sign of the Pelican on The Lady's chin. "I'm sorry," Mbali whispered as the mirrors from her prayer shawl scattered gold orbs across The Lady's face. "You know I didn't want this."

To my surprise, a tear dropped silently to The Lady's cheek. "I know, Mbali."

"Do you know the words?"

The Lady nodded. The Ending was a prayer most Arits learned as children: *Tonight I may join Egungun's Parade; tonight I may be purified. Am, who wrote my birth and death: Guide me to Core, the world without end.* The women swayed as they held each other, speaking in unison. "Tonight I may join Egungun's Parade . . ." Again, Mbali made a sign on The Lady's brow. "Tonight I may be purified. Am, who wrote my birth and death: Guide me to—"

The Lady seized Mbali under the arms, toppling them both to the ground. Still gripping Mbali with her lean, muscular arms, she swung the High Priestess to dangle over the edge of the tower.

The crowd below shrieked.

"Decision time, brother," The Lady panted. "If only—if only you had let us be a family."

The Emperor's Council surged forward, but halted in fear when The Lady's grip loosened. Olugbade placed his knife on the ground with calculating calm. "It's me you want dead," he said, "yet you cannot kill a Raybearer. This is futile, Lady. If you hurt Mbali, you will only die a villain. Come. Give her to us and end this with dignity."

"Someone is going over the edge of this tower," she replied. "Someone dropped, or someone pushed. I don't want to hurt her, but the choice is yours."

"It is not for you to give choices," Olugbade retorted.

But The Lady wasn't looking at the emperor. Her eyes were locked on Thaddace . . . who stood right by the emperor, and the edge of the tower. The High Lord Judge turned ashen.

No. She couldn't mean . . . It wasn't possible. How did The Lady even *know* that Thaddace . . .

Then my heart turned to lead.

She knew, because I had told her. I had wanted to make her laugh. I had betrayed Thaddace and Mbali's secret: the only leverage that could turn a council member against his emperor. I had sold Thaddace's soul for a smile.

"Don't do it," Mbali rasped at Thaddace. "Remember what you believe. There is no justice. Only order."

"You don't believe that," Thaddace whispered. "You never have."

Mbali gave a faint smile. "Some lies we believe to survive." Then she dug her nails into The Lady's arm, and The Lady yelped with surprise. Her grip on Mbali loosened.

"*No*," Thaddace bellowed. The whites of his eyes

flashed, and the air crackled as his heat-precision Hallow spiraled out of control. The energy was so strong, I could see his memories without touching him. A childhood of poverty and crime blossomed in my mind's eye, along with a freckle-covered Mewish boy who longed for stability. I floated through the day he arrived at the Children's Palace, gaping at the first clean clothes he had ever worn. I hurled forward years. Thaddace's heart swelled with disbelief: Olugbade, the young prince he had grown to worship, had just named him High Judge of all Aritsar. Him—a thief from the rat-ridden slums of Clough-on-Derry!

I flew forward again. The boy was a man now, enforcing law with the penitent severity of a former criminal. He fell for a priestess girl from Swana, for her eyes that saw the truth, and her kiss that tasted of mercy. With a single nudge from her smooth dark fingers, his idols of stability crumbled.

Years passed. He grew fond of a child who reminded him of himself. A feared child, born into dishonor: the daughter of a criminal. He watched her grow in the Children's Palace, smiling at her tenacity. He put his faith in her, and when the time came to pick his successor, he offered her the same chance at redemption that had been given to himself.

More years. Gray crept into the man's red hair as he struggled to live in the tension. He loved the law. He worshipped Mbali. He revered Olugbade, his lord and brother.

How could Thaddace know that the girl he had chosen—the child he had given a chance—would cause that tension to snap? That she would betray his secret? That she would topple everything he held dear?

"I'm sorry," I gasped. "I'm so sorry."

Then Thaddace, High Judge of Aritsar and beggar boy from Clough-on-Derry, sobbed, swiveled, and pushed the Emperor of Aritsar over the edge.

The Lady fumbled at the same time. With a cry of horror, she dropped Mbali.

It was quieter than I would have expected, the *crack* of a body meeting stone. Louder was the sound that followed, a continuous shrill that cut to my eardrums like needles. The crowds were stampeding, fleeing as cohorts of Imperial Guard warriors filled the courtyard. Thaddace was being dragged away by his council, limp as a rag doll, his green eyes deadened with grief.

A single *crack*.

Which body? My pulse roared in my ears. *Which body?*

Then a figure rose in the sky, blocking the sun's merciless rays. His jet hair floated, a corona in the wind. The symbols on his body glowed, curving down his sinewy arms, which held a shivering burden: Mbali.

Alive.

The man set the High Priestess down, and she scurried, gasping down the stairs leading back into the palace.

"You came back to me," breathed The Lady.

"I came back to you," Woo In agreed. Then he grabbed Olugbade's knife from the ground and swiped at The Lady.

"That's for lying to my people," Woo In cried as a

long, thin line of crimson blossomed on The Lady's cheek. "Now you're marked, like I am—like the thousands of Redemptors you would send to their graves. You can forget about Songland's help. When you're empress, I'll make sure they want nothing to do with you."

The Lady lifted her hand to her face, then stared with interest at the blood on her fingers. "You monstrous boy," she murmured. "I'm not going to be empress now. You've killed me."

Woo In's face screwed up with confusion. Someone lunged at him, screaming, wailing, beating his chest. The person was me, I knew, but the world had gone numb, and my vision had shrunk to tunnels.

"That was Olugbade's knife," I sobbed. "He poisoned it. You poisoned her."

The green stripe on Aiyetoro's mask didn't matter. The Lady had anointed Woo In, and so he could kill her—just as Thaddace had killed Olugbade. Against Woo In's hand, she was immune to nothing.

Woo In's face drained of color. Then a gaggle of warriors burst from the stairwell onto the rooftop, surrounding us. Woo In's arms connected like a vise around my torso. In a flash we were airborne, rising higher, higher, above the palace, leaving The Lady behind.

"Murderer." I sobbed against him, wanting to claw his chest but unable to move my pinned arms. "Monster. Murderer."

"I didn't know," he gasped. "I didn't know."

The warriors were shooting at us. An arrow grazed my

arm with a searing sting, and another landed with a *thump* in Woo In's side. Still we ascended, away, far from An-Ileyoba. Before I drifted from consciousness, the last thing I registered was the wind whipping my ears, and a sea of warriors, surrounding a splayed body in the courtyard far below. Drums echoed on sandstone, as cries rung from parapet to parapet:

"The emperor has gone to the village. He will not be back soon. Long live His Imperial Majesty: Ekundayo, King of Oluwan, and Oba of Aritsar."

CHAPTER 31

WHEN I CAME TO, IT WAS SNOWING.

I had seen snow only once before: on my council's goodwill tour, when we had traveled by lodestone to the mountains of Biraslov. I remembered thinking how surprisingly soft they felt—the flakes peppering my face, kisses that made me laugh and shiver.

There were no kisses now. Only icy slaps from the wind as we passed over a valley of ghostly white. Woo In still carried me, though his grip was loose, and I stayed afloat via a pulsing force I could not see. I still wore nothing but my First Ruling gown, barely shielded from the cold by Woo In's thin cape.

"Your arm won't bleed until we land," Woo In said. His voice was rough and weak. "Neither will my wound. The airstream stabilizes them, but I won't be able to keep us in the air for much longer."

"How long was I asleep? Where are you taking me?" I thrashed, and my arm brushed the arrow in Woo In's side. He howled in pain and we plunged toward the ground.

I shrieked and Woo In cursed, then we stabilized, hovering precariously in the air.

"Trust me," he rasped. "You don't want me to drop you."

"You left her." Moment by moment, the scene at An-Ileyoba returned to me. My arm ached where the arrow had grazed it. "You poisoned The Lady and left her there."

"My airstream can't carry that many people. I had to pick."

"Why me?" I demanded. "I'm not the one who's dying, you idiot. *She* is. Because of you."

He was silent for several moments, letting the wind scream in our ears.

"She isn't dying," I whispered. "She's dead, isn't she?"

He sagged against me. So I snuffed out every nerve in my body, muted every thought, and grew a shell of adamant against what he was about to say.

"She was dead within minutes of us leaving the capital," he said. "I knew it when the Ray left my body."

My ears refused to accept the words. So they washed over me instead, falling harmlessly to the earth beneath us. I would deal with them later—one impossibility at a time. "How long have we been flying?" I asked.

"You've been asleep for hours," he said. "Nine, maybe ten. We're almost to Songland; though, thanks to your storm, we might need to stop for the night."

"*My* storm?"

He gestured to the valley below, which was hedged by

frosted blue mountains. At the mouth of the valley, chiseled into the rock face, stood massive twin statues of a Songland king, hand raised in foreboding. Each sculpture was the size of several towers, and must have taken centuries to complete. "That's the Jinhwa Pass," Woo In explained. "It's the only way into Songland from the Arit mainland. Have you never wondered why Songland isn't part of the Arit empire?"

"They refused," I said, teeth chattering. "Enoba the Perfect accepted their choice, but cut them off from trade, since they wouldn't be governed by our regulations."

Woo In barked a laugh. "Accepted? Do you really think Enoba united this continent without shedding blood? Enoba convinced many realms to join him, yes. But the lands that refused, he conquered. All except Songland, thanks to my thrice-great-grandfather, King Jinhwa. His shamans enchanted the mountain pass so that only people of Songlander blood, or those personally invited by the reigning monarch, may enter. Every time Enoba tried to bring an army, the land rejected him, sending ice and snow. You haven't been invited by my mother," he explained. "Hence the storm."

"Why are you taking me to Songland?"

"I'm only taking you to the border," he said after a pause. "There's something you need to see."

Before I could ask more questions, the pulsing airstream sputtered, and we dipped violently. Woo In cursed again.

"I've grown too weak," he said through gritted teeth.

"We'll have to find shelter. Hold on . . . and I'm sorry about the pain."

"Pain?"

"Once we're out of the airstream, your wound will start bleeding. So will mine."

We spiraled down into the valley, my stomach doing backflips until we landed in a bracing puff of snow. Immediately my arm burned. Blood began to trickle down my forearm, and I tore my skirt for a bandage. Beneath Woo In, however, the snow had turned completely crimson. He moaned, but when I reached to pull out the arrow, he shook his head.

"Not yet. I'll bleed too much," he gasped. "We—we need . . ." He murmured something under his breath. Then his head fell limp in the snow, and his eyes fluttered closed.

"Don't you dare," I said, shaking his shoulders and slapping his face. "Don't you dare fall asleep and leave me here."

Woo In was still. I struggled to my knees and looked around wildly. Nothing but white, white, encasing us like a vast tomb, the sky melting into the ground. Woo In twitched, murmuring again.

Several yards away, a smudge of black and gold appeared.

I swallowed hard as it grew nearer, its glowing eyes fixed on me, a familiar lurid yellow. Snow melted beneath its wide, spotted paws, leaving a ribbon of green grass.

"Hyung," I whispered.

The emi-ehran stopped, inches from my face. Heat radiated from its pelt, making the ground beneath us soggy as ice turned to water. Feeling seeped back into my limbs, and the leopard-beast's meaty breath dissolved the frost from my lashes. Hyung cocked its head to examine me, tail twitching. Then it roused Woo In with an affectionately rough tongue to the face.

"I know, I know," Woo In groaned, as though the beast had spoken aloud. "No need to say I told you so."

Hyung made a sound halfway between a purr and a growl, and Woo In smiled.

"Admit it. If I wasn't so much trouble, you'd be bored."

The beast expelled an odorous huff similar to an exasperated sigh. Then it bent to its haunches. I helped Woo In onto Hyung's steaming back, then removed the arrow, bunching his cloak to slow the blood. Afterward, I pulled myself up, nervously clutching the beast's neck as Woo In slumped against me, and we climbed between hill and mountain.

The Jinhwa Pass ended abruptly on a steep ridge overlooking the valley below. Rooftops sprawled in a vast red patchwork, and roads spiderwebbed over the land in gray veins, pulsing with carts and horses. A river swept through the valley like dark blue ribbon, and long white boats shimmered on its surface.

"Welcome to Eunsan-do," murmured Woo In.

"It's beautiful," I said quietly. "I wish Kirah could see it." She had described Songland's capital vividly, citing phrases from her poetry scrolls. Golden faces shaded by netted hats, bustling through the streets. High-waisted silk robes sweeping the cobblestone. Fish and noodles wafting from market stands, and muscular women carrying wheat bundles on their backs, rolling their eyes as fishermen called from riverboats. Children scampering across the curved rooftops, chasing kites in the shape of tigers. Kirah had made songs for each image, crooning as she stared beyond Oluwan City. Each note seemed to form a tether, linking her heart to someone far away.

Woo In shifted on Hyung's back and attempted to sound nonchalant. "Why would your council sister want to come here?"

"I have no idea," I lied, and punished him with silence for the rest of the journey.

Hyung did not take us into Eunsan-do. When we climbed out of the pass, the frost abruptly disappeared, and green leaves crunched under the beast's massive feet as we climbed a ridge that hugged the mountainside. By the time we arrived at a small clearing, clouds had smothered the moon. Tents, plows, and animal pens loomed around us. A single house with a raised foundation creaked beneath a curved, broad-lipped roof. When we staggered inside, the winter air dispersed. Numbness melted away from my feet, though the room had no fire.

"Magic," I whispered.

"Songland," Woo In corrected. "We build fireboxes outside. Smoke canals lead under our homes and heat the floor." The inviting warmth increased when Hyung parked itself in front of the door, effectively sealing the entry shut. "Watch your step," said Woo In.

"Why should I watch my—"

Then I stumbled over a lumpy bundle. It moaned. My eyes adjusted to the darkness, and across the long, low-ceilinged chamber, tiny bodies sprawled on the floor, faces peering up at me sleepily. Children—every single one covered in blue birthmarks.

"What is this place?" I whispered.

Woo In paused before answering: "A refuge." Then he pulled me down a corridor to a windowless chamber that smelled of pine needles. "There's a pallet in the corner," he murmured. "Rest. We travel tomorrow morning."

"Where?" I demanded, dizzy with fatigue and council sickness. "Why am I here? What do you want from—" But he closed the sliding wooden door and clicked a lock into place. Only when Woo In's steps retreated down the corridor did the cries from An-Ileyoba sink in.

The emperor has gone to the village. He will not be back soon. Long live His Imperial Majesty: Ekundayo, King of Oluwan, and Oba of Aritsar.

"Dayo," I rasped as sobs came with sudden force. "No. I can't be here; he'll be alone." I pounded on the doorframe. "You have to take me back. I didn't get to explain. He'll think I abandoned him again. He'll think—" *He'll think I chose my mother after all.*

But I didn't have a mother. Not anymore.

I staggered back from the door, collapsing onto something soft: a thin leather pallet, piled with musty-smelling blankets. Then I cried my face stiff, sputtering in a pool of sweat and mucus as the empress and princess masks dug into my breasts. I moved only to twist my council ring, around and around until a red ring blossomed around my finger, and my demons dropped fitfully to sleep.

I winced at the morning light trickling in from the corridor. Children's voices and lowing animals sounded faintly through the walls, and my temples were on fire. I lurched upright from the pallet and regretted it. Nausea rolled over me.

I hadn't felt council sickness since my last year at the Children's Palace, during an outbreak of pox. The testmakers had quarantined Dayo's council, forcing us to sleep in separate rooms. Even Dayo had been required to stay away, because even though the Ray protected him from illness, he could still spread it.

As it happened, none of us had the pox . . . but we might as well have, since council sickness felt several times worse. Through the fog of my headache, I noticed that my hand throbbed, swollen where I had twisted my seal ring.

My heart skipped—another person was in the room. Above me stood a girl in a leather vest and patched trousers, with tan cheeks and stony brown eyes. Patterns shimmered faintly on her skin. No longer blue, as they had been nearly a year ago, but deep violet.

"Ye Eun," I breathed. "You're alive. You made it out. Of course you did; you're brave and strong, but Am's Story, I worried about you so much . . ."

I reached to embrace her. She caught my arrow-wounded arm with a small, firm hand.

"I have to clean this," Ye Eun said. Her face was a cold mask. "You could lose the arm if it gets infected. It happened to one of the younger boys."

She clutched a rag that reeked of astringent herbs, and shifted a bundle strapped to her back: a tuft-haired infant Redemptor, who babbled against her shoulder.

"Ye Eun . . . don't you remember me?" I asked. "We met at the temple in Ebujo. I—"

"Of course I remember you." Her voice was toneless, and her gaze was full of ghosts. "You're the one who was supposed to keep me safe."

My belly turned to stone. "I'm sorry. I tried—"

"We don't need you, you know," she said. "I'll save the others, just like I saved myself." The baby cooed and nestled into her back. More blue-marked faces, ranging from toddlers to older children, peeked into the room from behind Ye Eun's legs. Except for Ye Eun, none of them looked older than ten.

"Where are we?" I asked. "Where's Woo In?"

"You mean the Traitor Prince?" Ye Eun shrugged.

"He's checking the rabbit traps. He said to feed you, and to make sure you hadn't hurt yourself. I only checked your hands and arms."

I glanced down. Dried blood crusted at the base of my finger, where I had twisted my ring last night.

"I have to clean your wound and watch you eat," she said, and took my hand impatiently. Her small, deft fingers swabbed my wounds and wrapped them in linen. A bowl of gray porridge steamed by my pallet, as well as a bucket and washcloth. As I washed and ate, Ye Eun peered at me more closely and huffed.

"You're already infected, aren't you? Now Traitor Prince will be angry, and I'll have to hike down to the village for garlic. I'm already behind getting the others ready for the Underworld—"

"It's not infection," I cut in, wincing at the cotton sensation in my throat. "It's council sickness."

Ye Eun's scowl remained. "Then you should have brought someone. You're like Traitor Prince. He gets fevers when he comes without Kathleen, or one of the others."

"Well, he won't get fevers anymore," I snapped, making the girl jump. I swallowed and winced. "I'm sorry. I just meant . . . Woo In isn't part of a council anymore. The Lady is dead. And I'm his prisoner." I smiled weakly. "So I wasn't allowed to bring a sibling."

"If you're a prisoner, we all are," she retorted. "This is Sagimsan: the mountain where Redemptor babies are left. Sometimes it's easier to abandon us at birth instead of waiting till we're ten. Traitor Prince flies over the mountain and brings the babies here."

"Oh." My heart twinged at the tiny curious faces in the doorframe. "Why do you call Woo In a traitor?"

Ye Eun shrugged. "All Songlanders do. After he promised his soul to The Lady, and Crown Princess Min Ja disowned him. But I don't really care if he *is* a traitor. He's good to us." She paused. "I didn't think I'd come back to Sagimsan. After I escaped the Underworld, I thought I'd find my parents. They gave me to the mountain, but—I thought maybe—they might want me back." She smiled dimly. "They didn't. No one wants a girl who's walked through hell and back. So my emi-ehran led me back here. I help make the Redemptors strong. I teach them how to survive, like I did, so they're ready when it's time. It's not always enough. But it's better than waiting for people in capes."

I winced, remembering how reverently she had eyed my wax-dyed cape at the temple banquet.

"You should eat your breakfast," said Ye Eun. She watched my spoon, and I noticed for the first time how her cheekbones jutted, with no fat to soften them. "Traitor Prince will be back soon."

I held out the steaming bowl. "You finish it."

She swallowed, then shook her head. "If you don't want it, we should give it to Ae Ri." She turned, presenting her back to me. "Help me untie her."

I froze, terrified. I'd never held a baby for more than a

few seconds, when peasants thrust them into my arms on goodwill campaigns. I had kissed the infants, as expected, and returned them as soon as possible.

"She's hungry," Ye Eun insisted. "Don't worry, she's clean."

I huffed, gripped the baby's underarms, and wriggled her from the harness. She was alarmingly light, even wrapped in a homespun shift and loincloth. Her soft curly hair smelled of hay and milk, and curiously, her skin was several shades darker than Ye Eun's.

I squinted. "Is Ae Ri . . ."

"An isoken?" Ye Eun shrugged. "Maybe. There are illegal camps on the border, where Songlander merchants trade with Aritsar. That's how I learned to speak Arit: buying supplies there for the refuge. It's rare, but I've heard of merchants taking Arits as lovers." She looked askance at Ae Ri. "Maybe that's where she came from."

The baby squirmed in the crook of my arm as Ye Eun fed her, smacking up the porridge with pink, wet lips. Then she clutched the front of my gown and gurgled a greeting.

"Hello," I said uncertainly.

Ae Ri cooed, and examined me with brave, dark eyes set in a lattice of blue birthmarks. My heart swelled with a familiarity I couldn't explain. Suddenly, I was enraged.

What kind of treaty would end this tiny story, would snuff the light of her soul, after *ten* short years? What kind of peace cost a life that had barely begun?

A shadow filled the door, and Ye Eun reclaimed Ae Ri as Woo In stalked heavily into the room, clutching his freshly bandaged side.

"I checked her for wounds, like you said," Ye Eun reported. "She's sick, but clean." Then she turned to leave.

"Wait," I called out, not ready for Ye Eun to be gone. For so long, I had thought she was dead. It didn't matter that she hated me; she was alive—gloriously, vindictively alive. When she stopped, I stammered, "What was your emi-ehran in the Underworld? Was it a leopard, like Woo In's?"

"No," she said after a pause. "Mine is a phoenix."

"I'm not surprised."

The hint of a smile played with her mouth. "I named her Hwanghu," she said quietly. "Empress." Then she vanished from the room.

Woo In dropped a bundle of clothes at my feet. "Change into these. The journey will be short." His half-moon eyes were wan; he had passed a restless night. He was sweating with fever, and it was likely his head pounded as mine did. I felt no pity. The Lady's bloodied face still glistened in my mind.

Before leaving me he said, "Summon the Ray. You can't reach your council from this far, but it helps the headache when you try."

I obeyed him, letting heat build at the base of my neck, and sending an invisible beam of light in what I guessed was Oluwan's direction. The light faded and grew cold when met with emptiness. But Woo In had been right—the pain, for now, was no longer unbearable.

The garments were made of wax-dyed cloth, seeping with spice-scented memories of Oluwan, where Woo In must have bought them. He had brought boots for me as well, and a cloak—blue like his, cut from warm wool.

I dressed and passed into the house's main chamber, seeing what I'd missed the night before. Diagrams of beasts and Underworld passages hung around the room, and chalk slates cramped with Songlander script lay abandoned on cushions. A schoolroom. On the longest wall, a map of the continent stretched from end to end, lodestones marked meticulously in each realm.

Woo In and I left the camp on Hyung's back, and soon crested one of the pine-covered steppes. After an hour, we stopped at a curved crevice in the rock face, tall and narrow, like a cat's eye. The glistening blue veins that ran throughout Sagimsan seemed to meet here, joining to form lightning bolts across the mountain floor. Energy pulsed through the cold air, and when we dismounted, it hummed through me as well, exploring my body with relentless curiosity. The emi-ehran arched its back, its whiskers on edge.

What kind of place could unnerve a beast who had seen the Underworld?

"Hyung will wait outside," Woo In said, then bent to pull off his worn leather boots, one by one. "I would advise you do the same," he said, nodding at my feet.

"Why?"

"It's a way of showing respect."

"Until you explain what this is, I'm not going anywhere."

Woo In shot a tense glance at the crevice opening. "I'm not supposed to show you this place. Its location is known only to the Songlander royal family. But . . ." He let out a slow breath. "There's a story hidden deep in the mountain. It explains the Redemptors and Songland's curse. But it's spelled, so only certain bloodlines understand. According to the shamans, the Kunleos are one of them. So when The Lady came to Songland sixteen years ago, asking for aid with her coup . . . I brought her here. She read the story, but wouldn't tell me what it said. She said it was dangerous. She told me to trust her, and I did." His face hardened, then softened with desperation. "I need to know what's in there, Lady's Daughter. Please, we don't have much time. The Treaty Renewal is tomorrow night."

"You've never said my name before." I frowned, feeling strangely awake in that air, as though I'd been sleepwalking for months. "Do you know that? She's part of me, Woo In, but we aren't the same person. And we never will be."

He blinked, processing this, then nodded slowly and reached for my hand. "Please, Tarisai."

I let his fingers close around mine. Together, we slipped through the crevice, and descended into the heart of Sagimsan mountain.

CHAPTER 32

THERE WAS NO NEED FOR A TORCH. Translucent bolts of blue rock glowed from within the tunnel walls, and we moved as with a current, energy coursing in one direction as we climbed down, down, down.

We stopped in the mouth of a round stone chamber. The ceiling glittered with paintings of pelicans, halos radiating from their lifted wings. The floor was painted with the same symbol from the Oluwan Imperial Library, and from Aiyetoro's drum: two overlapping suns, bordered by a circle of linking hands.

My breath floundered. It was like the air had disappeared, and I inhaled nothing now but pure blue energy, thrumming through my temples. At the other end of the chamber, thousands of bright glyphs covered the wall.

"The heart of Sagimsan," Woo In explained. "Every blue vein you've seen in the mountain finds its source in this room. I can't read that wall. But you can."

"How?" I crept toward the wall, squinting at script so complex, it made my eyes cross. "I don't understand." But the words began to murmur, whispers that wrapped around me in a seductive lullaby. My hand rose, as though possessed, and I pressed my fingers to the wall.

The script jumbled in dizzying patterns—and then it shot from the wall in a beam. I gasped as the glyphs covered my body, clinging to my skin like running water. I shut my eyes. When I opened them again, the symbols had vanished . . . and instead, four words glowed on the wall.

WELCOME HEIR OF WURAOLA

"Focus," I heard Woo In yell, as though from a great distance. "Listen."

His voice grew mute as another filled my ears: a deep, lovely roar, like the voice of a fathomless ocean. It was not old or young, neither male nor female. But I knew, without seeing its face, that this power could unmake me with a single word.

Tarisai.

I fell trembling to the ground.

Do not fear me.

"Shouldn't I?" I whispered, my back against the cold floor. "You're . . ." My breath caught while I tried to wrap my mind around the impossible. But I knew it in my bones. "You're the Storyteller."

432

A considering pause.

I am a memory of the Storyteller, it replied. *Confined to rock, for when I am needed. You have ears. Will you open them?*

I nodded dumbly.

Then you shall hear, Heir of Wuraola.

The chamber fell away. Part of me knew I still lay within the energy-charged mountain, my body still as death as Woo In hovered, anxiously waving a hand in front of my open, unseeing eyes. But the other part of me hurled through a sea of images, smells, voices. I soared over a patchwork of realms: cities rising, falling, evolving as though I were riding on time itself.

Several thousand moons ago, the ocean-voice said, *a brother and sister, both warriors, watched their homeland being torn to pieces. Monsters rose from the deep, and contagions spread their fingers, and island turned on island. Enoba was brave, but Wuraola was wise. She saw how division weakened humans against the abiku. When she told Enoba, he enslaved an alagbato, demanding the power to unite twelve realms.*

I was back in the Swana savannah. I watched from above like a star, as a broad-backed warrior approached a dewy-faced alagbato: Melu, five hundred years younger. The immortal slept peacefully by his pool, shimmering wings tucked around his smooth, long limbs. With catlike dexterity, the warrior snapped an emerald cuff onto the alagbato's arm.

Familiarity chilled my spine. Through this story, I realized, The Lady had learned how to enslave Melu.

433

For Enoba's first wish, he asked the alagbato to grow land across the oceans, uniting the islands so they could be ruled as one. The alagbato-turned-ehru said, "It is done—" and for miles, earth covered the waters. Enoba was satisfied, and crossed his new continent with a formidable army. But lands so vast could not be conquered by Enoba's spear alone, and so Wuraola used her words to win the hearts and minds of the people.

Still, the brother and sister were unsure of victory against the abiku. Enoba returned to the ehru, and asked his second boon: the power to rule an empire for eternity. For this gift, the ehru climbed to the heavens and stole two rays from the blazing sun.

"No man escapes old age," warned the ehru. "But for every heart moved by your Ray, one facet of death's blade may not touch you. Your heirs shall be even more powerful, for they shall possess one immunity at birth. Take this Ray, and give the other to your sister and equal, for no being was made to rule alone."

But Enoba, seeing the nations his spear had won, said, "I have no equal," and devoured both Rays himself.

Melu's savannah vanished, and again, time whirled past me in a blur of color: forests razed, villages born, cities rising, rulers crowned.

Enoba's rule was long, and soon peaceful. His Ray caused him to outlive Wuraola, and though he mourned her, his pride scrubbed her story from the earth.

Under the Treaty, monsters from the Underworld disappeared from the continent. Redemptor children were born in every realm. But after years of parents wailing in the streets, weeping as their children were taken from them, the Arit people began to resent their emperor.

"Why should we sacrifice our children for peace," the Arit people began to rumble, "when the emperor need not sacrifice his own?" For Enoba had made the abiku promise that Oluwani children would never be born as Redemptors.

Enoba feared a rebellion. Hoping to mollify his subjects, he returned to the ehru and demanded his last wish: a way to ensure that only children from Songland, and never children from Aritsar, would be selected as Redemptors. Reluctantly, the ehru bestowed a new power on Enoba's Ray: the ability to make a sacred council, and unite eleven souls to his own.

The Treaty, the ehru explained, was sealed by blood—one drop from every ruler. He compared it to drawing straws in a game: So long as the blood was equal, no realm drew the short straw. The Redemptor curse favored no realm; all sacrificed equally. But now that Enoba had united eleven souls to his own, his blood held the power of twelve realms. He had added, so to speak, longer straws to the game. When the continent gathered again to renew the Treaty, Enoba's blood supplemented the power of the twelve Arit rulers, stacking the odds against Songland. Ever after, no Redemptors were born in Aritsar.

Suspecting foul play, the Songlanders rebelled, refusing at first to give up their children. But the abiku retaliated, ravaging the land with monsters and plagues until, with rage and grief, Songland submitted. The children were sent—three hundred each year.

Enoba's secret died with him. But every one hundred years, his curse on Songland is restored at the Treaty Renewal, when Enoba's descendants spill their blood into Enoba's shield.

Now the voice showed me another scene: not the

past, but a premonition. I saw the Imperial Hall, lavishly decorated for the renewal ceremony. I saw Enoba's shield being carried up to the dais. I saw Dayo in emperor's regalia, wearing his dead father's sun crown, and surrounded by a semicircle of rulers. I felt Woo In's haunted gaze, heard Ye Eun's screaming parents, and saw thousands of children thrown into a cold, yawning pit from which they would never return—as Dayo leaned over the shield, slit his hand, and let his blood fall.

"No," I screamed. "No!"

What story do you live for, Heir of Wuraola?

Then the scene faded to white.

Woo In's face came into focus, inches above mine. "You're awake," he sighed, shoulders sagging. "You were barely breathing. I feared . . ."

He trailed off, helping me sit up, and his hands felt hot against my clammy skin. My vision was uneven, as though part of me still floated above my body. The glyphs had disappeared from my skin, returning to the wall. But nothing looked quite the same—least of all Woo In, whose geometrically patterned features filled me with fresh horror.

"You're cursed," I croaked. "You, Ye Eun, the Redemptors—the Kunleos cursed all of you."

Woo In grew still as death. "I knew it," he whispered.

The world spun as he helped me up. "You can tell me more when we get back to the refuge. Let's go—the mountain is draining our energy. Try not to nod off. If you sleep while we're still in range of the cave, it will be hard to wake up."

We returned to the house in the Redemptor village, collapsing on the heated schoolroom floor. After Ye Eun restored our strength with steamed fish and broth, I told Woo In everything. His back grew more rigid with every word, and when I finished he rasped, "She knew." He was white with fever, tears of rage pooling. "The whole time," he yelled, "The Lady knew that the Treaty would curse Songland, and she was *still* going to renew it."

Children scattered from the schoolroom in fright. I pressed a damp cloth to Woo In's brow, and then to my own, remembering lines from my mother's journal. *I will pay the price of peace, as my ancestors have before me.*

I frowned in disbelief, then sat up straight. "Wait. Maybe Mother was trying to right the scale. She anointed you, didn't she? The Storyteller's memory described the Treaty Renewal like drawing straws, a game unequally weighted against Songland. But thanks to you, Mother's blood represents Songland as well as Aritsar. If *her* blood fell in Enoba's shield, the Treaty Renewal would be fair again. Redemptors would be born all over the continent, just like before."

Woo In considered, then shook his head slowly. "She never meant to anoint me," he whispered. "And once she did, she tried her hardest to erase my blood from her veins."

I bit my lip, then reached out to cup Woo In's cheek. "May I?" He nodded, and I tumbled into a memory of freshly fallen snow.

I am ten years old, and I have survived the Underworld.

I pace at the mouth of Sagimsan's holy cave, shivering, and smiling at the thought of *her*. Hyung's meaty breath toasts the top of my head, and its whiskers tickle my brow. My best friend—my only friend—growls, nipping my hair with disapproval.

"Don't look at me like that," I laugh. "I trust her, OK? Once she reads what's in there, she'll know how to help us. There will be no more Redemptors. No more kids like me."

Hyung only sighs, making fog in the frigid air. My head snaps up: footsteps echo from the cave. When The Lady appears, I rush to her side. She smells metallic, drenched in the energy of Sagimsan. For a moment, she stands erect in her fur-lined red cloak, majestic as the moment I first saw her. Then she sways on her feet; the Storyteller's memory has sapped her strength. Before she stumbles, I offer my shoulder.

"Thank you," she says, smiling with genuine warmth. "You saved me."

"Well, you saved me first," I reply, and she laughs, ruffling my hair.

"Yes, dearest, I suppose I did."

When I had first returned from the Underworld, I thought my life would grow wings, soaring like the cranes above the Gyeoljeong Sea. I thought I was free: no longer a walking sacrifice, instilling guilt and sorrow in all who saw me.

Instead, whispers of *hell-boy* had peppered the palace at Eunsan-do. Nursemaids stripped me naked each morning, scouring my birthmarks with salt and ice water. Nobles baited Hyung with swords and sticks, trying to drive the emi-ehran from the palace, and my relatives spat to ward off evil whenever I passed. Min Ja, my fierce sister, tried her hardest to protect me. But only Mother could put a stop to the bullying . . . and she did nothing but cry.

You smell of death, my baby boy, she sobbed. *My poor dead baby.*

But I'm not dead, I reminded her. *I'm alive. I came back.* But she only cried more, and I knew the truth then: Deep down, my mother wished that I had never returned.

My whole life, she had prepared for my death. It was her way of coping, bracing for her inevitable loss. But instead of a sacrificed angel, I had saddled her with a live, cursed son.

Well, I would saddle her no more. The next morning I had packed a meager camp and ridden off with Hyung to Sagimsan. If it weren't for my emi-ehran, I would have frozen to death within a month.

Then an angel climbed the mountain ridge, snowflakes

439

winking in her floating black hair. She called my name in a voice like music. When she found evidence of my camp, she unloaded her pack and started a cook fire. The mouthwatering smell of sweet fish and spicy noodles coaxed me from my hiding place—my food stores had long run out.

The angel nursed me back to health, wrapping me in panther blankets and spoon-feeding me stew.

"Who are you?" I croaked.

"A friend," she said, brushing the wind-whipped hair from my forehead. Her dark fingers were warm, as though she had brought the sun with her from Aritsar. "You may call me The Lady."

"You're a foreigner. You're the reason it stormed in Jinhwa Pass all week."

"I'm afraid I am. Queen Hye Sun would not invite me to her realm, no matter how many letters I sent." She frowned, pulling her crimson cloak closer around her. "Luckily, I wasn't trying to go all the way to Songland. I only wanted to find you."

"Why?"

"Tales reached the Arit border of a lost Redemptor prince, vanished into Sagimsan. Queen Hye Sun is worried sick."

I snorted. "I doubt it. She wishes I was dead." I explained about my treatment at the palace. The Lady's face, suddenly vulnerable, softened as she listened. Anger lined her elegant features.

"I know how cruel a palace can be to children," she

whispered, taking my hands and squeezing them. "Especially to a child it fears."

"I wouldn't mind the nobles. But Mother . . ."

"I understand, Woo In. My father didn't want me either."

For several moments we sat in silence, hands clasped, watching snowflakes drift into the fire.

"You're a lovely boy, you know," she said. "Queen Hye Sun doesn't deserve you, and she knows it. I've heard rumors that she's tortured with guilt. If you went back now," The Lady said thoughtfully, "she would give you whatever you wanted."

"I don't want anything from her."

"Ah," breathed The Lady, avoiding my gaze, "but I do. I want to keep children like you safe. And if you convince your mother to let me borrow her army for just a little while, I can make sure that no Songland child enters the Breach ever again."

My pulse quickened. "How?"

"That's where you come in, my dear. Somewhere on this mountain, there's a cave with a very special secret. I'm told only a few Songlanders can find it: the highest shamans and the royal family."

I gulped. Of course I knew how to find Sagimsan's holy cave. Every year, my family visited on a pilgrimage to leave offerings at the opening and pray for Songland's prosperity. No one was supposed to go inside, but I had once stolen into the tunnel, mad with curiosity. I found a room with glowing gibberish on one wall. Then I fainted, lungs floundering in the blue pressurized air. Eventually shamans came to rescue me, and I was barely conscious for two days.

"I can't tell you where it is," I said, drooping. "I'm only allowed to tell family."

"Not allowed by who? The bullies in Eunsan-do who called you names?" She let me ruminate on this before adding, "Besides, I can *be* family, dear. If you will have me."

And as I lay my head on her soft chest, she told the most beautiful story I had ever heard. There was a band of anointed children, outcasts just like me. They had raised each other, grown together, traveled the world sharing one mind. Their love was so strong, separation caused illness, and even death.

"Where are they now?" I asked in awe.

"Waiting at the Arit border."

"Do you miss them?"

"Yes, though council sickness does not affect the Raybearer. I could not bring them into the pass; the storm was bad enough with one foreigner. I have three Anointed Ones, and several more hopefuls." She smiled. "Someday, we will be twelve." The Lady could anoint me too, she explained. In her family, I would never be *hell-boy* or *sacrifice*. I would only ever be Woo In: liberator of the Redemptors.

I led her to the cave the very next day.

"Did you learn what you needed?" I ask her eagerly

442

now, my arms wrapped around her waist as we ride Hyung back to camp. "Can you free the Redemptors? Will you anoint me now?"

"I . . ." She rubs her temples. "I learned a lot of things. Let me be, Woo In. I need to think."

I ask her again the next morning, as The Lady retrieves a hare from one of her traps, absently snaps its neck, and cleans it to roast over our fire. "Are you done thinking, Lady?"

After a pause, she says, "You don't really want to be anointed, Woo In. It's for life, you know, and a lot of work, not to mention the council sickness. Why don't you join me as . . ." She thinks quickly. ". . . as an honorary member? It'll be just the same."

"It won't," I say, frowning. "I won't have the Ray."

The Lady laughs. "We don't need the Ray to love each other, child. Tell you what. Why don't you get bundled up and go back to Eunsan-do? I'll wait right here, and you can convince Queen Hye Sun to see me. Then I'll come to the palace and fetch you. We'll go away together, forever." She cleans her bloodstained hands in the snow, then comes to draw her cloak around me, murmuring into my hair. "Once the queen lends me her army, I'll need a handsome young prince to help me lead it. Just imagine—"

"You don't want me." To my embarrassment, my lower lip starts to tremble. "You're afraid to keep me with you. Just like Mother."

The Lady kneels to my level and grips my shoulders. "I am nothing like Queen Hye Sun," she whispers. She fixes me with those vivid black eyes, though for a moment she speaks to herself. "I would never disown a child out of fear. I'm not like Father or Olugbade. I'm better. I'm different."

"Then anoint me."

She stiffens, then brightens. "I can't. Not yet, anyway. You have to love me first, remember?"

"That's all right then," I say. "Because I do."

Her breath catches as she stares, features shading with wonder and grief. "Am's Story. You mean it, don't you?" I nod and she laughs bitterly, kissing my forehead. "No wonder the Kunleos have always anointed children. Love is so uncomplicated at your age."

She stands and paces for several minutes, avoiding Hyung where the beast sits nearby, cleaning its paws and baring its teeth at her. Then she stops, murmuring to the air.

"Isoken blood would balance it. Several strains from different realms . . . It's a risk, but it could work. There's still room on my council. I need only find the right ones. Yes . . . it's worth a try."

She draws a vial out from under her cloak, and it swings from a chain on her neck. Her full lips harden with resolution, then blossom into a sweet smile as she turns to me.

"Come, child." I run into her outstretched arms, and she wets my brow with oil as her Ray engulfs me. I wince as she draws a knife and slashes her palm, then mine, letting our blood run together. Then her words drip into my ear like beeswax, deafening and sweet. "Receive your anointing."

CHAPTER 33

WHEN I DETACHED FROM WOO IN'S MIND, I shivered, shaking off the phantom of my mother's embrace.

"For all her efforts, The Lady never did get Songland's army," Woo In murmured, smiling ruefully at the schoolroom floor. "I tried to convince Mother for years, but Min Ja always managed to talk her out of it." He chuckled. "Out of the two of us, my sister always had the brains. She tried to warn me about The Lady, but I wouldn't listen. So Min Ja washed her hands of me. I don't blame her."

After a tense moment I asked, "Kathleen isn't the only isoken on Mother's council, is she?"

"Of course not. They're all isokens, all except for me and the first three."

"So by strengthening her own blood—by representing Arit realms multiple times through mixed-race council members—"

"The Lady hoped to cancel out my blood, stacking the dice against Songland again. That's why she still hadn't anointed her last member. She had to find the *perfect blend* of isoken."

I shuddered. "It's so callous. Like choosing breeds at a market." My head spun in confusion. "And wouldn't isoken blood be weaker? A pure-blood council member represents their realm fully, whereas an isoken represents each realm by half—"

"Or their blood represents each realm fully. No one knows for sure how the magic of Enoba's shield works. But The Lady had to try. She knew Arits would rebel if their children were born as Redemptors. She would never have risked losing her throne."

A lump grew in my throat, so large I couldn't swallow. My mother was dead, and I didn't even know what to feel. Should I cry for the Kunleo princess, a child disowned by her father, exiled by her brother, and abused by the world? Or should I curse The Lady, a tactician who would willingly kill thousands of innocents? Perhaps it was wrong to choose. In any case, I had run out of time for tears.

"I can stop it," I said, gripping Woo In's arm. "The Treaty Renewal isn't until tomorrow at sunset. Take me back. I can stop Dayo."

His face brightened, and then dimmed to gray. "I'm too weak to fly," he said. "The arrow wound is bad enough, but my body is weakened, still adjusting to the loss of the Ray. I'd never make it to Oluwan. You could ride Hyung. But the only way to reach An-Ileyoba in time . . ." He broke off, glanced at the map on the wall, and avoided my gaze.

On the map, I counted the eleven realms between

Sagimsan Mountain and Oluwan. The world around me grew cold.

The only way to reach An-Ileyoba by sunset tomorrow was to ride through twenty-six lodestones.

After four crossings, my body would begin to disintegrate. If I was lucky, my lungs would start failing at ten. A man had once been known to survive fifteen, but had spent the rest of his life deformed and bedridden.

But twenty-six?

I would die within minutes of reaching Dayo. And that's if I made it to Oluwan.

"It's over," said Woo In. "At least, for these Redemptor children. Ae Ri. Jaesung, Cheul, and the rest. Maybe in a hundred years, Dayo's descendants will end the Treaty. Until then . . ." He smiled tightly. "At least we know who to blame for our nightmares."

That night I slept in fits and woke up just as exhausted as when I had first laid down. When Ye Eun offered me breakfast, I shook my head. The screams of phantom children still rang in my ears. "I need air," I said.

Ye Eun didn't move from the doorway. "You upset Traitor Prince." She looked haunted. "We heard him, late into the night. He was crying. Traitor Prince never cries."

"I'm sorry, Ye Eun. He'll be fine after a while. Don't worry."

"I never listen when big people say that. 'Don't worry.' As if they know. As if they can protect you from anything." The child watched me for a moment, taking in my tense shoulders and swollen eyes—and her hard expression softened. "Sometimes when I think of the Underworld, I scream for hours and hours. I have to. I can't do it in front of the little ones, but when it gets bad—I go to the shrine." She pointed through a window up to a stony, overgrown path that crept into the woods behind the house. "It's old. Traitor Prince says shamans built it centuries ago. It's meant for prayers, but when I cry . . . I don't think the Storyteller minds."

I nodded. "I don't think so either." And since my numb feet had nowhere else to go, they left the house, turned, and crept up the path.

Wind chimes echoed through the trees. Bits of color flashed, crystals hanging high above in the branches. They must have been tied decades before, when the skyscraping trees were close to the ground. The chimes grew in volume until the path finally ended, and I arrived at a lean-to with a peeling green roof, overgrown with vines. Stacks of smooth boulders marked the remains of a shaman's meditation garden. A mysteriously clean marble altar rested beneath the lean-to, and fading on the rotting green overhang was a mural: the Pelican of Am, splaying its wings.

I fell to my knees. Dew seeped through my trousers. I felt suffocated—trapped in a cage with no walls, stretching to the cloudy Songland sky. I had failed Aritsar. I had failed Dayo. And now, I would fail Ye Eun, Ae Ri, and countless others as well.

Monsters were nothing. The true terrors were people like me—the ones who saw suffering, who heard the screams of a hundred generations echoing for miles around them—and still did nothing.

Chimes jangled in the trees overhead. A delicate breeze rattled the shrine, and for a moment, the pelican's eyes seemed to flash.

"It's never enough," I told the mural. "The ones I save won't outnumber the people I've hurt. Not in ten years. Not in a hundred. Or a thousand . . ." The damp carpet of pine needles looked suddenly inviting. My voice slipped away to a whisper as I sank to the ground, resting my cheek by a mound of stones.

Hours could have passed, or minutes. I neither knew nor cared. The chimes grew louder and distorted, and with the growing cold, a new kind of sleep spread through my body: the kind from which many winter travelers have never woken up.

But before my mind could slip beneath that cold, still pool forever . . . Something glowed from the shrine. A pulse of heat rolled over me in waves, like the gale of an enormous creature beating its wings.

Then a tritoned voice—not old or young, not male or female, but warm as the sun on a clear savannah morning and resonant as a griot's drum.

Do not ask how many people you will save. Ask, To what world will you save them?

The voice, soft and calm, seemed to fill all of Sagimsan Mountain.

What world, Wuraola, is worth surviving in?

Then I woke, alone.

The chimes were silent as I sat up, and pine needles fell from my hair as I blinked dazedly. Gold streaked across the sky. The morning had aged to afternoon—mere hours between now and sunset.

I turned up the path and ran. I did not stop to wonder why my cloak was warm as a brazier, instead of damp from dew. I did not question why my limbs were lithe and swift, instead of rigid with the forest's chill. I did not ask myself if the tritoned voice had been real or a dream.

I knew only one thing: A world worth surviving in wasn't built on the screams of children.

When I returned to the camp, Ye Eun stood on the porch with Ae Ri, watching grimly as I mounted Hyung. "Goodbye," she said, and did not ask where I was going.

I whispered my destination in Hyung's ear, and used my thighs to coax the emi-ehran into motion. Then, propelled by the heat of Ye Eun's gaze on my back, I disappeared down the hillside forever.

Mountain air burned my lungs. My hair swelled in the wind, beating my shoulders in a black cloud as I clung to Hyung's neck. The emi-ehran bounded down into the Jinhwa Pass, leaving paw-shaped craters in the snow. The storm had stopped; the old magic must have sensed that I was leaving. Still, a white wasteland stretched for miles before us. In the distance, a fortified wall marked the border of the Arit empire, and beyond it, my first lodestone.

The Jinhwa Mountains bordered two Arit realms: Moreyao to the west, and Biraslov to the north. Hyung veered toward the latter, and pale-skinned border guards in fur hats watched in terror as I neared the wall. I flattened myself against Hyung's sinewy back as arrows sailed past. The guards were too far away to see my council ring— they had taken me for an intruder. But I would not stop. Ducking for cover, I wrestled the crown princess mask from beneath my tunic. Arrows grazed Hyung's unnaturally thick pelt, glancing off without piercing. Swallowing to moisten my throat, I held out the mask and read its name. I had to believe now. I had to believe what I said, or there was a chance the mask would not listen.

"*Iyaloye*," I hollered . . .

And nothing happened.

No light. No sign. Had it all been a lie? Perhaps Olugbade had been right. Perhaps I didn't have the Ray, perhaps . . .

Then I remembered: The Lady was dead.

I put away the princess mask and seized instead the mask of the empress.

"*Obabirin*," I yelled as Hyung careened toward the wall. "*Obabirin!*"

The mask's eyes flashed, emitting a blinding light that made the guards stagger back.

The stream of arrows ceased. "I am Tarisai Kunleo," I screamed, heart pounding. "I bear the Ray of Wuraola. *Obabirin. Obabirin!*"

And Hyung soared through the opening in the border wall.

The lodestone was yards away. Warriors were yelling, running to block our path.

I roared the old Arit word again, and with another flash of light the warriors halted. Hyung leapt over them in a bound that knocked the breath from my chest, and we landed running. A yard more—then another—and with a tremor that shook every bone, we had crossed through the first lodestone.

Through waves of nausea, I smelled the sweet, green perfume of rice fields, and heard new voices cry out in surprise. According to the map in Ye Eun's schoolroom, I was now at the northwestern tip of Moreyao, and my next lodestone was two miles south. Hyung plowed on, passing fields in a blur, leaping over carts and dodging petrified village farmers. We reached the next port in minutes.

"*Obabirin*," I cried, and again we were through.

Balmy sea air. The port had spirited us to the coast of Sparti. My insides threatened to rise up my throat, and against Hyung's rippling muscles, my ribs had begun to bruise. But there was no time for rest, no time for any thought but forward.

After the fifth crossing, my left hand grew numb. I flexed the fading fingers, willing them back into view as we flew across the foggy moors of Mewe, only to see my thumb disappear when we crossed a lodestone into Nontes. By the eighth crossing into Djbanti, I could not feel either foot, and when I inhaled, my chest shuddered with excruciating pain, as though a lung had gone missing.

Still, Hyung's paws beat against the ground. *What story will you live for? What story do you live for?*

The humid air of Quetzalan rainforests washed over me, and my vision swam. It was the thirteenth crossing. "*Obabirin*," I croaked as we crashed through the dense brush and vines, narrowly escaping the blow darts of hidden warriors. This time, my voice dissolved into a cough. Something gurgled in my throat. A stream of crimson trickled onto my chin and I wiped it away.

Crossing seventeen hurled me into the spice markets of Dhyrma. I wasn't sure whom the merchants feared more: the enormous Underworld beast, or its half-vanished rider, with her clothes stained with blood and vomit, and her ghostly hand outstretched, bearing a lioness mask with glowing eyes. Spots began to cloud my vision.

I lost count of the lodestones.

A wall of heat told me I had passed into the Blessid Desert, and the scent of camels and cinnamon reminded me of Kirah.

I wondered, dreamily, if I would ever see her face again.

Forward. The red earth and colorful awnings of Nyamba.

Forward. Grass, everywhere, and the distant hum of tutsu. Swana, I realized with a surge of fondness before blacking out again.

When I returned to consciousness, the air hummed with voices. Bodies pressed all around, and above me loomed the smooth onyx face of Enoba the Perfect. A statue in a grand market square.

"I'm here," I murmured through lips I could no longer feel. Oluwan City—I had made it to the capital. "Dayo. I'm . . . I'm coming."

The sun dipped toward the horizon, bathing Palace Hill in bloody gold. As I rode, the rulers would be lining up before Enoba's shield. Dayo would be last, so perhaps I could make it. I could—

Guards intercepted me at the An-Ileyoba gates, bellowing and pointing their spears at Hyung. *The mask,* I remembered dimly, as a faint ringing sounded in my ears. *The mask will make them go away.* But when I tried to reach for it . . . nothing happened. I couldn't feel my arms. Couldn't *see* them. No. *I'm Tarisai Kunleo,* I tried to say. *I bear the Ray of Enoba. See me. See me. I'm here.*

But I wasn't. Not anymore.

For the first time in hours, Hyung stopped moving. My body faded in and out of view, a dying firefly. I opened my mouth to speak—and then even that was gone, a hole in the air, a void of silence.

"It's an evil spirit," shrieked the guards. "It's here to curse the Treaty. Stay back. Don't let it near. Fetch priests from the temple."

I was so close. Dayo was just beyond those walls, about to commit the only atrocity of his life. Deciding the fate of thousands of children, draining an ocean of stories.

No.

I tried to yell. I fought the shadows creeping at the edge of my vision; I begged for my feet to reappear. *I am not a ghost*, I screamed without words. *I am not nothing. I am not nameless; I will not fade into graceful oblivion like every other Kunleo girl, every other Empress Raybearer.*

But I could not speak. I could not stand, and when I tried to summon the old anger, the indignant warmth of the Ray . . . I felt only emptiness.

I'm sorry. I sent the thought to Dayo, and Sanjeet, and Kirah, and Ye Eun, and every other person I had failed. *I wanted to write a new story for you. For all of us. I tried.*

I tried.

Then the remains of Tarisai Kunleo slipped from Hyung's back, and the world dwindled to gray.

I expected to wake in the Underworld, feeling the icy fingers of children that my ancestors had damned. I would let them take their vengeance, dragging me down to a world of lost songs and buried dreams, far from the heat of sunshine.

Instead, my ears roared with familiar voices. Ghosts from the story I had lived before, a life that had drifted far away.

Until you grant her third wish, neither you nor I will be free.

Do you love me now, Tarisai of Swana?

A bellysong: the cure for any soul in bondage.

You have never worried me, daughter. You have only disappointed.

Only one thing is more powerful than a wish, and that is a purpose.

I was levitating, thrashing in a warm lake of light. My skin, limbs, and organs had been lost in the lodestone ether. Now they returned, painful but whole, as though my parts were made of clay and a master potter reassembled me. When my vision cleared, I stared up at steeply slanted, gold-flecked eyes. My body was being cradled in pole-like limbs, and around them, transparent wings of cobalt blue gave off sparks.

"Melu," I murmured. "Are ehrus like the abiku? Can you visit the Underworld?"

"No." He beamed, shimmering brighter. "The abiku are spirits of death. Alagbatos are guardians of life. We are not in the Underworld . . . And I am not an ehru anymore." He lifted his long, dark forearm, and I gasped: The Lady's emerald cuff was gone. "You have set us free, daughter."

I took in our surroundings. We were still in Oluwan, just outside the palace gates. Hyung stood protectively between Melu and the palace guards as the sun sank in the sky. But the warriors were no longer raising their spears.

Instead, they watched in frozen reverence, kneeling, brushing their chins in the sign of the Pelican as Melu helped me to my feet.

My bloodstained clothes were gone. Instead, a wrapper of green and gold clung to me like a second skin, its fibers too fine to have been spun by human fingers. My arms glowed like they had been polished, and on my chest hung the two masks of Aiyetoro, their eyes shining.

"How?" I asked.

"You found a purpose." The alagbato reached down with narrow fingers, touching my cheek. "Wanting to be loved was not enough. Devotion to your friends was not enough. But wanting justice—to carve out a new story for this world, no matter the cost—that was enough. No human's wish may rule you now."

Tears filled my throat, but I only nodded, reaching for Hyung. The beast knelt, and I lifted myself to sit sideways on its back, unable to straddle it in my gleaming wrapper. "The story's not over yet," I told Melu.

He nodded. "Go. There is not much time."

I whispered to Hyung, and the emi-ehran sprang into motion. We bounded through the palace, crowds of guards and courtiers parting like water. I crossed courtyards, scattering peacocks and splashing through fountains. When we arrived at the towering doors of the Imperial Hall, I slid off Hyung's back. The warriors guarding the door brandished spears to keep Hyung at bay, and gaped when they recognized me.

"Anointed Honor," one of them stammered. The warriors wore red bands on their forearms, mourning for the late emperor. "We heard . . . you were kidnapped by a wicked Songlander. His Imperial Majesty will be relieved at your return."

I realized with a jolt that they meant Dayo. "I have to see him."

"Apologies, Anointed Honor, but the Treaty Renewal is underway. Once it's over, we're sure the emperor will—"

Hyung let out a deafening yowl, making the warriors leap back. Taking advantage of the distraction, I pushed past them, heart slamming in my chest, and burst through the double doors of the Imperial Hall.

"Stop," I screamed. "Stop the ritual!"

The heat of a thousand gazes bored into me. Shocked murmurs hissed like wind in a storm, but I didn't care. Only one person mattered . . . and when I saw him, every bone inside me threatened to buckle.

Before a sea of courtiers, Dayo stood in his father's clothes on the dais, just as the premonition on Sagimsan Mountain had shown him. The twelve rulers of the continent stood gravely behind him, while my crowned council siblings watched from the sidelines. Enoba's shield lay on a gilded stand, and Dayo's hand hovered over it, a knife pressed to his palm. He froze when he saw me.

"Stop," I said, sprinting to the front of the hall and evoking protests as I pushed through the kings and queens sharing the dais with Dayo. I seized his wrist. "Don't do this."

But before Dayo could respond, slimy voices raised the hair on my neck.

"Hello, killer-girl." Four abiku stood before the dais, hands interlinked. Their childlike bodies were dusty gray, as though they had rolled in ash, and their pupil-filled eyes glowed pink, like rats. They stood so unnaturally still, I had not even noticed them when I entered the hall. The abiku cocked their heads and spoke in unison. "Again, you interfere with our covenant? Were the lives lost at Ebujo not enough? Still, you thirst for more?"

"You are the ones who thirst for blood," I spat, then turned back to Dayo. "The treaty isn't fair. I can't explain now, but you have to trust me: Enoba rigged it. Kunleo blood overrepresents the Arit realms, so Songland loses every time. If you finish the ritual, thousands of Songland children will die."

Gasps echoed through the hall, and Dayo recoiled from the shield, dropping the knife on the floor.

"I knew it," one of the rulers gasped. From her accent, I realized with dread who the person was: Queen Hye Sun of Songland. Wrinkles framed her eyes like dragonfly wings, and gray hair shone from a high coronet. The corners of her mouth were fixed with vast, cumulative grief. "I knew the Storyteller could not have cursed us so." Her voice shook. "It was the Kunleos all along."

"Of course it was," snapped a young woman at her side. She was an unwrinkled version of Hye Sun, and I recognized her sardonic tone: it matched her younger brother's. I gulped, suspecting that when Crown Princess Min Ja took the throne, relations between Aritsar and Songland would not heal easily. I didn't blame her.

"Dayo didn't know," I insisted. "No one did, except Enoba. Woo In can vouch for me."

"You know where my son is?" breathed Hye Sun. "He is safe? Alive?"

I nodded. "He sent me." I didn't mention that I'd left him feverish and bleeding from an arrow wound.

"When it comes to the people he trusts, my brother has shown foolish judgment in the past," Min Ja pointed out. "Why should we believe that your emperor was ignorant of the curse? And what does it matter if he was? The Arit throne is soaked in the blood of our children." Her face was white with rage. I felt the prickle of what Woo In had called sowanhada in the air, and in one graceful movement, the princess summoned a wind that upended Enoba's shield. It landed at my feet, its crimson contents splattered onto the dais. The abiku hissed, but Min Ja showed no fear. "Songland withdraws itself from the Redemptor Treaty."

The abiku smiled, four identical sets of tiny pointed teeth, in mouths that unhinged at the jaw. "Then it is war you want," they said. "A return of the Underworld above ground. A millennium of death, and disease, and the earth teeming with flood and fire. Very well. We accept."

"No," Dayo cried out. "No more war. We'll make a new treaty, one that protects Songland." He bowed deeply to

Hye Sun, who inclined her head. Min Ja only crossed her arms. "We'll make new terms for the Redemptor Treaty," Dayo continued. "The abiku will continue refraining from attacks on the continent, including Songland. However—to make up for the unfair selections of the past—the next generations of Redemptors will be born in Aritsar."

I cringed, anticipating what happened next. Delegates and courtiers from every Arit realm yelled and shook their fists, protests deafening as they threatened to rush the dais.

"Please," Dayo breathed. "It's only fair—" But the din drowned him out, and he watched in a panic as the crowd grew in unrest. Below us, the abiku's grins broadened.

My council siblings fell in place to defend the throne. Sanjeet leapt on the dais, unsheathing his scimitars, barking orders to the Imperial Guard.

Over them all I announced, "No more children will be sent to the Underworld."

The hall quieted. I planted myself on the largest dais echo-stone so my words carried. Then I spoke slowly to hide the shaking in my voice. "Instead of innocent children," I told the abiku, "I offer you a true prize. A flavor you have never tasted, blood previously forbidden you. In exchange for permanent peace—for a treaty requiring no renewal and no more wars—I offer you the soul of a Raybearer." I swallowed hard. "I offer the soul of an empress."

"No," Sanjeet rasped.

I can walk through fire, I Ray-spoke to all my siblings. Dayo's face contorted as he remembered my words from so many years ago, when I had carried him from the burning Children's Palace. *All you have to do is trust me.*

"Empress?" scoffed Min Ja. "There has been no empress since Aiyetoro."

"And I bear her mask," I said, and invoked the ancient title: "*Obabirin.*" The mask's eyes flashed, and the hall took a collective breath, roiling with whispers. "I am Tarisai Kunleo, niece of the late emperor. The priests of Am may examine my blood," I went on, "and confirm that it flows with the Ray. But these are the only witnesses who matter." I pointed to the abiku and growled, "You know what I am, spirits. Do you accept my offer?"

For the first time, the abiku shifted, features piqued with greed. They whispered among themselves, and then fixed their pink eyes on my face. "What you are," they purred, "is the bearer of a weak Ray. Until your blood runs with the power of all twelve Arit realms, you would be a paltry prize for the Underworld."

"You require that I have a council?" My pulse pounded with hope. I could simply share a council with Dayo. My council siblings already loved me; they would have no trouble receiving my Ray alongside Dayo's. "Done," I said.

The abiku smirked. "Not just any council, *Obabirin*. We require potent realm blood. To be an acceptable Empress Redemptor, you must anoint the twelve rulers of Aritsar as your council."

Around me, the realm rulers began to cluck in protest. My heart sank. How was I supposed to convince twelve rulers to trust me? More than that, they would have to *love* me, or else the Ray wouldn't work.

But I set my jaw and said, "Done. But while I'm assembling my council, you can't claim any more children as Redemptors. Give me ten years."

The abiku scoffed, chuckling. "One."

I balled my hands into fists. "Five."

They considered, cocking their heads. "Two. Our final offer."

Slowly, I picked up the dagger that Dayo had dropped on the dais. Then, slitting my palm, I let my blood spill into Enoba's shield on the floor. "Done," I said, and my arms began to prickle.

I watched in horror as blue symbols grew like lace across my forearms, twisting in intricate patterns.

"A mark of your promise," the abiku tittered. Then they vanished.

The hall dissolved into frenzied whispers. Dayo took up my slashed palm, staring at it with grief and wonder.

"You're breaking your promise again," he said. His imperial sun crown, an upright gold disc, glinted in my eyes. "You're leaving."

"Not for two years. And who knows? Maybe I'll survive the Underworld." I tried to smile, but my lips faltered. "I'm sorry, Dayo."

"Don't be."

He swallowed hard, then clasped my hand and raised it in the air. Blood ran down our interlaced fingers.

He addressed the Imperial Hall, tears glistening on his half-scarred face. "Long live the heir of Aiyetoro," he said. "Hail your Empress Redemptor."

CHAPTER 34

AFTER THE TREATY RENEWAL, MY COUNCIL retreated to the Hall of Dreams, and I poured out all my secrets.

I stood as they sat around me on stuffed pallets, listening blankly as I confessed about my mother's wish. I told them how I had stabbed Dayo, discovered that I had the Ray, and freed myself from the curse by choosing justice, even to death, over my freedom. I longed to soften the story, drape it in downy caveats and excuses. But I resisted, letting the facts stand naked—that much, at least, they deserved from me.

They were silent for a full minute. I searched each of their faces with terror, expecting to find my damnation etched there. Then Emeronya came forward and touched my brow, mimicking the gesture I had used every night in the Children's Palace, giving her sweet dreams of snow and lullabies.

"As I lean on you, Empress," she said in her characteristic monotone, "you may lean on me."

Umansa touched my face next, wetting his fingers with

my tears. "As I lean on you, Empress," he said, smiling at the space over my head, "you may lean on me."

Then it was Ai Ling and Mayazatyl, Kameron and Thérèse, Zathulu and Theo ... and last, Kirah, who grinned impishly as she repeated the vow. "When you first came here, I had to teach you what *ice* was," she said afterward. "Don't forget that when you're big and mighty, Empress."

"I won't," I said, and my heart sank as I considered her. "Kirah, I think I'll need your help."

"You *think*?"

"I know." I laughed, though a lump was forming in my throat. "Between recruiting the continent rulers for my council and preparing for the Underworld, I won't have time to fix relations between Aritsar and Songland. But we can't just ignore them. Not after what we did to them for centuries. We need to send an Imperial Peace Delegate, someone familiar with Songland customs. Or at least— someone who's read a lot about them."

Kirah's lips parted, slack with surprise.

"It might take months. Years even," I continued. "But if you can convince them to trade with us, then we can install a Songland ambassador at An-Ileyoba. I suspect that once he's recovered, a certain sullen prince might be up for the job."

Say no, I begged silently. *Don't leave me, not now. Stay, be Kirah, the anchor in my storm of curses and secrets.*

Her hazel eyes misted. "I'll think about it," she said,

466

but the excited tremor in her voice betrayed her; she had already decided. When she folded me in a cinnamon-scented hug, I smiled into her shoulder. No more cages, I thought. Not for Kirah, anyway.

Last was Sanjeet. We hadn't been alone since I returned from Sagimsan, and ever since I had offered myself to the abiku, he had barely looked at me. Did he think I'd been reckless? When he came forward at last, anger and pain deepened the hard lines of his face. And instead of touching my brow, his hands clenched my blue-marked forearms.

"I will lean on you, Empress," he said in a guttural voice, "if you promise you'll come back."

I gulped. "Jeet—"

"Promise," he said, "that you'll fight to leave the Underworld. That this isn't some stupid, idealistic suicide mission to pay penance for a crime you did not do."

Kirah sucked in a breath. "Right. These two could use some time alone, I think. Let's go. There's dinner in the banquet hall." Forcefully, she herded Dayo and the rest of my council siblings away, leaving me and Sanjeet in the shadowy Hall of Dreams.

He released me and stalked to the tall arched windows. His tunic was long and sleeveless, black cloth crisp against his copper shoulders, and his profile sharp in the moonlight.

"This is where we first met," I said presently. "You were chained up."

His mouth lifted, a grimace and a smile. "Even then, you were bent on saving strangers."

"When Woo In flew me away . . . I was afraid you would come after me. I'm glad you didn't."

"I sent five Imperial Guard cohorts. I told them to scour every corner of the empire for where that Songlander could have taken you. I even saddled a horse, planning to lead the search myself—"

"But you didn't," I repeated, coming to stand beside him. "You stayed because Aritsar had just lost its emperor, and Dayo needed you. Aritsar needed you. It's who you are, Jeet. It's who I am too." I reached up, tracing his stubbled jaw. "We weren't raised to see the world as a small place, where nothing matters but our happiness. That isn't our story. And . . . I don't think it ever will be."

He leaned down, resting his brow on mine. "Death is a small world too," he whispered. "Even smaller than happiness. If this is your way of giving up—"

"I'm not giving up. If I don't go to the Underworld in two years, children will die. You know that. I'll have help, Jeet. I'll send for someone who can teach me to survive down there."

"Woo In?"

"Maybe," I said. But I was thinking about Ye Eun: how fiercely she had stared me down at that temple in Ebujo, small fists clenched as she faced the mouth of hell. If anyone could teach survival, it was Ye Eun.

I hoped, with a fleeting thought, that she would bring Ae Ri. The baby's large, intelligent black eyes surfaced often in my thoughts, a mystery that played on my heartstrings.

Sanjeet exhaled, crumbling like a pillar as he folded me in his arms, joining my heart to his. "The Underworld is not accustomed to losing souls," he said. "It will tempt you to stay. You will want to pay for the sins of your ancestors, even after you've fulfilled the treaty. I can't keep you safe. I won't bottle up who you are, not even for your own good. But I'm . . . scared, Tar. I need you to promise you'll come back. Please. I need you to—"

I laced my fingers around his neck and pulled his face down to mine. He tasted like salt, like grief and fear. When I deepened the kiss, he swept an arm behind my knees, depositing us on one of the pallets. His hands passed over my waist and hips, and I hummed, each curve taut beneath my finely spun wrapper.

"Promise," he said. His mouth hovered over mine.

"I will." My voice was a rumble in my throat; my body was a drum, and he had struck its core. "I do."

Then I reached down and touched my ankle. Without hesitation, he drew the cowrie shell chain from his pocket and fastened it in place. Slowly, his fingers traveled up my calves, strumming until my skin sang a song without words. Minutes passed, and when the music swelled at last, we collapsed in the shape of each other, drifting into feverish sleep. Our bodies remained entangled when our council siblings returned for bed, tiptoeing around us to claim their pallets.

I woke in the dead of night. The Ray had synced my siblings' breathing as they slept—in, out, a sigh, a shudder.

Relief seemed to hit me all at once. My throat welled up, and I buried my face in Sanjeet's shoulder, stifling happy sobs.

I belonged in this motley family, grafted together with blood pacts and mystery. I belonged in Aritsar, this empire of beauty and great suffering, teeming with stories like the gold-encrusted cells of a beehive. And I was no one's tool. No one's imposter.

I was Tarisai Kunleo, and this was my family.

In the distance, guards drummed messages on the palace walls: *Gorro-gun-pa, da-dun, da-dun, gun-pa-pa. All clear—eleventh hour—the emperor and council are sleeping.*

Thaddace's trial for Olugbade's murder was tomorrow. It would take a miracle, but as the new High Lady Judge, I hoped to reduce his punishment from beheading to banishment. Then there would be a coronation—mine and Dayo's, as well as the mantle-passing ceremony for the new Emperor's Eleven.

We would move from the Children's Palace into the Imperial Suites: a maze of interconnecting chambers, with a special apartment for the emperor. Already, Dayo had ordered more apartments built for me, though I had tried to stop him. I couldn't imagine being apart from my siblings. Though if I was to please the abiku, I would have new siblings soon.

The faces of the twelve Arit rulers flashed in my mind: old and young, dark and pale, all frowning at me with suspicion. I sucked in a breath. Some of the rulers were old enough to be my grandparents. They hadn't asked for this. How was I supposed to convince them to respect me? To . . .

Love me?

And what about the rest of the empire? Commoners, warriors, nobility . . . If I survived the Underworld, I would rule them alongside Dayo. Sanjeet had said that I was popular among commoners, and respected by the Imperial Guard. But surely there would be pushback, and the nobility had no reason to trust me at all. What if *no one* wanted the daughter of an ehru and a traitor, an empress-turned-Redemptor?

My stomach grumbled. I hadn't eaten since leaving Woo In on Sagimsan Mountain, and whatever Melu had done to rejuvenate me had worn off. Perhaps there was food left in the banquet chamber. I slipped out of Sanjeet's arms and padded barefoot from the Hall of Dreams.

I jumped—Imperial Guard warriors lined the corridor. What were they doing here? It was only the Children's Palace . . . Oh. Right.

They were guarding Dayo, the emperor of Aritsar. And me. The Empress Redemptor.

"Can I help you, Your Imperial Majesty?" one of the female guards intoned, stepping forward. Her head was shaved and her features were vaguely familiar.

"I haven't eaten," I said groggily. "It's all right, don't wake the cooks. I'll just—" The guard's gaze locked on mine, and I froze.

She was Oluwani, with ordinary dark brown features. But her face had changed just for a moment, a mask dropped, revealing a tawny face with green eyes. Then it returned to normal.

"Are you sure," the guard said, "that there's nothing I can do for you?"

"Banquet chamber," I whispered. She bowed smoothly and led the way.

The Children's Palace banquet chamber was as I remembered it: a mosaic-tiled floor and long kneeling tables with tasseled seat cushions. The servants had cleared most of the night's feast away, but baskets of kola nuts and oranges already lined the tables for breakfast.

"What do you want, Kathleen?" I asked the guard, taking a piece of fruit and peeling it with trembling hands.

"It's not about what I want," she snapped, dropping the illusion to reveal her true face. As in the disguise, her scalp was bare; she had shaved her head in mourning. Her voice broke with repressed tears. "It's about what you owe her."

Then she held out a burning oil lamp and a scrap of paper. I recognized my mother's script on the calfskin: a page from one of her journals. The hair on my neck rose as I realized what Kathleen wanted.

"No," I said, dropping my peeled orange and backing away.

"She was your mother," Kathleen spat. "And she's dead! Murdered! Don't you care?"

"Of course I care," I shot back. "But there's nothing I

can do. And don't you dare say I owe her. I'm not like you. I didn't swear my life to her service; I didn't choose any of this."

For a moment, Kathleen looked as though she might strike me. Then she inhaled, her voice measured with desperation. "Shades can only come back once. The rest of us—her Anointed Ones—we've all tried to summon her. To say goodbye, to make sure she's all right. But she won't come. She's waiting for you."

I swallowed, staring hard at the mirrored ceiling, my reflection murky in the shadows. Then before I could change my mind, I accepted the oil lamp. I held The Lady's journal page to the flames, completing the summoning ritual.

The air went cold.

I closed my eyes, and when I opened them, The Lady stood in the center of the banquet hall. Shadows draped her translucent form like a floor-length mantle. I fought a giddy, unnatural urge to laugh—even in death, my mother managed to look like an empress.

Kathleen burst into tears and ran to her, thrusting her arms around The Lady's shrouded figure.

The Lady embraced her, stroking her shaved head and kissing her cheek. Then she whispered in her ear. Kathleen glanced reproachfully at me, but nodded, and left me alone with my mother.

"Hello," I managed eventually.

The Lady ignored me, turning to pace the chamber.

Again I fought a manic urge to laugh. Some things never changed.

"The last time I was in this room," she murmured, running her ghostly fingers over the baskets and centerpieces, "my brother flipped over the tables. That was the night he banished me. When I showed the world who I was."

"What happened to you after Woo In took me away?" I asked. "What was it like when . . . ?"

"When I died?" Her voice was calm, and she faced me at last. Her serene expression shifted, as if recalling a deeply repressed memory. "Your friends . . . They bought me time. Yes. The Blessid girl sang to slow my heart, while that Dhyrmish lover of yours carried me to the palace infirmary. The Kunleo boy ordered the healers to give me an antidote. It was too late, of course." She paused. "I . . . did not anticipate that Ekundayo would try to save me. I tried to kill him, after all. But he ordered healers to my bedside. Simply because he knew you would mourn me. Olugbade was not so noble. But sometimes, I have learned, the fruit is unlike the tree."

It was the closest she would ever come to apologizing for hurting Dayo. I sighed and asked, "Are you in pain? The stories about the Underworld—Egungun's Parade, and the paradise at the earth's Core . . . are they true?"

And for the first time in my life, my mother looked afraid.

"Yes," she whispered at last. "To reach my eternal rest, I will join the parade of all dead souls. And for every step I take, I will feel any pain that I caused out of malice or neglect while I lived. But I was able to wait. I wanted to see you first."

"Why?" I demanded. "Because you still want me to overthrow Dayo? Because you want me to betray Songland to the abiku, like you were planning to?"

The Lady flinched, and then set her jaw. "You are my daughter," she said. "I wanted to say goodbye."

I examined her, expecting to see flickers of cunning: a hint that she was bending my emotions to her will again. But all I saw was a proud, lonely woman, frail from poison, searching my face for traces of the dream she had lost.

"It was a game, you know," she murmured. "I played it the only way I knew how. Aritsar would not have crowned me without an army, and so I made promises to gain Songland's support. But if I had let the abiku take Arit children instead of Songlanders . . . even an army would not have saved me. Woo In doesn't understand. I couldn't free the Redemptor children, but I would have been good to him. I would have . . ." She trailed off, her expression growing vacant. Suddenly, she looked very old and very young at the same time. "That boy must be suffering, all alone again on Sagimsan. I will send Kathleen to nurse him. He was helpless when I found him. I crossed realms to form my council, saved outcasts, prodigies that the world ignored. I gave them communities. I made them useful."

I smiled ruefully, remembering Melu's description of a young bandit queen.

"There are so many still out there: geniuses waiting

to be seen and recognized. My council can continue my work. You will be confined to this lofty palace, ruling Aritsar from above. But my people will be on the streets below, helping you rule from within."

I shook my head. "I don't need your—"

"My enemies think I have lost," she interrupted. "But they are wrong. I said I would put an empress on the throne of Aritsar, and I have." She pressed her lips together. "Through you, my legacy lives."

You didn't make me empress, I wanted to snap. *You didn't make me who I am. I am not the sequel of your story. You did not give me my name.*

Instead, I leaned up and kissed her smooth cheek. It was cold as stone. I slipped her a memory of a cooing baby in Bhekina House: a little girl who wanted for nothing, content in The Lady's embrace.

"Goodbye, Mother," I said.

"Goodbye, Made-of-Me." Water glistened in her brilliant black eyes, but she didn't follow me as I let her go and walked to the door. As I stepped out into the corridor, I closed off the past, embracing that murky horizon, my shore of unsung stories.

But The Lady spoke one more time, her voice quiet as a sowanhada wind, and as wonderstruck as a little girl, gazing from her only window at the vast savannah sky.

"Tarisai," she said, "Tarisai Idajo."

CAST OF CHARACTERS
AND THEIR HOME REALMS

Tarisai (TAR-ree-sigh), Swana
Sanjeet (Sahn-JEET), Dhyrma
Ekundayo (EH-kuhn-DYE-oh), Oluwan
Kirah (KEE-rah), Blessid Valley
Mbali (Mm-BAH-lee), Swana
Thaddace (THAD-us), Mewe
The Lady, Unknown
Olugbade (Oh-loo-BAWD-day), Oluwan
Theo (THEE-oh), Sparti
Emeronya (EHM-er-OH-nyuh), Biraslov
Ai Ling (Eye-leeng), Moreyao
Mayazatyl (MYE-ah-ZAH-tuhl), Quetzala
Thérèse (Tay-RES), Nontes
Kameron (KAM-ruhn), Mewe
Zathulu (Zah-THOO-loo), Djbanti
Umansa (Oo-MAHN-sah), Nyamba
Woo In (OO-een), Songland
Melu (MEH-loo), Swana
Hye Sun (HEH-sun), Songland
Min Ja (MEEN-jah), Songland
Nawusi (Nah-WOO-zee), Nyamba
Aiyetoro (EYE-yeh-TOH-roh), Oluwan

GLOSSARY

abiku (ah-BEEK-oo): Spirits of death that inhabit the Underworld.

abiku blood: A potent poison that can spread through earth, leeching life from everything it touches.

agbada (ahg-BAH-tah): A sweeping, floor-length men's garment with long, loose sleeves and cloth that drapes generously over each shoulder.

alagbato (ah-lahg-BAH-toh): A guardian spirit, or fairy, of a natural resource, such as a forest, river, savannah, or larger region.

An-Ileyoba (Ahn-Ee-lay-OH-ba): The palace at the heart of Oluwan City, the capital of Oluwan.

Biraslov (BEE-rah-slahv): A snowy realm in the far northern regions of the Arit empire, predominantly occupied by People of the Wing. Home realm of Emeronya, a member of Dayo's council.

Blessid Valley (Bleh-SEED VAL-ee): A desert realm of nomads in the Arit empire, located south of the center Arit realms. Blessid Valley occupants are predominantly People of the Wing and are known for herding, pottery, and strong familial clans. Home realm of Kirah, a member of Dayo's council.

Bushland: Supernatural stretches of land created by Enoba the Perfect when he united the Arit continent. Also called "the Bush." Bushlands play a role in regulating the climate of the Arit continent and are often inhabited by spirits.

Bush-spirit: An often-malicious spirit that inhabits the Bush.

chin chin (cheen-cheen): Sweet, bite-size pieces of fried dough.

Core: The ultimate resting place of all souls, a paradise located in a supernatural dimension at the center of the earth.

Dhyrma (DER-mah): A realm in the eastern reaches of the Arit empire, known for gemstones and luxury goods and predominantly occupied by People of the Ember. Home realm of Sanjeet, a member of Dayo's council.

Djbanti (Jih-BAHN-tee): One of four realms in the center of the Arit empire. Known for a culture of hunting and scholarship, and home realm to Zathulu, a member of Dayo's council.

Egungun's (Eh-GOON-GOON-z) **Parade**: The purgatorial march in which all souls participate before entering the permanent afterlife of Core.

ehru (EH-roo): An enslaved spirit.

emi-ehran (EH-mee-EH-rahn): A spirit-beast of the Underworld, typically sent to comfort lost or dying souls.

fufu (foo-foo): A food made of cassava flour and water, cooked to a consistency similar to mashed potatoes.

gele (GEH-lay): A headdress made of elaborately folded bright starched cloth.

Ileyoba (Ee-lay-OH-ba): The central district of Oluwan City, in which the palace, as well as the luxury villas of the nobility, are located.

iyaloye (EE-yah-LOY-ay): An Arit crown princess.

matemba (maht-EHM-bah) **fish**: A type of dried fish, often used in stew.

Mewe (Myoo): A northern realm in the Arit empire, known for its sheep herders, wool exports, and craggy green landscape. Home realm of Kameron, a member of Dayo's council.

moi moi (MOY-moy): Steamed bean pudding.

Moreyao (Mor-ree-yow): A northeastern realm in the Arit empire, known for elaborate silk textiles and prosperous rice paddy farms. Home realm of Ai Ling, a member of Dayo's council.

Nontes (Nawnt): A northwestern realm in the Arit empire, known for its lace textiles, rose gardens, and gray weather. Home realm of Thérèse, a member of Dayo's council.

Nyamba (Nee-AHM-bah): One of four realms in the center of the Arit empire. Known for its experts in divination and artisanal weaving, and home realm to Umansa, a member of Dayo's council.

oba (OH-BAH): An Arit emperor.

obabirin (OH-bah-BEE-reen): An Arit empress.

oloye (oh-LOY-eh): An Arit crown prince.

Oluwan (OH-loo-awn): The capital of the Arit empire and one of four central realms. The largest hub of trade, research, and cultural preservation and known for its orange groves and coastal fortresses. Home to the wealthiest Arit noble families and seat of the emperor.

Oruku (Oh-ROO-koo) **Breach**: The last known entrance to the Underworld, located in the Ebujo Temple in the realm of Oluwan.

Quetzala: A southern realm in the Arit empire known for its rainforests and highly advanced architecture. Predominantly inhabited by People of the Well and is the home realm of Mayazatyl, a member of Dayo's council.

Redemptor: A person born with maps on their skin, compelled by the Redemptor Treaty to enter the Underworld as a sacrifice to prevent attacks from the abiku.

Songland: A peninsula nation hedged by enchanted mountains that protect the realm from intruders. The only realm on the continent independent from the Arit empire. Known for its enchanted sowanhada warriors and Redemptors, and home to Woo In, the notorious "Traitor Prince" and son of Queen Hye Sun.

sowanhada (soo-AHN-ah-da): A powerful language unique to Songland that permits the user to control various elements.

Sparti (SPAR-tee): A southern coastal realm in the Arit empire, known for its fishing industry, sculptures, and musician-poets. Home realm of Theo, a member of Dayo's council.

sprite: A small, capricious spirit that inhabits fertile fields and forests. Often found in swarms and poached for use as a light source.

Swana (SWAHN-nah): One of four central realms in the Arit empire, known for its supernaturally fertile crops and powerful alagbato, Melu. Predominantly home to People of the Clay. Home realm of Tarisai, a member of Dayo's council.

wrapper: A long woven garment, often intricately dyed or embroidered, that wraps several times beneath the arms.

Yorua Keep: A coastal, highly guarded fortress in Oluwan that houses the Prince's Council.

ACKNOWLEDGMENTS

The paradox of writing a book is that most of the work is done in isolation, but none of it would be possible without an army supporting you every step of the way. My army fought for this book for over twelve years.

Thanks to Kim-Mei, my wonderful agent, who took a chance on an unknown writer, and then proceeded to advocate for this book with tenacity and conscientiousness like I had never seen.

Thanks to Maggie, my brilliant editor, who worked on this book with such genuine enthusiasm that every critique felt like a gift.

Thanks to Shasta Clinch, my copyeditor, who has an eye for detail that would *definitely* qualify as a Hallow, and who navigated the rules of my universe better than I ever could.

Thanks to Brooke Shearouse, who I'm half convinced is Supergirl and using her job as an extremely competent publicist as a cover. Thanks to the rest of the publicity, marketing, and editing team at Abrams for their brilliant hard work.

Thanks to Charles Chaisson for his breathtaking artwork, and to Hana Nakamura for her thoughtful and inspired book design.

Thanks to Mom, who kept her daughter well supplied in books and trips to the library. Thanks to Dad, who bought